MARKED FOR DEATH

MATT HILTON

Sempre Vigile Press

Matt Hilton

MARKED FOR DEATH

MATT HILTON

First published In Great Britain by Sempre Vigile Press 2018

1

ISBN Paperback: **978-0-9935788-3-0**
Also available in eBook

Dedication

This one is for Raymond William Hilton.
I miss your laughter, my little brother.

Prologue

Smoke, fire and corpses.

That was his world when his senses coalesced out of the fog of incomprehension. For minutes gone – or for an eternity, he wasn't sure – he'd floated outside his corporeal body, his mind tumbling slowly through a void of nothingness. He could see, taste, touch and smell nothing. In that place he was at peace. It's said that when death comes, the final sense to leave us is hearing. In that abyss there was sound, though it came from such distance that it barely scratched at the edge of his hearing.

As he tumbled through the colourless void he grew aware that he was straining to deny those sounds, because through acknowledging them it meant he still clung to life. He didn't want to hear. He wanted only to wallow in peace and leave everything behind…the fear, the agony.

But the more he tried to ignore the sounds the more insistent they became.

And as they grew louder panic swelled.

What was he thinking? *He didn't want to die!*

Now he clawed against the alternative, and his own voice rose to join the audible chaos surging over him. He screamed, a ragged, throaty roar of denial that snapped his ethereal mind into the present, and he was reeled in at a shocking velocity. Mind and body collided with the force of an exploding star, a phosphorescent white light splitting apart the void, and through the rents in its insubstantial fabric poured reality.

Choking smoke. Searing flames. Charred and bloody corpses.

He could taste his own blood, and smell the acrid tang of noxious fumes. But they were distractions compared to the crushing weight on his chest and legs. A huge slab of jagged concrete bore into him, his frail body the only thing denying its inexorable contest with gravity. He was on the verge of bursting, of collapsing under the immense weight, as had the building currently under bombardment by US missiles.

Even as he grew aware of his predicament, memory flooded in.

He had been standing alongside another two private military contractors, supposedly in Afghanistan to assist with the peace-keeping forces, but really using the opportunities that a nation in turmoil offered to those willing to step outside laws and morals. He'd partnered with the two Chechen mercenaries to work security while they brokered a deal with the Taliban. It was a deal that would open routes through Chechnya to the Western world. The mercenaries would grow rich on the raw opiates on offer. The meeting within the Taliban stronghold – a compound of high walls and a cluster of concrete bunkers abandoned by the Soviets years ago – had been tense, but promised to grow fruitful...until hell rained down from above.

The only thing that had saved him immediate evisceration was that the first missile to strike had targeted an adjacent building. The detonation had destroyed that building, and had hurled massive chunks of debris onto the one in which they met with the Afghans. Walls and parts of the roof collapsed on them even before they were aware of the concussive wave of sound and fury rolling over them. He had seen men picked up and thrown through the air, as if swatted by an invisible giant, their bodies pulverized by flying debris, even as he had been thrown down. Ears ringing, thoughts swirling, it took him moments to crawl up from the dirt and stand again. He was dazed, covered from head to foot in dust, but otherwise unhurt. Miraculously he had survived where so many others hadn't. Through the choking cloud of debris a hole in the wall offered an escape, and he staggered towards it. Beyond it a curtain of fire raged, and he backed away from the furnace heat that washed over him, throwing his arms over his face.

He was retreating like that when the second missile struck and the remainder of the ceiling thundered down on him, forcing his sensations into that foggy void. His arms were still before his face, but their strength wasn't what had spared him from being pulped. Other chunks of debris he'd fallen amongst helped prop up the crushing weight of the slab. Yet he was still trapped, and had no hope of dragging himself free. The slab promised to be his final marker.

Another missile struck towards the rear of the compound. The flash lit up the smoke that wreathed around him, and he felt the concussive force of the detonation almost instantaneously, the concrete on top of him thrumming like the skin of a drum, casting down grit and dust in his eyes. The corresponding boom compressed his eardrums. He screamed again...but it escaped his constricted chest as a plaintive wheeze.

'Elbek!' A voice responded, speaking in Russian. 'Is that you? Where are you, Elbek?'

Elbek was one of his Chechen partners.

Elbek was dead.

He could see the man's crushed face a few feet away, his body mashed under more fallen concrete. He could smell Elbek's blood and his voided bowel.

'It's me!' he croaked.

'Where's Elbek?' The voice had switched to English, for his sake.

'He's gone...please...you have to help me.'

Rocks clattered, and a figure loomed alongside him, crawling on hands and knees. He peered into the face of the man that would decide his future. The Chechen's face was streaked with dirt, and blood trickled down his cheek. His sharp eyes played over him, and then slipped away. He had been disregarded. The Chechen began to crawl away, to claw at rocks to help him stand.

'Please,' he said. 'Don't leave me here like this.'

He would die beneath the rubble, choked or burnt to death. Should he survive he faced execution by the Taliban – for in their minds, who else could have guided the US missiles to their stronghold – or capture and imprisonment by the US forces who would deem him a traitor and enemy combatant.

'There's nothing I can do for you,' the Chechen rasped. 'Except give you a swift death.'

The Chechen had returned to his side, this time standing over him with an assault rifle hanging down by his side.

'No,' he pleaded. 'Please. I don't want to die like this.'

'I don't see any other way for you.'

'I'm trapped. Yes. But you can get me free.'

'What's in it for me? I've wasted enough time here as it is.' The Chechen wasn't only talking about his need to flee before the US troops arrived to sweep the compound of survivors. He was angered that his deal with the Taliban, and the riches it promised him, was at an end. There was little to profit him in dragging another mercenary from the wreckage.

He strained against the rubble. It sank a fraction lower. 'Ask anything of me, and I'll do it.'

'I need to go.' The Chechen snorted and turned aside, not even bothering with delivering a mercy killing.

'Wait!' If he could, he would have lifted beseeching hands to the Chechen. 'Help me. Save my life. Do that and I swear to you I'll do the same for you a thousand times. Please, get me out of here, and I'll do anything you want. Anything! I'll fight for you. Even if it means dying for you!'

He didn't know it then, but his pledge would be tested many times in the coming years, but through every trial he stayed true to his word. Even when asked to do the worst things imaginable.

1

Splinters of glass cascaded across the sidewalk, a bed of needles on which the squint-eyed thug went to sleep. Seconds ago he'd been jumping around, as hyper as a speed addict, spitting froth from the corners of his mouth in his agitation, until I'd delivered the sleeping pill by way of a straight right to his jaw.

I hadn't planned on sending him through the window, but the subsequent explosion of glass, the slap of his body on the pavement, bought me a few seconds while his pals blinked in astonishment at his downfall. By the time their attention turned back to me, I was on the offensive. I upended a table, scattering food and condiments, and kicked it into the thighs of the two men nearest me. While they wasted time trying to clear the obstruction, I vaulted it and kicked the first of them over onto his back. While he was down I stamped on his groin. He jack-knifed at the waist, woofing in agony, and met my knee with his face. He sprawled out flat again.

The third guy should have hit me while I was still side-on to him, but he made the mistake of going for a two-hands grab, intending to yank me off his downed pal. He caught the collar of my jacket, began hauling, but that worked in my favour: I pivoted half-circle and rammed the tip of my left elbow into his liver. He lost all control of his grip, and likely his bowels, as his response was to squat and shudder out a deep groan. Reversing my pivot, I again employed an elbow, and this time his fat head made a perfect target. He crashed against the upturned table, his weight thrusting it back a few feet before he flattened out.

The violence had been shocking and sudden, and to the observers out on the sidewalks I might have looked as much like the instigator as I did the perpetrator of the brutal exchange, but I'd only gone there to enjoy a quiet lunch. I should have known better; I tend to attract trouble. If there's an idiot in the room they always gravitate towards me, and sadly I'm not the type to suffer fools.

And the trio of punks lying around me in varying degrees of messed-up had been drunken fools.

They'd come off the beach overheated, but instead of lining their stomachs with food and maybe taking a soft drink they'd elected for pitchers of beer. Too much hot sun plus too much cold beer: not a good combination. The alcohol made them boisterous, rude and belligerent. Squint-eye didn't understand that four-letter words were best kept between his own ignorant company, and he had no right to complain when asked by the manager to keep it down around the lunchtime diners. His way of dealing with the request was to get louder, and begin throwing his weight around, challenging anyone who thought himself man enough to shut him up. I told him to shut it.

Squint-eye – encouraged by his equally stupid friends – set his chin, then strolled over to my table with his fists clenched.

'You goin' to make me shut it, old man?' he demanded, one eye watering, the other pinched almost shut. Dried spittle formed scummy patches at the corners of his mouth. More spit was ejected when he wiggled his fingers and beckoned me to try it. 'C'mon, asshole, you want to have a go?'

'Let's take this out in the parking lot,' I said as I stood.

'Why not do things right here?' To punctuate his point, he snatched up a ketchup bottle from my table and swung for my head. Before the bottle was halfway through its arc, my fist impacted his chin and things kicked off.

It's one thing standing against bullies, but my problem was I didn't have much balance when dealing with them: once tripped, my switch was prone to overkill. Surrounded by the recumbent trio, I took abashed glances around, observing the shocked expressions of my fellow diners. I felt bad that I'd helped ruin their day out.

A family of three sat at the nearest table, shocked into immobility, loaded forks still raised. I could see the partly masticated remains of a cheeseburger in the wide mouth of a sturdy, ginger-haired kid. His eyes were huge and glossy with excitement.

'Sorry your boy had to witness that,' I said to the kid's parents.

The father, the progenitor of his son's red hair and freckles, glimpsed at the kid, then shook his head, as if an apology was unnecessary. 'Can't get him off those online shoot 'em up games, I'm betting he's seen much worse.'

The mother, a frumpy blonde, and obviously the parent that'd determined the kid's stocky figure, moistened her lips as she stared up at me. 'They asked for what they got, mister,' she announced.

Other diners were in agreement, some of them even offering a short round of applause. One old guy sitting close enough to spit on the thug I'd elbowed cackled softly in laughter. He used an immaculately white sneaker to prod the downed man. He spoke directly to him. 'If you're intent on throwing your weight around, you should expect a hard landing now and again.'

His words of wisdom rang as a personal warning to me. I looked for the manager, held up my hands in apology. 'I'm sorry about the trouble; I only planned on getting them outside and on their way. Things rapidly got out of hand, though.'

'This wasn't on you, Joe,' the manager said, his expression one of sombre reflection. I'd been visiting his beachside diner for years, and was on first name terms with Grant. 'That punk would've smashed your head with that bottle if you hadn't stopped him.'

'I was more annoyed that he called me an old man.' I smiled to show I was joking.

'Yeah,' said Grant, who was my senior by a couple of years, 'he asked for it. I only wish I'd opened the window first.'

'That wasn't planned either,' I assured him. 'I'll pay for the damages, Grant.'

He pointed down at Squint-eye, who was still dozing on the sidewalk. 'He can pay for the damages.' He checked out the overturned table, the spilled food and crockery. 'The rest is salvageable.'

'Maybe we should put them in the recovery position or something.'

'Let's drag 'em into the parking lot, let them sleep it off,' Grant suggested. 'It's garbage collection day, maybe someone will do me a favour and throw them in the trash.'

He was jesting. Plus he had a duty of care, as did I. Between us we got the trio of young punks propped in the shade at the side of the diner, and slapped them into wakefulness. I didn't hold a grudge. As long as they behaved – and shelled out ample reimbursement to Grant for the broken window – I'd allow our disagreement to end.

To be fair, when they did come to, they wore similar expressions of sombre reflection to Grant's countenance earlier. They knew they'd been in the wrong, having had some sobriety knocked back into their foolish heads. Squint-eye paid up, and even offered me an apology and his hand. I didn't believe for a second it was a trap to pull me into a headbutt, but call me cautious. I clapped him on the shoulder instead, directing him back to the beach.

As he had during previous visits to his diner, Grant again offered me a job, which I again declined. It had become a discussion point with us to a point where we sounded like a stuck record.

'I've already got a job.'

'You seem to have plenty downtime,' Grant countered. 'I sure could use you on the door over the summer break...'

'I'd make a poor doorman,' I said. 'I can't differentiate doors from windows.'

He shook his head at the lame joke.

'Besides,' I went on, 'I enjoy eating here; it wouldn't be the same if I worked here. I wouldn't be able to relax.'

'You never relax,' he reminded me. 'You should take up yoga or something, Joe, do some breathing exercises, or you're going to burn yourself out. You're not as young as you used to be.'

I blinked at him in mock surprise. 'I just knocked a guy through a window for suggesting I was old.'

'I didn't say you were old, just...well, not young either.'

'And you think me working a door, bouncing groups of drunken reprobates, is going to be good for my health? Thanks for the out, Grant.'

He extended his hand. 'The offer's always open.'

I had no reservations about taking his hand, and I winked my appreciation.

'Can I get you a fresh plate?' Grant offered. My lunch was currently being mopped off the floor by one of his serving staff.

'Lost my appetite,' I admitted. I squinted at my wristwatch for effect. 'Besides, it's time I was getting on...before age really does catch up to me.'

'Got a lot on?' His tone was doubtful.

'I'm a busy man,' I said.

I was lying. I was between jobs and was growing antsy. On another day I might have made do with slapping some sense into Squint-eye and his pals, not beating on them as vigorously as I did. Boredom had a detrimental effect on me, and a worse one on the fools that snapped me out of laconic mode.

The truth was, I was mildly embarrassed. Despite the show of appreciation from the diners, I was sorry that I'd acted so violently, especially in view of children, and was uncomfortable about returning inside. I couldn't eat while being eyed openly – or surreptitiously – by the other diners. I especially didn't want to field their questions or misguided accolades, let alone reproof once the adrenaline spike faded and they began thinking more clearly about the kind of person in their midst. I said goodbye to Grant and strolled through

15

Mexico Beach towards my beach house, seriously ready for a change of scenery.

I liked Mexico Beach and was loath to relocate, but it was beginning to look inevitable. During my downtime I enjoyed eating at Grant's place, and at Toucan's, or taking a cold beer at one of the other beachfront bars. I liked jogging up the beach towards Tyndall Air Force Base following the coast of Saint Andrew Sound. If I had a choice, my ideal would include mountains, forests and shimmering lakes, but this was Florida. Sitting quietly on the deck outside my beach house, watching pelicans skimming the cerulean waters of the Gulf, was as close to my idea of second best as I could imagine. But I was quickly becoming the serpent in this particular paradise. More than once trouble had followed me home, and extreme violence had been the outcome, and I knew that the residents would only tolerate me in their midst for so long before they began muttering behind my back and wishing I was gone: after that it'd be pitchforks and flaming torches. Grant's continued offers of employment was a case in point; he liked me – for now – but he also feared me. My potential for sudden and extreme violence hadn't engendered me an offer as a fry cook or front of house greeter. He offered the doorman's job simply because I'd turn it down, and that subtle message reminded me of my value to him, and probably to the other residents and business people he regularly conversed with.

My friend Rink had encouraged me to move nearer Tampa, closer to our base of operations, to cut down on the commute time. In the past I'd refused, countering that the drive allowed me to put the necessary space required between my day job and where I laid my head at night. But the hundreds of miles were moot when trouble rode my shoulder, as heavy a burden as a sack of bricks.

Before reaching home I stopped off at a beer and oyster bar on Highway 98, where you could buy T-shirts emblazoned with the legend 'I Got Shucked In Mexico Beach!' but I didn't need a new shirt or oysters. In fact, following wisdom Squint-eye and his pals should have heeded I made do without beer, electing instead to nurse a large black coffee. I sat in the shade of a porch so that the screen on my smartphone didn't reflect the glaring sun, and logged on to their free Wi-Fi. My mind wasn't fully engaged on perusing the real estate webpages I'd bookmarked, and I kept gazing out to sea, or observing the vehicles passing by on the highway, or the diners coming and going to the adjacent parking lot, the reptile part of my brain anticipating further trouble.

I almost dropped my phone when it rang unexpectedly, but settled down quickly when the caller ID flashed up Rink's grinning face.

'Enjoying your weekend off, brother?' he asked without preamble.

'I was.'

'Geez, Hunter, and I thought you'd be happy to hear my dulcet tones.'

I grunted in humour. 'It's not you, Rink.' I told him about how my lunch had been spoiled. 'These days I seem to knock more heads here than I do at work.'

'And you don't even get paid for your services. Those bar owners up there should send around a hat and ask for donations for you.'

'It more likely they'll ask for donations for a bus ticket out of town for me.'

'Nice to be appreciated, huh?' Rink brushed off the matter. 'I'm gonna ask you a ridiculous question I already know the answer to.'

'If you must.'

'Do you own a tuxedo?'

'You're kidding, right?'

'There was always the long shot you'd have one packed away in mothballs somewhere.'

'Yeah it's hanging alongside yours, hidden behind all those Hawaiian shirts and board shorts in your closet.'

'Warned you it was a ridiculous question. You're gonna have to rent one once we get down to Miami.'

'What's the gig?'

'Remember when McTeer was on that minding job down there a few months back?'

'The one where he was supposedly rubbing shoulders with the Beckhams?' Jim McTeer was an employee of Rink and a good friend. He was an ex-cop, and during this downtime with Rington Investigations he'd worked private security for some visiting sportsman down in Miami. He hinted he was looking after David Beckham while he was in town trying to set up a soccer team, but I thought he was pulling my leg. Football in Miami? I didn't see it working out.

'He wasn't blowing smoke up our asses,' Rink said. 'He genuinely was part of Beckham's entourage, and must have made a good impression. He's been asked to supply some extra guys to work security at a gala dinner evening in some swanky hotel on South Beach. He thought we might enjoy a coupla days in Miami on somebody else's ticket. What do you say, brother?'

'Swanky hotels aren't my scene.'

'You're just afraid I'll make you shave and have a haircut.'

'Is that part of the deal?'

'It's easy money, Hunter. Our remit is to be there, fill out a coupla suits, and look mean and moody. It reassures the celebs that they won't be bugged by the great unwashed while they eat abalone and drink champagne.'

'Do we have to eat sea snails?'

'No.'

'OK then. My palate has grown more refined in the past few years but I still won't put a bloody snail in my mouth.'

'The things you've eaten in the field…'

'That was different, Rink. That was about survival, not choice.'

'I hear you.' He was silent for a few seconds, as he contemplated the things he too had been forced to devour while on deep cover missions. He once admitted to me that swallowing a handful of beetle larvae wasn't so bad; swilling them down with his own recycled urine was what had left a bitter aftertaste. 'Kind of gives you an appreciation for momma's home cooking, right?'

'When are we needed?'

'I'm flying down tonight with Raul.' Raul Velasquez was another of Rink's employees. Some time back he'd been severely injured during the rescue of an abducted kid from his Mexican cartel boss father, and Rink had kept him off the front line while he recuperated: that meant Rink didn't foresee this job as too strenuous or risky, an ideal way to get Raul back in the field. 'We're meeting with McTeer this evening. Think it's doable from your end?'

'We're working tonight?'

'No. If you can be in Miami for early afternoon tomorrow it'll do. I'll have a suit ready for you, but the haircut and shave's over to you, brother.'

'You'd best give me an address.'

'I'll email the details across to you.'

'Good stuff,' I said with no sentiment in my tone. 'I'll see you tomorrow.'

'Great to hear you're already working on *mean and moody*.' Rink chuckled. He hung up.

Mean and gloomy, more like. Ennui had been my frame of mind for some time. Not only was I growing unwelcome in my hometown, I didn't want to be there any more. Although I'd joked with Grant about feeling old, I wasn't quite over the hill yet, just acting like a surly washed-up fighter looking for one last battle. I needed to get moving, kick my butt into gear and shake off the doldrums. Standing around at a gala evening wasn't exactly the kind of action my heart sung for, but it was preferable to waiting to be shucked in Mexico Beach.

My phone defaulted back to the webpage I'd last been perusing, but I'd no interest in it now. I swiped it off-screen, and looked up a flight to Miami. I was tempted to drive, I enjoyed being behind the wheel rather than cramped on a plane, but Rink had intimated that he wanted me wide-eyed and bushy-tailed for the job. I found a six a.m. Delta Airlines flight out of Panama City that would get me to Miami for lunchtime, despite having to make a connection in Atlanta, Georgia. All told, a journey time of less than five hours wasn't too bad for a Sunday. By the time I'd finished booking, Rink had emailed over the details of the swanky hotel, plus the less salubrious one where we'd be staying for the duration of the trip. He also reminded me to bring my Speedos with me for a day on the beach the guys were planning. Yeah, right. Getting me in a tuxedo was pushing things as it was.

3

The hotel commanded a position at the centre of the Art Deco District adjacent to Ocean Drive, overlooking Lummus Park and the world-famous beach. It wasn't one of the massive edifices of steel, glass and concrete I had expected, but housed in a luxurious mansion setting that made the term 'opulence' redundant. It reminded me of an Italian villa, formed of arches and mezzanine floors around a central courtyard: everywhere I looked there were fountains, mosaics and gold gilt and plush wood that glowed under soft lighting. It was exclusive, boutique-style, with only a small number of sumptuous suites. Even dressed for the occasion in my rented tux I was as conspicuous as a blind cobbler's thumb. This was the domain of the uber-rich, not some ex-squaddie who'd grown up on a tough housing estate in Manchester in the north of England. Saying that, there were others at the gala evening that hadn't been born with a silver spoon in their mouth, but had worked their way up to an elite status through hard graft or great looks. I'd be name-dropping if I mentioned some of the famous faces in attendance: just let it be said that a certain rap artist was so enamoured by his girl that he had put a ring on it.

A-list celebrities rubbed shoulders with sports stars, politicians, mega-successful business people and other bright and shiny individuals whose inclusion I couldn't work out. Perhaps they were talent agents, literary editors and movie producers: that, or they were criminals. Some of the guests had arrived with their own retinues, and some of those included security details, but their remit was different from ours. The boys from Rington Investigations were largely expected to man the doors, stay in the background and remain beneath the notice of those dining on Michelin-quality food and drinking champagne. Reading between the lines, this was supposed to be a sponsorship drive to help fund a charitable institute: in my opinion the dinner and bar tab would keep a Third World country afloat for a year.

Earlier we'd met at another hotel, ours. It was part of a chain affiliated to the Hilton brand, four stars at a push and all the buffet breakfast you could eat. Even so, it was plush compared to some of the dives I'd stayed in during other jobs. Because our employer was covering expenses, we'd taken a room each, but had met in Rink's for a job briefing and last-minute instructions from McTeer. Primarily he asked me to try not to break anything, and I promised I'd keep my hands to myself. He was only partly joking. We were subcontracting to the hotel security team, and McTeer was hopeful of further contracts in the coming months; the last he wanted was to be struck off their approved supplier list because we didn't meet their high-calibre of service staff. 'Mean, moody, hands in pockets,' I reassured him. 'I get it.'

'Actually, keep your hands out of your pockets,' he countered, with a grin, 'or you'll make the place look untidy.'

Once we'd got suited up, and the James Bond jokes were out of the way, we reported for duty at the villa, and were directed to the rooftop lounge – the regular dining room wasn't spacious enough to contain the numbers at the gathering – and shown our posts by one of the in-house security men who reminded me more of a butler than a bouncer. He even had a fake British upper-class accent, and when I asked where he was from he looked at me as if I were the one speaking a foreign language. I guessed he was a Yank who spent his spare time watching reruns of *Downton Abbey* on BBC America.

The rooftop lounge was only partly open to the elements, a portion of it enclosed by a retractable marquee-style roof usually employed should one of the frequent lightning storms blow in from the Caribbean. Tonight it was in place to ward off the prying camera lenses of paparazzi buzzing overhead in helicopters. Ceiling fans worked to keep the guests cool as they imbibed over-priced plonk, but I was stationed very near to the door that gave access to the elevators, so was a victim of the sultry heat: the humidity was a swine, and I was frequently in need of a mopping down so that I didn't look as if somebody had upended their champagne flute over my head. I tried to remain surreptitious as I dabbed sweat from my eyes, and blew it out the corners of my mouth. Velasquez and McTeer were on the far side of the roof, but Rink was stationed near to me. When I looked over at him he appeared cool and detached, untroubled by the heat. Dressed in his tuxedo he cut a dashing figure, and on one occasion I'd overheard a Botox-enhanced beauty ask her girlfriend if she was positive Rink wasn't actually Dwayne Johnson, the movie star and ex-professional wrestler. He had the physique, the tawny skin tone and exotic looks, though on closer inspection Rink's features were more Eastern, with the epicanthic folds of his eyelids denoting a Japanese rather than Samoan heritage. I grunted in mirth at the girl's star-struck wonderment as she sidled past Rink a few times, and was tempted to ask her who I reminded her of, but was afraid she'd respond with 'My grandfather'.

The girl was one of about a dozen young women in attendance whose reason for being around was simply to be pretty and laugh in all the right places. Some of them would be professional star chasers – hoping to snag themselves a husband or a sugar daddy – and some I guessed were there on another professional basis. They called themselves escorts but they were still hookers, however they dressed and preened for the occasion. But good luck to them. They were employing their assets to get them through life; was that much different than me hiring out my fists because I could throw, and take, a punch or two? However I looked at it we were all whoring our skills.

Servers minced around the guests, both male and female, all of them as pretty as the celebrities and escorts alike, but were largely invisible until a glass required replenishing or grape required peeling. As they passed me I nodded in greeting, but I was beneath their notice. If there was a scale by which those on the roof were measured, me and my colleagues stood on the lowest notch. But that suited me, because I thought every last one of them were pretentious sons of bitches playing at giving a shit. Deliberately, I noticed, the fame-hungrier of the guests made it their mission to periodically step from under the anonymity of the marquee to ensure the paparazzi got a good shot of them posing in the glare of strategically placed fauna and furniture. As often as I mopped my face, I glanced at my wristwatch, counting down the hours until I could go off-duty and return to the real world.

As more alcohol went down, the volume levels rose. I could barely hear the string quartet that played on – as ignored as I felt – under a pavilion at the far end of the roof. Conversation was now at an excitable, tipsy buzz interspersed by stilted laughter, and once by an angry bark when a narcissistic prick commanded his female companion to shut her mouth while he was talking, which she did. The babble was getting on my nerves, as was the trickle of sweat rolling down my back, and I was pleased of the respite when finally it was speech time. The organiser, who reminded me of one of those plastic-faced cosmetic surgeons that advertise their services on the cable channels, thanked and fawned, made a few lame jokes, then thanked and fawned again for a few minutes before he received a hearty round of applause and then was instantly forgotten as glasses were again replenished. His speech was largely pointless, but had been delivered to remind his guests that signatures on cheques were a requisite parting shot at the end of the gala evening. I made myself a silent bet that more than a few of those swilling down Dom Pérignon or whatever were freeloading or would have an unfortunate lapse of memory before skipping off to their waiting limousines. The charity drive was as much a show as any of the posturing of the rich and glamorous, anyway. Any donations given would be to offset tax bills, not out of philanthropic generosity. The entire pathetic and facile disguise to the event sickened me to the stomach: this was pretence, the rich and famous acting rich and famous while protecting their wealth and fame.

I was happy when the midnight hour finally approached. I suspected that the guests wouldn't hang around; they'd be scooting off to other parties held in exclusive clubs in other parts of the city, and good riddance. Apart from non-reciprocated greetings, I'd barely shared more than a few passing words all night. Ordinarily I was happy with my own company, but it was different when ignored by those who believed themselves my betters. My father, a hard-working man who'd scraped a living all his shortened life, used to tell me that wealth didn't make a man better, all it meant was he could afford softer toilet paper. 'We all squat to take a crap, our kid,' he told me, 'and never forget it, and I think the man who has to have his arse wiped for him is the lesser for it.' He had a way with words did my dear old dad.

Keeping my word, I kept my hands to myself. Even when tipsy dinner guests tripped past, still aloof to my presence, on their way to the elevators down, I stood unmoving, hands clasped at my waistline. A quick glance at Rink showed he was more comfortable with the job, and appreciated the parade of beauties strolling by. The girl who had mistakenly believed he was The Rock sidled up and passed him her phone number, and Rink gave her one of his patented grins and an arched eyebrow as he placed her card in his front breast pocket, the sly devil. As the girl sashayed past me, Rink offered a surreptitious wink that said 'What happens in Miami stays in Miami.' Good luck to him; he was currently romantically unattached, so there was no need for him to be a monk. I was only pleased that we'd booked separate rooms back at our hotel.

Once the majority of guests had left, McTeer and Velasquez meandered over, McTeer via one of the servers who still held a tray of canapés. He approached me with flakes of filo pastry dotting the corners of his mouth, and holding aloft something unidentifiable on a cocktail stick. My best guess was escargot, and I had to swallow down on a little bit of bile that made its way up my throat.

'Perks of the job,' he announced as he wagged the snail – or whatever it was – at me. 'Go grab yourself a snack, Hunter. It's delicious and free.'

'Thanks,' I said, 'but no thanks.'

'Your loss, Hunter. Leaves more for me and the guys.'

'Knock yourselves out,' I said. 'I'll grab something from room service when we get back. Is this us done, Mack?'

'Yeah. Told you it was easy money.' He took an approving look around at our surroundings – the detritus of the evening was rapidly being spirited away by the servers – and nodded in satisfaction. 'I could get used to this line of work. You did an exemplary job, guys, thanks. I'm pretty sure there'll be more where this came from.' He wasn't talking about the escargot he wagged again, but future employment at similar events. He then glanced sheepishly at Rink. 'If it comes to it, you sure you can spare me, boss?'

'I won't stand in your way, Mack. You have to follow the money, brother,' Rink told him philosophically.

Not me, I thought. Job satisfaction meant a whole lot more to me than any amount of remuneration or leftover finger food I could eat. But I kept my opinion to myself. Velasquez also looked thoughtful, and he perhaps was thinking along similar lines as me, but then he placed both palms on his face and rubbed some life into his rubbery features. 'Man, I'm bushed,' he said. 'Who knew standing still for five hours was such hard work?'

He had a point. I had aches in places I didn't know I had places. Rink though appeared untroubled: but he had mastered the art of stillness both mentally and physically, which was why he was one of the best recon scouts I'd ever met, and I'd met hundreds. When he was in the zone, he could make a fence post appear hyperactive.

'I have to have a quick debriefing with the security manager,' McTeer announced. 'See you guys downstairs in a few minutes?'

27

We began moving for the elevators while McTeer went in search of Jeeves the butler, Rink and Velasquez a couple of paces ahead of me. Being the thoughtful employer, Rink checked that Velasquez was OK.

'I'm good, Rink. Ready for more action though. I think I've spent enough time answering phones, don't you?'

'As long as you are ready, brother.'

'Ready for anything.' He sneaked a look back to check McTeer didn't overhear. 'Just not something as mind numbingly boring as this BS again.'

'I second the motion,' I put in.

'It's not every job where we get to chew fat with probably the most famous couple in the world,' Rink said. He meant the undisclosed rap artist and his singer/actress wife. The fact he hadn't actually spoken to either didn't matter; they'd shared the same oxygen for a few hours.

'I dunno,' I said. 'I once met and had my photo taken with Mickey and Minnie at Disney World.'

Rink laughed, and shook his head at me over his shoulder. He'd reached the elevator and hit the call button. I glanced along the short corridor. 'Is there a toilet round here? I need to pay a visit before we get in a cab.'

'I think the ones on this level are reserved for feted guests,' Rink said.

'Fuck 'em,' I said wryly, as I recalled my dad's wise words. 'We all have to take a crap, Rink, and I want to check out the quality of the toilet paper. Perks of the job, right?'

Rink screwed his face. 'Just make sure you remember to flush, brother.'

'And don't go signing your autograph on the stall,' Velasquez added. He mimed dipping his finger and swiping it on an imaginary wall. Now I screwed my face.

'Gross!' Rink said, but he was grinning.

Boys will be boys, despite the fancy surroundings.

While they boarded the elevator, still trading toilet humour, I went off in search of the men's room. Raised voices led me to it.

I paused outside the door. I knew it was the right washroom because of a fancy brass plaque depicting a gentleman in a top hat; there was an adjacent ladies' room further along the corridor. So it surprised me when I identified both voices as emanating from within the men's room. The loudest was male, the other higher-pitched, and definitely feminine, not to mention frightened. There was a sharp crack that the closed door barely dulled, and the woman yelped in pain.

What happens in Miami stays in Miami. The over-abused axiom didn't hold much meaning if something could be stopped from happening.

I pushed open the door and stepped inside.

It was a decision a wise man might live to regret, but call me impulsive.

'Is there a problem here, ma'am?' I asked.

It was the type of washroom where a polite attendant would hand out damp towels and hand cream, maybe even a spritz of expensive cologne, in exchange for a generous tip, but now that most of the paying guests had retired to bed, so too had the attendant. There were individual stalls, a row of urinals and a bank of washbasins, all the golden fixtures and fittings glimmering under soft lighting. At the end nearest the door there were even plush leather loungers, and a docking/recharging post for laptops and tablets should there be any waiting time. In retrospect I'd wager that the ends of the toilet paper were individually folded into neat little triangles. It was as pretentious a shithouse as any I'd visited.

The man had a woman arched backwards over the washbasins. But as I announced my entrance he turned to face me, one hand flat against her chest as if she required protection from me. The woman's eyes were tearful, and her left cheek blazed with the imprint of a palm, but otherwise she was incredibly beautiful. She was dark-haired, tall, buxom, and her legs were lengthened to almost impossible perfection by the addition of stiletto heels. Her gold dress shimmered as it hugged her curves in all the right places. I'd noticed her earlier, though she was seated at the far end of the rooftop lounge, and had also noted her fair-headed beau when he'd snapped at her to shut her mouth when he was speaking. Throughout the proceedings I'd noticed he'd remained largely neutral to those who'd attempted to engage him in drunken chatter, pulling off the mean and moody look so well McTeer should have employed him for the evening. Reclining on a chaise lounge, he hadn't given much hint of his size but I could see now that he was a good four inches taller than me, athletic rather than muscular, and about ten years my junior. He wasn't intimidated one iota by my appearance.

'There is no problem here,' he told me. His voice was accented, clipped. 'Your services are not needed. You can leave.'

It was one thing being ignored by rich punks, quite another when they chose to talk down to me as if I was a dog.

'I wasn't speaking to you.' Purposefully looking past him, I caught the woman's tear-filled gaze. 'Ma'am, I'm sorry but you're in the wrong washroom. If you'd like I'll escort you out of here to somewhere safe.'

The man gave her a shove, so that he could fully face me. 'You are intruding in a private matter,' he warned. 'Leave now or you'll be sorry.'

He'd pale eyes, almost yellow, but that could have been an effect of the mood-setting lights. Despite hair the colour of weak tea his skin was nearer white coffee, and it wasn't a recent tan from being under the Floridian sun but genetics. His rangy build, his appearance, hinted at a mixture of Middle Eastern and Russian heritage, which fit his accent. If I had to punt my best guess I'd say he was originally from Georgia or Chechnya or another of the former Soviet states between the Black and Caspian Seas.

'If I leave I will be sorry,' I countered, and again searched the woman's gaze, letting her know it was the last thing I'd do. I held out a hand for her. 'Ma'am.'

She looked fearfully at the back of the guy's head, then at me. She shook her head gently. 'I'm...I'm fine. Really. You should leave like Mikhail said.'

'Can't do it,' I said.

'You can and will,' Mikhail snapped and took an aggressive step towards me. My palm shot up flat between us, and he halted. His fists bunched at his sides.

'Take it easy, buddy,' I warned him. 'You need to calm down.'

'Where do you come off telling me what to do? You are a damn performing monkey in a suit, and a cheap one at that.

Here's what is going to happen. I tell you what to do, or I'll have your damn job and your fucking balls.'

'You're welcome to the job,' I replied, but left the rest unsaid.

'Damn right I am. I could buy you, like that!' He clicked his fingers. 'I could buy this fucking hotel. Do you think I'm a man to be told what to do?'

'I think your ears are so full of your own pompous bullshit you wouldn't listen anyway.' I took a step deeper into the room. His fists tightened a few notches and I shook my head in disdain. 'But you should. Go ahead, buy the hotel, but never...ever assume you can own anyone. Nobody is property you can do whatever you want to.' I indicated the woman. 'Nobody.'

He thumbed back at her. 'She's mine, and I'll do whatever the fuck I want to her. And no punk ass rent-a-thug is going to tell me different.'

This contract was important to Jim McTeer, and I'd promised to behave so I didn't spoil the prospect of future work for him. I'd especially promised to keep my hands to myself but the guy was seriously testing my resolve. McTeer would be pissed off, but he'd also understand. If it were he in the washroom, McTeer wouldn't walk away and allow the punk to continue beating the girl either. But I had a sense of what to expect if I put Mikhail on his arse. Squint-eye and his pals had taken their beating because they knew they'd been jerks; this arsehole would probably hit me with a lawsuit and a bill for his dental work that would ensure I'd be existing on minute noodles and refried beans for the foreseeable future.

I moved a pace to one side, so I didn't present an immediate hostile threat. I again offered a hand to the woman. 'Ma'am,' I said softly, 'you don't have to put up with this.'

'I...I can't leave,' she croaked.

'You are not leaving, Trey,' Mikhail emphasised, so it was clear who was the decision maker.

Trey – I took it that was the woman's name and not a Russian swear word I was unfamiliar with – placed her manicured fingernails against the sore spot on her cheek. Her tongue played along her bottom lip. She was checking for injury, anticipating more to come. 'Mikhail,' she said reasonably, 'this is not the time or place. We both should leave.'

'You should listen to her,' I added. 'But you should leave separately.'

'The only one leaving is the interfering asshole.' As he made the declaration he sneered down at me. 'You have three seconds, my friend. And I'm counting.'

I'd tried diplomacy.

It had failed miserably.

Now the inevitable was unavoidable, because I could tell he wasn't even going to wait until three.

As he twitched, I hit him.

The best form of defence is offence. Never let it be said otherwise.

My uppercut caught him under the chin before he'd even loaded up his arm for a swing, and he sat down heavily on the floor. He was stunned but not out. When he glimpsed up at me I saw the yellow tinge to his eyes had been a trick of the light. They were blue, as cold as ice, but in direct contradiction they simultaneously radiated volcanic heat. This was a man unused to being struck, and he hated the sensation as much as he did me.

'Stay down, pal,' I warned him as I again extended a hand for Trey.

She didn't immediately accept my offer of safety. She was as stunned by Mikhail's downfall as he was, and probably as afraid as he was angered. She looked down at him, one hand now almost stuffed inside her mouth. She took a faltering step towards him, her heart and mind at war. But then she halted and a shudder went through her. When her gaze switched to mine her dark eyes were wide and begging the question of me: *do you know what you've just done?*

'He asked for it,' I told her. 'If there's one thing I despise it's a bully. Now come on. He can't hurt you any more. I won't let him.'

Tentatively she edged around Mikhail. He made a half-hearted grab for her but she dodged out of his reach, and he transferred the hand to his mouth. He dabbed his lips with the back of his wrist. There was blood on it when he raised the hand to point at me. 'You have made a big mistake, my friend.'

'You're the one on your arse with a sore jaw,' I pointed out.

He shook his head, then slowly dribbled bloody saliva between his knees. 'Your mistake was not finishing me. Believe me, I won't make the same mistake.'

'For any threat to work, your victim needs to be afraid it will come true. Stand up, I'll knock you down again, and yeah, I just might have to finish you so we don't have to keep going through the same old rigmarole. Believe me?'

He ignored me. He stared at Trey, who'd taken cover behind me but hadn't yet fled the room. 'You have made a big mistake too, Trey. You've been places, been party to conversations, and been trusted. Go with him, but your betrayal will not go unpunished.'

I placed a protective arm around her waist, could feel her shivering, and gently urged her towards the exit. But she was resistant and for a moment I thought she was going to rush back to her fallen beau and beg for forgiveness. But she was made of sterner stuff. Her shivering grew to a tremor, pent up fear morphing into excitement at her imminent escape, or maybe into anger that she'd taken his shit for so long. 'You son of a bitch!' she snarled as she touched her fingers to her swollen cheek. 'That's the last time you will ever hurt me, Mikhail.'

He didn't reply; he only sneered up at me as he dribbled more bloody spit on the tiles. When he knew he'd caught my attention, he showed me his bloody teeth. 'Be seeing you again, champ.'

'Remember what I warned you about threats?' I asked. 'Oh, that's right. You don't listen.'

I allowed him to mull over my parting shot in private, while I ushered Trey out of the washroom and towards the elevators.

'I have to go back.'

Trey's proclamation wasn't exactly a surprise. Fearful of the future, many victims of abuse chose familiarity over the unknown. Women beaten mercilessly by their partners often made excuses for them, even believing that they themselves were somehow responsible for pushing their partners to such bad behaviour. Often they'd lie on the abuser's behalf, resist help, and even defend their abuser when push came to shove. Some victims ended up dead at the hands of those they wouldn't say a wrong word against. I had caught a glimpse of tougher mettle in Trey and hoped she wouldn't cave in, but her words were hardly unexpected.

'If you go back things will only get worse. Trust me. Besides, you don't owe that punk a damn thing. Let him think about how much of an asshole he was to you while nursing his own sore mouth.'

'He only slapped me.' Her downcast expression betrayed the lameness of her words.

'This time,' I said, and gave her a forthright look, but she refused to meet it.

I hadn't yet pressed the down button, only closed the elevator doors, giving her a few seconds breathing time to get a grip of herself before we reached the ground floor and had to mingle with other people. Trey leaned wearily against the rear wall, both arms folded behind her lower back. Her neatly styled hair had come away from its fixings and hung loose over her features. I couldn't see her eyes, only her quivering bottom lip. She was the definition of forlorn.

'You weren't working tonight,' I said.

She glimpsed up at me from under her sweeping bangs. 'I was a guest.'

'Yeah.' Initially I'd made the assumption that she was one of the professional escorts hired to accompany the rich guests, but Mikhail's assertion that she'd been places, been involved in conversations, and been trusted, had informed me otherwise. Her relationship with him had been lengthier than a few paid-for hours. I decided it best to keep quiet about presuming she was a hooker. It might not endear me to her, could even earn me a slapped face too. That she was his long-term partner also explained why she felt so bad about his comeuppance and wished to return to soothe his bruised ego.

'Mikhail is your boyfriend, right?' I went on.

'More than that.'

'Husband?'

She showed me a diamond-encrusted ring on her wedding finger, and she shuddered in regret. 'This isn't just for show.'

'Then I can understand you feeling bad about walking out on him, especially with me, a stranger. But you need to give him some space, let him cool down and sober up before you speak to him again. If you go back now he'll only take up where he left off, and this time he's got something to be really angry about. Why did he slap you like that?'

She had the grace to look embarrassed as she tucked her locks behind one ear. 'He didn't take me into the men's room so that we could talk while he was in the stall.'

'Oh,' I said. I'm broad-minded, but could still be embarrassed when missing the obvious.

Despite the flushed cheeks, Trey wasn't really shy – she was angry. 'I told him that we weren't going to do it in any washroom and I didn't care how fancy it was. He wasn't happy, said the least I could do was get down on my knees for him.'

I cleared my throat.

She stared at me dead in the eye. 'I'm no slut.'

'I didn't suggest you were.'

'You intimated it. *You weren't working tonight*, huh? I get what you meant now. What? You're regretting stepping in between a man and his wife's business?'

'Not at all. It's like I said, he doesn't own you, wife or not. He had no right to hit you like that.'

'You hit him. What makes you any different?'

'He deserved a punch in the face, you didn't.'

'Wow,' she said, and stared between the toes of her stilettos. 'Don't you think that's all a matter of personal opinion? In his culture it's a wife's duty to see to her husband's needs. Perhaps I did deserve a slap for my wilfulness in refusing him.'

'No way. In some cultures men put the welfare of their goats before their wives or children. Doesn't make it right, just because it's the way it's been done for generations. And if you want to argue cultural ways, then in mine I cherish women and children. I protect them.'

'Oh yeah. Where are you from: freaking Utopia?'

'I'm British.'

'Yeah. I got that. Men don't hit their wives in England?'

'Some, but they don't deserve to be called men in my opinion.'

'Your opinion,' she said, but this time smiled sadly. I was slow to catch on that she was teasing, or perhaps reminding herself that not all men were bullies.

'I meant what I told Mikhail,' she said, growing more serious. 'That was the last time he'd ever hurt me. The last time I'd allow it at any rate. But you heard him, right? He said I'd be punished and Mikhail isn't one for making idle threats.'

'I'd argue that point,' I said, and offered a smile, but it really wasn't the time for jokes. Trey genuinely was concerned that her husband would follow up on his promise to hurt her.

I finally hit the down button and the elevator surged as if eager to please. We were only three floors up, travel time to our destination only seconds away.

'I won't let him hurt you,' I said.

'That's quite something,' Trey replied. 'You don't know me. You don't owe me a thing. And hey! Thanks for getting me out of a sticky situation but really, you've done all you need to do. Hell, I don't even know your name, and here you are pledging to be my protector.'

'I guess I was being a bit presumptuous,' I agreed.

'Presumptuous, huh?' She made a sound of disdain in the back of her throat. 'I'm half expecting you to demand a damn blow job for your help.'

'I'm sorry if I gave you that impression. I don't want anything from you.'

'Then why promise to help me, saying you won't let Mikhail hurt me? How can you do that? We only just met. I don't even know...'

'My name's Joe Hunter. Most of my friends use my second name, but you can take your pick.'

'You're still a stranger to me.'

'Then tell me your name.'

'Tracey Vis... No, don't call me that. I'm Tracey Shaw. Most of my friends call me Trey.'

I nodded. 'There, we aren't strangers any more.'

The elevator settled at the ground floor and the doors swished open.

'This is my stop,' Trey announced. 'I wish I could say it was nice meeting you, Hunter, but under the circumstances...'

'Do you have a room here?' I asked.

She gave me a look of reproof. 'Didn't I mention I wasn't a slut?'

'And didn't I mention you got the wrong impression of me? I only ask because it'd be a better idea for you to move elsewhere. Stay here and Mikhail will be kicking down your door in no time.'

'I'm not staying here. It's like I told you, I was a guest. We have our own home here in Miami.'

'Which you really shouldn't return to either if you intend avoiding this punishment that Mikhail promised.'

She hadn't yet stepped out of the elevator car, which was a good sign. 'So where should I go?'

'Come back to my hotel.' Before she could again remind me that she wasn't a swooning damsel – or loose woman – to be taken advantage of, I calmed her. 'You can stay in my room, but I'll double up with one of my buddies. It'll allow you some thinking time, and if you decide you want my help, then you can let me know in the morning. Deal?'

She thought about it for a long beat. 'No deal. Thanks, Hunter, I do believe your intentions are honourable, but it's like I said, we barely know each other. I think it's best for us all if we just say goodbye.'

I was disappointed, but her response was understandable. I was just some guy who'd bust her husband in the chops. What right had I to offer to be her protector? She didn't know about my true line of work – how could she? She could be forgiven for suspecting I was some seedy creep who'd latched on to her with hopeful delusions about what the future could hold for us both.

'Here.' I passed her a Rington Investigations business card I'd slipped from my wallet, on which I'd previously written my personal cell number on the rear. 'In case you change your mind.'

She eyed the card, then snapped it thoughtfully against her thigh. 'You're a private detective?'

'I'm not just a performing monkey in a cheap suit,' I said, quoting Mikhail's insult back to her. 'And I'm not only in the investigations department, I specialise in...' I thought about it. 'Other areas.'

Trey left the elevator and strode away, head up, shoulders back. I stepped into the grandeur of the central courtyard and watched as she headed for the exit. I was glad when she didn't throw away the card at the first artfully disguised trashcan she passed. She wasn't carrying a regular purse, just a tiny clutch bag, so cupped the card in her palm and held it tight alongside her right thigh. She understood its value, and I think that she got that Mikhail wasn't the only one whose promises should be heeded. Before she exited the hotel she glanced back. Our eyes met, and she mouthed the words *thank you.* I winked. Then I turned to watch the elevator and adjacent stairwell should Mikhail appear in swift pursuit.

Instead I spotted McTeer coming down.

'Sorry for the holdup,' he said by way of greeting – he again toted a bunch of liberated canapés folded in a napkin, 'but some inconsiderate asshole was holding the elevator.'

I didn't admit to being said inconsiderate asshole. But he still eyed me suspiciously. 'What did you do, Hunter?'

'Me? I didn't do a thing,' I lied. 'Just thought I'd take a look around, admire my surroundings while I got the chance. You know, just in case I don't get asked back again.'

'Oh, man,' McTeer wheezed. Visions of being added to the hotel's approved supplier blacklist must have cavorted through his mind. 'Now I know you goddamn did something.'

6

Mikhail Viskhan stooped over, dribbling bloody saliva into the porcelain washbasin, periodically hitting the faucet with the heel of his left palm to sluice away the evidence of his humiliation. He worked his tongue around his mouth and was certain that the security man had loosened two of his teeth: he was livid, when really he should be grateful that his jaw wasn't broken. The man's swift uppercut had been delivered more with sharp intent than for brute impact, designed not for lasting injury but to concuss him and drop him on his ass. Mikhail couldn't recall being hit. One second he was winding up to punch the guy's face, next he was sitting down, brain flashing scarlet to white to scarlet again. He must have been knocked unconscious, but only for the briefest of times. Mikhail had experienced similar knockouts in the past, but he'd always managed to stay on his feet long enough to recover, and then rally, and go on to defeat his opponent. He was an undefeated kickboxer. As a youth he'd fought many incredibly skilled opponents in the ring and on the streets, and others after that where no rules applied and the arena was formed of bloodstained concrete and bomb-blasted walls. In those life or death matches Mikhail had killed with blades, guns, grenades and, only where unavoidable, his hands. Those battles were in the arena of warfare. He considered himself a seasoned warrior, and it shamed him that a lesser man had humiliated him with such ease.

He spat blood once more, then teased at one loose tooth with the tip of a finger. He swore savagely in his native tongue.

'You'll have to slow down, Mikhail, I'm not following you.'

The voice emanated from his smartphone, where he'd set it aside to avoid the splashing water.

'Then listen closer,' Mikhail spat, again in his native language.

'English please,' said the man at the other end.

'I want him found and humiliated, the way he humiliated me!'

'This comes at a most unfortunate time,' the speaker reminded him. 'Do you really want to get mixed up in this when we're on such a tight deadline?'

'I promised him I'd have his balls and I fucking want them.'

'Mikhail, carrying out a personal vendetta jeopardises the successful outcome of the operation.'

'Fuck the operation!'

'Mikhail, be reasonable, my friend. Months of planning have gone into this; to disrupt our schedule now could prove disastrous. Let this man go, there'll be other opportunities to salve your bruised ego after the operation's completed.'

'Salve my bruised ego? Is that what you think I'm concerned about: my fucking ego?'

The man kept silent. It was apparent from his lack of response that he did indeed believe that the dent in Mikhail's ego was what was most troubling to him. Mikhail was narcissistic in the extreme, and any blemish to his reputation was as bad as an ugly wound on his handsome features.

'I'm pissed, Sean. And rightly so, but I don't want him dead simply because he knocked me down; didn't you listen when I said he took Trey with him?'

'I heard.' Sean Cahill's tone was nonplussed. 'But from past experience, she'll be back.'

His wife had tried to walk out on him before, but on those occasions it had been different. She had nowhere to go, nobody to turn to and everything to lose: rapidly she'd come crawling back, begging forgiveness and had taken her punishment for her defiance. This time she had left arm in arm with a gallant white knight. Who knew what she'd tell the security man if she thought she'd found a sympathetic ear to cry into for the first time.

'If Trey speaks, she'll jeopardise more than the fucking successful outcome of the operation. We'll be hunted like rats through this sewer of a country.' Mikhail spat a final time, then grabbed at a tissue dispenser on the wall; he yanked out a wad and wiped his lips and chin. He returned and bent over his smartphone. 'She cannot be allowed to speak.'

'If she tells anyone what we've planned then she too will be scooped up by the FBI. It's in her best interest to keep her mouth shut or risk spending the rest of her life in prison.'

'She is a woman,' Mikhail snapped. 'When does a woman ever show good sense? No, Sean, she will talk. I know this. She'll talk to spite me! The way she spited me this evening! It's in her nature, she knows no other way.'

'I warned you about taking a wife...especially a wilful wife.'

'I was confident I could bend her to my will. I did bend her. But I won't lie, she always strained to resist me.'

'And now she has sprung back,' replied Cahill.

'She has outlived her value. Whether she talks of our plan or not, her betrayal shows where her true loyalties lie, and they're not with me. I have given her everything, and I'll take it all back. I should have killed her the first time she tried to resist me, not married her.'

'Yes, I did suggest it at the time.' Cahill grunted at the memory. 'But she was of more value to you alive than dead back then. We both knew that. But you might be right, perhaps now is the time to end your marital agreement. Divorce is not an option, I guess?'

Theirs was a marriage of convenience. Mikhail sought US residency, and therefore required an American spouse. Tracey Shaw was a desperate young woman forced into white slavery in a former Eastern bloc state who needed free passage home. Mikhail had yanked her from one form of sexual servitude into another albeit more glamorous one, at the price of her hand in marriage. Love had never been a factor in their relationship, only a seething undercurrent of hatred, but both had got what each of them desired. But Mikhail had been in Florida for a decade now, having supposedly forsaken Chechnya for his new American wife. He had established himself as a valued contributor to the economy, a highly successful businessman –

at least that was his public persona. It was unlikely he'd be deported if his wife perished. Not that deportation would ever become an issue, when he was already on the cusp of leaving.

Ten years.

Not once in that decade had he ever felt that Trey appreciated what he had done for her. Without his intervention she'd be a drug-addled hag still whoring to stinking labourers in a Bulgarian brothel, or dead. She deserved no less now that she had scorned him so badly.

He no longer needed her.

As it was, should she die, it would matter not if his residency status came into question, because it would be too late to make a difference. Once his plan came to fruition he intended returning to Chechnya a hero, so fuck the American Dream, and fuck his American wife.

And fuck the pig that had loosened his teeth. He wanted that bastard dead too and his balls brought to him in a pickle jar.

'We have other assets on standby,' he reminded Cahill. 'Use them. Trey and her white knight must die painfully.'

'You want me to run two operations at the same time? You're asking a lot of me, my friend.'

'No. I can manage the final details of the operation, and coordinate our teams, and will have them ready. Trust me, Sean, things will go with a bang. A colossal fucking bang! You can oversee the second operation.' His tone grew sarcastic. 'I trust you'll be more successful if you are not guided by a bruised ego.'

Cahill didn't reply. His words had insulted Mikhail – hardly surprising of a narcissist – and he was now calling in penance.

'I expect you to be at my side when the parade begins and things get noisy, Sean,' Mikhail went on, 'and will not accept tardiness. You have a little less than thirty-seven hours to complete your mission and bring me proof of both their deaths. Cut off the man's balls, do what you will to Trey, I don't care, but she must be punished before she dies. I gave them my word; see to it that it's fulfilled.'

'This is a distraction we could both do without,' Cahill replied cagily. 'But it shall be done. I owe you, Mikhail, and I always repay my debts.'

'Thank you, Sean. You've saved me the trouble of reminding you. So here...I'll give you a head start. Trey won't have returned home, she'll be in hiding. But if you find the bastard that punched me, you'll find her. He worked here in a security role. Speak with the security manager, Greville-Jones, and find out who he is. He will have the names of all those on his payroll and where they are currently staying. When you find them, kill them both and make it painful for them. Do not let me down.'

Cahill began to say something, but Mikhail cut the line with a hard jab at his phone screen. He straightened up, dabbed his chin a final time and dropped the wadded tissues in the nearest washbasin. He tested his rakish smile in the mirror over the sink. The right side of his face was inflamed, but otherwise he was as ravishingly handsome as he always had been. He straightened his tie and cuffs.

He left the washroom, found the elevator down. The courtyard was empty as he strode across it, as was the reception area. He stepped outside under the awning, and was immediately blanketed by heavy damp heat. He was the final guest to leave the gala event, but was not neglected. A valet, dressed in a button-down vest and bow tie despite the intense humidity, jumped to it and went to fetch his Ferrari.

Mikhail deftly spirited a folded hundred-dollar bill into the valet's hand while they exchanged places in the driver's seat. The valet nodded his gratitude even before checking the denomination of the tip, and felt he must say something. 'Thank you, sir, and please take care driving home. I hear there's a hellish storm coming.'

'That there is,' Mikhail responded from the driving seat. He gunned the gas and the supercharged vehicle surged away.

'And I am the bringer of thunder and lightning,' he added, thinking of the storm of his making that was about to hit Florida.

7

An hour after arriving back at our own hotel, McTeer forgave my heavy-handed response to the idiot in the washroom: he knew of the playboy from previous events where he'd proven an insufferable boor, and McTeer conceded he was overdue a punch in the face. Possibly through shame, or more likely through a need to protect his own reputation, Mikhail hadn't admitted to being knocked on his backside for acting like a dick. There was still the possibility that he'd make a complaint once he'd slept on it and sobered up, but for now all was well. Despite the very late hour McTeer received a telephone call from the head of security to thank us for our invaluable service at the gala event – we'd apparently pulled him out of a pinch where sourcing the necessary level of experienced security cover had been proving difficult – and to reward us with a personal gift. McTeer said it was appreciated but not required, but Albert insisted. He had offered to send over some expensive champagne, and McTeer had caved in after agreeing the caveat that a pack of beers would suffice. We were in the wee small hours, but that I learned wasn't a problem: parties extended through until dawn in this part of town and Albert didn't expect we'd be retiring soon. He said he'd send over a courier with our beers *tout suite*.

'Is that guy for real?' I asked.

'He's a pompous asshat,' McTeer said, 'but when he's sending us over free beer he's OK in my book.'

'Albert?' I asked, thinking of the butler in the Batman comics.

'Albert Greville-Jones no less.'

'With a highfaluting name like that he was born for the role, I guess.'

Velasquez had a set of eyes like split pomegranates. 'Don't know about you guys but even the thought of an ice-cold beer isn't enough to keep me awake. I'm gonna hit the sack. Any objections?'

I wasn't that excited about a couple of gratis beers either. 'None from me, buddy. I might not be too far behind you.'

'Jeez, where's Rink when I need him?' McTeer sneered in mock distaste. 'I'm stuck with a couple of lightweights while he's off dancing till dawn.'

Rink had rung his lady admirer and been invited to join her at a party at a nearby club. We didn't expect him back until morning.

'C'mon guys,' McTeer cajoled us. 'We should go along to that party too. Rink's not the only one can give a pretty girl the People's Eyebrow.'

'It's not his damn eyebrow Rink plans on giving that hottie,' Velasquez told him. 'Let him be. We'd only cramp his style.'

'Speak for yourself, melonhead.' McTeer leered for effect, and his grizzled features puckered up like Winston Churchill's after a hard night on the booze. 'The girls can't resist my Irish charm.'

'My grandma is more Irish than you, McTurd,' Velasquez said. 'And has more chance of pulling a date for the night, and she's been dead for ten years.'

McTeer spread his palms in a *whaddayamean* gesture. He looked at me. 'C'mon, Hunter, the night's still young.'

I didn't bother reminding him that I'd had a long day. I'd risen at 3 a.m. to make my flight out of Panama City, so had been on the go for the best part of twenty-three hours already. 'You're on your own, I'm afraid.'

'Oh, man...' he groaned, but then McTeer shrugged and brightened. 'More beer for me, then.'

My room was the one next to McTeer's. Velasquez had the room across the corridor from mine, and Rink's was next to his. We went our separate ways, Velasquez almost stumbling into his room out of fatigue. Although I should have been equally worn out, my head was buzzing and I doubted I'd sleep any time soon. I got out of my tux and splashed some cold water over my face, finger combing the moisture through my hair. I wasn't ready for bed so pulled on some jeans and a shirt, and laced on my boots. I'd no intention of going in search of a party but the idea of a stroll on the beach called to me like the fabled siren's song. Viewing the sea at night held a certain magical quality for me.

Before I slipped out of my room, my cell phone rang.

Unidentified caller.

But I had an inkling who might be calling at this late hour.

'Hello?' Trey's voice held some trepidation.

'Hello,' I responded.

'Is that Joe Hunter? You, uh, gave me your card?'

'You decided to call then?' It was rather a pointless observation, but it gave her a way to continue, without any awkwardness.

'You said you could help me?'

'I'm a man of my word.'

'I...well, I guess I need your help. I...' She paused, gathered herself. 'I don't know what to do.'

'Where are you?'

'Right now? I'm in a cab. But I don't know where to tell the driver to stop.' Her voice lowered; she didn't want the driver to overhear her next proclamation. 'I can't go home, and I've no credit cards or enough cash with me to rent a room. Mikhail always controls those things.'

I gave her the name of my hotel and my room number. 'Come here. You can take my room.' Rink's room was vacant; I would use his. 'I'll come down and pay your fare when you arrive.'

'I've enough cash on me for the cab,' she reassured me, 'just not enough for the rest.'

She didn't want to meet me at the front door. Somebody might misconstrue the arrival of a pretty young woman meeting in the early hours with an older man from out of town. 'OK. Come up to my room.' I gave her the number once more. 'Trey?'

'Yes?'

'You can trust me,' I said. 'Not all men are like your husband.'

'You don't know the half of it,' she said, and left her ambiguous comment at that as she hung up.

Trey was at my door within fifteen minutes. She was still dressed in her shimmering party dress and stiletto heels, but that made sense considering she'd had no opportunity to change. I stand a shade less than six feet tall, and in her shoes Trey could almost meet me eye to eye. The shoes forced her posture rigid, but that wasn't the main reason for her standing so tall. She was trying not to look frightened. Her fear wasn't because she had presented herself at the door of a relative stranger, one who'd proven he had a violent streak. She was so fearful of her husband that she had not gone home to gather her things in case he returned before she could leave. All she carried was her clutch purse. Inside it, I guessed, was the cell phone she'd called me on from the cab, and a few bits of makeup for freshening up, perhaps a few extra dollars Mikhail had allowed her. Her cheek was no longer inflamed from the slap she'd taken, and the other colour had drained from her features. She was as pale as alabaster, and looked more fatigued than even Velasquez, though still prettier with it. There was another obvious difference since last I'd seen her: the diamond ring had disappeared from her fourth finger. The missing ring was a statement of intent. I didn't mention it.

I moved aside so she could enter my room. I'd hung my tuxedo in its bag pending return to the rental shop, and slung it from a coat hook on the wall. Otherwise my room looked clear of my belongings; I'd packed them in my bag ready to cart across to Rink's room, and the bag was out of sight on the far side of the bed. The room was neat, clean and comfortable, but probably less than she was used to. But who knew how she usually lived. I'd met individuals who presented themselves immaculately but lived in hovels unfit for a dog.

'Take a seat,' I said.

She had a choice between a tub chair in front of a counter that held the TV and telephone, plus a coffee maker, or the bed. She chose the latter. Habit forced me to take a look out in the corridor. There was the faint murmur of voices from a TV in a room further down the hall, but that was the only hint of life. I closed the door and turned to check Trey out. She was staring back at me, eyes glistening with moisture, but it was a sheen of hope, not fear. Neither of us could find the appropriate words, so I indicated the coffee maker. 'Can I get you a cup?'

She shook her head politely.

'OK then,' I said, and went over and dragged around the tub chair instead. I sat, so I wouldn't offer an imposing figure looming over her while she was seated. Trey turned side-on so she could meet my gaze, and crossed her legs. She clucked her tongue, reached down to her shoes. 'Do you mind? These things are killing me.'

I'd no objections. She eased out of the shoes and set them aside. I noticed they had red soles and recalled that was a trademark of some highly expensive designer brand. My soles were dung-coloured rubber. Trey bent to massage her heels and toes, and I averted my gaze from the flash of creamy skin of her inner thighs. I'd said I was to be trusted and would give her no reason to suspect I'd an ulterior motive for helping. Though it wasn't an easy task.

When I looked again at her she had her face in both hands, and her bare feet digging into the carpet as she rocked back and forward. I waited for sobs but they didn't come. She straightened and stared back at me, her eyes glistening but now with a pointed intensity. 'If Mikhail even suspected I came here, he'd kill me.'

'Then we keep it between ourselves. He doesn't need to know where you are, and in the morning I'll move you somewhere safer until you can decide what you want to do.'

She touched the pale spot on her ring finger. 'I've already made up my mind. I'm never going back to him.'

I nodded. Good decision.

'That doesn't mean he won't try to force me to come home.'

'Then you go to the courts and get a restraining order.'

She blinked in surprise. 'You're kidding, right? I didn't think you were so naive.'

I wasn't naive, I was pumping her for information, but in a manner in which she'd offer it willingly. If I asked her outright what kind of enemy I'd made then she might not be so forthcoming with the truth. To be honest I was also trying to determine exactly what kind of trouble I could be getting into.

'I've a friend up in Tampa, called Bryony. She's a police detective; I'm sure she can put us in touch with professionals who can help you get away from your abusive husband.'

She snorted. 'You're talking about social workers? I think I made a mistake coming here after all. When you said you could help, well, I was thinking in another way. Do you seriously think Mikhail Viskhan's the type to take this lying down?' She said his name as if I should recognise it.

'Viskhan?' I clarified. 'He's not called Shaw like you?'

'I prefer my maiden name; alas, our marriage was not one blessed by a holy man.'

'More a contract of convenience?' I ventured.

'For him it was convenient, for me...well, I'd little choice in the matter.'

'There's no love between you?'

'You saw what he was like in that washroom: does Mikhail strike you as a person who loves anyone but himself?'

'I'm only asking...'

'You want to know if I'm going to have a change of heart and go running back to him in the morning? *Trust me*, Joe, that isn't going to happen. Hell, I've been looking for an opportunity like this for years. Since...well, since even before I met Mikhail.' It was clear there was more she thought about adding, but I was still a stranger to her, and she wasn't yet ready to give up all her past. That was OK, because, reading between the lines, she had not been a willing party to the marriage, but had been pressed into it. Similar arrangements were made daily across the planet, and often for the wrong reasons. I decided not to speculate. She would tell me her story when she was ready. But I wanted to learn more about Mikhail, the person I was making an enemy of.

'He's obviously a wealthy man,' I said. 'Russian new money?'

She frowned at the term.

'Dirty money?' I pressed.

'He's an entrepreneur, made his fortune in importing and exporting. His rise from poor Chechen immigrant to successful businessman is celebrated by many, proof that the American Dream is still possible for those willing to work hard for it.' She barked a scornful laugh and looked me dead in the eye. 'You know what I mean by "import and export"?'

'Drugs? Weapons?' I shook my head in regret, realising the obvious. 'Something even more valuable?'

'A good percentage of sex workers in this city are owned by Mikhail. I told you we were invited to that gala dinner as guests...it wasn't entirely true. We were there to ensure that Mikhail's girls behaved appropriately. Unfortunately he was the one that ended up embarrassing himself.'

'He supplied those escorts, huh?'

'It's typical of him. All of those girls on hand, and he still dragged me into that bathroom.' A shiver went through her and for a moment I wondered if in some absurd way she was envious of some of the younger women. But I was wrong. She was ashamed; angered that Mikhail still treated her like a whore to obey his dirtiest command. I recalled her assertions on more than one occasion where she'd iterated that she wasn't a slut.

'How long have you been his prisoner?' I wasn't going to play things down. She had been held and controlled against her will, so what else was she?

'Ten years as his wife, two more before that.'

'Mind if I ask what happened?'

She inhaled deeply, folded her hands on her thighs. 'Stupidity, I guess. Yeah, stupidity. I suppose I have to take some responsibility for what happened.'

I shook my head. Hers was the typical response I'd been expecting. 'No, Trey. You are not to blame.'

'I left myself vulnerable, got split up from my friends, and made the mistake of trusting the first smiling face I met.' She halted there, perhaps wondering if she was making a similar mistake again. She nibbled her bottom lip, then decided to carry on. 'I was on a gap year from college, and went on a backpacking trip with some friends and ended up in this nightclub in Bulgaria. We were a bit wild, got drunk, but we were young...it wasn't enough for us. We got stoned. I don't remember much after that besides speaking with this kind girl who offered to show me the way back to my hostel. Next I remember is waking up in a room with a chain round my ankle and needle holes in my arm.' She stopped then. Her story after that could only get much worse. I wasn't going to press her on it for now.

'Mikhail found you there?'

'I'd been moved to another brothel by then, but still in Bulgaria. He chose me from a bunch of other girls, but primarily because I was American. I acted stupidly and got taken, but I'm not a fool. I knew immediately that servitude to Mikhail wouldn't be pleasant but it was my way back home.'

Now I was the one with my head down and my hands folded in my lap. Trey had halted again and she allowed the silence to add gravitas to her situation. I raised my gaze. Even haunted by her plight, she was stunning. I assumed the narcotics she'd been purposefully addicted to were a thing of the past, a more potent weapon used to bend her to Mikhail's will since: terror.

'You couldn't reach out to your family for fear Mikhail would harm them?'

'He swore that if I tried to contact my parents he'd have them burned alive in their home. I believed he was capable of doing that. He has made many threats over the years, and I'm sorry to admit I kept my mouth shut out of fear.'

'Turning to the local vice squad was also out of the question,' I supposed. 'They would have protected you as an informant, but that wasn't enough to save your parents or others Mikhail threatened to harm.'

Trey didn't reply; she didn't have to.

'So why now?' I asked.

She looked at me.

'You've turned to me for help,' I went on, 'despite the consequences.'

Her tongue darted between her lips. 'Two reasons,' she said. 'You're not a cop, and Mikhail needs to be stopped. Permanently.'

I exhaled. 'I don't know what impression I gave you but I'm no hitman.'

'Aren't you?' The way in which she said it she was inviting me to peer deeply into my own soul. 'If you knew what Mikhail is planning, I bet you'd have a different opinion.'

I sat straight in the chair. Stared at her while she stared back. She wouldn't know it from my outward appearance, but I was fizzing with adrenaline inside. I hated torpor, and it was a reason I couldn't help getting in trouble. Earlier I'd wondered what I was getting into having interjected on Trey's behalf, but with little concern about the consequences. Her latest announcement had certainly given me a metaphorical kick in the butt where I sensed there was an opportunity to lift me out of my self-imposed doldrums. The more dire the answer to the mystery she posed, the better for me.

'Tell me,' I said, eager to hear.

'I need to know I've reached out to the right man first,' she said.

'Tell me about Mikhail and we'll see.'

'He's not only a pimp, a criminal. He's a very dangerous man.'

'How dangerous?'

'Let's put it this way. Once he puts his mind to something, there's no stopping him. And if I'm right about what he's planning...there will be casualties. Many casualties.'

Her announcement sent a jolt through me, but its only outward manifestation was a nerve jumping in my jaw. 'You need to tell me everything, Trey. Right now.'

Trey's mouth opened, but before she could say another word I heard movement in the corridor. I glanced at the closed door, just as there was a soft rap on wood. The knock wasn't on my door, but on McTeer's, the adjoining room. That'd be the courier arriving with his beer, I supposed. My friend's voice was partly muffled as he responded to the knock, and only marginally clearer when he answered the door. He sounded ebullient enough...at first. But then McTeer cursed harshly, there was a drumming of feet, and a gun barked. By then I was already leaping to grapple Trey, taking her over the bed and onto the floor beyond. She landed on top of my overnight bag, and I pressed her down with my body covering hers even as chaos reigned in the adjoining room. A gunshot cracked again, followed by a drawn-out moment of silence, before something crashed down. I felt the heavy impact as a shudder through the floor and the trickle of adrenaline through my body became a deluge.

8

Seconds ago, Jim McTeer had been reclining on his bed, shoulders and head propped on pillows stacked against the headboard, secretly pleased that Hunter and Velasquez had declined a night on the tiles. He'd been talking BS, because it was what guys did when they were together and didn't want to be perceived as the lamest of the bunch. In his mid-fifties, his partying days were over. He was happier sitting in his jockey shorts with his dress shirt unbuttoned over his hairy belly, while he watched some nubile young things cavorting on-screen on one of the pay-per-view channels. He'd kept the sound muted, so was robbed of some of the enjoyment, but was spared any embarrassment should one of his buddies overhear the TV. Hunter's room had one of those adjoining doors, so the soundproofing was minimal. In fact, he'd been enjoying his movie while keeping half an ear cocked to the soft murmur of voices filtering through from Hunter's side: no wonder Hunter didn't want to go out when he'd already organised some female company.

'Lucky bastards,' he'd whispered, thinking of both Rink and Hunter, 'but all power to you.' McTeer had a wife, his second wife actually, and hell, despite theirs being a long-distance marriage, if she learned what kind of movies he enjoyed while away from home she'd string his balls in a sling for a month. When he heard the approach of feet, and the knock at his door, he first made sure to power off the TV before going to greet the courier. He'd downed a couple of miniature vodkas from the mini-bar, was ready to wash them down with a few cold ones before settling down for the night. 'Who's the lucky bastard now, guys?' he grinned.

McTeer was no dope. He'd been a big city detective for the full twenty-five, and had worked as a private dick and security consultant since taking retirement from the force. Usually his internal instinct to danger pinged warnings, but his senses were dulled by the thought of cracking open a beer and getting back to the cavorting beauties on-screen, and, by then, vodka that had already set his brain buzzing: he wanted the courier gone quick time. He leaned to glimpse through the security peephole in the door, caught the warped image of a guy holding up a box, and pulled down on the handle before his brain registered that other figures loomed beyond the courier. The door was already on its inward swing before his inner voice told him, *Set up.* And then it was too late.

'The fuck is this?' McTeer snapped.

Three men pushed into the room, the first – a mean-faced Latino – thrusting the boxed beers into McTeer's exposed stomach so that he'd no option but take them in his hands or allow them to drop on his bare feet. It allowed the 'courier' to free up his hands and yank out a revolver.

'With the compliments of Mister Viskhan,' the Latino sneered, and brought up the gun.

McTeer thrust the beers away, directly under the barrel of the gun, just as it barked. The bullet found the box and the bottles inside and there was an explosion of amber froth. McTeer lunged in as the leaking box tumbled down the gunman's body to the floor, the sound softened by the resistance of his slightly bent legs and also McTeer jamming up against it. McTeer grappled for the gun, twisting around with his assailant so he faced the other two men also holding guns. They couldn't get off a shot for fear of hitting the Latino. McTeer reared backwards, dragging the gunman with him, then managed to yank his hand round and insert his own finger through the trigger guard. He popped the nearest man in the chest, and there was a moment where silence descended over the tableau as realisation hit. The would-be assassin toppled slowly and then gathered speed as gravity took hold of his dead weight. The corpse's impact sent a thrum of vibration through the floor that McTeer felt through his bare soles.

The sound was the catalyst for the death struggle to resume.

The Latino grunted and cursed as he contested for the gun, and McTeer's language was equally colourful. The third man in the room, a white kid with a scraggly beard and beanie hat settled low on his brow, danced back and forth looking for a clean line on his target. The revolver spun from the Latino's grip, skidded under the bed somewhere out of reach. McTeer jostled with him, then headbutted him savagely. Resistance went out of the Latino's knees, and he sank, almost dragging McTeer down with him, but they spilled apart, and now McTeer was an open target. The beanie-hatted kid fired.

Blood freckled the side of McTeer's chin. He glimpsed down at a spewing wound on his left shoulder. 'Fuckin' punk-assed little junkie,' he snarled at the kid.

The kid fired again, and this time with better aim. The bullet took McTeer in the gut, and he stumbled back, his knees colliding with the bed, and he sat down heavily. He looked down under heavy eyelids at the Latino, who was scrabbling around, one arm beneath the bed in search of his dropped gun. McTeer was tempted to kick him in the ass, but he couldn't lift his leg. He looked down at his belly. The puncture site was a small puckered hole, but it pulsed blood, sopping his boxer shorts and upper thighs. Internally the damage would look more significant. It didn't hurt yet, but if he were spared a few minutes more the pain would be coming in spades.

McTeer wasn't ready to die – he hadn't seen the end of his picture, goddamnit—but it didn't look as if he had much choice in the matter. The only thing buying him a few precious seconds was that the kid looked as equally stunned by what he'd done. He wasn't as keen on pulling the trigger a third time. But the Latino was incensed and had given up on his gun, was reaching to grab the one dropped by their dead pal. As soon as he got his hands on it, it'd be *goodbye, cruel world*.

McTeer shook his head, begged the question: 'What the fuck did you do, Hunter?'

As the Latino spun on him, mouth open, saliva sewing together his exposed teeth, he paused at McTeer's words. His expression changed to gloating as he eyed the two pulsating wounds painting McTeer crimson. 'You fucked with the wrong people, asshole!'

McTeer grunted at the irony: the Latino thought his question had been introspection. 'Dickwad,' he announced, 'you don't know the fuckin' truth of it.'

The connecting door burst inward, even as another figure hurtled in through the open door from the hall and slammed the beanie-hatted kid into the Latino.

'Stay down, Trey,' I whispered harshly, 'and don't make a sound.'

Her eyes were directly in line with mine, reflecting my features. My face was set in a rictus. I pushed up off her, then grabbed the bedding off the mattress and dumped it over her so she was concealed in the narrow space between the divan and wall. Next door the shit was going down and it was deadly.

I didn't have time to plan, so went on instinct. I swept up the nearest weapon to hand even as I padded silently to the connecting door and pressed my ear to it, just in time to hear a voice tell McTeer he'd fucked with the wrong people. It was the kind of thing that cowards tell a victim they have at their mercy. McTeer wasn't going to die in cold blood if I could help it. I drew the privacy bolt, decided that there'd be similar bolts on McTeer's side, so reared back and smashed my heel in the door below the handle. The door hurtled open, and I was a split-second behind it into the room.

The tableau imprinted on my senses in the next millisecond. McTeer sitting bleeding into his shorts, a gangbanger with a gun a foot from his face, another young punk in a woolly hat with his gun down by his side, and a corpse splayed on the floor alongside a spilled box of beer bottles.

Time snapped taut in my mind, then accelerated forward, and my mind caught up to my actions as I lunged for the gunman, even as Velasquez hurtled in from the corridor and hammered both clasped fists between the woolly-hatted guy's shoulders, who slammed his pal sideways. The young guy went down with Velasquez on top, still hammering, now on the back of the guy's neck.

As the gangbanger stumbled to find his balance, my left hand grasped the barrel of his gun and thrust it skyward. The guy's finger squeezed the trigger and he wasted a round in the ceiling: it didn't stop him pulling the trigger again, and more bullets zipped through the air and buried themselves in the furniture and walls as we momentarily tussled. I didn't want the gun off him, just away from McTeer. I didn't need it. I battered one of Trey's stiletto heels into the man's neck, yanked it out and then buried it deep into his incredulous left eye. The heel didn't reach his brain, but again that wasn't my intention; for what he'd done to McTeer I wanted the bastard to suffer before he bled out through his severed carotid artery. As he sunk down, moaning in abstract terror, one hand patting at the body of the shoe embedded in his blinded eye, I held his gun hand aloft until weakness assailed him and his finger slipped free from the guard. I let him fall back unceremoniously on the carpet alongside his dead friend, even as I watched Velasquez stomp his heel repeatedly on the back of the young punk's neck. The hat had come off during the tussle and lay wadded alongside his shaved head on which had been etched swirls of tattoo ink.

Velasquez returned my gaze. His fatigue had fled, and he now looked wired. His normally olive skin was the pallor of a fish's belly.

'What the fuck just happened?' he intoned. A minute ago he had been sound asleep, now he'd killed a man by shattering his vertebrae. It was unsurprising that he looked at me as if he was still caught up in a nightmare.

It *was* a nightmare, and it wasn't over yet.

We both raced to McTeer and helped him lie flat on the bed. The shoulder wound wasn't life threatening, but the one low in his abdomen was. I slapped a palm over it, but staunching the blood flow wouldn't save him, not when he was probably leaking pints of the stuff internally. 'Val,' I commanded my friend, using his nickname, 'call an ambulance, then call Rink.'

'What the hell, Hunter? What the hell?' Velasquez was almost as shocked as McTeer.

'Get a grip, Val,' I shouted. 'Do as I told you. Ambulance!'

He snapped out of it, but was still in flux. I stabbed a hand at the telephone on the counter opposite the bed. Velasquez stumbled towards it, while I went back to tending to McTeer.

'An ambulance won't help, may as well send for a priest.' McTeer's voice was reed thin, but he found humour in his words and he chuckled at them. Bloody saliva popped between his lips.

'I won't let you die,' I promised him.

'Don't think you have much say on the matter. I think that's between me and my God.'

'Since when did you find religion?' I asked, trying to keep his mood jovial. 'Don't go bothering God now, not while I'm around, we might end up in another fistfight.'

'I'm a good Catholic boy, a pure angel,' he told me, which, when I thought about it, was unsurprising. 'I guess I've just let my halo slip now an' again, huh? Wonder if St Peter will let me in?'

'I won't let you die!'

He smiled up at me. 'Hunter, you're a good man, a good friend, but even you can't do miracles. I'm going, buddy, and if it happens to be downstairs, well, so be it. Can take up with these three assholes again where we left off.' He craned for a look at the trio of bodies littering his floor. 'They're all dead?'

'Every last one of them.'

'Good. Fuckers deserve it for shooting up my beers.' He laughed again but this time it was pained and more blood frothed between his lips. I maintained pressure on his wound, but was fighting a losing battle. I searched for Velasquez. He'd downed the phone, had finished his call and I hadn't heard a word of it.

'Are the medics coming?'

He nodded.

'Rink?'

'I couldn't get him.'

'Try again,' I told him, 'but use your cell. He probably just ignored an unknown number, but won't with yours. Get him here, Val.'

'I...I shouldn't leave you alone.'

'I'm not alone. I'm with Mack. Go on, Val, get Rink here.'

Velasquez eyed his friend – he was closer to McTeer than I was, had worked alongside him and Rink long before I joined their motley crew a few years ago – and it was probably right that he was the one to hold McTeer's hand while he died. But I didn't want to put that on Velasquez. I'd caused this, because I couldn't keep the promise I'd made to McTeer to keep my hands to myself. Velasquez had to dodge around the corpse of the man he'd stomped to death to return to his room, but his gaze never left McTeer's until he spun away and across the hall.

'He won't be the same after this.'

McTeer's voice was now so faint I could barely hear it.

'Val isn't cut out for this shit,' he went on. 'I told Rink, Val ain't suited to this, not any more. He's going to take this badly, Hunter, going to need help getting over it.'

'And you'll be around to help him,' I said.

'Cut the crap, Hunter, we both know I'm done. Fuck me, man, I should be pissed at you.' He reached trembling fingers and placed them over the hand I had on his wound. He patted me gently. 'But I'm not. If it was me in that bathroom I'd have knocked that pukeball on his ass just the same. Those punks, they said they were sent by that asshole you told me you hit...Viskhan, but they weren't sent after me, brother.'

'I know.' My throat thickened around my words.

'That girl you've got hidden in your room, she's this Viskhan's wife, right?' He snorted in pained humour. 'You don't have to hide it, I heard you guys speaking. Don't let her go back to him, don't let him take her.'

'I won't.'

'Promise me you'll protect her.'

'I already did.'

He nodded at that. Then he grimaced, and the contortions didn't stop. He moaned and his legs squirmed. They looked oddly pale and thin, hairless above skinny little ankles. Impending death was cruel, making a robust tough guy like Jim McTeer appear pathetic in his final moments. I wished that I had time to pull on McTeer's trousers for him, to gain him a little humility. He settled slightly, and his hand again found mine, this time turning it over so our bloody palms were cupped.

'Any of...those beers...unbroken?' he asked.

'Yeah.'

'Get me one, will ya?'

'I don't think that's a good idea, Mack.' I was hoping the medics would miraculously arrive in time, and the complications of alcohol in his system wouldn't help.

'You worried about me damaging my liver?' He laughed, but it ended in a sob.

I slowly backed away from him, and stooped for the box. I'd to pull back the lid to find an undamaged bottle. I popped the cap and returned to the bed.

McTeer was gone.

Not physically. His body was exactly where I'd left him, but of his spirit there was no sign. His open eyes were as dull as the sense of aching loss that filled my chest.

'To you, Mack,' I whispered, and tilted the bottle to my lips.

Velasquez was back in the room.

He charged over and almost flung himself on McTeer. He shouted hoarsely, shaking McTeer, trying to rouse him. I let him. He had to get it out of his system. But after a short while I put a hand on Velasquez's shoulder and squeezed gently, and he rested back into me. Sobs racked his frame. But when he turned and looked up at me, he'd gotten a grip on himself.

'You have to go, Joe,' he said.

I shook my head.

'You have to. This isn't finished. You know that as well as I do.' He indicated the woman standing in the open doorway between my room and McTeer's. Trey had disobeyed my instructions and had come to inspect the fallout. She leaned against the frame, looking tiny and forlorn, and little of her stature was to do with missing her shoes. 'Those bastards killed Jim because of her.' There was no recrimination in his words, just plain truth. 'When they hear they missed her, more of them will come. You need to take her somewhere safe.'

He was right, but I had no intention of leaving.

'Rink's coming,' Velasquez reassured me. 'But so are the cops. I had to tell the nine-one-one operator about the shootings, so the cops will be sent too. You can't keep that woman safe if you're locked in a cell.' He leaned in conspiratorially. 'Nobody knows you were in here—' he cast an arm around at the three dead men '—I'll tell the cops this was all on me, buy you some time.'

'I can't let you take the rap for this, Raul.'

'You can, you will, because I'm not doing it for you. I want to do it for Jim. I heard you promise him you'd keep that woman safe, and you better well keep your promise too. And, Joe—' he reached out and gripped my wrist tightly '—if you get the chance you're gonna avenge him. You get me?'

I stood, his grip tightening on my wrist. I offered the tiniest of nods. 'I get you.'

'Good.' He took the forgotten beer bottle from my hand, then tilted it in a silent dealmaker to his own lips and drank. 'Now move it.' He almost pushed me towards Trey.

I grabbed Trey as I passed, scooped an elbow around her waist and almost hauled her across the room with me. When she'd come out from hiding she'd pushed the bedclothes back on my bed. I snatched up my bag of belongings and headed for the door with her.

'Wait,' Trey said. 'My shoes!'

'Leave them.' I had no desire to go back and yank the heel out of the dead gunman's eye socket.

Everything had gone to hell. But that was what came of using untried assets for any operation. There was always the possibility that one or more of the men Sean Cahill sent to complete the hit would be injured, but not all three and not fatally. The deaths of the three gangbangers was no great loss, not personally, and their link back to Mikhail Viskhan and himself was tenuous, but that was always dependent on them killing their target outright and getting clean away. Useless bunch of shits! He'd done the hard work for them, had set up a feasible approach for them to gain access to the target's hotel room through Albert Greville-Jones. The head security guy owed favours to Mikhail, and Cahill had called one of them in. Greville-Jones supplied the names of the team he'd subcontracted out to during the gala event that Mikhail and Trey attended, and between them they'd identified the guy who knocked Mikhail on his butt as Joe Hunter. Greville-Jones set up the in for Cahill's hit team by ringing his contact, James McTeer, and identifying where the team was staying while in Miami, and offering to send over a token of his appreciation. Hell, he'd even supplied a box of quality beers to add authenticity when Cahill's bogus couriers turned up. All the useless hitters had to do was wait until the door was opened, and then shoot dead everyone in the room. They had no way of singularly identifying Hunter, so the collateral damage was a necessary precaution. Cahill had even driven the useless punks to the hotel, supplied the untraceable weapons they needed to get the job done, more or less pointed them at the correct door and told them, 'Go get 'em boys.'

They killed one guy, but not the right one, and paid a heavy price. Cahill didn't know the specifics yet, but none of the three had survived the encounter. Maybe, considering the alternative, that wasn't such a bad thing. If they were dead, they couldn't talk, or lead the cops back to him. The surviving members of the team from Tampa would easily piece together

Greville-Jones's betrayal; the head of security was a loose end that needed tying up. He fully suspected Greville-Jones would fold under interrogation, and in hindsight he'd bet the security man wished he hadn't been as generous in supplying the top end beers; if the gangbangers had carried an anonymous empty box up to the hotel room door it would have sufficed for their disguise, and would have left an evidence trail Greville-Jones could easily squirm away from. All he need do then was send a crate of beer over by a reputable courier and he could swear his innocence: but largely that idea was fucked, because the uniquely labelled beer was traceable back to the six star hotel he worked at.

The job had been rushed, and had gone down the toilet because of the lack of forethought. Cahill wasn't overly surprised, and it was why he'd warned Mikhail about trying to run two separate operations when they were on such a tight schedule. That he'd been warned wouldn't mean a damn thing to Mikhail. He had placed Cahill in charge of the second op, and it was his responsibility to fulfill his duty. Mikhail wasn't a forgiving boss: in fact, Cahill could expect punishment if he didn't pull something out of the bag and achieve a speedy and satisfactory result.

Perhaps driving the hit team to the hotel had been the lesser of his mistakes, because it meant he was in position when all hell broke loose and was able to take stock of the immediate aftermath. Feigning the image of a concerned hotel guest he'd been able to mingle with others milling around outside the hotel foyer as the medics and police arrived, hearing excitable chatter about McTeer's murder, and how he and a colleague had managed to turn the tables on their attackers before he perished. It also meant he was in position when Trey Shaw – accompanied by a man he suspected was Joe Hunter – slipped unnoticed by the authorities from a service exit and stole away across the cultivated gardens adjacent to the hotel. Had he not been watching for them he wouldn't have noted their furtive escape either. Because the hotel was the scene of a multiple homicide, the police would soon set up a cordon, and all guests and hotel employees would be held pending questioning and clearing of any involvement. Cahill couldn't allow himself to be caught up in the noose, so he too slipped away, returning to his car, which he'd fortunately left a block away from the hotel. The job had gone to hell, but at least fortune favoured him. From his car he could still see Trey and her protector as they crossed Ocean Drive and hurried along the sidewalk fronting Lummus Park. To all intent and purpose the couple could be any returning from a late night party: Trey even looked the slightly inebriated girlfriend with the guy's jacket slung over her shoulders and her bare feet padding timidly along the concrete, his arm wrapped protectively around her waist to usher her safely home.

Cahill saw his opportunity. He could drive his car at them, mount the kerb and mush them under his wheels. Job sorted, as Dan StJohn, an English buddy of his, might say. But that was rushing things again. He couldn't be positive that Hunter wouldn't hear his approach, and divert Trey into the park out of harm's way. If they dodged into the park then he'd have to pursue them on foot, and what then? He was currently unarmed. Hunter had already shown his mettle in knocking down a hard-ass like Mikhail, and who knew if he was the one responsible for taking out the hitters who killed his pal. Cahill was no slouch in a fight, but why bloody his knuckles when other opportunities to kill them would come, opportunities he could walk away from uninjured? *Show caution*, he warned, *and think.*

He required backup and weapons.

That was fine, because even in the dead of night he had access to both. Keeping an eye on the couple, he took out his cell phone and began rounding up assets far worthier of his trust than the punks he'd agreed to pay with all the cocaine they could snort over a weekend. He sent two of the first guys who answered his call to silence Greville-Jones. By then

Hunter and Trey were almost out of his line of sight, so he set his car rolling after them. But only insofar as he gained on them enough where he could pull over once more and continue with his arrangements. He powered down his window. It was hot and humid, but before the night ended Miami was going to grow much hotter for his targets. So hot, he thought that Mikhail's assertion that he wanted to be on a flight out of the country before the bodies were discovered sounded like the best prospect for Cahill too...and that was before anything came of Mikhail's plans for that damned parade.

Trey was flagging and it had little to do with the intense humidity. She stumbled along as if drunk, murmuring incoherently at times, and her head hung forward as if she lacked the strength to hold it upright. Shock could do that. I'd noted her downward spiral from the instant I dragged her from my room and threw my jacket over her shoulders. She'd progressively weakened, and I suspected she was almost at a point of collapse. She needed time to come to terms with what had just happened, and to gather her wits and strength, but time wasn't a luxury available to us. Despite what Velasquez had said, other people did know we'd been at the violent scene, because on exiting my room it was into a corridor flanked by open doors and anxious fellow guests peeping out to ensure they weren't next to be caught up in the gun battle. Exiting the room adjacent to the one where the fight had occurred might put off a few suspicions, because we could look like an innocent couple fleeing the horror next door. But once the police were on scene and the connecting door found smashed open and Trey's shoe embedded in the gangbanger's eye, it would only be a matter of time before somebody recalled our rapid departure. Velasquez had offered to take the rap for killing those who murdered McTeer, but any investigator worth their salt would know he was covering for a friend, and likely one registered to one of the rooms rented by McTeer. Rink had an alibi, I didn't: ergo Joe Hunter would be a wanted man, and so too his female companion who'd supplied the impromptu murder weapon. I'd tried explaining that to Trey as we slipped away through the hotel's grounds, but she'd only stared back at me with a glaze of incomprehension over her slack features.

Counter-surveillance comes as second nature to me, but it was difficult losing myself quickly when struggling to hold Trey upright. I had to dump my overnight bag – once I'd removed my jacket and other necessary belongings and secreted them about my pockets – in order to help her without it becoming an extra encumbrance. I had my phone, my wallet, some loose cash, and that was about it. I'd been tempted to take one of the guns from the dead men, but that would have confused the issue for Velasquez and made it look as if he'd killed an unarmed man. He would claim self-defence, and also that he was trying to save McTeer from armed and dangerous individuals, but he'd be treated like a cold-blooded killer if all the weapons weren't accounted for.

I was still torn about leaving him behind to suffer the fallout alone, but it was a choice I'd been pushed into. He was right about Trey needing my protection, and the only way I could offer it was to get her out of harm's way. The cops could only do so much to ensure her safety, and little for mine. The majority of cops are decent folk, but some are susceptible to corruption, particularly by an individual with the influence Mikhail Viskhan wielded, be that by reward or threat. A turnkey paid to leave a cell door unlocked, to turn a blind eye, while an assassin slipped into my cell wasn't an unfeasible prospect, the assassin possibly wearing an official uniform or prison coveralls. Handcuffed and cornered, I'd be hard put to save my skin, let alone Trey's. I'd made a promise to my dying friend and another soon after to Velasquez, and my greatest fault is the value I lay on my word: it often comes back to my detriment. But I'd vowed to protect Trey from her husband, and to avenge McTeer's death. So be it.

Lummus Park was to our left, Ocean Drive stretched out before us, and I'd no destination in mind. The sidewalk made for easier barefoot walking than the park's gravel paths would, so I stuck to it for now for Trey's sake, but we had to get off the main strip and fast. It was nearing 3 a.m. so there were few other pedestrians around; early birds were tucked up in their beds, partygoers sequestered in nightclubs. Vehicles still prowled the streets, mostly cabs and limousines, and most recently emergency crews responding to the hotel we'd just fled. Soon, I bet, police patrols would be following a grid search pattern as they attempted to bring us to ground. I steered Trey into Lummus Park, and towards the beach. The sand underfoot would be better for her comfort, but that wasn't my only consideration. We could make distance along the beach without attracting too much attention from passing squad cars.

Trey sat down abruptly. She huddled over, wrapping her arms around her knees, face concealed under her hair.

Sobs racked her frame.

'We have to keep moving, Trey.'

'Please...' Her throat was full of mucus, and her voice a series of popping bubbles. 'Just give...me...a minute.'

'We have to get somewhere safe.'

'Where?' She looked up at me and her dark eyes were pools of despair. 'It doesn't matter...where we go, Mikhail will...will find me.'

'He won't.'

'You don't know him the way I do.'

I was more than curious about Mikhail Viskhan; already I'd had the inkling there was more to him than the big-mouthed braggart I'd first assumed. Sending hitters after us had proven he didn't make empty promises and that he wasn't afraid of a fight. Paraphrasing Sun Tzu's *The Art of War* – 'Know yourself, know your enemy, and you shall win a thousand battles' – I couldn't agree more with the master warfare tactician. To take on and beat him, I needed to know more about Viskhan. 'You can tell me about him as we move.'

'He...he has these *people*.'

'Yeah, he's already shown that.'

I took it that she meant employees, and clients, and those in his pocket, and even those he could press into his service through fear or reward. Yes, he'd have dozens at his beck and call but he wasn't omnipresent, and certainly not omnipotent. I wished now I'd proven that by slashing the edge of my hand across his trachea instead of simply giving him a love tap on his chin. Hopefully I'd get the opportunity to put things right again, but not if I allowed Trey to remain seated on the grass while the cops moved in.

I pulled her up. She was a dead weight in my arms, but to be fair she wasn't the heaviest of burdens either. I hooked one arm under her knees and the other around her back and lifted her to my chest. 'We have to keep moving, or he will find you.'

I didn't have to carry her far. It wasn't her physical body that had burned out, just her will, and perhaps my closeness comforted her enough that she began thinking clearer again.

'You can set me down now,' she whispered against my shoulder.

'Maybe best I carry you until we get onto the beach,' I said, but didn't return her to her feet.

'I...I can walk. Sorry. For being a burden.'

'You're not a burden.'

She coughed out her disbelief. 'I shouldn't have come to you. I've put you in danger.'

'I think I did that to myself when I intervened in that bathroom.'

'Yes. You should have walked away.'

'My bad.'

'I wish I could have too. Before this, I mean. Then your friend wouldn't be dead...or those three men.' Her voice hitched in her chest.

'Those three deserved what they got.'

'No. They were there because Mikhail sent them. Maybe they had no choice in the matter...the way he forced me to do things I didn't want to do.'

'My fucking heart bleeds for them,' I growled.

'Please, Joe. Put me down.'

I lowered her feet carefully, checking first the ground underfoot wasn't littered. She leaned against me, and yes, my closeness was a comfort to her. 'I'm so, so sorry your friend died. I feel responsible, and...'

'He was called Jim McTeer,' I told her bluntly. 'He was a good man. He didn't hold you responsible and I don't either.

Neither should you. There's only one person at fault, and he'll get his comeuppance. But only once we're out of here. Are you sure you're OK to walk?'

'Yes. I'm sorry for being such a weakling.'

'It took bravery to walk out of that washroom with me,' I reassured her. 'Especially when you've feared the consequences for years. We're going to have to send your parents a warning, make sure they go somewhere safe until this blows over.'

'My parents died. First my dad a year ago, my mom only a month ago. It's the only reason I had the guts to follow you, because Mikhail can't reach them now.'

'Aah, I see,' I said.

'Yeah,' Trey said, as she took a wavering step away. 'Now you know I'm not as brave as I seemed a minute ago.'

'You still understood the consequences of leaving him, though, so the decision couldn't have been easy.' I offered her a hand to rest on while she found her balance. 'It was a brave move.'

'Or desperate?'

I shrugged. 'It's moot. You walked away, and if you're determined to keep walking, then you're OK in my book.'

'Then let's walk.' She gave me a trembling smile before pushing her hair back behind her ears. She snugged my jacket over her shoulders and began picking her way across the grass beneath the trees. I smiled at her. Then turned to peer back the way we'd come. There was a car idling at the kerb where we'd veered into the park. I couldn't make out any detail of the driver but for a pale splotch of skin, slightly blued by the glow from a cell phone screen. In a less paranoid reality I might have believed it was simply an innocent guy who'd pulled over to safely make a telephone call, but I didn't buy it. He could be a cop, a witness who'd felt it his civic duty to follow us while guiding the cop to our position, or it could be someone worse. One of Mikhail Viskhan's *people*. In my perfectly paranoid reality, I'd choose the latter until proven wrong. I hurried after Trey, swept my arm around her waist once more and propelled her into the shadows beneath a stand of palm trees. Confident our observer couldn't spot us in the darkness, I halted and turned to study him.

'What's wrong?' Trey craned for a look.

'Nothing,' I lied, because the car was driving slowly away from the kerb, continuing along Ocean Drive. Not because the driver had lost interest in us; I believed he was hoping to head us off. 'You said you could walk,' I asked Trey. 'How do you feel about running?'

The obvious strategy was to double back the way we'd come and try to slip unseen behind our hunter. But he might be savvy enough to expect that, so it was better that we go for broke, continue in the direction we were headed but at a faster clip. Once we were on the sand the driver would be at a disadvantage behind the wheel and would have to get out on foot if he'd any hope of spotting us again, and following closely. If I could get him alone on the sand, I could possibly hide Trey while I turned the tables and became the hunter.

Trey shrugged into the sleeves of my jacket, then hitched up her dress to a point it barely protected her modesty but freed her legs. 'Now I can run,' she said.

'OK. Then run.'

She was fleet-footed, assisted by a fresh surge of adrenaline. I kept pace easily enough, keeping between her and Ocean Drive until we approached the end of the park and found ourselves in among shrubs planted at the edge of a wide beachfront walkway. I quickly scanned to the right: if our hunter had made it to an appropriate parking spot at the end of Lummus Park in time, he could already be on the walkway and heading our way. I couldn't see anyone. A brief glance left showed we didn't have the walkway to ourselves, though; a trio of youths was walking along, drunkenly swaying, but they had their backs to us.

'OK, Trey,' I said, halting her urge to rush onto the path. 'I'm going to cross first. As soon as I give you the sign, cross as quickly as possible and get over that wall.' I indicated a low balustrade that separated the walkway from the beach, along the top of which were seats where beachgoers could sit while wiping sand from between their toes. 'Then I want you to duck down behind it.'

She didn't argue, so I trotted across the path and sat on the wall. There I folded my arms on my chest, just an ordinary nonchalant guy taking a rest before continuing his beachside stroll. It wasn't a convincing disguise, but it would suffice for my purposes. When I was positive we were unobserved, I gestured Trey across and she came at a loping run, then went over the wall in one swift vault. I heard her feet thump into soft sand below. She didn't have to duck, because the drop was more than I'd expected, the wall taller than her. I waited, still observing, then swung my legs around so I was facing the beach and dropped down after her. Trey turned as if she was prepared to run for the sea, but I caught her. I turned her north, to her surprise, as it was back towards the direction of the hotel we'd recently fled. 'No. Stay close to the wall where you can't be seen.'

'Why not go that way?' She pointed south.

I didn't tell her about the man in the car who could be waiting for us down there. He'd put paid to my escape plan. 'They'll expect us to try to put as much distance between us and the hotel as possible, I'd rather not be predictable. Go on, that way.'

She did, and I hung back a few paces. I had enough height to peer over the wall, but due to the angle I couldn't see all the way to the far end of the park. I followed Trey. She picked her way tentatively, and I wanted to usher her on, but I could see her problem. The beach was regularly cleaned of detritus and trash, but up so close to the boundary wall the sand was littered with tinier pieces of trash and carpeted by spiky lengths of palm leaves and other flotsam. In her bare feet Trey must have felt as if she was negotiating a bed of nails. It was small discomfort considering the alternative, but perhaps unnecessary. I hadn't been able to determine if the guy from the car was following us, so maybe I was putting Trey through discomfort for nothing.

'OK,' I said. 'Head down towards the surf.'

Trey glanced over her shoulder. Lamps on the walkway painted a gleam of gratitude in her eyes. She began cutting across the sand, running with determination. I allowed her to go. Continued moving along at the base of the wall until she was at the surf line, then stopped. I again peered over the top of the wall, craning to see all the way down the walkway. The lamps formed interlocking pools of shadow and wan light. A figure moved through them: there briefly, gone for longer, then back in view again. I had no way of telling if it was the man from the car; he could be a guy like myself who enjoyed a walk by the sea at night. He wasn't in a hurry, and though his gaze regularly swept out to the sea, he could have been enjoying the sights. Occasionally he glanced into Lummus Park too, but again his actions were natural enough. However, my Spidey Sense was tingling. As he stepped into the latest pool of light and paused to look around him he was about fifty yards distant, but close enough that I could make out his colouring and body shape. I could pick a soldier out of a crowd of civilians any time.

He held himself erect, as if standing to attention was his default pose. He was muscular, strong, but his wasn't a build cultured in a gym. Most of his power was in his shoulders and thick forearms, and the muscles of his legs that swelled against his jeans. His musculature was similar to mine, though he edged me on bulk. He wore his reddish hair short, but not aggressively, and a neat moustache. A pale blue shirt was tucked into his belted jeans, a bit prim looking, but he'd casually rolled his sleeves up his forearms. Because they were permanently attached to their smartphones, subliminally aware of the hour and date at all times, fewer people wore wristwatches these days, but he did, and I thought that was out of habit. No other jewellery, though, and no distinguishing tattoos I could spot. I made myself a bet he was tattooed, but like mine they were hidden under his clothing.

It was one thing being harried by drug addicts and gangbangers that Mikhail could press into service, another when it came to a professional soldier. But to tell the truth, it wasn't a surprise: some of the wealthier criminals employed the services of veterans and mercenaries as their closest line of defence. I wondered about this man's story, and how he'd fallen into the servitude of an abusive scumbucket who'd made his fortune off other people's misery. Not that I cared, or had any affinity with a brother in arms, just that knowledge is power when it comes to facing any enemy. And yes, this man was my enemy. I knew it in the depth of my bones, and that was before he moved to the edge of the walkway, stared across the sands and pulled out his cell phone from his pocket. Under the blue wash of his screen, and in profile, he presented the same image I'd noted not long ago when spotting him seated in his car.

I checked for Trey.

At first I couldn't see her – not a bad thing, because it also meant she couldn't be spotted by the soldier – but then noted a small hummock of shadow against the tumbling surf. Realising that I hadn't followed, she'd taken my instructions by the letter. She'd headed for the surf, then waited there, crouching down to offer a smaller target. The natural contours of the beach obscured her from the man's view. But if I cut across the sand to join her he'd spot me. Hoping she was staring back at me, I held my left hand horizontally, gesturing for her to stay down. She didn't. She couldn't see the man I was observing and, misinterpreting my gesture, she stood. That simple action was enough to catch the man's eye and he turned abruptly. I watched his head crane forward as he pinpointed her in his sights. He was under no illusion that he was looking at Trey Shaw, but it gave him pause. Last time he'd seen her she was accompanied, so where was I? He checked the obvious, and I'd nowhere to hide. I stepped away from the wall, set my heels in the sand and openly regarded him.

He was stock-still.

So was I.

It was a tableau that must change.

I was tempted to approach him, see how things played out. I was confident he was unarmed. He had no idea if I'd a gun or not. He began walking away, backwards, his gaze never leaving mine as he lifted his phone to his mouth again and began speaking rapidly.

Others were coming.

The best form of defence is offence. But sometimes you just have to run for it. I hailed Trey, sweeping my arms at her to get moving and was pleased she complied without argument. She raced along the wet sands, sending up plumes of phosphorescent spray as she plunged through pockets of surf. I churned through drier sand, the going a little tougher. I kept glancing back, noting the position of our hunter. He had halted his backwards march the second we took off, and was progressing at a steady clip along the walkway. I noted, though, that he was careful that he didn't gain too close on us, and I doubted it was through cowardice. It made sense: why risk a confrontation when he could raise the odds in his favour by coordinating reinforcements? I was certain that when they arrived they would have weapons, and numbers. But with the best will in the world they would take time to arrive, so we still had an opportunity to slip the noose the man was tightening.

I called Trey to me, and we met about midway between the sea and the walkway. There the beach was at its darkest. There was a storm moving in from the Caribbean, bloated clouds the colour of old bruises piling overhead. Off on the southern horizon lightning flickered, sending tendrils of luminescence across the sea like fiery veins. We were, at most, a few minutes away from being blasted by its entire fury. I wasn't fearful of being struck down by a thunderbolt, but gunfire.

'We have to get off the beach,' I told Trey. 'We're too exposed out here.'

'Who is that man?' she asked breathlessly.

'I'm guessing he's one of your husband's men. Looks tough, and capable. Ex-military.'

'Cahill,' she said in a way that I knew I'd correctly read him. 'I wasn't sure, but hoped it wasn't him.'

'Dangerous?'

'More dangerous to me than Mikhail,' she assured me.

A pithy part of me wanted to joke that being more dangerous than Mikhail was no great feat, but that would have been misinformed bullshit. I'd rattled Mikhail with a swift uppercut when he'd made the mistake of underestimating me. To make the same mistake with him would be the greatest sin in battle. Instead I said, 'I was hoping you'd tell me he was someone benign like Mikhail's accountant.'

She shook her head, and her throat crackled as she tried to raise a sensible reply.

'I'm joking,' I said. 'Now let's keep moving. There.'

I pointed out an opening from the beach between low-lying dunes back onto the walkway. There was a series of concrete steps, and a platform on which there was a freestanding shower. I only noted the latter because I briefly considered tearing down its pole as a makeshift weapon, but it'd take a stronger man than I. Speed and mobility was still our best bet. The guy – Cahill – was disinclined to chase us down in a foot race, though his insidious advance told me he wasn't for backing off either. He caught my eye, and nodded in silent promise. I jerked my head, inviting him to come on.

But then we ran again, kicking up sand even as thunder rumbled overhead. I hoped for rain, a tumult that might help conceal us from view. But for now the heavens clung to their heavy load.

We charged up the steps, and onto the walkway. It was smooth pavement, so no hindrance to Trey's bare feet, but sooner or later I'd have to do something about them. Barefoot she could be injured too easily, and an injury would slow her down. I didn't want to have to carry her again when it meant compromising my fists.

We caught up with the trio of drunken youths, and flashed around them. They hooted and hollered, possibly misconstruing the reason for an older guy chasing after a pretty young thing with her dress rucked up around her hips. On another occasion it might have been funny. I urged Trey across the path, placing the trio between Cahill and us. Any small inconvenience to his view was still an inconvenience. I pictured him craning, ducking side to side for a better look at where we were.

I grabbed Trey's elbow and yanked her into Lummus Park. Lewd comments followed us from our drunken friends. Then we were pushing through exotic fronds and could hear nothing but the swish of our bodies through the foliage. Trey made a pained yelp, but kept going, hopping slightly until she found her rhythm – footwear for her was becoming a priority. As finding a weapon was for me.

There were small saplings in abundance, and huge trees, none of which would be of much use as a club, so I didn't bother trying to tear anything down, but on reaching a cinder path I ducked down and worked at a loose edging stone. I hefted it even as I took up the chase after Trey, who'd carried on. It was about the size of a baseball but twice as heavy.

We raced out of the park at 15th Street, and to my annoyance found it quite busy with late night revellers spilling out from a nightclub. More people meant more opportunities to lose ourselves in the crowds, but it also offered more witnesses. The way we bounded out and across the road caught a number of eyes, and they didn't stop staring as I pressed Trey into a service alley alongside a boutique-style clothes store. Cahill had any number of witless allies to point out our direction when he arrived. Fleeing the way we were, he could claim to be a cop and nobody would challenge him, but they'd eagerly point out where we'd gone. That was OK by me. Because as soon as we entered the service alley I again caught Trey and made her halt.

'Over there,' I said bluntly.

I pointed at a tall stucco wall that separated the alley from an adjacent hotel's grounds. It stood seven and a half feet tall.

'I can't climb that!'

'I'll boost you over,' I promised. 'Now come on, quick.'

Trey glanced down at her bared legs. Looked up at me, her gaze scolding.

'I'll avert my eyes,' I reassured her.

'You'd better.'

I underhanded the rock over the wall and heard it thud harmlessly on a lawn. Then I leaned with my left shoulder against the stucco wall, cupped my hands. 'Use it like a stirrup,' I told her. 'Left foot in, and then I'll lift so you can swing over your right leg.'

Balancing with one hand on my shoulder, she stepped up and I took her weight. Her sole was gritty in my interlocked fingers. 'Ready?'

'Ready.'

She aided my lift by flexing her supporting leg, and I almost hurled her aloft. She swung her trailing leg backwards, more like a kicking mule, and her knee knocked painfully against the top of the wall. But, gritting her teeth, she grasped hold with both hands and squirmed over so she was lying astride it. She peered down. 'Who's going to boost you over?'

'Just keep clear.' I backed up a couple of steps, then charged forward, springing up and hooking both elbows over the wall. I swung my legs the opposite direction from her, then came to rest facing her, a leg swinging over space on both sides of the wall. 'Need to be lowered down?'

'Ordinarily I could make that drop myself, but not without my sneakers on.'

The hotel grounds were beautifully cultivated, well maintained, but, exactly where we'd chosen to go over the wall, they'd employed the area as some kind of storage ground for unused lawn furniture and other sundry items. Chairs and tables were stacked loosely directly below us, alongside a lean-to type shed. I shuffled closer to Trey, took a quick look back to ensure Cahill hadn't caught up too soon, and then offered her both my hands. Her palms were soft, cool, her fingers slim, but there was the strength of determination in them. She gripped tightly as I supported her while she brought round her trailing leg, then lowered her until she was standing on top of one of the tables. From there she hopped down, stumbled and almost fell. A couple of ungainly lunges and she'd caught her balance. She looked back at me, embarrassed by her clumsiness, but saw no reproof from me. She blew out loudly at her near miss. I swarmed down, and also jumped off the table. My boots sunk inches into soft earth. Thankfully the forgiving landing dampened the thud, as from the other side of the wall came the soft slap of jogging feet on asphalt. I snapped a finger to my lips, and Trey played at being a statue.

The footsteps continued past where we'd scaled the wall, the sound diminishing. It was Cahill, or it was a cop or security person who'd spotted us heading into the service alley and followed to investigate what we were up to. It didn't matter who it was; they'd taken the bait. I found the baseball-sized rock I'd chucked over the wall, then ushered Trey away silently, whispering that she should lower her dress now. She did so without question, and to my relief the shimmery material retained its luxuriant form around her long legs. Not that her bared legs weren't a pleasing sight to me, just that she no longer looked like a woman on the run. I also took my jacket back from her and slipped it on, and pushed my rock in a front pocket. It pulled down on the material but it wasn't obvious I was carrying a blunt weapon.

Soles slapped asphalt again, the sharp cracks resounding off the boutique's exterior wall. I halted Trey, listened and heard a faint but hurried one-sided conversation, picking out only sporadic words. Whether the speaker was Cahill or not, he was sending his reinforcements to cut us off on Sixteenth, the adjacent street to our north. Good enough for now. I urged Trey west, towards the side entrance of the hotel.

We walked inside as if we were regular guests – my reason for the rapid change of appearance – and I slowed Trey to a stroll. Rushing would draw unwanted attention; best we appear as if we had a right to be there and all the time in the world to enjoy our stay. Trey's feet made little sucking noises on the tiles. We took a left turn and we were in the main entrance foyer. There were a few guests around, lounging in plush chairs, almost nodding asleep or too intent on their cell phones or tablets to give us any notice. They were guests taking early flights home after their vacation, and some had their suitcases poised for action for when their cabs to the airport arrived. I spotted one young guy dozing in his chair. He had a bag on the couch alongside him, but a hand rested protectively over the top of it. But for his comfort he'd kicked out of his sneakers. Without stopping I stooped and snatched up the shoes and kept moving, concealing them under the front of my jacket. Thankfully nobody took note of the brazen theft, and the young guy didn't even stir. I hoped he'd an extra set of shoes in his bag for his journey home.

I took Trey to one side, hiding from view in an alcove at the entrance to a ladies' restroom. 'Put these on.' I pushed the shoes towards her.

She took them, inspected them momentarily with bemusement painting her features. 'They're too big.'

'Pull the laces tight,' I told her. 'They're better than running around in your bare feet all night.'

She saw the sense in my words, and crouched to brush sand from between her toes.

'Trey, we don't have time for that. Just put on the sneakers, OK?'

She sighed in exasperation, but again did as commanded without argument. It struck me then that obeying without question had probably been the template of her life for so long that she knew no other way. I suddenly felt a pang of guilt at treating her the way Mikhail had. But it was short-lived. As soon as she'd laced the sneakers, I checked we were still unobserved then nodded at the front exit. 'We go out that way.'

'Back onto the main strip?'

'Yep. Cahill thinks we've snuck off through those back alleys to the north, so we go the way he'd least expect us.'

There was logic in my plan, but not a little daring. Emerging from the front of the hotel, we'd be only four or five blocks away from the hotel we'd recently escaped. But I was hoping that the proliferation of cops in the vicinity might deter Cahill or his people from making an attempt on us if we were identified.

We headed back out into rain.

But it wasn't the deluge I'd hoped for. Electrical storms were a feature in this neck of Florida, but often they were more noise than substance. Then again, some raging tempests did occasionally scour the area during the hurricane season. Things could turn nastier yet.

Lightning flashed and thunder rumbled, and the rain pattered on the hot pavement and on Trey's bared shoulders. Further to the south the red and blue gumball lights of emergency vehicles added their own light show to the early morning hours. I distractedly wondered how many people currently stood around the body of my friend, and his killers, back in that room. It also made me think about Velasquez, and where he was now: probably downtown in some cell awaiting interrogation. And where was Rink?

Velasquez and McTeer were my friends, but Rink was a whole lot more. He was more like a brother to me, more so than my deceased half-brother John had ever been and, discounting my ex-wife Diane and my aloof mother, the nearest thing to family I'd ever had. I'd bet that right then Rink was going crazy at my disappearing act, but for all the right reasons. Rink wasn't stupid, though; he'd bide his time before trying to make contact, allow me to find somewhere safe before we spoke. I made a mental note to ensure that happened as soon as possible.

To add to our disguise, I offered my elbow to Trey and she hung on. Supporting her assisted her to walk in her flapping sneakers. She kept her gaze stoically ahead, so she didn't attract any attention, but I could tell she was mortified that she was stepping out in clown's shoes.

'I'll find you something more appropriate to wear as soon as possible,' I whispered out the corner of my mouth.

'Can't you just steal us a car or something instead?' She was joking, but to be fair it wasn't the worst suggestion of the night.

I nodded towards a path between two buildings. My limited knowledge of the neighbourhood was being tested, but I was sure the path would give access to further shops and boutique-style hotels serving the Art Deco area. Beyond that would be another major highway called Collins Avenue, and I wanted to gain its freedom.

Sadly Cahill hadn't easily been fooled. Putting himself in my shoes, he must have figured out the false trail I'd set, and backtracked to where we went over the wall. Considering that we would then have used the hotel for cover, he needed to only watch for us exiting again, and his vigilance had paid off.

When I happened to glance back, he was a hundred yards distant but paralleling us on the opposite side of the street. We had no option to turn towards the police cordon unless we wanted to throw ourselves at their mercy, so we had to carry on, and I suspected we were heading directly into a confrontation. I told Trey to keep walking, then dug my hand in my pocket and tested the lumpy edge of the rock I'd carried with me from the park. Let the bastard follow us down that path and I'd smash Cahill's skull to pulp.

Cahill still wasn't prepared to make his move. If he followed up that path he'd just bet that Hunter would be waiting for him. Ordinarily he was a proponent of the old adage that if you're afraid of what lurks in the cave then walk in and challenge the beast, but he wasn't stupid. You could only overcome fear by taking positive action, but his decision wasn't based on fear but sound reasoning. There was another old saying he was fond of: 'You don't buy a dog and bark yourself.' His reinforcements were almost on the scene, some of them heading to rendezvous with him, others to cut off Hunter and Trey. His prey was pinned between the two converging forces, so why risk injury when he could assure it for Hunter within minutes?

Cahill was full of old sayings as he pursued Hunter. *We are like peas in a pod, two sides of the same coin, and* – another saying learned from his English pal – *six and two threes*. Yes, he'd recognised Joe Hunter as a man cut from the same cloth as he. Physically they were alike, at least, and he suspected they had similar training and life experiences. They were both ex-servicemen, warriors. They were both killers. If he pursued Hunter into that alley he would guarantee that only one of them would emerge alive and, frankly, he had no wish to die to simply soothe Viskhan's damaged pride. And it was a possibility. Shit happens: another saying he was prone to.

He'd gotten his first inkling of Hunter's mettle when spotting him lurking behind the wall at the beach. Hunter's instinct wasn't to scurry off, to try to conceal himself in the shadows; he'd stepped out in the open, meeting Cahill and offering a direct challenge. Hunter was a man who knew his abilities and played to his strengths. It wasn't macho posturing; his stance had said *come and try to kill me, but be prepared to die in the attempt*. They had been like reflections in a warped mirror. Cahill had been tempted to close the gap, but logic won out.

This was only a secondary operation, and the first took precedence over his desire to test himself against his twin. Apparently, similar logic had forced Hunter to flee, and he would keep running while he too had to prioritise – Trey's welfare trumped a battle to the death for bragging rights – but their clash was an inevitable one, Cahill hoped. All of the running around was pissing him off, and the fact he'd almost lost his prey back there where Hunter had played a blinder in scaling a wall had only added to his displeasure. Luckily he thought the way that Hunter did, and was fortunate enough to spot them emerging from the front of the hotel they'd backtracked through, as he might have done if their roles were reversed, so he was still in line with getting his fight. As he coordinated his team, he truly considered telling them to keep Hunter alive for the time being, but then that would be a selfish request. Or would it? He must first discover how loose-lipped Trey had been concerning Mikhail's plan. Had she had time to mention it yet to her protector, or worse still, to any of the others from Tampa who might even now be spilling the beans to the police? He doubted the latter, but she could have told Hunter about what was about to go down.

Then again, prior knowledge of their operation would have given Hunter leverage with the cops responding to the attempted hit on them at the hotel. He wouldn't have fled with Trey if he could negotiate the protection of the FBI or Homeland Security in exchange for what he'd learned.

Fuck it, he decided. Hunter couldn't know yet. And besides, anything Hunter knew could die with him, and with Trey as well.

He spoke into his cell, telling his B-team to move in now.

Even as he did so he checked and spotted his A-team speeding along 15th Street towards him. He glanced towards the flashing police lights, but nobody down there was aware of the Mercedes' haste. Nonetheless he turned to wave at its driver to slow down.

The Mercedes was filled to capacity with men Cahill had worked alongside for years. He briefly wished it was they he'd sent to the hotel to carry out the hit, but the past was the past and there was no changing it. He didn't waste any time repeating descriptions of their target – he'd already done so over his phone – but immediately ordered two of the men, Monk and Hussein, out of the back seat and sent them up the path in pursuit while he leaned across and accepted the semi-automatic pistol from the third man previously crammed in the back seat. Out of habit Cahill worked the action on his gun, checking a round was in the chamber, and then dropping the clip and making another quick check that it was fully and correctly loaded. He'd nothing to worry about, because it was another ex-soldier that'd prepped it for him, his English pal, Dan StJohn. In the front were two more colleagues from back in the day when you could merrily cap a rag-headed Jihadist and not worry about the politically correct ramifications. He grunted in humour at the memory: ironic that they should now make bedfellows of their previous enemies.

'Let's go get 'em, boys,' he announced as he slipped in alongside StJohn. He grinned at his colloquialism-spouting buddy, slapped the headrest of the driver's seat and added, 'Don't spare the horses, mate.'

Distantly there was the throaty roar of a speeding vehicle. A dull *wumph*! Thunder grumbled overhead, almost rattling the Mercedes on its wheels. If the thunder had come a second sooner he wouldn't have discerned the impact for what it was. All humour was lost from his next command. 'Go! Go! Go!'

14

'Run across there and hide in the doorway of that shop.' I pointed her destination out to Trey, a darkened alcove at the front of a store selling artists' supplies.

'They'll see me.'

'Exactly.'

'You're using me as bait?'

'It's either lure them towards you or we get caught in the mouth of this path. There are guys coming behind us; we can't fight them all. Please, Trey, this is our best chance. Go, run.'

Less than fifty yards away a large silver SUV was prowling along Collins Avenue, having completed a sweep of 16th Street. Even as I exhorted Trey to get going, the driver must have received fresh instructions from Cahill, because he hit the gas and the SUV surged forward to head us off at the end of the path. I actually slapped Trey's backside in my urgency. There was nothing lascivious about the gesture and I'm certain she didn't take it as a cheap grope. She grabbed at the hem of her dress, dragged it up and galloped across the road, ungainly in her over-sized sneakers. She was the proverbial startled doe as the SUV's headlights caught her in their glare. Thankfully she didn't halt in terror but kept going, mounting some steps and charging into the darkness of the alcove. Nobody fired a gun at her, which was fortunate. But I hoped all eyes were on her. The SUV began a tight swerve towards the kerb on that side of the road. That was when I bobbed out of hiding, and hurled my rock with all the strength in my arm.

If the rock had been bigger and weightier it would have fallen short, if smaller it would have ricocheted harmlessly off the windshield, but this was a Goldilocks rock: just right. It punched into the windshield directly in line with the driver. It didn't go all the way through, but busted a crater in the glass, and sent jagged cracks in a starburst pattern over the rest of the screen. The noise was surprisingly loud. For the briefest of seconds the driver was shocked into incomprehension, in the next he misconstrued that he was under fire, and only after that he recognised the hurled rock for what it was. But by then he'd reacted on instinct to the attack, and that was what I'd prayed for. The SUV swerved wildly as the driver took diversionary tactics. The front slammed the rear of a parked van at the roadside.

The SUV had already been slowing to disgorge its occupants in pursuit of Trey, so the impact wasn't as devastating as I'd prefer, but it was bad enough. The van was lifted off its back wheels, shunted around in a tight arc, and the SUV bounced up onto the sidewalk, so it ended up jammed against a low wall. Instantly steam plumed from its ruptured engine compartment, and something whirred in protest.

All the while I hadn't stopped moving.

There were the vague shapes of three figures within, and they were still recovering from the impact. The driver was nearest me, so he was my initial target. I yanked open his door, and as he swung round to meet me, mouth open in a wordless curse, I pounded my hand into the side of his neck. In the front passenger seat was another man, and I didn't pay him much attention, too intent on the gun in his fist that he swung towards me. I shoved his swooning pal in his way, and he made the mistake of trying to reach past to shoot me in the face. I grasped the barrel of the pistol – noting that it was fitted with a screw-on suppressor – and drove it towards the windshield even as he pulled the trigger. My hurled rock had smashed the glass, but the bullet didn't. It ricocheted off the glass, perhaps hit the steel of the doorframe, and ended up in the driver's left thigh. The driver was blasted out of semi-consciousness by the sudden agony, and he reared back in his seat, further entangling the gunman's arms with his. I tore the gun out of the man's grip even as their backseat passenger lurched over and tried to grapple me. He should have decamped the vehicle and gone for a clean shot. I easily avoided his reaching hands, took a half step back and shot him first. It was a small calibre round, a .22, but at that range it had killing power. It hit the guy in the right orbital socket, immediately beneath his eyeball, and that did it for him.

The two living men were vocal. The front passenger was now unarmed, but the driver pushed his pal out of the way so he could reach under his jacket for his own pistol. I shot the driver twice for good measure, one bullet in his side, the next in his neck where I'd recently struck him. The passenger threw open his door and fell out onto the sidewalk. He was on the far side, momentarily concealed by the car, and I let him scramble away. I dug under the dead driver's armpit and drew out his gun. This one hadn't been prepped with a silencer. The escaping passenger was the would-be silent assassin tasked with killing Trey and I. I felt justified in shooting him in cold blood, and would have if not for the two men who hurtled from the mouth of the alley I'd recently come from. They both held guns. Neither of them was Cahill.

The first was wraith thin, with the hollowed-out features of a mummified corpse. His expression was centred on pinched raisin eyes, so black that they were like pinholes in his skull. The second man was thicker-set, with wavy black hair and a darker cast to his skin. Their initial reaction to the devastation I'd wrought among their friends was to take stock, their next to separate so they didn't offer a single target, and then they went for concealment. I didn't try to shoot either because I too went for cover, scrambling over the buckled hood of the SUV to the far side. Instantly I sought the fleeing passenger, and if he'd run around the back of the wreck and across the road he might have survived my wrath. But the fool went up the steps, directly towards Trey's hiding spot. I shot him in the back, and he sprawled before hitting the top step. He rolled over, writhing in place, injured but not dead, not even crippled. I shot him again, and this time he lay still.

I then started taking rounds. Or rather the SUV did. The shots weren't designed to kill me, but pin me down as the two hitters attempted to flank my position. I swarmed up the steps on my hands and knees, a gun in each hand, bypassing the recently slain man. I didn't even glance at him. As soon as I hit the sidewalk, I hurtled up, momentarily vulnerable to a shot to my back, but made it into the relative safety of the alcove. Trey emitted a little squeak of alarm as I crushed up against her. She was tucked down into the deepest corner of the doorway. If we stayed there the two gunmen could move in on our blind sides, and we'd be trapped. I'd still give them a fight, but only until Cahill and whoever else he was with arrived.

I helped her up. 'Stay tight,' I told her, 'and ready to move.'

The door to the art supplies store was locked, probably bolted too, but was never designed with more than minimal security in mind: who robbed a shop of its paint and pencils? I threw my shoulder against the glass and it fell out of its frame, crashing down inside the shop and tinkling in a thousand pieces. I was glad I'd managed to get Trey some footwear, because she'd be walking on broken glass. I helped her through the gap, then had to force my own thicker set frame inside. We set off motion detectors and an alarm began wailing. I didn't mind too much. If the car wreck and gun battle outside wasn't enough to bring the police then the alarm would, because it would probably be connected to a remote monitoring station, and the security company would dispatch people to the scene. It narrowed down the time Cahill's team had available to catch us before they'd have to make a speedy retreat.

I'd no intention of making a stand in the shop, waiting for the cavalry to arrive. Despite our close call, I still felt that for either of us to survive the night, it was better to keep moving than submit to a jail cell. I backed from the door, the silenced gun in my right hand, while I waved Trey towards the back with the other. 'Find us an exit,' I hissed.

I followed her deeper into the shop, bypassing shelves filled with acrylics and oil paints, brushes and palate knives, canvases and other artists' paraphernalia. There was a unique, clean aroma in the air, and it struck me how fecund the atmosphere outside had grown since the onset of the storm. My hair was dripping with rain.

A shape loomed at the right edge of the doorway. Someone taking a peek inside, and by the shape of the head it was the Middle-Eastern guy. He dodged out of the way, and then his scarecrow pal bobbed out and loosed three bullets into the shop's interior. None of them troubled me or Trey, who had already gone to the right into a back room. I didn't bother trying to hit the skinny man, because he was already taking cover. I waited a beat, and then his buddy leaned out and extended his gun. I fired, and he jerked back to cover. They didn't show for long seconds after that. I was deep in cover, while they presented as silhouettes against the back glow of streetlamps and lightning: I had the upper hand in any exchange of rounds. I heard them whispering to each other, guessed they were already planning to cut off our escape. One would stay out front and draw my fire while the second gunman made his way around the back. Time to go. I rushed after Trey and found her in an office-cum-staff kitchen, standing in front of a fire exit door fitted with a push bar. The bar had been double secured by way of a chain and padlock. We wouldn't be leaving by that way. But there was a window high up. Without pause I pushed my guns into my waistband, grabbed a printer off a desk and lobbed it through the glass. I used the barrels of my guns to knock out the larger chunks still stuck in the frame, then kicked a chair across the floor for Trey to climb on and through the window. She hissed sharply as she clambered outside, picking up scratches on her bare arms and legs. He dress caught momentarily on a sliver of glass, and I yanked it loose for her. She dropped out of sight.

Before following her, I returned to the showroom and fired a blind shot, using the un-silenced pistol for effect, to keep those outside guessing where we were. From beyond the broken doorway I caught the squeal of tyres on wet asphalt, but there was no alarm from the duo of shooters. Cahill and other reinforcements had arrived. I charged back into the staffroom as someone commanded a hard entry to the shop. I guessed Cahill would also direct someone to the back. Without pause I stepped on the chair and went bodily out of the window, my heels kicking the chair over on the floor in my urgency. I hit the ground in an ungainly heap, knocking my left shoulder on something indeterminate in the dark, but solid all the same. Small hands grabbed at me to assist me up. I almost fell into Trey's arms, and felt her loose hair adhere to the slick skin of my face. I blew more strands out of my mouth, then checked I still held both pistols. 'Can you shoot?' I asked breathlessly.

Her eyes were moist glimmers in the darkness. They shook side to side.

'Never mind.' I shoved the silenced pistol into my waistband and transferred the other to my right hand. I hadn't had a chance to make an inspection of the gun, but knew from experience it was a bog-standard Glock 17, and judging by the weight it came with a fully loaded magazine of nine rounds – less the one I'd fired blindly in the shop. At that moment in time I'd no idea how much ammunition was still in the silenced gun. More than I'd had five minutes ago when all I could throw was a Stone Age weapon. *Don't knock the rock*, I thought whimsically as I searched for the most direct route out of the small service yard we stood in.

There was a small door at the back, bolts thrown, but no obstruction from this side. I poked my head out first, and discovered a narrow alley that serviced a number of the surrounding buildings. It was almost full to bursting with trashcans and dumpsters, hidden from the view of tourists and wealthy residents of the neighbourhood. The fecund stench was back, and so was the rain. Thankfully none of Cahill's team had made it there yet. I urged Trey out and ahead of me, just as a clatter resounded behind us. Gunmen were in the art supplies store, and would soon be on our tails. I shut the door, and then dragged over a couple of dumpsters and jammed them in the way. In the shop, they didn't try to scale out through the open window; I heard somebody hammering at the lock and chain, and then the door being thrown open. A moment of trepidation followed while they checked they weren't running out into an ambush, but then I caught their harsh words and rumble of feet as they rushed for the door. By then we had made it to the end of the alley, and turned left up the next. We spilled out into an unused patch of ground, separated from the next building across by a chain mesh fence. I stared up at the building looming ahead. Smiled at Trey and said, 'Remember when you suggested stealing a car?'

15

Rink was icy cold, and it had nothing to do with the pelting rain. He stood rigid at the side of the road peering up at the second-floor apartment home of Albert Greville-Jones, in the same spot he had for a full minute since paying his fare and watching the taxi pull away. The rain had plastered his dark hair to his brow, and dripped from his scarred chin. He was an intelligent man, and understood that what he was about to do could end badly for him, but there was another part of him that spat in the eye of consequences. The bastard moving back and forward behind the second-floor windows had sent the three gangbangers after Hunter, and they had murdered Jim McTeer. Rink felt justified in ripping the unctuous piece of shit limb from limb.

Rink had arrived at McTeer's room too late to get more than sketchy details from Velasquez before the police arrived and took him into custody. But he'd learned enough: that the man who'd set up the hit was the self-same security manager they'd worked for only hours earlier. Rink heard about the woman who'd turned up at Hunter's room, and how she'd most likely been an intended target of the hit, along with Hunter, as a consequence of his run-in with her husband at the hotel. To protect her from harm Hunter had booked with her, and Velasquez intended buying him some time by taking the rap for two of the dead – the third killing was on McTeer, and nobody but his God could judge him now. With Hunter on the lam and Velasquez locked up pending interviewing and processing, it was on Rink to right the wrong done to them by Greville-Jones, and hopefully help both his friends out of the pinch they were in. He'd woken another friend a few states away in Arkansas, but after hearing what Rink needed, Harvey Lucas didn't complain about the ungodly hour. Harvey was a wiz when it came to interrogating the web, and had supplied Rink with Greville-Jones's home address much faster than if Rink had returned to the villa-hotel and turned the place upside down in search of the employee files. Harvey also promised to make tracks for Miami to assist in any way he could. To buy Rink time, Velasquez had promised to play ignorant about who was behind the delivery of beers to their room, but the cops would figure it out soon enough and arrive at the security man's apartment.

If he was going to learn who had motivated Greville-Jones's betrayal, he must do it now. He wanted to know the name of the man Hunter had knocked on his ass in the restroom, and he'd get the answer by similar – but more vicious – means. McTeer was dead; Greville-Jones might not be so fortunate.

He had to consider that Greville-Jones was armed, and dangerous. He had come across as a pompous fop, but you didn't attain the position of head of security at an exclusive six star hotel on cultured manners alone: Rink assumed the man had been around the block a few times, and would be no walkover. But it didn't matter. If the bastard fought back, then it would only justify being hit all the harder.

Rink's fists curled at his sides. He still wore his rented tuxedo, but had doffed his tie and loosened his collar. The shoulders of his jacket were sodden. He took it off and dropped the jacket among some shrubs as he approached the stairwell up to the second floor. As he ascended he undid the buttons at his shirt cuffs, and cinched his belt a couple of notches.

The SoBe apartment was a home from home for Greville-Jones, who also owned a larger condo north of Miami. Rink had no desire to terrorise any innocent family members, but through Harvey he'd also learned that the security man was divorced and childless. He was confident that Greville-Jones had returned home alone after leaving work earlier, and his perusal of the windows gave him no reason to doubt his summation. He'd watched the man pacing to and fro, speaking animatedly into a cell phone, but his had been the only figure to cast a shadow on the windows. However, as he ascended the stairs he thought he could discern men's voices – plural.

Greville-Jones didn't enjoy sole occupancy of the building, only the uppermost second floor, so hearing the voices of other people wasn't too unusual, but it raised Rink's hackles. He had to consider that there was more than one way up to Greville-Jones's place, not only the stairwell he'd come onto.

Expecting trouble from one party or another – and likely the police – had Greville-Jones summoned assistance of a legal team, or indeed a couple of his employees to back him up? The former would prove more troubling for Rink: he'd seen the calibre of Greville-Jones's uniformed-monkeys and they didn't sweat him one little bit. In fact, wailing on them would help some of his pent-up rage before he set on Greville-Jones. Otherwise he might be in danger of destroying him prior to learning anything useful.

Prepared for violence, he nevertheless didn't allow his anger to get the best of his senses. He ascended the final few risers on cat's feet, and approached what appeared to be a secondary exit door from the apartment. A covered balustrade allowed access along a short corridor to the other side of the building, where Rink supposed the main entrance was. The voices – excited whispers, he now realised – originated from the far side. Whoever was doing the speaking, they were being careful not to attract the attention of the other tenants of the building. Doubtful, then, that it was Greville-Jones's legal team or in fact police officers who'd gotten there ahead of Rink.

It felt as if his blood was running like ice melt through his veins; suddenly it almost solidified, growing colder again. Rink ignored the back door and padded along the corridor. Overhead the rain pattered on the semi-opaque ceiling, covering any faint noise he made, but not the voices. Gaining the corner, he could now see that the front of the building featured balconies adorned with hanging baskets overflowing with exotic flowering plants, and overlooked an equally twee garden. It was not a scene conducive to violence, but that was what it had become.

Two indistinct figures hulked over a third, who had collapsed in the open doorway of the apartment. Even as the slumped man shuddered in agony, one hand pawing the air ineffectively in defence, the two over him stooped and plunged knives into him repeatedly. Greville-Jones's blood glistened darkly on the steel blades.

Rink had gone there to exact violence on the man, but was conversely moved by his plight. The two assassins appeared to be taking great delight in making the security man suffer before he died. They goaded each other with prods and slaps of encouragement to stab him again, which they did, slowly and surely. It occurred to Rink that perhaps Greville-Jones had not been an enthusiastic party to the attack on Hunter and the woman after all, but had been coerced or threatened, and this was his payment for involvement. Whoever was behind the hit on his friends, Rink realised, they were now cleaning shop.

He was unarmed.

It mattered not.

Rink sprang on the two killers, mashing them together as he drove them off Greville-Jones's body and onto the balcony. His fists hammered in, a blow to each of the nearest man's kidneys, which arched him backwards in agony before he understood he'd been set upon. Rink's left elbow pounded in, taking the man in the side of his neck and knocking him against the balcony railings. Instantly Rink pursued the second killer, slamming the toe of his leather shoe deep between the man's legs. Because the man still had his back to him, Rink's kick was wholly unexpected and was more effective. The knifeman dropped to his knees, moaning in anguish as his hands dropped to cup his injured groin. His bloody knife clattered on the concrete floor in the same instant that Rink's right knee powered into the nape of his skull. The force sent him face down on the ground, and he didn't stir afterwards.

Rink forgot about him. Spinning, he sucked in his gut as the first knifeman slashed wildly at him. For the first time Rink got a look at either of his opponents' faces, and it was a face he instantly fixed in his mind as one to be hated with a passion. As the man took another wild stab at him, Rink caught the extended arm on his upraised forearm, and swept it aside. The palm of his other hand drove into the knifeman's chin, but not with stopping power. It was a move designed to keep the knifeman confused and off balance. Rink's left hand snapped down on the knife-wielding hand, and yanked it down and across in a deep sweep between their bodies, and then the hand was somewhere overhead, the elbow flexed over Rink's shoulder. He wrenched on the lever of the man's arm and there was only one way the man could go unless his arm was yanked loose of its socket: up and over.

Rink stepped back half a pace as the man disappeared over the balcony railing, and didn't need to see him impacting the ground two floors below to know the killer had gotten his just desserts. The exotic plants below didn't offer much resistance, and the body hit the ground with bone-smashing force.

Rink gave the second killer a cursory glance. He hadn't moved and wouldn't soon. Rink was temped to finish the job his knee had started, and a quick heel stamp would part cranium from vertebrae. But killing either man was unwise unless he wished to become the subject of a manhunt the way Hunter was.

He went to one knee alongside Greville-Jones. The man was a mess of blood and torn clothing. But miraculously he was alive, though not for much longer. His hand that had pawed so ineffectively at the air before now reached for Rink. He grasped the front of Rink's shirt as if it holding tightly enough would stop him slipping over the precipice.

'P-please help me,' Greville-Jones croaked. He knew he was dying, and was scared of going.

'I should let you die, you son of a bitch,' Rink growled. He wasn't certain that the man recognised him. But apparently he knew exactly why he'd been repeatedly stabbed.

'I...I was pushed...into helping them.' Blood popped in Greville-Jones's left nostril. 'Cahill said...'

'Who is Cahill?'

'Sean Cahill. The Irish bastard...' More blood popped, this time from his mouth. He began to drool.

'He's the one that ordered the hit on Joe Hunter?'

The hand on Rink's shirt flexed, then lost what strength was left to it. Greville-Jones began to slip away. Rink slapped the side of the man's head and his eyelids fluttered. 'Stay with me,' Rink commanded brusquely.

'H-help me...first.'

'Tell me what I want and I will. Is Cahill the one responsible for murdering my friend?'

'He has murdered me!'

'You're not dead yet. Jim McTeer is. Do you remember my friend Jim? He's the one you sent those bastards after. You helped murder him.'

A sob broke from Greville-Jones's lips, and more bloody saliva streamed down his chin. Rink doubted his grief was driven by guilt.

'Cahill said...if I didn't help...Vish...Viskhan would have me killed.'

'Viskhan. Who is he?'

'He...he is...a *bad* man.'

'I want his full name.'

'Mikhail. His first name is Mikhail. He's...he's...'

'Yeah, yeah, a bad man. Well, *buddy*—' Rink couldn't form the dying man's full name on his tongue ' —he doesn't scare me. He made the wrong enemies when he chose to kill one of our friends. You're dying, not much I can do about that; not sure I would help you if I could. But know this, and it might give you some peace: Cahill, Viskhan, they won't be far behind you.'

There was scant life left in him, but Greville-Jones nodded as if in gratitude. Rink snorted; he hadn't made the promise of vengeance on his behalf. He glanced at the open doorway. The cell phone Greville-Jones had been using minutes earlier lay on the floor, dropped when he was ambushed at the door. Rink snatched it up.

He hit 911.

When the operator picked up he said, 'Help...I've been stabbed...two men with knives are forcing their way into my apartment...' He dropped the cell phone and allowed it to clatter along the floor, cancelling the call. Then he picked it up and wiped his fingerprints clean with his shirttail. He lay the phone down beside Greville-Jones. 'I didn't do that for you, buddy,' he said.

The cops would trace the call back to Greville-Jones's address, but Rink would be long gone before they arrived. Let them assume that the two injured killers had fought a tougher victim than they'd expected. The unconscious man had no way of identifying Rink and the one lying broken downstairs – well, what could he tell the police? If Greville-Jones did miraculously survive, then he might finally admit to Rink being there, but by then Rink would be involved in a whole other mess anyway. He didn't think Greville-Jones would survive. He'd been stabbed upward of a dozen times and at least two of the wounds were fatal...he'd bleed out long before the emergency services arrived.

Rink retraced his steps, found his tuxedo jacket where he'd left it in the bushes, and shook off most of the rain. He pulled into it to conceal Greville-Jones's bloody handprint on his shirt and walked away, while taking out his own cell phone and calling Harvey Lucas.

'I've got some names for you to check out, Harve,' he said.

16

I was hoping that the parking garage would be utilised overnight by local residents, and therefore contain plenty of vehicles to choose between. It turned out that it was a private enterprise, where cars could be parked by the hour, and had closed before midnight. Our choices were few, and of the sporadic vehicles we came across most were too modern to steal without a lot of time and effort. We'd almost given up hope of finding something I could hotwire before Cahill's team began a systematic sweep of the split-level garage. But I spotted an old panel van. It was parked in a recess adjacent to an access stairwell. Plastic cones, and a trestle used by a painting crew who had been freshening the directional signage on the low ceiling, surrounded the van. The crew must have clocked off work the previous Friday evening, but left their van and gear in situ for their return to work on Monday morning. The van was sufficiently aged that I didn't expect to have to thwart a computer to get it going.

Trey didn't look impressed by our getaway vehicle, but followed me to it anyway. She went round to the passenger side to try the door. It was locked. It mattered not. I smashed the driver's window with a rap of the Glock's barrel and soon had both doors unlocked. I warned Trey not to get in, but keep watch. I'd rather she was able to run if our hunters discovered us before I got us moving, than get penned inside an immobile van. She hopped from foot to foot, scanning the length and breadth of the parking floor for sign of movement. Nobody had made it up to the third floor yet, but we could hear them below us. Cahill's people risked being cornered by the police responding to the break-in at the art supplies store, but weren't ready for quitting the chase. I'd probably incensed them by killing three of their number, so could understand their determination. I was as equally pissed about McTeer's death that I wasn't for quitting the fight either. In their story, they undoubtedly believed themselves the protagonists.

I had to wrench at the steering wheel to disengage the lock, then arch backwards under the steering column to get at the electronics, and felt vulnerable with my legs and abdomen exposed to attack. Trey did a good job of standing guard, though, so I thought I'd be able to bring my guns to bear before anyone got close enough to shoot my balls off. It'd been some years since I'd had reason to hot-wire a vehicle, but old habits die hard. The engine roared to life, and I urged Trey to get in quick. As soon as she was on board I reversed the van over the cones, flattening them under the tyres. The sound of the engine would bring Cahill's men running. Not Cahill, though. He'd shown caution before: I took it he'd returned to his vehicle to cut off our escape route after sending his expendable men after us into the parking garage. He could already be in place to block any escape from the building.

The van was designed for lugging around scaffolding and paint pots, not for speed or manouevrability, but what it lacked in finesse it made up for in brute force. Its tyres squealed in protest as I took the sharp turn onto the first down ramp, and the van rocked wildly, throwing over some equipment in the back. Trey clung to a handle above the door, but I told her to get down as close to the floor as possible. Presented against the window she'd offer too irresistible a target. She squeezed down on a rubber foot mat dotted with speckles of dried paint, her backside and lower torso beneath the dash, arms bent on the seat, and head tucked into them. The doors wouldn't stop a bullet, but at least hidden our pursuers wouldn't know if she was in the front or in the cargo area behind. Driving, I was the obvious shot to go for. The first one wasn't long in coming.

There was no direct route down between the levels, and I was forced to take the van in a wide semicircle between thick concrete stanchions to attain each ramp down. As I sped for number two, a gunman tracked our progress, shooting with calm surety. The first bullet shattered Trey's window and sprayed her with glass. She yelped, even as I gritted my teeth and squinted my eyes: all I needed was flying slivers to blind me. The second bullet drilled the body of the van and ricocheted around the cargo area before its force was spent. The next bullet hit the back doors, which meant I'd powered the van past the shooter, but he'd get another chance as I swung towards the next down ramp.

Bullets caromed off the hood this time, one of them nicking the windshield. The van's tyres shrieked in torment as I torqued the van for the ramp. It went down at speed and the front fender clattered off the concrete floor before I could right the van. I yanked the steering to the left, glancing in my mirrors at the last second and seeing a stocky figure rush onto the ramp behind us. Another volley of bullets riddled the van before we were out of his firing line. I checked on Trey. Her impulse was to blink up at me, her mouth held in a taut grimace. 'Stay down,' I grunted brusquely.

'You're bleeding.'

'It's nothing. A bit of flying glass.' I could feel the sting in my right cheek where my dermis had been sliced open. Warm blood trickled down the side of my neck. I tested the integrity of my inner cheek with my tongue. The glass hadn't made it all the way through.

I ignored the minor injury, concentrated on racing the van through the next half circle. A crazy guy – the same skeletal figure who'd tried to shoot me earlier – lurched out from between two stanchions and set himself directly in our way. His gun flashed repeatedly, the strobe effect of his gunshots lighting up the parking garage, mimicking the lightning flashes outside. The windshield was holed twice in quick succession. The spent bullets didn't strike me, or Trey, but I dread to think how close they came. I stamped the gas and sent the van ploughing towards the shooter and he dove for cover at the last second. A bump told me he wasn't fast enough to avoid all injury; I think at best I clipped his heels, but he wouldn't be as spry after that. He didn't get off another shot as I swung hard towards the exit ramp.

A security barrier controlled access from the parking garage. It was no serious obstruction to the van. It was smashed loose, although not before the van's hood crumpled at the impact, and the windshield imploded. Parts of the shattered barrier clattered over the roof and rattled to the floor behind us. A few splinters found their way inside, but they were lost among the glittering nuggets of glass that landed heavily in my lap and over Trey's shoulders and hair. Trey shouted wordlessly – I think I might have too. There was a short incline up to street level. Thankfully the road was deserted of traffic as the van rocketed up and performed a graceless bound off the uppermost end of the slope. It bounced and jostled as I fought with the steering wheel, throwing most of the heaped glass off my thighs onto the floor, then the back end swung out and slammed a signpost on the far kerb. We were on 16th Street by my best guess, facing back towards Collins. I didn't want to go that way, because if Cahill had returned to his vehicle he'd be coming in from that direction. I tore the van around in a tight arc, and was again facing the exit ramp.

The thicker-set guy with wavy black hair was lumbering up the ramp. In his dark features his eyes practically seethed with determination. He came to a halt, taking a shooter's stance, and aimed directly at my exposed face. I leaned down hard on the wheel, stamped the throttle, felt his bullet whizz by the back of my skull before it buried itself in the padded upholstery of the passenger seat. By the time he got off a second bullet, the van was hurtling away in the direction of Washington Avenue, trailing its rear bumper along the asphalt.

In my mirrors, the gunman charged out onto the street, raising his gun, but didn't waste any rounds. His skinny pal limped out behind him, plus a third man who I hadn't laid eyes on before. I couldn't determine how many pursued us. The third man could have been the same who'd fired at us on the second level then raced to join his friends, or this could be another man. Including Cahill there was upward of four hitters on our tail at the very least. And perhaps there were more coming. Our best bet was to get away from Miami Beach at first order, and that should be before the police got their act together and set up a cordon. Miami Beach was effectively a barrier island adjacent to the mainland, built on one of a series of off-shore keys all interconnected by a series of bridges. If the police deemed the night's events serious enough – considering the number of dead, they'd be fools not to – they could effectively shut down the entire island, then set up a search pattern to run us to ground.

I spun the van onto Washington Avenue, speeding north towards Dade Boulevard and the first opportunity to cross Biscayne Bay to the mainland. There was a plethora of intersecting streets we could have followed west and found access onto Venetian Way, but I was more intent on putting distance between our pursuers and us first. I was driving without lights, and still trailing a bumper that clattered and sent up a shower of sparks, so the possibility of being stopped by the police was high, but just then the lesser of two evils. Trey clambered upright into her seat and set about shedding the accumulation of glass and splinters from her hair. They tinkled softly in the footwell.

'You OK?' I asked, glancing across at her.

She returned my look with a startled expression, her mouth pouting. The breeze gusting in through the broken windshield made locks of hair dance around her head.

'Some night, huh?' I said, and squeezed her a smile.

'I take it you're not talking about the weather?'

It was good that she could still joke considering all that she'd witnessed.

'I bet you're reconsidering your decision to seek help from me now?'

'Quite the contrary,' she replied. 'I'd be dead by now if not for you. Instead, I only look like I've been through a war.'

Despite her hair being snagged, dotted with splinters of glass and other debris, her arms and legs scraped, and her beautiful gown dirtied and torn, she looked incredibly beautiful to me.

'This isn't the way I hoped things would play out,' I admitted. 'We've been constantly on the move since the hotel and I haven't had time to do much more than react. My original plan was to get you somewhere safe, though, and I suppose that hasn't changed. Didn't expect I'd be moving you in a van full of bullet holes.'

'Better than us being full of bullets,' she said, but then her features grew pensive. She was thinking of the trio of men I'd killed outside the art supplies store. She grimaced at me. 'Back at the hotel, before your friend was killed, you said that you weren't a killer for hire...'

'I think the term I used was "hitman". I'm not.'

'The way you stopped those men...'

'That was self-defence. If I hadn't stopped them then they'd have killed us. Even the unarmed man tried to shoot me first, before I got his gun and turned it on him when he went after you in the doorway. My conscience is clear.'

'I wasn't criticising, Joe. I'm glad you're the way you are. It's going to take someone like you to stop Mikhail.'

'He'll get what he's due.' I recalled something else she'd said back at my hotel room an instant before all went to hell. 'You said something along the lines of if I knew what Mikhail was planning, I'd have a different opinion about killing him.'

She nodded, but allowed her chin to dip towards her chest. She busied herself with picking some stray slivers of glass out of her décolletage. She was clearly uncertain about how to tell me. I waited her out, and she finally looked over at me. Tears welled in her eyes. 'I'm afraid if I tell you the truth you might kick me out and leave me for Cahill to catch up.'

I sniffed. Contemplated what she meant, and was about to say 'Try me,' but then headlights glared in my mirrors as a Mercedes SUV rocketed in from a side street and accelerated after us. 'OK, we'll speak about it later. Right now you should put on your seatbelt,' I commanded. 'Cahill isn't finished with us yet.'

The van was an old workhorse – the only reason I'd been able to hot-wire it – but it wasn't built for the demands of a high-speed chase. It was weighty enough that it wasn't easily rammed off the road, but wasn't infallible either. A smaller vehicle could push a bigger one all over the place when strategy and tactics were applied. Some police drivers trained in how to stop a moving vehicle during a pursuit by the application of tried and tested techniques, as did various military and private security personnel. Cahill's man knew his stuff. Twice already he'd almost had our van fishtailing as he applied his front fender to the van's opposite rear side. Luckily, I too had undergone training in defensive driving tactics and, coupling them with luck and daring, I managed to keep us on the road as we sped onto Dade Boulevard. Unfortunately, we were headed in the opposite direction than I'd originally planned, and was being pursued further into the interior of the island. Or was it fortunate? I didn't really want them pursuing us to the mainland, so perhaps it was better that I tried to lose them in North Beach or elsewhere, before making an attempt to get Trey off the island via one of the bridges.

I pushed the van to its highest speed, which topped out at a little over seventy miles per hour; the Mercedes we competed with was a flying machine by comparison. On the highway, staying ahead of it became a task in itself, and I'd to swerve across lanes to prevent it speeding past. If they got in front of us, we'd be forced to a rolling stop and would be under Cahill's and another passenger's gun sights. The trouble with swerving was that it offered fresh opportunities for the Mercedes to ram us at an angle and cause the van to spin out.

Earlier, when stealing the van, I'd had to put down my weapons, but I'd since had Trey wedge the Glock between my thighs while she held on to the silenced pistol in reserve. On the two occasions that the Mercedes had already attempted to blast past us, I'd snapped up the Glock and dissuaded them with a couple of ill-aimed shots – the bullets had failed to hit the Mercedes but the flashing of the gun had been enough to discourage them from driving alongside me. I knew it was only a matter of time before they attempted to force a path by on Trey's side.

Dade Boulevard became Pine Tree Drive as we hurtled past the Miami Beach Fire Rescue HQ. Intersecting streets offered ways for others of Cahill's team to join the pursuit, but my hope was that they had only two cars, and one of them was currently out of commission where my flung rock had sent it ploughing into the stationery vehicle outside the art supplies shop. We passed a high school, and I thanked an unheeding God that it was still the early hours and no kids were in our path. A golf course flashed by on our left, and then the road made a couple of kinks and I hauled the old van through the chicanes like a seasoned rally driver. The Mercedes slammed into our back end and the van jumped a little, the tyres losing traction and skidding one way and then the other before I could get it fully under control. I dropped a gear, stamped the gas pedal and gained a lead of a few precious feet on the Mercedes.

A major intersection loomed dead ahead where 41st Street bisected the island. During the day I'd be risking a collision if I didn't obey the lights, but there were very few vehicles on the road so the risk of mangling us in a wreck was worth it. I shot through a red and across the intersection without slowing. Behind us the Mercedes followed our lead, so close to our back end that I briefly wondered if they'd got caught up on the trailing fender – but more likely the fender had been ripped loose following their first attempt at ramming us.

We were fortunate that most of the cops in Miami Beach were tied up at the two homicide sites we'd left behind, otherwise the competing roars of our engines would have alerted plenty of patrol cars who'd join the chase. As it was, we largely had the roads to ourselves. The surface water stood in wide puddles and sheeted up behind us as we plunged through. The Mercedes caught our spray, deluged by it, forcing the driver to back off a little so he could see beyond the wipers battling to clear the screen. But I didn't have a much cleaner line of sight: droplets stung my face, made me squint, as did the wind blasting inside the van through our shattered windshield. Trey huddled, as much from the cold as the threat of a bullet through her side window.

Pine Tree Drive curved sharply to the left, and just beyond the bend there was another intersection, this time with two streets converging on the main route. On the approach to the intersection the opposing lanes of the road were separated by a beautifully maintained median, green with grass and sculpted trees. The Mercedes suddenly took an unexpected move, shooting across the median into the oncoming lane, missing a tree by inches, and then the driver hit the gas. It flew past us, and I'd no clear shot at them. But I caught a brief glimpse of Cahill's face and the smug wink he offered me. The Mercedes could easily outrace the van, but we weren't competing for pink slips: this was more a demolition derby than a drag race. As they reached the convergence of the three roads, the driver braked, hitting a controlled skid that brought the Mercedes directly in front of the van. I could plough into them or I could swerve. We might survive an impact, but probably not. Instinct forced the latter response. As I yanked down on the steering wheel, I again got a brief snapshot glimpse of Cahill and the gun he fearlessly aimed at me despite the probability we were all going to die in a rolling wreck. He popped off a round. It caromed off the frame of the windshield and I flinched, expecting to be drilled by the ricochet.

The van, peeling right, still caught the back end of the Mercedes, shunting it around in a half circle in a manner the driver had attempted to spin us on a number of occasions. But my grip on the steering wasn't firm, and I felt the wheel spin under my fingers. The van darted up the sidewalk and crashed through a temporary fence erected around a construction site. Corrugated metal sheets flew as we slammed through a pile of stacked timber. The van almost went airborne. Cursing, I fought for control, eyes darting for a clear path through the site. I couldn't see one, but the van was uncaring. It smashed through another pile of timber, and I expected to be impaled at any second. Trey shrieked beside me and, with no other way of trying to save her, I grabbed her and forced her down. She wrapped her arms over her head. The concrete foundations of a building were dead ahead, and if we hit them that'd be it. At the last second I spotted the only thing that might save us from being pulped against the concrete. A ramp had been constructed to allow trucks to reverse onto the edge of the foundations, in order for them pour their loads of concrete. I tore down on the steering and got three wheels on the ramp. Before we took flight, the back right wheel clipped the edge of the foundation wall, tore chunks of cinder block off, and also blew out the tyre.

The next few seconds were dominated by a cacophony of sound – bumps, squeals, creaks, thumps – as the crippled van bounced and smashed a path through recently laid cinder blocks and rebar. The van began coming apart. I felt the driver's seat twist beneath me, and knew I was seconds from being hurled through the open windshield. I held tightly to the steering, bracing for the final impact. But it didn't come. We went airborne once more, the van making a lazy barrel roll as it finally gave up the race.

Time slowed, and everything was crystal clear to me. I had a sense of direction, and Trey was above me, the centrifugal force of our roll working to throw her against the passenger door and up towards the roof. I was pushed down and against the driver's door. At least I wasn't being forced towards the shattered windshield any more. We obliterated a second temporary wall of corrugated steel sheets, and I gritted my teeth against the imminent impact with the earth beyond.

There was no earth, only a flat sheet of deep sapphire dotted with myriad colours where it reflected the lights on Collins Avenue, which was about a hundred yards distant.

The van slammed into Indian Creek, and I experienced the impact as a shock wave that passed through my body like a cannon blast, and it continued through the van, warping and twisting and tearing it apart. Foaming water blasted into the interior of the van, totally blinding and overwhelming. There was no lazy settling of the van on the water. It plunged beneath the depths even as it exploded, throwing open the rear doors and allowing the creek to flood in at all angles. I was hammered, my brain was whirling in shock as I choked on briny water, fighting for breath that wouldn't come, and...shit, I was drowning.

18

Stripped to his boxer shorts, Mikhail Viskhan swore at his cell phone, and was a second from throwing it across the room. He caught sight of his reflection in a wall mirror, his fattened lip drooping: he looked like an idiot! Instead of smashing the cell phone against the wall, he stabbed buttons again and re-dialled Sean Cahill's number. The son of a bitch was purposefully ignoring his calls, growing too big for his friggin' britches – a term that Dan StJohn was fond of. Cahill would have to be reminded that they weren't peers; Cahill was an employee and he must respond when his boss hailed him.

'Pick up, damn you!' he seethed at the ringing phone, but then relented with a sigh.

You should remember that Sean is not a dog at your beck and call, but your second in command, he thought. You ordered him to complete an important mission and now you complain that he has fully submerged himself in its completion?

'He should still answer when I damn well call him!' he snapped aloud in his native tongue.

You allowed your hot head to get the better of you, his internal voice argued, *so you can only blame yourself. Like he'd said, Sean's time would be better served here, finalizing plans and preparations than off hunting your bitch of a wife and her protector. Why have you not learned the value of Sean's counsel when it has proven so beneficial in the past?*

'Because he does what I say, not the other way around!'

The phone continued to ring unanswered.

Mikhail threw the cell phone away in disgust, but took care that it landed on the plush bedspread so was undamaged. The naked woman beneath the sheets peered back at him wide-eyed, her bottom lip caught between her teeth. Mikhail's annoyance at Cahill found a new target. 'Get up,' he spat, this time in English, 'and get the fuck out of here, you filthy whore.'

The woman blinked at him in astonishment. Minutes ago they'd been in each other's arms, and he'd been an aggressive but fulfilling lover. She still wore a sheen of perspiration from their exertions. She had believed him a satisfied customer.

'I said *get out!*'

Before the woman could comply, he lunged at the bed, grasped the sheets covering her nakedness and yanked them in a bundle onto the floor. The woman squeaked in alarm, and pulled inward defensively, arms across her breasts, thighs crossing. Her pose had nothing to do with modesty, because she'd already proven she'd perform the most depraved of acts at his instruction. Mikhail snarled the fingers of his right hand in her hair, while his left snapped down on her upper arm. He yanked her as violently off the bed as he had the sheets. His phone clattered onto the floor along with her.

'Get out,' he growled again, then kicked her away so he could snatch up his phone from under her.

'What about...'

'Payment? You dare to ask *me* for money?' The ligaments in Mikhail's throat worked like plucked strings. 'Do you forget who the fuck *you work* for too? Now go, before I have to remind you.'

This time the woman obeyed with haste. She scrambled to collect her discarded clothing, and had barely grabbed enough to protect her modesty when Mikhail emitted a growl like an enraged beast and chased her through the door. She fled along the corridor naked, her clothes bundled in her arms. The whore didn't know how fortunate she was: she got to run away in a manner that Trey had never been allowed to himself. He felt like chasing her down and beating her until she bled from every orifice, but resisted the urge. Disposing of her corpse would be an inconvenience he could do without. If Sean was there, he could be given the task of clearing up the mess, but Sean wasn't...where the fuck was he?

The sound of the front door slamming echoed through the otherwise empty house.

Mikhail instantly forgot about the whore.

He inspected his cell phone. The screen had darkened, but as he swiped his thumb across it he again saw Sean Cahill's details, though the call had timed out.

He thought about hitting the call button again, but instead a weary sigh washed through him. He placed the phone down on a bedside nightstand, and went to select fresh clothing from his walk-in dressing room. Dawn was fast approaching, so he selected appropriate daywear. He was about to dress, but could smell himself. He stank of whore.

He showered.

Returned dripping to his room, and saw that a faint glow was in the process of fading from his cell phone on the nightstand.

He'd missed a call from Sean Cahill.

He was tempted to ignore it, let Sean wait, the way he'd been forced to wait like a mongrel begging scraps from its master's table. But he stabbed at the call button.

'Mikhail?'

He ignored the inquiry. 'Why the fuck didn't you answer me sooner?'

'I've been busy.'

'Too busy for *me*?'

'Yes, even for you, Mikhail.'

A snort of derision blasted from Mikhail's nostrils. 'Then you'd better have a fucking good reason, Sean. I do not like to be ignored.'

'It's done. Is that reason enough?'

'Done? You mean...'

Before he could press for details, Cahill had a caveat. 'It's not all good news. We lost some men – Harris, Waller and Sierra – and Monk has a busted ankle.'

Mikhail could not give a fuck for any of the mercenaries Cahill mentioned. They were as expendable as every other sack of meat on his payroll. But he understood there could be repercussions from losing those men if their bodies were traced back to him. Another thirty hours or so and it would not matter who the cops connected to him, but the premature deaths of some of Cahill's crew was troubling at this early point. Miami Beach would be awash with investigators, and that could prove a hindrance to their main operation.

'One man managed to kill three of your soldiers? Huh, maybe I did not show this Joe Hunter the respect he was due, after all?'

'He proved himself a capable and wily opponent,' Cahill said, with grudging respect of his own. 'But it didn't matter in the end.'

'If he hadn't sucker punched me earlier, things would've been different,' Mikhail was quick to add.

'He was tough and skilled,' Cahill added, and Mikhail wasn't sure exactly why – perhaps it was to convince Mikhail that there was no shame in being knocked on his ass by a worthy opponent.

'It's a shame we had to be enemies, then,' Mikhail said, without an iota of sincerity. 'Had we met under other circumstances he might have been a worthier addition to your team than the useless punks he killed.'

Cahill changed the subject. He didn't think of any of his men as useless, then? To him their lives had been wasted on soothing Mikhail's bruised ego? Mikhail grinned snarkily at the thought.

'Another man surprised us tonight,' Cahill went on. 'Greville-Jones.'

'You said you'd have him silenced before the police could speak with him.' Earlier, while following Hunter and Trey into Lummus Park, Cahill had appraised Mikhail of the connection with the failed hit on them, and the beers sent to the hotel by Greville-Jones, but he'd assured him that the security man would be silenced before the connection was made.

'Don't worry; he won't be speaking to anyone. He's dead. But not before he put up one hell of a fight. He knocked one guy out and threw the other off a balcony before succumbing to his wounds.'

Mikhail breathed heavily into his cellphone. 'I find that surprising indeed. I didn't think Albert had it in him.'

'Me neither, but there you are. Two more guys taken out of the picture.'

'The police have them?' Adrenaline trickled through Mikhail's system, and he shivered at the sensation.

'They're both in hospital under police guard. Neither of them is in a fit state for interview at this time, but it's inevitable that it will happen. But don't worry, Mikhail, they have no direct connection to our main operation, and know nothing about you.'

'I'm not worried. Not for me. They can lead the police to you?'

'Perhaps.'

'Then they require silencing.'

'When does it end, Mikhail? There are only so many links in any chain...will we reach a point where I'm the one requiring silencing?'

'Stop acting like a petulant child, Sean. I value you too much. I haven't forgotten that you saved my life – more than once – and for that I'm eternally grateful.'

'You saved my life first.'

'Yes, I did, and I've never allowed you to forget it.' Mikhail laughed too hard. 'Would I now have you killed just because of your inability to handle a simple clean-up job like this?'

Cahill's silence said everything.

Mikhail had saved his life, dragging him from the rubble of a bombed building and carrying him to safety. In return for his life he'd served Mikhail for fifteen years. His debt was repaid tenfold, most recently when he took the bullet intended for his boss, but he still got Mikhail to safety before he collapsed from blood loss. Mikhail's debt to him was massive, and yet Cahill was no fool: if it came to it, Mikhail would sacrifice his closest friend to save his own ass. Back when they were guns for hire, things were very different. They were brothers reliant on the other to guard their backs. These days Mikhail was wealthy enough to command all the protection he needed, and Cahill as expendable as any other gunman on his payroll. Of late, he felt that Cahill had entertained delusions of grandeur, and it would serve as an important message to anyone who thought otherwise if Mikhail had him executed. But not until after the successful completion of their operation. Cahill was too integral a player in its success to have murdered yet.

'You are too valuable to me, Sean,' he repeated. 'And I can forgive your mishandling of your other tasks now that you've achieved your prime objective. I hope you suitably punished Trey and her white knight before they died?'

'They are dead, drowned at the bottom of Indian Creek, that's the main thing.'

'I wanted you to bring me Hunter's balls in a jar…'

'Didn't get the opportunity, but trust me, before they died they both understood they'd fucked with the wrong man.'

'Good,' said Mikhail. 'Now get yourself back here. Dawn is approaching, and we have much to complete before tomorrow.'

'I haven't slept in twenty-four hours,' Cahill began.

'Have I slept?' Mikhail responded harshly. 'You're not the only one who has made sacrifices for the completion of the operation. Do you think I've been idle while you have been taking your time chasing Trey and Hunter?' He glimpsed back at the tousled sheets on the floor, and smiled to himself. 'I have expended sweat too and am tired. But this is not the time to slow down. Now get back here. No argument.'

Mikhail cut the call.

Cahill glanced at Dan StJohn, and caught his friend's wry expression. They were a mile away from where they'd forced Hunter and Trey into Indian Creek, waiting for a fresh vehicle to arrive and collect them. Cahill's driver had sped off in the Mercedes to make sure it was out of sight should any early bird witnesses have reported the high-speed pursuit to the police. While he had a moment to catch his breath, Cahill had decided to update Viskhan, and StJohn had overheard everything.

'Mikhail's his usual grateful self,' Cahill said as he shoved away his cell phone.

'He's such a prick,' said StJohn.

'Yeah. But he's the prick that's paying us.'

'I vote we shoot him in the head and find ourselves a new employer.' StJohn sniffed, as though the idea wasn't the worst one he'd ever had.

'Not until after the money's in our hands, Dan.'

'Do you really think he's still good for it?'

Cahill wondered what the Englishman was hinting at. 'Why wouldn't he be?'

'This fucking operation.' He wasn't talking about killing Hunter and Trey. 'Viskhan has this town tied down, is pulling in cash left, right and centre, and the fucker's grown minted off the proceeds: but he's prepared to give it all up for the sake of some fucking raghead plot? You ask me, he has fucking lost it.'

'Ours is not to reason why,' Cahill quoted.

'Fucked if I'm gonna die for some jihadi bullshite.'

'But you don't mind the *doing* part?'

'You know me. Pay me enough, I don't give a fuck who's in my gun sights. But the emphasis is on "pay me". Viskhan made the deal with the Syrians, but all we've heard are fucking promises to be delivered after the deed is done. Ever get the impression we're being played like those fucking suicide bombers who are promised more virgins than they can handle when they reach paradise? Don't know about you, mate, but if I were them, I'd like a go at those virgins before my bollocks got blown off.'

'You think the Syrians won't pay up afterwards? That's for Mikhail to worry about. He's the one who pays us, and trust me, I know he's good for the cash.' Cahill faced his old friend. 'You can trust me, Dan.'

'I wouldn't be here if it wasn't for you.' StJohn clapped a hand on Cahill's shoulder. 'After this, tell me you aren't following that arsehole back to Chechnya? You know, mate, we could run a gig like Viskhan has going here ourselves. We could pick up where he left off once he's out of here...but not if we're tied to what the crazy bastard has planned for tomorrow.'

'You want us to pull out at the eleventh hour?' Cahill shook his head. 'That's one way of making certain you never get paid, Dan.'

'Like I said: we shoot him in the head. Sink him out in the Atlantic and feed him to the fishes. Take what he has, and everything will be sweet. If he goes through with this bollocks tomorrow, the shit's going to hit the fucking fan. Big time, mate. There'll be Feds crawling all over the place for months. Miami will be off limits for us. We won't be able to scratch our arses without it being jotted down in a file someplace, let alone move any of our merchandise. It'd be in our best interests if Viskhan doesn't make it till tomorrow.'

'If Mikhail heard what you're saying he'd have you skinned alive.'

'He won't. It's like you said, Sean, I can trust you. Viskhan only thinks you're his pal, I know you're mine.'

Cahill rocked his head. 'I still owe him.'

StJohn grunted in scorn. 'Do you bollocks! You've pulled him out of the fire more times than he can even remember. He only saved you once.'

'I still wouldn't be here if it wasn't for him.'

'That's true. You could be the king of your own kingdom instead of having to kiss his arse all the time.'

'I enjoy my work.'

'Aye, right. Bet you'd enjoy it more if you were your own boss.'

Cahill concurred with a nod. 'But you'd still be happy kissing my ass?'

'I was thinking more along the lines of partners.'

'I wish I could say yes, and who knows, after this there will be opportunities for us. But for now, we have a job to do. I gave my word to Mikhail that we'd see this operation through, and my word is my bond. Soon as it's done and the money's in our accounts, we can do whatever the hell we like.' He held StJohn's gaze. 'You still with the programme, Dan?'

'I'm with *you*. Just don't expect me to strap on a fucking suicide vest like those other fuckwits we're helping.'

Indian Creek is only one of several waterways intersecting the collection of smaller barrier islands forming Miami Beach. It was fed by the waters of Biscayne Bay and tidal. The water was deep enough even at low tide to moor a boat alongside any of the many private piers dotted along its length, and easily deep enough to submerge a van. It was high tide. We were about ten feet below the frothy surface, and that was more than enough water to drown in. If it had been broad daylight, Cahill could have peered down through the water and watched us perish, but thankfully – if that word was even apt – it was still dark out. To him we'd be invisible. That was our only saving grace. In hindsight I believe he came and checked that there was no coming back for either Trey or me, then fled the scene in the Mercedes before any emergency services responded to the scene of the crash, but while I was underwater I didn't give him much thought. I was too involved in trying to keep us alive.

Initially I'd been battered into confusion by the impact of the van plunging into the creek, and the deluge of water flooding in from all egress points of the van left me reeling as we sank deeper. I couldn't breathe, couldn't see, and my other senses were all overwhelmed by a tumult of competing stimuli. Only the fact that I'd sucked in a lungful of air in anticipation of slamming into unforgiving earth did I have any hope of survival at all. I hadn't been wearing my seatbelt. I floated free, but who knew where? I forced my eyelids to open, but everything was a frothy blackness full of popping bubbles that sparked like phosphorus and added to my confusion. My palms slapped at metal, at jagged glass adhering to a rubber seal, and I twisted away, knowing I was heading the wrong direction. My hands groped around again, and I felt something slick and yielding: Trey's shoulder. She wasn't moving. Dead or unconscious, I didn't know, but I grabbed at her to haul her...I didn't know where. But I couldn't move her.

I recalled earlier warning her to strap in. I ran my hands down her body, found her thighs and retraced back to her waist. Undoing a seatbelt is such a simple task, but under the circumstances it almost thwarted me. But then the clip snapped out of the retainer and I hauled Trey into my arms. She flopped against me, buoyed by the water. I tugged her towards the shattered windscreen. Met a collapsing bank of sand that cascaded around us in a blinding cloud. The van had nosedived on its side into the water, and had buried its front end in the creek bed. It gave me hope that air had been forced into the rear cargo area, to hang there in a life-saving bubble I could draw from. I swam over the buckled seats into the cargo hold, fighting with floating paintbrushes and who knew what else as I dragged Trey through the gap. The back doors had been blown open by the force of the water, but because the van had come to rest on its side, one of them had fallen shut again. Any hope of finding an air pocket inside the shell of the van was slim, but I pulled along the uppermost side of the van to a point in the corner adjacent to the shut door.

I screamed in grateful delight as my features broke the surface, and found oxygen. I sucked in deeply, then bobbed down, and pushed Trey's head in my place. I heard her skin squeak as I forced her against the metal siding. She was inert. So I circled my arms around her body and yanked forcefully against her abdominals in a desperate Heimlich manoeuvre. What air had been compressed into her lungs was dispelled in a spluttering cry of alarm, but then Trey instinctively sucked in air. I could imagine her desperation and terror at that moment, so could forgive her for trying to fight free. Her nails clawed at my hands. Ignoring the discomfort, I squeezed her into the corner then pushed my head up alongside hers. My lips cleared the water but that was pretty much it. I sucked in air. Then spoke to her in a series of rapid commands. We couldn't make for the surface yet: I was certain that Cahill would check we were dead before fleeing. If we broke for the surface then, we'd be shot to death. But Trey panicked, and began clawing for escape, this time her fingers pushing me down. I roughly got a hand under chin, pressed her tightly into the air bubble, all the while almost drowning myself.

I held Trey there for what felt like an eternity, but must only have been a minute at best. Then I forced upward so I could replenish my breath. The air was stale and tasted bitter, but it was the most incredible air I'd ever breathed.

Twice more I repeated the process until I felt Cahill must have given up on seeing us alive again.

The final time I forced my lips out the water, I found there was nothing left to sustain either of our lives.

'Hold your breath,' I hollered, but all it sounded like was a garble of swarming bubbles.

I wrapped an arm around Trey's waist, pushed backwards, and found the closed door, though it was swinging loose on its hinges. It was lying crosswise across my shoulders. I backed, kicking at whatever foothold I could find, and we surged out of the gap. The door handle smacked me painfully on the nape of my neck, then gouged over my skull before I was free of it. Bubbles raced for the surface, and if I'd had any clear sense I could have discerned up from down. But my only thought was to get away from the van, so I dragged Trey with me, kicking like a frog, one arm swiping at the water. With no idea how much distance I'd put between the wreckage and us, I finally broke towards the surface, towing Trey with me. She kicked and squirmed in my grasp, and I'd little strength left to hold her. She broke free and clawed her way upward.

Moments later it was her arms around me as she helped drag me from beneath the creek and onto a muddy sandbar that pulled and tugged at my limbs like quicksand. I think I must have blacked out – not fully gone unconscious, but lost all sense of reality – because for a moment after my face broke the surface, I wanted nothing more than to dip back under and give in to the inevitable. Trey smacked me, the full width of her palm across the side of my head. The blow was enough to kick-start my survival instinct, and I sucked in fresh air.

Immediately Trey's palm clamped down over my mouth, and my eyes must have been as large as golf balls as I stared at her.

'You have to be silent,' she whispered into my ear. She jabbed a hand towards the bank. From twenty feet away, but hidden from my line of sight, I heard voices dwindling as Cahill and another of our pursuers retreated from the creek's bank, having seen all they needed to. If they heard me gasping like an asthmatic they'd return, and I was in no fit state to fight back.

I nodded at Trey in understanding, and she reluctantly withdrew her hand. I shuddered and fought the urge to shout for joy that I could breathe again. Worming over on my back, I was less likely to sink, and was able to breathe normally. I had a brilliant view of the stormy sky – lightning still flashed to the north but the bad weather had passed.

From some distance off I picked out the warbling strains of an approaching siren. Nearby a vehicle accelerated away, and I guessed it was the Mercedes putting distance between them and the responding cops. Though it was still early somebody must have heard the van's chaotic progress through the construction site, and telephoned it in. Within minutes people would gather on the bank and observe the point where the van had gone in the creek. We had to be far away by then. At that place, the creek was about a hundred yards wide. We could swim across it, but not quickly enough to escape more observant witnesses. So I pointed upstream, urging Trey to get away.

'We should wait for the police,' she argued.

'We're not safe in jail,' I told her.

'We're safe out here?' She looked at me, eyes wide with incredulity.

'It's been a hell of a night but you're still alive,' I said. 'I can't guarantee you'll survive another day behind bars. Viskhan and Cahill are determined fuckers, and they won't let a few bars stop them getting at you. For now they think you're dead. If we let them carry on believing that for now, it gives me a chance to get you somewhere safer.'

The small muscles around her eyes constricted. Something I'd said had hit home. 'OK. But where do we go from here?'

'Stay close to the bank, and head upstream.' I knew that Indian Creek widened and then split around a small island further to the north, giving us more options where we could climb out of the water than if we headed downstream. But my idea wasn't to wade all the way to Biscayne Bay.

We'd made it about a hundred yards when the first emergency crews arrived at the construction site. Their flashing lights danced on the bellies of the low-lying clouds. A minute after that, someone began shining a spotlight over the surface of the creek, having found where we'd crashed through the temporary fence and plotted our impact point. The beam began making wider sweeps, searching for evidence of survivors, and I hoped they concentrated on the area downstream from where the van entered the water.

Dripping wet, I grasped Trey's hand and led her towards the bank. We had come upon a jetty that extended out over the creek. A speedboat was moored on the far side, but I'd no intention of using the boat for a speedy – yet noisy – getaway. I had another idea. On the bank was an overturned rowing boat. It looked as if it hadn't been used in years, and in the dark I wouldn't be able to determine the hull's integrity until we tried to float it.

I asked Trey to wait in the water, but she followed me out, stood dripping in her ruined dress and sopping over-sized sneakers. Her hair was a bedraggled mess hanging round her shoulders, and there was no trace of make-up on her face but for bumps, bruises and scratches. She caught my bemused glance, and took a brief look down at herself. I expected her to sob dismally, but she surprised me with a chuckle. 'Gee,' she said, her expression a little manic, 'I think the shop's going to go mental when I return this dress. It's Versace.'

'Versace, huh? Is that the local slang word for messed-up?' I quipped. 'Or am I being too polite?'

'If that were true, then you look a little Versace'd-up too.'

I was a mess. My exposed skin was a patchwork of scratches and bruises, and my clothing was saturated and clinging to me in all the wrong places. That was only externally. Inside I felt like a tenderized beefsteak. 'At least I don't have to go back to the shop.'

She laughed again, genuinely pleased, as she plucked at her ruined dress. 'What the hell? It's Mikhail who will get the bill. Serves him right.'

It was good to hear her laughter; many other people would have collapsed under the strain of the events she'd endured, let alone retained any humour. She might have been a virtual prisoner for more than a decade, but Trey Shaw had stayed strong. After witnessing the aftermath of the violence where McTeer and his attackers died, I'd feared she was on the point of collapse, but that had proven a momentary wobble. Now that she'd made a positive break from Mikhail, I suspected she'd fight tooth and nail before she was ever dragged back to him.

'Help me with this?' I motioned at the upturned boat.

Trey complied, squatting alongside me as we heaved the boat over. There was no outboard motor or even oars, but it didn't matter. We pushed it into the creek, and I waded in and held it steady while Trey boarded. I kind of fell over the gunwale and crawled upright, seating myself on a bench facing the prow as the boat settled in the water. Trey was up front, facing me. I paddled us out into the creek with my hands, taking care not to splash or make much noise.

All the while thinking that enough time had passed that I should contact Rink: I needed his help. When the van crashed I'd lost both guns I'd acquired, but the bigger problem was my cell phone was as soaked as my clothing, and the one in Trey's clutch purse had been abandoned in the sunken van. I'd cash and credit cards in my wallet, and they could be dried quickly enough, but they were little good to me while we were literally up a creek without a paddle.

Harvey Lucas was en route to Miami, but before catching his flight out of Arkansas, he called Rink. He'd been up all through the early hours collating as much information on their enemies as he could find, and what he reported didn't come as too surprising to either of them, but it did give some pause. Sean Cahill wasn't your average criminal, and Mikhail Viskhan more than just a narcissistic playboy. They were both sons of freedom fighters – but that depended upon whom you spoke to. Seen from the opposite end of a rifle barrel or exploding bomb, they were terrorists. Both men had followed in the footsteps of their fathers, and if the rumours were true they had committed more atrocities than either of their forebears.

'So we have the bastard sons of the Real IRA and CRI working together?' said Rink. The Real IRA were a paramilitary terrorist group, a more violent offshoot of the original Irish Republican Army, who kept the fight going after the IRA came to peace terms with the UK. On the other hand, the CRI or Chechen Republic of Ichkeria was the catch-all term for a self-proclaimed state at war with their Russian enemies, to which many of the diverse Chechen and Dagestan rebel groups paid allegiance. 'It's not exactly a marriage made in heaven, Harve.'

Rink was in a nondescript hotel room in downtown Miami, having made tracks to leave the resort island following his visit with Albert Greville-Jones hours earlier. His reason for leaving Miami Beach for the mainland wasn't an attempt at running away; it gave him more breathing space to plan and organize his return.

'They might be separated by religion and idealism, but the allure of money is a great motivator,' Harvey said. 'Besides, I'm not sure they give a damn for what their fathers stood for, I'm betting they have their own agenda...getting richer.'

'Sounds right,' Rink said.

'They met as PMCs—' Harvey was referring to private military contractors, also known as mercenaries '—supposedly fighting on opposite sides in Afghanistan. You ask me, though, they were united in the illegal drugs trade. From what I could dig up Viskhan saved Cahill's life during a US bombing raid on a Taliban stronghold, and Cahill returned the favour while helping his new pal escape the country. You have to ask yourself what they were doing cozying up to the Taliban, and I'd say it was about securing transportation routes of raw poppies to the narcotics trade. But who can say? I'm only working off unfounded rumours from other PMCs I spoke with.'

'I'm surprised Homeland isn't all over their asses,' said Rink.

'Perhaps they are. Guys with their backgrounds don't get to enter the US without being added to terrorist watch lists. But if that's true, why haven't they already been rounded up and sent to Gitmo?'

'CIA assets?' Rink suggested.

'You have to wonder.' Harvey paused, deciding if he should broach the subject. 'Do you think contacting Walter could be our right move?'

Rink gave a short, sharp grunt.

'Just saying,' Harvey said quickly.

'I'd rather keep that weasely little frog-gigger out of this.' Rink had no love for Walter Hayes Conrad. In the "official" role of a CIA subdivision director, Walter was also an active member of the ultra-secret counter-terrorism group codenamed Arrowsake, which both Rink and Joe Hunter once worked for. Hunter still held on to misguided affection for their old boss, whereas Rink had only contempt. His dislike hadn't lessened after Walter actively used them both to thwart an attack by a white supremacist group in Manhattan – an attack sponsored by Arrowsake in an attempt at raising the domestic terrorism threat level and with it their funding and viability as an invaluable security resource. But Rink had to admit, as an ally Walter was a necessary evil to have in their corner. His highest-level interference had kept both Rink and Hunter out of prison before, and the way the night had shaped up, perhaps calling him wasn't the worst idea he'd ever heard, at the least on Raul Velasquez's behalf. 'Just for the time being,' he added.

'If they are CIA assets, or the FBI are on to them and just waiting for their chance to pounce, we could be stepping into the middle of a shitstorm,' Harvey said.

'I could give a damn for spoiling the CIA's or the Feds' plans for them. They killed Mack, and for all we know could have killed Hunter too...' Rink paused on that thought, decided he didn't like the sound of it. 'They've tried to kill Hunter, until we know otherwise we assume they've been unsuccessful. But that's beside the point. Mack's dead, Velasquez's locked up and they're after Hunter and some innocent girl, and I swear those bastards ain't getting away with it.'

'Do the cops know who they're up against yet?'

'Beats me. I'm confident that Velasquez hasn't told them about Viskhan yet, but it won't take them long to piece things together. I've been watching the local news channels, but the reports are sketchy and the cops aren't commenting. Some of Cahill's guys were shot dead not far from where things started, and apparently a high-speed chase ended up with a van crashing into Indian Creek. It'd take an idiot not to connect the three incidents, but as yet, I'm confident the cops don't realise that they're looking for either Hunter and the woman, or Cahill and Viskhan.'

'They haven't connected the attack on Greville-Jones to everything else that's happening?'

'They must have by now. Albert didn't survive, but I made sure his attackers did, but not in a fit state to speak. The punks won't admit to being sent by Viskhan, or Cahill for that matter, but the cops will have figured it out. They'll know there's a bigger picture, and when they connect the hit on Mack to that on Greville-Jones, they'll soon figure out it all goes back to the work we did for him at last night's fundraiser. Once Viskhan's name jumps off the guest list at them they'll be on to us all.'

'So time's short before they start pulling you and all the others in for questioning?'

'Yup. Which makes it difficult for me do something about those bastards. But I won't let that stop me.'

'Y'know, I have to be the voice of reason here, Rink...' Harvey laughed cynically – usually it was Rink cautioning Hunter against rash decisions '...but why not just go to the cops and tell them the truth? Those guys that were killed in Mack's room, that was self-defence. Reading between the lines, the ones you mentioned getting shot nearby, and that chase that ended up with the van crashing, they have to involve Hunter trying to save that woman's life. None of you are the bad guys in this.'

'Some cops won't necessarily see things our way. If Viskhan has the manpower and influence to order a manhunt like this, then you can bet your ass he has a few cops in his pocket. I don't want a corrupt officer with an itchy trigger finger anywhere near any of us.'

Harvey didn't reply. He hadn't the same experience of working in the shadows as Rink and Hunter, and still held to the belief that most cops were honest and honourable. Largely they were, but you only needed one bad cop to pull a trigger, and Rink bet that Viskhan knew the bad ones. He was openly running business ventures that required that certain officials turned a blind eye to them.

'This got personal when those bastards murdered Mack,' Rink added.

'Then I pity them,' Harvey said. 'Look, I'll be with you before the afternoon's out. They're starting to board my flight so I'd best get moving. I'll email everything I have on Viskhan and Cahill to you; it might give you an idea where to start looking for them. Just let me know where and when you need me, Rink.'

'Thanks, brother,' said Rink, and he gave the address and room number of his hotel that he'd booked under a bogus name. 'Don't send anything over just yet; I'm going to switch to a burner phone soon. If the cops have tied me to all the trouble they might try to trace me via this one. I've kept it on for now hoping Hunter might call me, but he hasn't. Once I've a burner up and running, I'll leave an anonymous voicemail message on your office phone with the number. Check in with it, grab yourself a burner and answer me on it.'

'Sure thing,' said Harvey. 'I'll do it soon as I'm in Miami. But it means you'll have to wait for the info.'

'Just gimme Viskhan's home address,' said Rink. 'I'll go from there.'

Harvey read out the address as he headed towards the flight attendant checking boarding passes at the gate. Rink thanked him. Harvey said, 'Good hunting, brother.'

Dressed down, Trey Shaw was a different woman, although no less beautiful than when I first saw her. Her designer dress had been replaced with jeans and a plain grey long-sleeved shirt that concealed the scrapes and bruises on her arms, and her stilettoes – and more recently cumbersome boys' sneakers – with a pair of slip-on deck shoes. She'd styled her hair into a loose ponytail, and pulled on a ball cap and shades. Very tomboyish. But there was no disguising that she was a gorgeous young woman. She'd the kind of figure that looked good in any clothing. In fact, I had to admit that I preferred her casual look to the stunning-but-faux ideal forced on her by her husband. At heart I believed this was the real Trey Shaw, and I'm sure she felt the same. Her smile was one that flickered with embarrassment when first she'd emerged from the public restroom, but had slid into place when she noted my approving perusal. She'd barely stopped smiling since, even though we'd little to be happy about yet. Perhaps that was untrue: she'd escaped her husband and had regained a portion of control over her original self, and she was grateful for that. The smiles she offered me were maybe because I'd helped her reach this turning point in her life. I hoped I could keep her alive to enjoy it a while longer.

I too had changed clothing, but apart from now being dry I didn't look much different. But then I wasn't the type to stand out in a crowd to begin with, and would continue blending in. I'd dumped my soaked clothing in a trashcan in a men's bathroom, and had advised Trey to discard hers too. I'd been taking a chance when I shopped for the clothes we needed, but maybe the sales assistant was used to seeing disheveled guys replenishing their wardrobe after a heavy drinking session in this neighborhood, or she simply didn't care. I'd worried that reports of the van crashing into Indian Creek might have made the news channels already and people were on the alert for dripping survivors, but the young girl who took my damp cash was more interested in encouraging me to take out a store credit card – which would give me a twenty per cent saving on my initial purchases – than wondering why I was also buying a set of girls' clothes. I had a cover story ready should she ask, about being caught out in the storm, but it wasn't needed. She smiled and nodded and thanked me for my custom, all the while blank-eyed and robotic. I was confident that she'd already forgotten me as she pushed the store's credit card deal onto her next customers.

I'd changed before handing over Trey's outfit to her, then sat in an open seating area opposite Normandy Isle monument, nursing a coffee while I waited. There were CCTV cameras throughout the commercial area, and no way of avoiding them without skulking in dark corners, but I was unconcerned. In retrospect the cameras might be checked later, but only if there was a reason for the cops to go to the trouble. There was also mobile security, but the one uniformed guard I'd noted looked as bored and disinterested as the sales assistant had been in the shop. Fugitives were not expected to enjoy coffee in a busy public place.

Trey sat opposite me at a table, positioned so she could watch the thoroughfare behind me for any familiar faces. I could see past her down two converging roads. I'd bought take-out coffee for her, plus a muffin and a pre-packed taco wrap for each of us. At first she'd skirted around the food, but I'd advised her to eat. She needed the energy. Once she set about it she wolfed down the food, and looked for more. I passed her my muffin.

'Well, Joe,' she said around a mouthful of moist cake, 'you certainly know how to show a girl a good time. The fun doesn't stop with you, does it?'

It was good to hear her joking. I knew she was still balancing a fine line between euphoria at our escape and despondency that we weren't still in the clear. It was best that I kept her upbeat. 'Don't let it be said I'm ever a boring date,' I quipped.

'You won't get any argument from me.' She smiled again, then tore off another chunk of cake. Before popping it into her mouth, her expression grew more thoughtful. 'Actually, I've one slight misgiving. I've spent a wild night with you and I barely know a thing about you beyond your name. Huh, I'm not even sure Joe Hunter's your real name.'

'It's my real name.'

She shrugged marginally.

'Seriously,' I said. 'I'm called Joe Hunter.'

'That's exactly what you'd say if you were a spy using a pseudonym.'

'A spy?'

'The skills you've displayed throughout the night, you're more than just an average private investigator.'

I laughed. 'I can't even claim to be an average private eye; I'm pretty useless when it comes to investigations. That's the remit of the other guys in our team.'

'Well…' She paused to find the correct words. 'You've impressed me. There were times I thought I was along for the ride with Jason Bourne.'

I snorted in good humour. 'Don't be too impressed. I was winging it most of the time.'

'You did all right by me.' Through her sunshades I couldn't see her eyes, but from the tilt of her head she was studying me keenly. 'But what happens now, Joe? Where do we go from here?'

We'd paddled north in the boat, and took the right-hand spur of the creek around Allison Island, under the West 63rd Street bridge, looking for somewhere to make landfall. I was tempted to put ashore at Brittany Bay Park, but flashing emergency lights on the adjacent Indian Creek Drive put me off. Avoiding the police cordon, we slipped by on the creek and put ashore instead on another of the barrier islands that collectively formed Miami Beach called Normandy Isle. Being on the island limited our escape routes – we could go west on

79th Street to the mainland, or east to North Beach and that was it, unless we took back to the water.

'We sit tight for now. I need to contact my friend Rink. We need off this island, but if we take a cab we'll possibly be identified and arrested at the next police checkpoint.'

'How are you going to do that? Won't the police be monitoring your friend's cell phone?'

'You really have watched too many Bourne movies, haven't you,' I joked, but to be fair I was worried about the possibility. If we had been identified as the fugitives, and potential murderers of up to six victims from the fights at our hotel and at the art supplies store, then the cops might very well be keeping a tight eye on my closest associates. With Velasquez already in custody, that only left Rink at liberty, and the cops would expect us to try to make contact with him: so they might very well monitor his calls. Also, there was the possibility that Rink had been pulled in for questioning and was currently in custody too; despite having a checkable alibi, Rink's connection to the events leading up to the attack on McTeer and afterwards would be deeply scrutinised. But I had faith in Rink's ability to avoid detention. And we had our ways and means – if I told Trey the details now she'd be convinced she was on the run with an international spy or hitman. Our friend Harvey Lucas was a tech genius, and could have set up an anonymous communications channel via the dark web, but sometimes you only needed a burner phone and a discreet call monitoring service.

'I need to purchase a cell phone and prepaid SIM. So let's finish up and get moving.' Her earlier protestation at having no appetite was fully dispelled now. Trey ate the last crumbs of both muffins, and even picked some stray nuggets of chicken that had come adrift from my taco. It was understandable: she'd been running on adrenaline for hours, so her body would now be at a low ebb, and she was in need of a protein and sugar boost. She grimaced guiltily when she noticed me watching.

143

'I'm ravenous,' she admitted.

'We'll pick up something else to eat as well. We need to keep up our strength.'

There was a pizza restaurant on the nearest corner, and she eyed it dreamily. But it was still too early in the day for pizza. I collected our empty cups and wrappers and deposited them in a trashcan: the plastic lid off one cup fell loose, and I stooped and grabbed it and made sure it went in the can. I caught the disbelieving shake of Trey's head. 'What?'

'You're a man of such contradictions.'

'How come?'

She glanced all around, checking there was no danger of being overheard. 'You've left a trail of bodies behind us, smashed your way in and out of a shop, stolen a boat, a van and even some kid's sneakers, been involved in a high-speed car chase and crashed the van into a creek, but woe betide the day you'd ever be caught littering.'

'Yeah, you have to draw the line somewhere.' I smiled. 'Otherwise some people might call me a criminal.'

'Man,' she said, 'why the hell do I always end up attracting bad boys?'

I took her jest as intended, but she must have realised what she had intimated. Her head went down quickly, and colour flushed her cheeks. To save her any embarrassment I said, 'I do the same with idiots.' And then I realised what my words must have sounded like. 'Uh, not that I'm saying...'

Trey laughed heartily, and stood abruptly. She slapped me playfully on the shoulder, said, 'I think you had the best idea: let's get moving before we make complete fools of ourselves.'

'Yeah,' I said, sobering quickly. 'And while we walk, you can finish telling me what you started in my room about your bad boy husband.'

'Why bother? If we continue running away from the police, who's going to stop him going through with it tomorrow?'

I halted, forcing Trey to turn and face me. My frowning face was reflected in the lenses of her shades: it wasn't a pretty picture. 'Stop him from going through with *what*, Trey?'

She exhaled slowly. 'You've got to believe me that I have no part in any of this, but when you've been around them as long as I have they tend to ignore your presence, or they're confident that you're so under their thumb that you daren't speak a word to anyone else. Joe, I don't know exactly what it is they're planning for the celebrations, but I overheard Mikhail speaking with Sean Cahill, and he bragged that it was going to be *spectacular*.'

I thought about the date. 'I'd bet he wasn't talking about an Independence Day fireworks show.'

She peeled off her sunglasses so I could see the sincerity in her. 'Not the fireworks,' she said in a barely audible whisper, 'but I did hear something about a parade.'

This was only my second day in Miami Beach, but even I knew about the upcoming 4th of July celebrations centred around Collins Avenue and Ocean Drive – I'd have to be blind to miss the proliferation of banners and US flags flapping overhead, even while running in the dark. As well as numerous individual celebrations, parties and family events, a parade of floats and marching bands was due to take place to mark the holiday.

'Are you saying there's going to be some kind of an attack on the parade?'

'That's what I'm fearful of. Especially when Mikhail promised it would be more spectacular than what happened in Paris, Berlin or London.'

Rink parked his rental car in the shadow of one of a trio of gleaming towers in the beachfront community of Sunny Isles Beach, not too distant from where Hunter and Trey Shaw were situated. Glancing up at the looming buildings comprised of luxury condominiums, he thought that the current president might be controversial but there was no denying he could build an impressive set of towers. He wasn't visiting any of the condos; he'd pulled into the parking lot of an adjacent hotel set on the waterfront of a marina on the Intracoastal Waterway. He was within striking distance of Mikhail Viskhan's residence on a nearby islet connected to Collins Avenue. A quick stroll through Intracoastal Park would take him to a bridge onto the islet and from there he could walk directly up to Viskhan's house and knock on his door. He was sorely tempted to do so, but he wasn't yet ready to take the fight directly to the enemy. Not while the cops were still there.

He'd diverted into the hotel's parking lot when a patrol car shot by him and took the turning onto the islet ahead. He couldn't be certain that the cops were going to speak with Viskhan but, considering the previous night's events, it was a safe assumption. Whether or not Viskhan had been tied to the attack on their team yet was still up for debate, but Rink thought that it was only a matter of time before Tracey Shaw was identified as the woman seen entering the hotel a short time before, and was subsequently unaccounted for after a man had died with her shoe's heel jammed in his eye socket. If anything, the cops would want to question Viskhan concerning his missing wife long before they made a connection between Albert Greville-Jones's fatal assault and him, or even Greville-Jones to the attack at the hotel.

The cops beating him to Viskhan was inconvenient, but it was not an insurmountable problem. He simply had to wait the police out. They'd question Viskhan, take down his bogus account of his wife's disappearance and then leave. He doubted that Viskhan would become a guest of the Miami PD, the way that Velasquez had, because he had the clout, wealth and possibly the dirt on key politicians to ensure he never saw the inside of a police station. Rink could care less if Viskhan was ever convicted of his crimes, because he knew as well as Hunter that there were other ways to see that justice was done. He slipped his hand under the tail of his shirt, felt the hilt of the knife in a sheath on his belt. It was a D2 Extreme Fighting/Utility Knife from the KA-BAR workshops: justice would come at the end of its seven-inch clip point blade if all went as planned.

Planning violent murder wasn't in Jared Rington's character, not in his current guise as a civilian, but that hadn't always been the case. As an Army Ranger he'd killed enemies on the battlefield, and after his induction into Arrowsake, his skills had regularly been utilised on more pinpointed and specific targets. His kills were collectively termed 'military sanctions', but shake the terminology any way you wished and the actual definition of Rink's actions was assassination. Back then his targets had been terrorists, key enemy combatants, tyrants and dangerous international criminals, but it was easy for him to equate Mikhail Viskhan with any of those designations. Plus, there was the fact Viskhan – through Sean Cahill – was the motherfucker who'd ordered a hit on his friends, and that designation was enough for Rink's mind to rest easy with his plan.

As he waited for the cops to vacate the islet, he marked the time by the shrinking of the shadow from the nearest of the three Trump Towers condos as the sun arced higher in the heavens. After the storm, there was a distinct pastel hue to the sky, but soon all trace of humidity would be scorched from the air. Rink worked best in the dead of night, but being in stark daylight didn't faze him. He wasn't dressed in battle fatigues, or in a black jumpsuit – often his *costume de rigueur* back in his former life – but in a loose-fitting shirt and chinos, and would blend easily with the rich dudes preparing for a day on their yachts and cabin cruisers.

Forty minutes after they arrived, the cops left the island, turning right on Collins Avenue and back towards Rink's position. As they passed he glimpsed at the cops, but they didn't return his scrutiny. As expected, Mikhail Viskhan wasn't locked in the back of the patrol car. He took a deep breath, reached for the door handle. Another car following rapidly on the cops' tail halted him from climbing out of the rental. It was a large SUV, powder blue, the same hue as the sky. It also took the turn towards him, and was driven past. Two figures sat up front, with a third in the back. When Harvey first identified their enemies, he'd sent photographs of Viskhan and Cahill to Rink's phone. He got only the briefest look at the red-haired man with a neat moustache in the front passenger seat, and was certain it was Sean Cahill. In all likelihood the driver was another of Viskhan's henchmen, while their boss took his comfort in the back.

It was an assumption about the backseat passenger at best, but Rink decided on the imaginary flip of a coin, and pulled out after the SUV. Catching both his targets in one go suited him, and if it turned out Viskhan wasn't in the car then Rink could always return after dealing with Cahill. He fell in behind the SUV as it followed the highway through Haulover Park and on through the districts of Bal Harbour, Surfside and North Beach. The opportunity to catch the SUV, run it off the road with a slam of his fender against its rear side, and then bring hell to those within didn't arise. But that was OK: his intention for following had altered, he had no inkling where the SUV was heading, and he wanted to find out.

The SUV took a right at 71st Street, and crossed the water onto Normandy Isle. Separated by a delivery truck and one other car, the SUV was fifty yards ahead of Rink's rental as he passed Normandy Isle Monument, and Rink took the briefest of glances at the monolith set at the heart of a small palm tree-fringed park, before his attention fell on the SUV again. He had no way of knowing that less than a hundred yards away, on the other side of a commercial strip, Joe Hunter and Trey Shaw were in the process of purchasing a reconditioned cell phone and SIM card from a pawn shop. Minutes after that, the SUV led him over Biscayne Bay through North Bay Village to the mainland. Allowing other vehicles to fill the gap between them, Rink held back aways as the SUV went south: if the driver was counter-surveillance savvy he would have spotted the tail before now, and although that didn't appear to be the case, Rink knew that complacency could be a killer. He followed at a more discreet distance all the way down the coast until the SUV cut back into Biscayne Bay and onto Dodge Island, also known as Miami-Dade County Seaport. The island housed the terminals of a number of cruise ship operators, but was also the domain of dozens of cargo shipping companies. More than two thirds of the island was a concrete expanse buzzing with industrial activity, much of it stacked high with shipping containers, some newly arrived, others holding cargo destined for foreign lands.

There was only so far that Rink could follow. He was forced to pull into the long stay parking lot of one of the cruise lines while the SUV continued on past the US Customs inspection and processing area and into the industrial port. From his vantage, Rink watched as the SUV was waved through the security checkpoint, through which he couldn't follow. At least not in the rental car and without good reason. On foot he was at a disadvantage, and risked discovery, but he'd come this far and wouldn't be deterred by a few wire fences and bored security guards.

He'd lost sight of the car he'd followed but Rink got out, ensured his KA-BAR was sufficiently concealed under the tail of his shirt and then headed over the port boulevard. Within a minute he'd found entrance into the secure industrial area, walking boldly through a gate into a dry dock area containing yachts and cabin cruisers. Behind a large crane and boom employed to lift boats from the water, he scaled a chain-link fence by using some thoughtlessly stacked steel drums as a launching platform. Inside the secure area, he continued walking boldly: he'd discovered long ago that hiding in plain sight was often the best strategy. Look like you had a right to be there, and with a purpose in mind, and you were rarely challenged. He cut across the expanse of concrete, aware of the buzz and hum of heavy machinery around him. He was passed twice by workers in vehicles, and twice was paid no more attention than the briefest of cursory nods in greeting.

The last sighting he'd had of the SUV was when it had cut right towards a large warehouse, and then driven beyond it towards a dockside shipping container lot. He headed in the same direction. The atmosphere was dusty and hot, with no trace of last night's storm left on the baking concrete. He entered the container storage area unchallenged. There was no sign of the powder blue SUV. He gave the warehouse a brief look, but was confident his targets weren't inside; otherwise their car would be parked adjacent to it. He went left, walking with purpose along a pedestrian walkway marked out on the concrete with yellow paint. Taking care to appear as if he belonged there, he strode along, as if heading for a specific destination, but at the same time he took note of each row of shipping containers he passed. He spotted the SUV a hundred yards down one row, but there was no sign of its passengers. If he turned directly down that row he might be spotted long before he reached the car, so continued on past for two more rows before cutting across the road and into the storage area. He couldn't see another soul, but from nearby he could hear voices, too faint to discern the words.

Closing in on his enemies, his demeanour changed and he progressed stealthily. He positioned himself adjacent to where the SUV was parked two rows over. Gaps between the metal containers allowed him to snatch glimpses between the rows, and for sound to filter through. The configuration of the containers played games with sounds, and at first he couldn't pinpoint exactly where the voices originated. But he decided that it wasn't from near the SUV but further towards the dockside. He padded along the row of containers, and then set his shoulder against the final one as he again listened. The voices sounded muffled and hollow as if the men were inside one of the containers, but that wasn't it. Leaning out from his hiding place he spotted a building alongside the dock. It looked a temporary structure, some kind of prefabricated office. Parked next to it was a refrigerated van, emblazoned with a mixture of Cantonese characters and English decal, denoting it as belonging to a distributor of fresh produce. Peering beneath the van's undercarriage, Rink made out the feet of three individuals. The trio of men was the source of the muffled conversation. The whining of a crane at work nearby made hearing their words impossible, but he guessed that this was no innocent meeting. As far as he knew, Viskhan's business portfolio didn't extend to catering Miami's Chinese restaurants – unless he supplied illegal immigrant workers for their kitchens.

As he observed them, the trio moved together towards the back of the van. A slim, severe-looking Chinese man also walked out from the office, his attention on the trio, but he must have been motioned out of the way. He walked around the front of the van, lighting up a cigarette. From his angle Rink got a look at the nearest of the trio, but only briefly, before he unlocked the nearest of the van's back doors and swung it open. It concealed the others from view as they joined him at the back. The thing that immediately struck Rink was that the man in sight wasn't the third guy from the SUV: he was dressed in a security company uniform. But one thing that Rink was certain of was that he wasn't checking the van for illegal contraband, but displaying its wares. Rink would have liked to get a look inside the back, but it was impossible from his position. Moving to a better vantage wasn't an option either, not without backtracking all the way down the row of shipping containers and returning via one much further along.

Or he could walk directly out, confront the men at the van, and get down to his original reason for stalking Viskhan.

The temptation was great, but he had reservations. The Chinese guy was likely an innocent in Viskhan's schemes, and although the security guard was most definitely corrupt, he hadn't done a thing to attract Rink's personal ire. And then there was the third and most important fact: where was the last man from the SUV?

His survival instincts *pinged*.

Beneath the constant sounds of industry, the loudest of which was the mechanical wailing of the nearby crane, he'd picked out the scuff of a shoe on concrete.

He snapped around.

The third man from the SUV, his face rosy from the heat, was caught mid-step barely ten feet from him. He wasn't startled, more pissed that he'd been detected as he crept up on his prey. Clutched in his right hand he held a blade not dissimilar to the KA-BAR Rink carried. He also carried a pistol, holstered under his armpit beneath his thin jacket, but had chosen a knife for its silence. Viskhan might have bought the security man, but that wouldn't extend to all the customs officers on site and the sound of gunfire would bring the authorities running.

Whether he'd intended slitting Rink's throat from behind or if he only intended using the blade to force co-operation from him wasn't important. Their dynamic had changed the instant Rink spotted him. The man aimed his blade at Rink. 'What the fuck's your game, mate?'

The man's accent surprised Rink. It was British, but unlike the gruff northern English of Joe Hunter he'd grown familiar with, more a whiney twang. The guy was one of those 'poncy southerners' Hunter occasionally joked about.

It was pointless hiding the fact he'd been spying on the group at the van. Rink had been in a half crouch as he turned, but he rose up. Squared his shoulders. The man squinted at him, but didn't seem fazed by his size. He had a knife and a gun, and backup.

'I'm here to ruin Viskhan's day,' Rink answered.

'You think so, mate?' The man strode towards him, his blade held close to his right hip. 'We'll see about that then.'

'Yeah,' said Rink, and pulled out his KA-BAR. 'We will.'

The guy slowed his advance, but only as he dropped into a fighting crouch. Rink, five feet away, adopted a similar stance.

In Rink's trouser pocket, his cell phone chimed to announce an incoming message. It served as the bell to get their match underway.

24

Twice his day had been intruded on and Mikhail Viskhan was not pleased. First he'd had to go through with the charade with the police when they came to speak with him about Trey. He had acted shocked and dismayed, but not a little philosophical about the fact she'd been involved in a violent incident at a hotel, and was now a fugitive at large. He'd partially told the truth, claiming that they'd had a bust up the evening before and his wife had left him, but then he'd outright lied, intimating that it didn't surprise him that she'd run to the arms of another man, as it would not be the first time. He gave the cops the impression he was the put-on husband who was the recurring victim of an unfaithful spouse. His reason for not reporting her missing? She often disappeared for days on end, and didn't return until she'd satisfied her lustful nature, or she'd maxed out her credit cards. That the cops didn't believe his story wasn't cause for concern; it was enough for their report, and they had left. Once the actual truth came out, it wouldn't matter because he would already be back in Chechnya, so they could go to hell.

The visit by the cops was to be expected, so he'd allowed for the inconvenience to his busy schedule, before having Cahill and StJohn accompany him to this meeting at the port. Despite arriving later than originally planned, he couldn't care less, because those he was meeting with danced to his fiddle, not the other way around. The security man, Jeff Borden, was on his payroll, and had stalled the Chinese driver until their arrival. Viskhan was pleased with the goods he checked in the van, and was satisfied to go on Borden's word that the items concealed in boxes of frozen seafood would go undetected should Customs decide a thorough check was in order: he'd already greased enough palms that only the most cursory checks of the van would happen. Borden was confident that they could openly transport the goods on a flatbed truck and no questions would be asked. Viskhan was giving instructions for them to be moved to their final destination when the second unwelcome intrusion to his day occurred.

The first inkling that something was amiss was when he heard a savage curse ring out, and he stopped mid-sentence. The coarse words were followed by the bright clang of steel striking steel, then a duller sound of a body colliding with a shipping container. The container tolled like a funeral bell. Viskhan snapped his gaze on Borden.

'What is happening?' he demanded. 'You swore we'd have this area to ourselves!'

But it was apparent that Borden was as equally in the dark.

Ignoring the guard's perplexed expression, Viskhan looked to Cahill, who was already moving past them for a clearer view. Viskhan told Borden to lock the van doors and get it the hell out of there. Borden padlocked the doors then raced around the van in search of the driver. Viskhan went after Cahill. They'd only to take a few oblique steps to their right to see into the aisle between the nearest rows of shipping containers, and what Viskhan witnessed was concerning.

During their meeting, Dan StJohn had been tasked with perimeter guard duty. Although Borden had assured them that they would go unobserved, Cahill wasn't one for taking a man's word as the gospel truth, and nobody could ever be entirely positive an outside party wouldn't stumble across them. StJohn was supposed to dissuade anyone from eavesdropping, and ordinarily it was a task he excelled at.

But StJohn was lying prone, unmoving on the concrete, while a figure sprinted away down the aisle.

Viskhan withdrew his sidearm, as did Cahill, but neither of them took a shot. Hitting the running figure at that distance wasn't impossible, but still difficult. But it wasn't the improbability of taking down the fleeing figure that stalled them, but that the gunfire would bring unwelcome attention. The customs officers might have been paid to turn a blind eye to an illegal shipment, but not to a murder on their watch.

The stranger raced around the end of the row of containers and out of sight.

'Who was that?' Viskhan demanded, but his words were as wasted as those he'd aimed at Borden moments ago. Cahill had no way of knowing.

Cahill rushed to StJohn's side, crouched over him. He shook the downed mercenary.

Viskhan eyed StJohn dispassionately. 'Is he dead?'

'No,' said Cahill, 'he's still breathing.'

'Wake him. I want to know who that was and why StJohn let him escape.'

Cahill glanced up at him, and ordinarily he didn't display emotion when challenging Viskhan, but this time his nostrils flared, and his lips screwed. 'For God's sake, Mikhail! Does it look as if Dan didn't try his goddamn hardest?'

Viskhan noted the livid bruise forming on StJohn's forehead, and the bloody wound on his left thigh. 'His hardest wasn't good enough. Wake him, Sean, before I do.'

Cahill shook the unconscious man. StJohn moaned, stirred, suddenly jerked into full fight mode. Cahill had to force him down again, both hands grasping the front of his jacket.

'Dan. Take it easy. It's me. Sean.'

StJohn lifted a palm, showing he was in control of himself, and yet he blinked in dazed confusion as he sat up. Cahill helped him shuffle across and settle his back against the nearest shipping container. StJohn dabbed at the blood leaking from his thigh, then held his fingers in front of him. His gaze still appeared unfocused. His fingers went to the lump growing on his forehead. 'Fuck me,' he groaned.

'What happened?' Cahill asked.

StJohn exhaled wearily. 'Bit off more than I could chew, mate,' he admitted, then laughed weakly. 'I'm surprised to be alive.'

'What happened?' Viskhan's demand was more biting.

'Dunno, mate. Some huge Jap just kicked my arse.'

Viskhan and Cahill shared a frown.

'A Japanese man?' Cahill asked for clarity.

'Yeah, well, maybe a half-caste,' StJohn said. 'An Asian-American. He looked like a Nip but spoke with a Yank accent.'

'You spoke to him and you didn't stop him?' Viskhan snapped.

'I challenged him, and he told me he was here to fuck up your day.'

'My day? Really?'

StJohn only looked up at him as if Viskhan was stupid. But then his gaze swept the area around him. 'Where's my blade?' His hand slapped at his jacket, beneath his armpit. 'Shit. He took my gun, too!'

Cahill again offered Viskhan a frown, but it wasn't reciprocated this time. Viskhan peered down the aisle, almost in expectancy of the mystery man's return. When he was a no-show, he returned his attention to StJohn. By now he was struggling upright, Cahill assisting him to stand.

'What was he doing when you came across him?'

Taking his time before answering, StJohn leaned against the container while he dabbed at his leg. The wound was superficial, but enough to make his muscles stiffen. 'He was spying on you, but I don't think he could have overheard what was said. Listen to that racket.' The crane continued its mechanical whining. 'And from here he'd have no idea what you were looking at. At first I thought he might be a nosy copper, but only till he pulled his blade. Coppers don't usually come at you with a military grade pig-sticker.'

'He was good,' Cahill said. 'Least he was if he got you.'

'Yeah, he pulled some fancy Jackie Chan shit on me,' StJohn said. 'Took away my knife, cut me with my own blade, then threw me upside down against that fuckin' metal wall. He nearly bust my skull open, mate.'

'Impressive,' said Cahill.

Viskhan snorted. The way his men spoke he'd believe they respected the mystery man's skills. 'Are you about to die on us?' he asked StJohn.

157

'Not yet.'

'Good. Then let's go.' Viskhan turned his instructions on Cahill. 'Make sure that Borden has got the goods safely out of here, and then join us at the car.' As Cahill went to check that the van had already left, Viskhan added to StJohn, 'Maybe it's best that Sean drives us this time.'

'I'm all right, mate,' StJohn reassured him. 'Once I've given myself a shake...'

'It's not open to debate. Sean drives. I want to chase down that Jap son of a bitch.'

'We don't know where he's gone to,' StJohn argued as they began retracing their steps to the SUV.

'I don't care. You said he was here to fuck up my day. I assume you meant he referred to me by name? Well, I want to learn his and what he was doing here. Then I want him dead.'

'I'm happy to oblige,' said StJohn, 'but you ask me we won't find him. We'd be better off getting the fuck out of here, mate, in case he was a copper and brings back his pals.'

'As you already said, he was no cop. But you said he wanted me, and that is worrying. If he's after me because of what I've planned for tomorrow...'

'How could he have a clue about that?'

Viskhan shrugged. 'Some reason brought him here. He saw the van, and might have guessed what was inside. If he tells his suspicions to the cops, we're finished. We'll never get the goods where intended if the cops are on the lookout for that van. We need to step things up a bit.'

'Then are you open to a suggestion?'

'I'll listen,' said Viskhan, but he wouldn't necessarily take the advice.

'You could knock this Jihadi bullshite on the head, mate, and go back to doing what we do best.'

Viskhan didn't reply.

StJohn shrugged. 'Or you could shift the weapons to a less identifiable van. That way it won't matter if that Jap tells a friggin' soul what he thinks he might have seen or heard.'

The refrigerated van had gone. Cahill was giving final instructions to Borden, but he left the security man standing as he jogged over to join them.

'The van's in the clear,' he announced. 'Borden just checked with his buddy at Customs. He was going to put out an alert on the guy that took you out, Dan, but I told him not to.' Directly to Viskhan he added, 'I didn't think it's a good idea to mention him in case it brings us attention we could do without.'

'Hush,' Viskhan grunted. 'What is it with you two; suddenly thinking you can make all the decisions for me?' He snapped a hand to one side, to halt any argument. 'But I have to admit you both make valid points. Let's get out of here with as little fuss as possible; I want those weapons shifted to another less identifiable vehicle. That was your idea, StJohn, so you can oversee it. Sean, I want you to find out who that bastard was, and why he's got it in for me. Then I want him dead.' He looked pointedly at StJohn. 'Then we can concentrate on...what was it you called our multi-million dollars operation? The *Jihadi bullshite* I've invested my future in.'

'Brother.' Rink wrapped me in his huge arms and squeezed. It was a manly and perfunctory hug. 'It's good to see you.'

It was good to see him too, except the situation meant our greeting was more sombre than usual. Jim McTeer's death had hurt us both. We'd lost companions before, during our military careers and since, but under those circumstances there had been an expectancy of loss of life, and therefore the ability to compartmentalise our grief had pulled us through. But McTeer's murder had happened during what should have been an easy weekend for us. Looking mean and moody in a tuxedo at the gala dinner event was about as difficult as the job spec went, and hadn't required much effort – particularly on my part – and in hindsight it had been as dreary as I'd anticipated. Despite the number of celebrity guests there had been no real risk of trouble, and if I hadn't come across Mikhail and Trey in the bathroom the night would have gone without incident. Trouble of the worst kind should not have followed us back to our own hotel. Since the brief skirmish in the room, and the deaths of four men, I'd had little time to dwell on the loss of our friend, but the same couldn't be said for Rink. The senselessness of McTeer's murder had been allowed to simmer in his thoughts for hours, and one glance told me that he was on the brink of explosion. I hadn't seen him that riled since the murder of his father a few years ago.

One glance from him and he recognised the guilt in me. I'd earned Viskhan's enmity, and those punks had been sent to the hotel after me: McTeer should not have died.

'It's good to see you,' I said. 'I only wish it weren't under these circumstances.'

He looked away, but only to study Trey.

She took off her sunglasses. Her eyes were glossy. Perhaps she was feeling guilt too, because all that had happened had been as a result of my coming to her rescue.

'I'm sorry about your friend,' she said, her voice hoarse. 'I feel partly...*responsible*.'

Rink's mouth tightened a fraction. But he shook his head. 'Let's not play the blame game. We are all victims here, and nothing is on any of us. There's no hard feelings, all right?' He held out his hand. 'I'm Rink.'

'Tracey Shaw.' Her slim hand was engulfed in his huge callused mitt. 'But like I told Joe, everyone calls me Trey.'

'Trey it is then.' He appraised her anew, and I noted how she stood taller and squared her shoulders.

Rink would have spotted her at the gala event – she'd struck an eye-catching figure in her shimmery gold dress – but she looked very different now, so this was akin to a meeting of strangers. Although I'd shared her company for less than twelve hours I felt as if I'd known her for years. When we spoke on the phone I'd described Trey to him as a victim. But he saw the strong woman she'd proved to be.

He indicated his rental car, a Chrysler. He'd left it in a parking lot on the corner of the commercial strip near the Normandy Isle Monument. 'We should get outta here. We need to get you out of harm's way.' He was referring to us both.

Once I'd purchased a burner phone and pre-paid SIM, I'd rung an anonymous web-based voicemail service that had pinged an alert to Rink's cell phone. Using another similarly anonymous burner phone he'd called the service where I'd left him a coded message containing my new phone's number that he'd then called me back on. He'd been surprised to hear where we were, as he'd driven past us not long ago while following Viskhan and a couple of his cronies to a dubious meeting at Miami-Dade County Seaport. He'd immediately told me to sit tight and that he'd come to collect us. We'd only shared the barest of details of our actions throughout the night, but we'd both come to understand that we'd identified our enemies, and that we'd gotten involved in something much bigger than any of us first realised.

As soon as we were in the rental car, Trey in the back, Rink in the driving seat, I asked about Raul Velasquez.

'Still upholding his word, you ask me,' said Rink as he fired up the engine and pulled out of the parking lot.

He meant that Velasquez was staying firm on his promise to buy us some time to get Trey to safety, and to avenge our fallen comrade.

'He hasn't used his phone call yet,' Rink added. 'I assume he'd have warned me if the cops were on to us.'

'They must be looking for Trey and me by now,' I said, 'whether or not Velasquez has kept schtum about what happened in that room.'

'It's likely that you're both persons of interest,' he said, 'but I ain't heard your names on any of the news bulletins yet. The media's treating the shoot-out at the artists' shop and the high-speed chase as separate incidents to what happened at the hotel, but you ask me, the cops have already tied the two events together.'

'So it's only a matter of time before they identify the men I killed, and follow them back to Viskhan?'

'They probably already have, or are close to doing so.' Rink mentioned that the cops had visited Viskhan at his home, but that they left soon after, and Viskhan was still at liberty.

'I'm betting Sean Cahill organizes the manpower so that a dirty trail doesn't lead back to his boss.' I checked with Trey, and caught her soft nod of agreement. 'I guess the reason the cops went to speak with Viskhan was about Trey's involvement at the hotel.'

'Last I saw on the news was that they're dredging Indian Creek for bodies...for now, those from the crashed van are presumed dead. For a while there I kinda feared the worst myself, especially when you took your time making contact.'

'Yeah, that was my bad. But to be fair, Rink, I was kind of busy.'

'Yeah, there was that.'

By now Rink was driving us across Biscayne Bay via the JFK Causeway toward the upper east side of mainland Miami. Leaving the collection of barrier islands behind felt good, I felt less like a trapped animal now I'd an entire continent to hide Trey in. He began to narrate his own eventful night. Beginning with his aborted interrogation of Albert Greville-Jones.

'So Viskhan's cleaning shop,' I said. 'Hardly unexpected. And he had him stabbed to death as if he was the victim of a failed home invasion?'

'Yeah, by a couple of crackheads with blades. I'm betting they don't know the name of the guy who sent them, but before he died Albert told me it was down to Sean Cahill, on Viskhan's instructions.'

'You said both his attackers survived? I'm surprised.'

'They weren't in a fit state to talk when I left them.'

'I wasn't criticising,' I said. 'I really meant I'm impressed. Are either of them able to identify you?'

'One of them got a glimpse of my face before I threw him off the balcony, but what's he gonna say? He won't admit to bein' caught in the act of murdering Albert. He's going to plead the Fifth.'

'Let's hope so. It keeps you in the clear for now.'

Rink took us down Biscayne Boulevard, through the Upper East Side and towards downtown. As we spoke, Trey was silent in the back: probably absorbing everything we were saying with a mild sense of shock. Rink began relating the details of his recent activity at the port, and how he'd been forced to abort that mission too when surprised by one of Viskhan's men.

'He was skilled,' he added. 'Almost got me with his blade before I took it off him and knocked out his lights. In fact, I don't mind admitting I might've ended up dead if he'd wanted to kill instead of capture me. He was a dangerous enemy to leave behind. Was tempted to finish him off, but it would have forced a gunfight with Viskhan and Cahill and that wasn't the right time or place. I might've punked out of the fight but sometimes retreat is the better part of valour.' Rink gave due credit to the knifeman, which meant we were up against another potentially deadly foe. He described how he'd escaped from the secure area of the port to his car, and how he missed out on following the refrigerated van Viskhan had been so interested in. 'Sure would have liked to have had a look inside.'

So I told him about what I'd learned from Trey, and that something spectacular was planned for during the 4th of July celebrations.

'*Spectacular* is terrorist speak,' he said for Trey's sake.

I'd already made the connection. It was code for an attack that guaranteed massive destruction and loss of life. Usually involving a soft target – aka unarmed civilians. I hadn't related my fear to her that Viskhan was planning a terror attack akin to those in Europe, but I think she'd already made the connection herself, especially considering the cities that Viskhan had reeled off.

'This guy that you beat up,' I said, 'was probably one of Viskhan's inner circle. Maybe even one of the bastards with Cahill when they ran us into Indian Creek. Military background?'

'Yup. And he was a Brit like you. A southerner, though. Spoke more like one of those gangsters out of a Guy Ritchie movie than Ned Stark.'

'That sounds like Dan,' Trey offered. 'He's originally from London. He's a friend of Sean. He's only recently come to work here in Florida...but from what I heard they go way back and have worked together before. Mikhail doesn't like him much, and I think the feeling's mutual.'

'D'you know his full name?' Rink asked.

'Daniel Saint-something-or-other.' She mulled it over for a few seconds. 'StJames...no, it's StJohn.'

Both Rink and me added StJohn's name to the roster of bad guys. Rink aimed a finger at the glove compartment. 'Check it out. I took those off Danny Boy for you.'

There was a combat knife and a Glock 17 Gen-4 chambered for 9x19 mm NATO standard rounds. Both were British Army issue, but not exclusively: the Glock was one of the most popular and widely available pistols in the world. A quick check over the gun confirmed it held seventeen rounds, one already chambered, a practice once forbidden for British troops armed with the Browning sidearm, but permissible due to the Glock's modern safety mechanisms where a misfire was practically impossible. I preferred my trusty Sig Sauer P226 to the Glock – as much through familiarity and nostalgia than anything else – but the gun had just raised our defensive capacity from the Stone Age I'd relied on last night to the modern era.

'Seems as if Viskhan's pulling in PMC operatives,' Rink said, and told me that Harvey Lucas had dug up intelligence on Viskhan and Cahill's backgrounds. 'I'll have him check out this StJohn dude once he arrives. Strikes me as unusual that Viskhan's hired pros to do his dirty work like this, unless...'

'The pros are there to train the patsies who are going to take the fall for them,' I concluded. Again I glanced at Trey for confirmation, and she watched me with wide eyes. 'Viskhan traffics female sex workers into the US, but I'm betting that isn't the extent of his human trafficking business?'

'He also supplies immigrant workers to other industries,' she confirmed. 'From South America and Mexico primarily, but recently he's been dealing with Eastern European and Middle Eastern traffickers.'

'It's all it takes,' Rink said. 'Some homegrown sympathisers and a bunch of brainwashed or coerced slaves, and you've got yourself a dangerous sleeper cell, ready to blow themselves up at the drop of a hat.' He looked dourly in my direction. 'This is getting kinda serious, brother.'

'Too serious to sit on?' I knew my next suggestion wouldn't go down too well. 'Serious enough to call Walter?'

'We should let someone know.' He skirted away from involving Walter exactly as I suspected he would. 'But it's going to be difficult getting anyone to take us seriously if you and Trey are still in the wind.'

I understood where he was coming from. An anonymous tip-off to the local police might be ignored as the usual ravings of a lunatic reading conspiracies coded in their alphabet soup. Before the police took our warning seriously they would need proof, but at that moment in time all we had was snippets of overheard conversations related to us by Viskhan's estranged wife. In fairness, Trey had no reason to lie to us, but to anyone else she could be deemed as someone with a hefty chip on her shoulder, who might concoct a story in order to make a monster of her husband. The fact that Viskhan was behind the spate of violence occurring throughout the previous night could be a matter of conjecture. Even if we were able to convince the cops he'd been behind those attacks, they didn't bear any connection to a forthcoming terrorist attack. He might be investigated, but it would not be enough to derail his *spectacular* from going ahead if other respective players were already in position.

'We can warn the cops,' I suggested, 'but Trey can't surrender to them. On her own, I trust she could convince them that Viskhan and Cahill need arresting for their other criminal activities. But that wouldn't get the result we need quickly enough. The cops will take their time building rock-solid cases against them, and by then the fourth of July will have come and gone. It'd be too late to halt the planned attack.'

'Unless she fingers them for the murders last night,' Rink argued.

'True. But I don't trust them to protect her long enough to stand witness. Viskhan hasn't gotten away this long without having some guys on the inside. If Trey surrenders to the police I'm betting she'd be dead before the day was out.'

For a moment I'd almost forgotten that Trey was sitting in the back of the car listening to everything we said. I turned to regard her. 'Don't worry. We're not going to let that happen.'

Rink exhaled deeply. He glanced in the rearview mirror to catch Trey's attention. 'Tell me you don't hold on to even the tiniest bit of love for your husband.'

'You mean my pimp, my jailer, my abuser?' she responded, and it was all that was necessary to confirm her hatred of him.

Rink nodded slowly then transferred his attention to me. 'OK. We tell the cops nothing about Viskhan's plan yet,' he said. 'We'll rendezvous with Harvey, get Trey somewhere safe, where they can work together on finding some tangible proof we can offer to the cops. While they're doing that we'll go after Viskhan and Cahill.' It was obvious why he'd checked with Trey first before suggesting his plan. By *go after*, he meant *kill the fuckers*. 'If we don't stop them in time then we'll call Walter. You know I don't trust the old bastard, but he does have his uses. Someone with his influence could prove helpful if we need to rally the troops.'

'Having him in our corner beforehand will help too,' I said. 'It'll help our cases if we intend dodging the lethal injection.'

My friend fell silent. Our plan to halt a possible mass murder was to conduct one of our own. Under certain aggravating factors the capital crime of murder was punishable by death in Florida, and what we planned ticked a number of boxes on the list. If we could show that our actions were motivated by the necessity to stop a worse atrocity then we might just survive the legal aftermath. Waiting until after the deed before bringing in Walter Conrad would be too late to help us. Finally Rink turned down his mouth. It was a precursor I recognised. 'Do what you need to do, brother,' he announced, 'but I don't care what he asks for in return, it doesn't get in the way of us avenging Mack.'

Sean Cahill paused to pick grit from the corner of his eye. He inspected the accumulation of orange gunk on the tip of his finger before flicking it away. He hadn't slept since the night before last and was beginning to feel the effects of fatigue in his bones as the day began segueing into evening. Viskhan expected a lot from his right-hand man, but this was taking the mick. He chuckled too hard at the irony of his thought, and realised he was going a little nutty through lack of sleep. He stopped laughing, and returned his attention to the more serious act of organising his people for tomorrow. As did Dan StJohn, some of his men were feeling uneasy about following Viskhan's latest scheme, and it was on Cahill to convince them to stay with the programme. Even for hardened mercenaries like them, launching an attack on US soil was dangerous, risky and, let's face it, he thought, immoral, but reminding them of the promise of a multi-million dollar payday would reignite their incentive to get the job done.

He was standing inside a deserted Chinese restaurant two streets back from the main strip on South Beach. Dan StJohn wasn't there, but four other PMCs were. Ernest Monk sat with his bony butt perched on a dinner table, taking the weight off his sore ankle: luckily for him, when he'd been struck by the fleeing van his ankle hadn't been broken, only twisted painfully against the joint. Omar Hussein leaned his elbows on a countertop, his thick, hairy wrists crossed beneath his chin, supporting his large head as he peered at Cahill. The other two men were called Jed Frost and Craig Parkinson – the men who'd assisted in chasing Joe Hunter and Trey Shaw in the early hours of the morning. Including StJohn, the four were all that remained of the mercenaries under Cahill's command. Three of their number – Waller, Sierra and Harris – had been slain by Hunter, and their loss had added to all the survivors' workloads. By now the cops would have identified their deceased comrades, and it wouldn't be long until they were all subject of manhunts. Both Monk and Parkinson had already voiced the idea of booking out of the US before the heat came down on them, but Cahill was having none of it. Viskhan's motive for lashing out at the US might be personal to him, but they'd signed on for the operation and it mattered not that it was the plot of a madman to rain terror on his adoptive country; their agreement based on massive reward was their bond. If they reneged on their word, their careers as professional soldiers-for-hire would be in dire jeopardy from then on: they'd be lucky if they could secure tenure minding a punk-assed drug dealer in some backwater Third World country.

Neither did it matter if the job they'd accepted from Viskhan went against the grain and sensibilities of some of his team; a job was a job, and they couldn't allow their personal morals, politics or religious beliefs to get in the way of a weighty paycheck. Nor should they allow private vendettas, but Cahill was aware that his team hoped for payback against the bastard that'd killed three of their number, and it now looked as if they would get their opportunity. After the failure of the emergency services to recover any bodies, it was probable that Joe Hunter had survived crashing the van into Indian Creek. Admittedly, Cahill too wanted to end things finally for Hunter. Even if they didn't have a personal reason to want him dead, Hunter had to be dealt with. Allowing him to live might jeopardise the success of their operation.

'If Hunter survived, then it's likely that Trey did too,' he announced. 'Mikhail wasn't always careful around Trey and she knows too much about the op to allow her to live. Hunter and Trey were both marked for death and that order hasn't yet been rescinded. But we have to handle the situation without it having a negative impact on our other responsibilities.'

'Everything else is in order.' Ernest Monk's tiny eyes glittered like volcanic glass in the subdued light. 'Viskhan doesn't need us to hold the hands of his volunteers. We've got them in place, and equipped them for the op, like we promised: I don't see why we have to babysit them any longer when Viskhan's own guys can do it.'

'You know why, Monk.' Cahill didn't expound. Not all of Viskhan's volunteers were willing volunteers: they could cut and run for the hills if they weren't continuously reminded of what backing out of the deal would mean for their families. Viskhan's hired thugs were OK when it came to standing guard, but not in motivating reluctant suicide attackers, or in stalling those too eager to strike against the Satanic West: a preemptive attack would place the security services on high alert and effectively stop the main operation from going ahead.

Cahill brought out his smartphone and hit buttons. 'Check it out,' he announced. 'I've sent you all an extra target.'

'Who is this dude?' Jed Frost squinted at the image on his cell phone's screen.

'Jared Rington,' Cahill said. 'I got his name from Greville-Jones last night before everything went to shit; he's the head of the outfit hired to bolster security at the event where Mikhail first came into conflict with Hunter. He wasn't at the hotel when I first sent those gangbangers after Hunter, but apparently he's made himself busy since. He followed us to the port earlier, and beat the shit out of Dan – Dan has since confirmed the man on your phones is the same one he fought with. I'm happy Rington didn't get a hint of what we were doing there, but it doesn't matter. From what he told Dan, he's got a boner for Mikhail. He's on some revenge gig on behalf of his buddies, you ask me.'

'Says here he was an Army Ranger,' Craig Parkinson pointed out as he went over the attached intelligence file. 'Currently runs a PI outfit out of Tampa. But I see a black hole in his service record. Only one reason I can think of for him to have his military record sealed. Special Ops?'

'Could be,' said Cahill. 'Does that concern you, Parky?'

'Why should it?'

'Brothers-in-arms and all that honourable bullshit?'

'My only brothers-in-arms are right here in this room—' Parkinson nodded to each of the others in turn '—and on slabs down at the county morgue. I feel no affinity to Rington just because he's another ex-Ranger. I was only wondering what kind of skills he brings to the fight.'

'He kicked Dan's arse in about three seconds. That should tell you something.'

Parkinson shrugged, as if unconcerned. But he still exchanged a glance with Frost, whose eyebrows had arched to his hairline. Dan StJohn was a hard bastard, and neither of them was his equal in a blood and snot fistfight. Therefore Rington's skills should be respected.

Cahill offered an unfounded theory. 'I sent a couple of punks over to deal with Greville-Jones. Before they finished him off, somebody kicked their asses too. I'm guessing that Rington did a number on them, and then got Mikhail's name out of Greville-Jones before he died. Explains why Rington knew who to come after.'

'It's more likely he'd have gotten your name,' Frost said.

'Yes,' Cahill agreed. 'I don't like the idea that there's a pissed-off soldier out there who could be after my blood.'

For the first time since he arrived at the restaurant, Omar Hussein entered the conversation. He rose from the counter, freeing up his hands so that he could cock and point an imaginary pistol. 'Doesn't matter how good this soldier is, he'll die when I put a bullet in his skull.'

'Yes,' said Cahill, and offered a mocking smile. 'Good luck with that, Omar. Perhaps your aim will be better than it was last night when you missed Joe Hunter.'

Hussein's imaginary gun took on a fresh configuration as he parted his thumb and forefinger by a whisker. 'I came that close to shooting him in the face,' Hussein said, 'even when he was driving that van directly at me.'

'Chill, Omar,' Cahill told him. 'I'm not doubting your shooting skills. Just reminding you all that you can't take anything for granted. I've seen Hunter in action, and it sounds like Rington's equally as dangerous an enemy.' He thought briefly about his recent pursuit of Hunter, and how he'd held back from a direct confrontation, and how his reticence had now come back to haunt him. 'You see either of them, you take no chances. You put them down fast, hard and permanently.'

Viskhan owned the restaurant, although an employee managed it on his behalf: Viskhan's involvement strictly kept to an invisible capacity. As a business it was a front through which Viskhan moved some of the workers he brought via illegal channels into the country. It had been closed since just after the Chinese New Year celebrations, and hadn't yet reopened to the public even though South Beach was full of vacationers. The premises acted instead as a base of operations for Cahill's team. The meat lockers in the kitchen served them as multi-purpose lock-ups, sometimes containing those recalcitrant sex workers in need of reminding of their duties. Cahill would have liked to fetch both Hunter and Rington to the restaurant, string them up in those lockers and butcher them like the annoying pigs they were. But he would obey his own instruction: next time they met, there'd be no messing around, no trusting to a watery grave for anyone. He would ensure that both men were dead this time.

He ordered his men to gear up and ship out. He gave each one specific directions to follow a channel to discover the whereabouts of any of their targets, including Trey Shaw. Now she, he thought, he'd love to get alone in one of those meat lockers. Mikhail was done with her, and Cahill didn't mind sloppy seconds, though he'd no interest in her femininity. He'd kill her as instructed by his boss, but it didn't mean he couldn't have a little fun with her first. He couldn't think of a better way to spend his final night in the US than in the company of a beautiful woman, one whose beauty he'd like to strip away inch by inch of flayed skin. No, he corrected himself. Sleeping would be the best way to spend the night, except there was little hope of that.

Mikhail had tasked him with discovering the identity of Jared Rington. He could check that off his list. Mikhail had also told him he wanted Rington dead...that was still to be seen. Latterly, after Cahill shared the news that the police divers had failed to discover their bodies in Indian Creek, they had to assume that their original targets were still at large. Mikhail had been displeased. Actually, that was a supreme understatement: he'd been apoplectic, and most of his rage had been directed at Cahill. For the briefest moment he was tempted to go along with StJohn's suggestion and put a bullet in Mikhail's head and take over the moneymaking empire that his old friend had built, and was about to topple. But putting aside his misgivings about personal beliefs – moral, political or religious – he was still a man of his word, and he'd sworn to serve alongside Mikhail after being dragged from the rubble of a Taliban compound devastated by a US drone strike. Perhaps in hindsight it had proved a kneejerk reaction but, for saving his ass, Cahill had sworn his life to his rescuer. Mikhail had called him on his promise on a number of occasions since, but in return he'd made Cahill wealthy, shown him a life far removed from that which he'd known as the son of an immigrant who'd fled Ireland with a price on his head. Shooting his old friend dead would be ungrateful, an untenable idea.

His pistol had remained in its holster, he'd taken the enraged berating, even kept his cool when Mikhail furled his hands round his shirt collar and slammed him against a wall. Mikhail's hot spittle had rained on his face, yet he took his scolding calmly. Then assured Mikhail that he'd personally continue to oversee the hunt for Trey, Hunter and Rington. Mikhail's temper was soothed and he'd even made an apology of sorts for taking out his frustration on his *dearest brother*. Cahill had then convinced him that he should lie low until their enemies had been stopped, and after the weapons had been moved to an alternative vehicle and on to their final destination StJohn had been tasked as his personal security detail. Cahill didn't fear StJohn taking the initiative and shooting Mikhail dead as he'd counselled, because StJohn would never betray his trust. All members of his team – even those who'd been killed by Hunter – were highly efficient warriors, but his second in command was the best of them. He'd failed in his first confrontation with Rington, but StJohn wouldn't make the same mistake a second time: Mikhail was in safe hands.

Alone in the deserted restaurant, Cahill again rubbed at his fatigued face. He exhaled deeply. Then he shook out his tiredness, mentally tightening his bootlaces. He began placing calls on his cell, pulling on numerous contacts he could bring into the search. He thought barking like a dog was a waste of assets, so why do the boot work when dozens of street-level workers could do it for him?

My second evening in Miami found me in a bar at the eastern fringe of the Little Haiti neighbourhood. The drinking hole was on the bottom floor of a three-storey building that also housed a welfare hotel and a pizza shop. The front window commanded a view over a railway track and an unofficial parking lot where cars were drawn up on the verge alongside 4th Avenue, where the last vestiges of foliage had been crushed into the white sand and railway ballast. Rink had briefly parked his Chrysler out there to drop me off, before moving the car around the side of the building. He'd elected to wait outside, as he was too distinctive to show his face inside the bar. He couldn't be certain that Jeff Borden hadn't got a look at him after his tussle with StJohn at the port earlier.

Borden obviously enjoyed a beer or two after getting off shift. We'd followed him directly from the port to the bar without him making any diversion home. His beaten-up pickup truck was abandoned on the hardpack alongside the railway track, left parked askew in his haste to wet his whistle. After Rink disturbed his clandestine meeting with Viskhan and his goons, Borden had probably done a lot of dry swallowing. In the ten minutes since he'd entered the bar he'd downed two beers and was onto his third. He still wore his security company uniform underneath a thin canvas jacket, but had unsnapped his clip-on tie. In the sultry warmth of the bar his features glowed with a thin sheen of sweat. His uniform hadn't attracted the attention of anyone else in the bar, so I guessed his attendance after work was a regular occurrence. Then again, it was my first time there and I hadn't risen as much as an eyebrow from any of the drinkers, or the two young Hispanic guys playing pool. Even the bartender had largely ignored me since delivering my Corona. I sat quietly at the end of the bar nearest the exit door – in view of Rink – while I drank measured sips of beer. Unless Borden had a bladder the size of a beach ball he couldn't keep up drinking in such quantity much longer. Even as I watched him in my peripheral vision, he chugged down his third beer and signalled for a fourth. I wondered if this was the norm after getting off shift, as it went some way in explaining the beaten-up aspect of his truck if he regularly drove back to his house after a skinful of beer. More likely was that the current overconsumption of alcohol was about calming his nerves. Was he aware of the impending terrorist attack, and was he anticipating being brought in on conspiracy charges? He was certainly drinking like a man who suspected his next beer might not be until many years hence, or with his final meal if he was given the lethal injection.

The two young Hispanics finished up their game, laid their cues on the beer-stained baize and left for parts unknown. At the same time, Borden pushed off from his bar stool and headed for the rear of the bar. As he passed the pool table, he unconsciously reached for the nearest ball, gave it a shove, and it ricocheted off the side cushions a few times before settling. By then Borden had pushed through the door into the men's room. Trusting that Rink observed me, I got up and followed Borden. As I passed the pool table I also reached for the nearest ball. But I didn't roll it away.

Before entering the men's room, I checked out the rear exit. It was a fire door with a push bar. But I needn't open it: the door was wedged open by a mop and bucket, allowing a draught to cool the stifling air in back. Through the open exterior door I heard the squeak of rubber on hardpack. I shoved inside the men's room. Borden studiously ignored me as he took a leak at a trough on one wall. A stall stood open beyond him. I moved towards it, and Borden was aware of my presence but didn't give me as much as a glance. He leaned with the flat of one hand supporting him on the wall: emptying his bladder was proving both strenuous and satisfying, judging by his grunts of relief. I slipped my recently acquired Glock from under my shirt and pressed the barrel to the nape of his neck. Borden's stream cut off mid-flow. He gave another grunt, but this one held no relief.

'You know what that is, right?' I whispered in his ear as I dug the gun barrel into his neck.

'Wh-what's this about, buddy?' His voice was a sibilant croak.

'Zip up,' I commanded him. 'Literally. Put your old man away, and stay quiet.'

I could feel him trembling through the gun. He zipped up, then held his hands out to his sides.

'Good,' I told him. 'If you want to stay alive you continue doing exactly as I tell you. Nod if you understand the severity of the predicament you're in.'

He nodded, but not enough that he escaped the pressure of my gun.

'Good,' I repeated, intent on cementing our relationship of captor and captive. 'Now put your hands behind you, palms out, and shove them down inside your belt.'

'I...I'm not wearing a belt,' he croaked. He was speaking the truth; he'd taken off his equipment belt before leaving the port.

Nevertheless I bumped the gun barrel on his skull. 'I told you to stay quiet. Shove your hands down the back of your pants.'

He tensed at the sudden pain in his head, but he nodded again, didn't comment. He inserted his hands into the back of his trousers as instructed.

'Now open up.' With his back to me he didn't quite understand my order. He stirred and was in danger of facing me. I gave him another rap of the gun barrel. 'Your mouth, open it wide.'

He followed my instruction, and I wrapped my hand round him and inserted the pool ball between his teeth. It was a struggle for him to open his mouth wide enough for it to go in, but I shoved it and it popped behind his teeth. 'That's just so you don't try anything stupid like shouting for help while we leave,' I told him. I transferred my grip to his collar, and aimed him at the door. 'I'm going to be right behind you, Borden—' using his name was a deliberate ploy to breed further fear '—and will shoot you if you do anything stupid. Are you going to behave?'

He nodded, and garbled out an affirmative around the pool ball.

'A nod is sufficient. Once you're out the door, turn immediately to the right and through the fire exit. My friend will meet you.'

Reaching past him, I opened the door, then took a brief look down the short corridor towards the bar. Its patrons astutely ignored us. So I shoved him out and propelled him towards the fire exit.

I held back a pace so I'd block any view of him should the bar man or a customer glance our direction. Borden followed my instructions to the letter, and stepped outside. Rink met him, slapping a strip of duct tape over his mouth before Borden indicated any recognition. Then he spun Borden around so he could see the gun I aimed at his chest, and made him ease his hands out of his pants. Rink wrapped more duct tape around his wrists. Borden looked sufficiently terrified, but apparently he hadn't got a look at Rink at the port, because his expression was bewilderment.

Rink had already positioned his rental car up against the fire exit alcove, with the trunk standing open. He shoved Borden towards it. 'Get in, and make yourself comfortable. We're going for a ride.'

The corrupt security guard was resistant for a moment. His head shook from side to side. He probably pictured the car's trunk as his final resting place.

'It's your choice, Jeff,' I said. 'You can get in the trunk and live, or you can die right here.' For emphasis I jammed my gun into his spine. Truth was, killing him was the last I wanted, but he couldn't know that. I pushed, and he went forward, climbing gracelessly into the trunk: a difficult task with his hands tied behind his back. Rink grabbed him, jostled him around so he could get on his side in a fetal position. 'Where are the keys to your truck?' I asked.

Borden peered up at me, stricken by his predicament.

'Your keys,' I repeated.

He nodded in the general direction of his right hip. I dug in his pocket and took out the truck's keys. Bounced them on my palm. 'Enjoy the trip, Borden,' I announced as Rink closed the trunk on his bewildered stare.

I followed in Borden's pickup as Rink took him north, then west away from the residential areas along the Biscayne Bay coast and into an old boat yard. When I say old boats, I mean the boats were aged, and probably unseaworthy. The yard was surrounded by chain-link fencing, long ago trampled down in places. One of the boats had been set alight by an arsonist. Weeds surrounded its blackened husk. Two sheds had also been burned, but not so badly that they'd collapsed. One of them had retained some integrity, and still boasted a tin roof and singed walls. Borden was pulled from the Chrysler's trunk and led towards it. Both Rink and I had earlier scouted an appropriate location before beginning our stakeout at Miami-Dade County Seaport. We knew what to expect when going inside the shed, but Borden faltered at the threshold when we entered the dim and stinking place. Burnt trash and old rusting bits of equipment littered the floors. The evening light found its way inside through chinks in the walls and roof, slanting like daggers towards the earthen floor. Motes of dust hung in the glowing beams. The interior of the shed had taken on an eerie, unreal quality since our earlier visit. It was the ideal stage for a snuff movie.

Rink sat Borden down on an old office chair positioned towards the back of the shed. He had our captive hang his arms over the back, and used the remainder of the duct tape to wrap around his chest and arms, securing him to the chair. Then Rink took out his KA-BAR and showed its keen edge to Borden. 'I'm going to take off your gag. You're going to be allowed to speak now. But if you shout...' He wagged the blade and didn't need to expound. He untied the gag and hung it over his hand for Borden to spit the pool ball into.

My gun was out of sight in my belt. Instead I wielded a small GoPro camera supplied to me by Harvey Lucas from the bag of equipment he'd brought with him from Arkansas. Harvey was currently babysitting Trey at a safe house in Flagami, a neighbourhood a hard stone's throw south of Miami International Airport. Together they were collating an evidence bundle we could hand to the authorities, alongside the more tangible proof we intended on getting out of Jeff Borden.

'OK,' I told the security man as I switched on the camera and pointed it at him. 'It's confession time. Now, you can later argue that your testimony was forced from you while under duress, but the plain and simple fact is I don't give a fuck if you get off on a technicality. You are going to tell the police everything you know about Mikhail Viskhan's plot to launch a terror attack on US soil.'

Borden's stricken expression was enough to make even me believe he'd no knowledge of such a plot, but it mattered not. He could deny any involvement in a terror plot, it made no difference, but not in assisting the acquisition and importation of illegal weapons to be used in the attack. To save his ass – and hopefully to later cut a deal with the cops – he immediately began babbling about having no idea what Viskhan wanted with the guns, and promised to co-operate fully and willingly with the authorities to halt an attack. To listen to him, anyone would think he was a patriot instead of an avaricious scumbag who didn't actually give a crap where those illegal firearms were destined or to what terrible use they'd be put, as long as his pockets were suitably lined.

Rink drove the battered pickup back to downtown Miami while I followed in his rental car. His destination was a five-storey building on 2nd Avenue, a victim of atrophy if ever I'd seen one; erected in the mid-1970s, it was in an early state of collapse long before it had begun looking anachronistic. Nonetheless, it was still the headquarters of the Miami Police Department, where the chief of police kept his office. We could have gone to any of the satellite police stations, and in particular the one in South Beach, but we wanted our package to be taken seriously, so it was best to go direct to the top man.

Rink found a parking spot adjacent to the steps leading up to the main entrance, gave Jeff Borden a fateful squeeze of his shoulder, then got out of the truck and walked swiftly to where I waited on a perpendicular side street. As soon as he was in the Chrysler I pulled out from the kerb and took us away from the police station. Not too far before I stopped, took out my burner phone and made a 911 call. I told the stunned emergency operator that the truck parked outside contained both a would-be participant of a terrorist plot named Jeffrey Borden and evidence of his guilt could be found in the glove compartment of said truck, and also in the sworn testimony of a witness winging its way to the chief via email. I'd have loved to see the faces of officers responding to the call when they found Borden trussed, gagged and blindfolded in the passenger seat, but we couldn't hang around. Borden would probably claim that he was the innocent victim of abduction, but he wouldn't be released before the cops discovered his confession on the GoPro camera I'd left along with Borden's cell phone in a plastic bag in the glove compartment. Hopefully, once the gears of officialdom began turning, resources would be poured into South Beach to confound Viskhan's planned *spectacular*. I had to ditch my burner, which I did with little finesse, simply chucking it out of the car window. Somebody would find it, probably pocket it, and if the cops traced its signal then fair enough: I wouldn't be the one they found it with. Rink used his phone to call Harvey and put him on speaker.

'Email the package, brother,' Rink announced.

In the safe house in Flagami, Harvey was poised to send the witness statement Trey had recorded to the same police office, and had been awaiting our signal.

'On it,' Harvey announced. 'That's it, it's done.'

'Be back with you soon,' Rink assured him. 'Everything OK at your end?'

'All's good.'

'How's Trey holding up?' I asked.

'She's doing fine, Hunter,' Harvey replied. 'She's showering and then going to take a nap.'

I wouldn't have minded a nap myself, but didn't envy Trey getting some sleep. She'd been awake for almost as long as I had. Staying on my feet, and busy abducting and forcing a confession from Borden, had kept my head clear. I felt sorry for Trey: collating a witness statement with all the necessary facts would have been a mind-numbing experience, I bet.

'She say what we needed from her?' I asked.

'Even more so. She gave a full account from when she was first abducted in Eastern Europe and forced into the sex trade, how she was coerced into marriage for fear of her parents' lives, up until the point where Viskhan sent those gang members to the hotel to kill you both. Man, I'm not sure I've ever typed so many words in one sitting. I was thinking of turning my hand to writing novels in my spare time, not sure I've got the stamina for it now. I might have to take a nap myself.'

I grunted at his levity. I really needed to sleep, but such a luxury could be a long time coming. 'What did she say about the terror plot?'

'Only what she told us earlier. Much of what she said is based on overhearing bits of conversations, piecing together phrases and key words. But she was able to give a concise account of how Viskhan and his people are involved in the human trafficking trade, and that lately he's been working almost exclusively with a broker connected to some group in the Middle East.'

'Did she specifically mention Islamic State?' Rink asked. Trey hadn't mentioned any terror group in direct terms to me, but I'd assumed she was talking about the most active terrorist organisation based in the region. They had been behind other soft target attacks, the type that we believed Viskhan was helping to facilitate in Miami Beach within the next twenty-four hours.

'No. She could only confirm that Viskhan and his buddy Cahill talked about "Syrians". I ensured that relevant buzzwords were included in her testimony; I don't think you need worry that what we've given the cops will be taken seriously.'

'She still wasn't able to pinpoint the planned attack, though?' I went on.

'Only that Viskhan mentioned a *parade* and that it was going to be *spectacular*.'

Yeah, that was the extent of what she'd already told me. I'd made the connection with the planned 4th of July celebrations in South Beach. I thought of the IS-promoted attack in Germany where a truck was driven directly into shoppers at a Christmas market. A similar act during a parade would have terrible consequences, and that was before we included the presence of weapons. Jeff Borden was no weapons expert, but he'd been able to tell us that the truck at the port had contained handguns, automatic rifles and also larger armament boxes.

'Pity it wasn't Viskhan we trussed up and delivered to the cops,' Rink said, 'instead of some greedy-assed security guard who had no knowledge of the actual plot.'

'Yeah,' I said, 'but that wouldn't be as satisfying as killing the fucker ourselves.'

Rink's mouth formed a tight line. Killing Viskhan was our go-to plan. But I'd earlier contacted Walter Hayes Conrad and brought him up to speed on our situation, and it was at Walter's urging that we followed a process where we could warn the authorities of the impending attack, supply the proof that would trigger a positive response and show us – including Trey, Velasquez and McTeer – as innocent victims caught up in the situation. He warned that if we went *cowboy* on this, there was little he could do to save our collective butts. Holding out on knowledge of an attack that might otherwise be prevented made us complicit in the plot, he'd reminded us. Even burning with a desire to avenge our fallen comrade, Rink had acquiesced to good sense.

We'd done our bit to get the wheels moving now, and Walter had suggested that our best move afterwards would be to surrender to the authorities, and assist their investigation any way we could. He swore he'd do everything in his power to protect us, but unfortunately – because things had already progressed too far, and I in particular had been involved in a fatal shooting – he couldn't supply an official cover story to us the way he had when we'd assisted Arrowsake in foiling the domestic terror attack in Manhattan.

Despite Walter's advice, there was no way I was going to surrender to the cops. Neither would I place Trey under their protection until I knew that Viskhan, Cahill and their people were firmly out of the picture. It sounds egotistical to say that she was safer in our care, but it was true. I had existed in a world where assassination and murder regularly occurred in supposedly safe environments, and occasionally committed by those trusted to protect the victims.

'I'm with you, brother. Viskhan's going down *hard*,' Rink said.

'Guys,' Harvey cautioned, 'I just heard the shower shut off.'

His heads-up was so that Trey didn't overhear us plotting to kill her husband. It didn't matter. Trey would never feel safe while Viskhan lived. There didn't exist an iota of loyalty – let alone love – for her husband in her. She would be a willing partner in plotting his death. It was the very reason why we were returning to the safe house in Flagami: I needed to interrogate Trey for everything she knew about Viskhan's movements. He was connected, and doubtless he'd be alerted that he was about to be arrested, and would go into hiding before the cops got their hands on him.

I said, 'Harve, go tell Trey she can't take that nap just yet. We're only minutes out and we need to speak with her first.'

I drove us to the safe house. The title was a misnomer. It was a room in a dreary motel buried behind a strip mall off 8th Street. As a neighbourhood, Flagami was characterized by neat, brightly painted and well-kept homes, and the motel was a blot on the landscape. Ours was the last room in a row of single-storey dwellings, rented – if you wished – by the hour, and with no questions asked. The kind of place where they boasted pay-per-view adult movies and coin-operated vibrating beds. It wasn't very defensible, but we were currently off the cops', and hopefully Viskhan's, radar. I pulled the rental car into the space directly in front of our room. There were other inconspicuous vehicles arranged before other rooms. Some of them I assumed belonged to travellers who didn't want to pay the exorbitant prices of the hotels closer to the airport, some of them by people taking benefit of the hourly rate. Nearby there was a mobile home-cum-trailer park, and it had an open-air swimming pool: through the car's open window I could hear people enjoying the facilities, despite the fact it was growing dark.

Harvey had the lights on inside the room. I could tell because he took a peek out between the blinds and a laser beam of light darted over the Chrysler's hood. I flashed our lights in a pre-arranged signal, and watched him crack open the door and lean out. The lights behind him struck highlights off his bald head as he checked left and right before fully opening the door. We joined him inside.

Harvey always looked immaculate. His dark skin glistened; his features were as perfect as those of a movie star. Even with his shirtsleeves rolled to his elbows and his tie loosened, he still managed to look classy: as if the casual look was one ascribed to him by a team of professional costumers. Next to him I always felt shabby by comparison. He was statuesque, photogenic, and could have been a Hollywood star if he'd followed that dream, but instead he'd enlisted to protect his country. He met Rink as an Army Ranger, before Rink was drafted into Arrowsake. These days he split his workload between IT consultancy, private investigations and piloting helicopter trips for tourists – occasionally he teamed up with us when we required his particular skill sets. He was as much a part of the team as Velasquez and McTeer.

Trey had finished in the bathroom. She stood toweling her hair dry, watching us expectantly as we circled in the room, looking for a place to come to rest. She'd dressed again in the clothing I'd hastily purchased early that morning; she looked and smelled fresh, though. If I didn't know otherwise, I'd have pegged Harvey and Trey as a good-looking couple. Having had no opportunity to shower, I probably stank of creek water and sweat, and looked rough. I decided not to check in the mirror. The many small wounds on my face itched and I trusted they had formed tiny scabs on my skin.

There was a large bed, a small chair. Harvey had spread his equipment on a small counter that ran down one side of the room, also used to house the TV, telephone and an archaic coffee maker. More of his equipment was on the bed. It didn't leave much room for four of us to sit. There was no pecking order to our current team – even if Rink's surname was in the letterhead of the company – but I let Rink take the chair. I dropped on the end of the bed, then lay back in the narrow space clear of Harvey's stuff. I exhaled in relief, but then forced myself to sit: had I closed my eyes for a second I'd have probably fallen into a deep sleep.

Rink narrated how things had gone with Jeff Borden, and I briefly interjected to clarify or strengthen a few points, bringing the others up to speed. All the while Trey watched us, the towel forgotten in her hands. Every now and then she winced, usually when the subject of torture came up. The truth was, Borden's mistreatment had primarily been mental – notwithstanding the fact he'd been abducted at gunpoint, trussed up in the trunk, then tied to a chair in a burnt-out shed. We didn't beat him; there had been no need. The simple fact that Borden believed we would happily hurt him was enough for him to comply with our demands.

'He swore he'd no knowledge of a terrorist plot,' Rink finalised his story. 'He admitted only to arranging the transportation of the weapons from a shipping container onto a truck bound for some restaurant. Borden's a punk-assed coward, and I believe him. Viskhan wouldn't make someone as easily manipulated as Borden part of his bigger plan. Plus, I saw the truck he was talking about.'

The two of us had discussed the truck during our drive back. Borden didn't know the truck's destination. Rink recalled that the company name had been on the side of the refrigerated box, written both in Cantonese and English, but he hadn't committed any detail to memory. Borden had elected information we hadn't prompted from him: he told us that after Dan StJohn and Rink fought, Cahill had told him to get the truck out of the port, but that they would have the contents transferred to a different vehicle in short order.

'It would have been handy knowing the details of that truck,' Harvey said. 'I might have been able to track it down before those weapons are offloaded.'

'I might have slant eyes,' Rink grunted in irony, 'but I don't read Chinese.'

'Mikhail owns a Chinese restaurant,' Trey offered.

'Really?' Harvey perked up, his fingers working unconsciously as if he was already at his keyboard.

'Well, I say owns. The restaurant was off the books as far as I could tell, but Mikhail had an interest in it. He moved some of his newcomers through the restaurant before they were shipped out to other venues and lines of work.' She didn't go into the grimy details of what those lines of work entailed, but we all knew. 'The restaurant was closed down months ago. I don't know why.'

'Where is it?' I asked.

She gave an address in South Beach, not a million miles from where the planned 4th of July celebrations were due to take place.

Rink and I shared a nod of agreement. Before doing anything further, though, I asked for Trey to sit with Harvey and collate a list of other premises that Mikhail Viskhan had an interest in. It was hardly likely that he'd be found at their Sunny Isles house from where Rink had earlier followed him. Specifically I asked that she think of places that weren't easily identifiable as boltholes to which he could scurry while avoiding the police.

I stood from the creaking bed, inserting the Glock taken from Dan StJohn into my waistband. Rink was armed with his KA-BAR and the second blade he'd acquired. We weren't exactly equipped for taking on a bunch of armed mercenaries, or who knew how many would-be terrorists, but we didn't care. We'd done our bit to satisfy Walter's idea of lawful process; now we wanted to do our bit to satisfy ours.

I hadn't eaten since sharing a meagre taco and muffin breakfast with Trey on Normandy Isle. I was ravenous, despite the effects of adrenaline in my system that dampened down my digestive system as it prepared my body for fight or flight. I could have wolfed down any number of the enticing dishes displayed in glossy photographs arranged on the restaurant walls, but that wasn't about to happen. Trey had been correct when stating the restaurant had been closed for a number of months: there wasn't even the slightest hint of aromas from the kitchens to suggest any of those mouthwatering dishes had been served in ages. Yet it was also apparent that the restaurant had been used more recently, except for other reasons.

Instead of garlic, five spice or soya sauce, I detected a smell I was infinitely familiar with: gun oil. The scent was prevalent in the atmosphere; a number of firearms had been unpacked, oiled and assembled within the dining room. There was nothing as incriminating as crates or packaging left lying around, so I had to assume that the weapons had been repacked and moved elsewhere. Having first been brought from the port to the restaurant, the weapons had been transferred to another vehicle – as Jeff Borden had claimed they would be – and taken to another storage location. Or had they? There were rooms in the restaurant we hadn't searched yet. Rink was stealing through the kitchens conducting his own search.

I turned towards the front of the dining room. Large windows faced the road outside, but sheets of brown paper covered them so that pedestrians couldn't get a glimpse inside as they passed. Streetlights cast their dim figures on the almost opaque paper so that they took on insubstantial shadow forms. All kept moving; nobody was out there attempting to find a chink in the coverings that they could spy through. The front doors were similarly obscured, but this time with drop cloths. We hadn't entered by the front door but by a window around back that Rink had prised open with his knife. I doubted that we'd tripped a silent burglar alarm, but was alert to anyone turning up with a set of keys. Actually, I welcomed the prospect of someone turning up, because our brief recce of the premises hadn't turned up any clues as to where we'd find Viskhan or his stash of guns, and they could help.

I moved deeper into the building, skirting around a service counter that adjoined the kitchen area. Rink had already moved on. I could hear his faint progress as he moved through an adjacent corridor. I went in the other direction, found a flight of stairs behind a closed door. They led down to a basement. It wasn't a large space. We were barely above sea level, so basements weren't a regular feature in that part of town. I found a dim room that was little more than a crawl space, almost filled to capacity with drooping power cables, copper pipes and machinery. I returned to the first floor. Another flight of stairs led up: there were rooms above the restaurant used – I guessed – as accommodation for the manager and his family when they were still in residence. For all I knew the guns could be up there, but before I got a chance to investigate I heard Rink call my name. I went to join him.

'The hell is this?' he asked as soon as I entered a room to the rear of the kitchens.

It was a storage area. A number of refrigerators and chest freezers took up spaces along one wall; opposite them were large metal racks. Some of the shelves still held stained cardboard boxes and random pieces of kitchen equipment. But Rink wasn't referring to them. He indicated a huge cooler that dominated the back end. It was almost like a room within the room, a large pale cuboid dominated at the front by two vacuum-sealed brushed steel doors. Neither was Rink's question rhetorical. He stood before one door that he'd tugged open, and meant what was inside. I moved alongside him before I could tell what had disturbed him.

On first perusal I could be forgiven for thinking the metal bars were parts of a secure cage system designed to hold fresh meat and produce; even the padlocks weren't too sinister in that context. But the bars weren't placed to keep thieves out, but to hold captives within each telephone box-sized cell. There were six individual cells, three to either side with a narrow space between down which a jailer could walk. In each cell there were two buckets, and God help the prisoner who mixed up their drinking water with their waste in the dark.

We looked at each other.

Trey had warned us that Viskhan moved trafficked slaves through the restaurant, but neither of us had suspected they'd be caged like feral beasts before they were moved on. I'd been thinking along the lines of them being forced into labour, washing pots and peeling potatoes, not this.

Rink opened the next door.

That compartment of the walk-in cooler was a single cell. There was a stained futon on the floor, some rumpled sheets. The ubiquitous buckets. But there was another addition that instantly soured my gut and put aside all thoughts of food. A large steel ring was bolted to the ceiling, and from it hung straps, on the end of which were buckled wrist restraints. On the slip-proof floor lay more restraints, and judging from their position it would force a standing captive to straddle while their arms were held aloft.

Rink juggled his KA-BAR to a firmer grip. I pictured his thoughts. If they were similar to mine they involved gelding the bastards who'd used this room while raping their captives.

We again exchanged a lingering look.

'Even if he didn't have Mack murdered I'd still cut off Viskhan's balls for this,' Rink said.

'I'm with you,' I whispered.

Ghoulish fascination made me lean inside for a better view. Dried blood spatters dotted the floor and the rear wall. There was another smear of blood on the wall above the futon, and it was the handprint of a small woman or child. Repulsed, I'd seen enough.

We backed away from the cooler. The stink wafting from inside was unlike any normal refrigerator I'd ever smelled before. Had there been people confined in the cooler while unsuspecting diners gorged on noodles in the dining room only a few yards away? Once those doors were sealed tight the cells beyond would be almost soundproofed. But I guessed not. The makeshift cells must have been used outside of trading hours.

Backtracking through the kitchen, we whispered about having Harvey drop an anonymous email to the cops about what we'd found in the storage room: the more evidence against Viskhan we could send their way the better for us when it came to explaining our actions. Cops frowned upon vigilantism, but who could blame us for taking up the sword against a monster like Viskhan?

I wanted to make a closer inspection of the dining area as that appeared to be where there'd been the most recent activity, and also the rooms upstairs, but again the opportunity didn't arise. From somewhere to our right a door squeaked open and we both ducked for concealment behind the kitchen counters. I craned for a view through the service area adjoining the two rooms.

Two figures entered the dining area through a side entrance on the far side of the building.

Worst-case scenario: the cops had arrived to investigate a break-in. That wasn't it. The best case: Viskhan and Cahill had returned to the scene of their crime. But that wasn't it either.

One of the men, a solid figure with wide shoulders and a head shaped like an upside-down bucket, moved with familiarity through the dim space, avoiding tables as he went directly to a store closet at the edge of the dining room. Behind him a slimmer, shorter figure limped in pursuit. I shot Rink a look, held out two fingers to my side. He nodded in understanding. Returning my attention to the new arrivals, I watched as the thickset guy returned from the closet lugging a weighty kitbag. He placed down his burden, and then began digging in the bag. His skinny pal moved beyond him, out of my line of sight. I scanned their back trail, anticipating more men to enter with them. But after I'd made a slow count to thirty in my head, it was likely they were the only ones to worry about.

The skinny man joined his pal.

They stood in a pocket of darkness, but they were backlit by the amber glow through the window coverings. I recognised their shapes. It was the two gunmen who had arrived too late to stop me shooting their pals outside the art supplies store. The skinny man I'd shortly hit with the getaway van I'd stolen – which explained his limping gait – while the stocky one was the Middle Eastern gunman who'd tried to shoot me in the head through the van's windscreen.

I could feel the heat radiating off Rink. Or maybe it was my imagination. Still, he was tense and ready for action. But I stalled him with another silent gesture of my hand. The bigger man had pulled from his bag a machine pistol with a folding stock. He tossed it to his pal, and then delved again in his bag. He withdrew a second machine pistol. Judging by their shape, both guns were identical and recognisable as Ingram MAC-10s fitted with two-stage SIONICS suppressors. The inclusion of the suppressors helped with noise abatement, and also control of the guns when fired on full automatic. Civilian ownership of the guns had been illegal in the US for more than two decades. But it was doubtful that PMCs in Viskhan's employment cared about gun laws.

The two men began inserting box magazines, and dependent on the calibre they were long enough to hold thirty .45 ACP or thirty-two 9x19 mm rounds. Whatever, between them they easily quadrupled the firepower available to us in my Glock. They had the upper hand if it came to a shootout, but we had the element of surprise on our side.

The two conversed, random bullshit that usually passed between friends comfortable in each other's presence, although there was urgency as if they were short of time. As they bounced comments and curses back and forth they checked the actions on the machine pistols, and the manner in which they did so told me they were experienced handlers. All the while, we waited, allowing the mercenaries to relax as they worked at routines they could perform with their eyes closed. As each weapon was given their approval they were set aside on a table, then the bigger man delved in the bag again. While his head was down and the skinny guy turned away to watch the shadow-play on the front window, I gave Rink a nod. Without comment he slipped away, using the counter as cover as he moved for the far end of the kitchen and a swing door that allowed the easy movement of servers from kitchen to dining room. He rose up, out of sight of the mercs, and checked I was ready. We shared a brief nod, and with it we moved.

Rink kicked the swing door open and pounced into the dining space. He held his KA-BAR in a reverse grip, the point angling down towards his right hip. He emitted a guttural challenge. The immediate effect was that the big mercenary jerked in surprise, both his hands deep inside the kit bag. The skinny man spun around, stunned by the sound and bluster and, caught in indecision, he looked at the nearest MAC-10, but his hands flew out from his sides, showing empty palms. It took a second or so for their brains to process the situation, see that Rink was armed only with a knife, and come to a collective decision. As the first guy began pulling free of the bag – choosing to go for a prepped weapon on the table next to him rather than assemble a gun from the bag – the skinny guy began a loping run for the machine pistols.

I darted up, the Glock extended in a two hands grip, and I shot Skinny in his right thigh. With no good leg under him, he collapsed down on his front and almost slid beneath the table holding the guns. I swung my aim on the big guy. He halted, fingertips an inch or so from snagging a gun.

'Go on,' I challenged him. 'Reach for it, you son of a bitch. See if you can dodge my bullet.'

His fingers withdrew.

He lifted his open hands to shoulder level.

'Good decision,' I said. 'Now move away from the table.'

He did as commanded. Rink rushed him, grabbed the collar of his jacket and kicked the backs of his knees, forcing the man down.

'Hands on your fucking head,' Rink snapped at him.

The big guy glared back over his shoulder, and Rink sneered at him. Laid his KA-BAR alongside the man's swarthy jawline. 'How's about I cut off your damn head instead and have done with it?'

His hands went on the back of his head, thick strands of blue-black hair jutting between his fingers. Rink rapidly patted him down and found a pistol holstered under his left armpit. He used the merc's gun to cover him with.

In the meantime, I'd come out from behind the service counter, gun again aimed at the skinny guy. He grimaced, his hands slapped over the wound in his leg. I bobbed the barrel of my gun, silent instruction for him to move from under the table. 'I...I can't move,' he snarled. 'You shot me, you bastard.'

'Move,' I warned, 'or I'll shoot you again.'

He played up the agony, making a meal of dragging his lame legs from under the table. He grasped for stability with a bloody hand, and only a blind man would miss that he was groping for a weapon. I curled my lip at Rink, and my friend got the message. He lunged, stabbed down with his left hand, and his KA-BAR went right through the questing hand and into the table. While Skinny howled, his body thrashing for freedom, I collected the MAC-10s and deposited them on the counter behind me. Next I grabbed the kitbag and swung it out of reach, allowed it to drop on the floor.

The big guy cursed us. He spoke in his own tongue, but you didn't need to speak Arabic to get the sense of his words.

'Shut it, scumball,' Rink hissed, with a tap of the gun barrel against the man's cheek. He checked Skinny, who had fought to his knees and had his free hand hovering too near the hilt of the knife impaling his hand. He only wanted free, but he was a soldier, and might go for broke if he did manage to tug it out. Rink leaned over, grabbed the KA-BAR and yanked it loose. The skinny merc fell backwards, his injured hand cupped inside the other against his chest. He moaned in dismay.

'Quit your damn grumbling,' Rink told him.

I grasped the injured man, hauled him around the table and deposited him alongside the kneeling merc.

'Get up like a man, Monk,' his friend encouraged him. I made note of the name.

'Yeah, *Monk*,' I said. 'You should kneel like you're praying to God.'

'M...my leg...'

'Suck it up.'

I grabbed him and jostled him onto his knees. Blood pulsed anew from the wound in his thigh. It was dark red, so not oxygen-rich blood from an artery. He wouldn't bleed to death quickly enough for me. I stepped back and observed our prisoners, while Rink was an unseen, dangerous presence behind them.

'You know who we are, right?' Both men had chased me, but they also had to understand the implications of making an enemy of Rink. He'd already displayed his willingness to hurt them, but it was better they understood the full urgency of their predicament. The big Middle Easterner nodded, his eyes seething. 'Then you should know that we aren't the type to pussy around. You will answer our questions, or you will die. What's it going to be?'

'I'm not afraid to die,' the big guy announced, this time in accented English.

Rink beat me to the punch. He set the KA-BAR against the man's jaw again. 'How's about I cut off his ears, Hunter?'

The big guy snorted. 'Then how would I hear your questions?'

'We only need one of you to answer us, pal,' I told him.

On cue, Rink sliced upward with his knife.

Despite his tough guy attitude the merc exhaled sharply, and was desperate to slap a hand to the side of his head – to check if his ear was no longer attached.

'Chill, dude,' Rink grunted in mirth, 'I've cut myself worse shaving.'

In truth the cut was deep enough, a raw strip that extended behind his left earlobe and into his thick hair. Warm blood dripped onto his collar. If the guy was seething before he was now volcanic. But – unlike some of his brethren – he wasn't suicidal. He forced himself to remain kneeling, hands locked on his head.

'What's your name?' I asked.

He didn't reply.

'Monk,' I directed at his cringing pal, 'what do you call your buddy?'

'Fuck you,' he replied, but with little force.

'That's an odd name. Oh, wait! You were being defiant, right?' I aimed the gun directly at his skeletal face. 'Like I said, we only need one of you, pal. Is your life worth keeping his name a secret when really it doesn't matter to me? I can just call him asshole and it'll do.'

'My name is Omar Hussein,' the big guy finally snapped. 'Why does it even matter that you know our names?'

'So we get them right in your damn obituaries,' Rink growled in his ear.

I thumbed over my shoulder. 'Either of you like to explain what the hell we found back there?'

Neither elected to answer.

'See, if either of you were involved in what I suspect what went on in those cells, I'll happily cut off your ears and feed them back to you.'

'Man, we ain't into that shit,' Monk said. 'We're like you guys, we're just old soldiers earning a living.'

'You're nothing like us,' Rink said. 'You're murderers.'

'And you are more virtuous?' Omar laughed. He turned his accusatory gaze directly on me. 'You shot three of my friends in cold blood.'

'Yeah,' I agreed. 'With the guns I took from them that they intended using on me and an innocent woman.'

'You shot Sierra in the back. To me that was the action of a coward and a murderer.'

'I also recall you trying to shoot me in the back while I was at it,' I countered, and offered him a snarky smile. We were arguing semantics. It wasn't helping anything, so I switched tack. 'Where is Mikhail Viskhan?'

'We don't know.' Omar was too quick to lie.

'I don't believe you. Where is he?'

Monk shook his head. 'He's in hiding. Seriously, man. We don't know where he is.'

'Bullshit,' said Rink.

Monk shook his head again, emphatically. 'It's part of the arrangement, man. We take our instructions from Cahill, not directly from that Chechen prick.'

'So where's Cahill so we can ask him?'

'Searching for you,' Hussein said.

'To kill us?' I asked, and didn't need an answer. 'Shame he didn't save us all the trouble and come back here with you. He send you here to prep those MAC-10s for tomorrow or was that an executive decision?'

The two mercs glanced at each other.

'You were arming yourselves, right, and for something much sooner?' I shared a quick glance with Rink, and his eyelids narrowed in understanding. It was beginning to feel like a scene from a spaghetti western. I firmed up my stance, my gun unwavering as I aimed it at Hussein's face. 'You got a location on us?'

He only raised his eyebrows, and a smile flickered across his mouth.

'Son of a bitch!' Rink quickly stepped away, shoving away his appropriated gun. He wasn't expecting an imminent attack on us. That wasn't what we'd realised at all. He snatched out his cell phone, hit buttons. 'Harvey? Don't ask me a thing, brother. Just get Trey the hell outta there *right now*!'

Before he'd even finished warning our friend, Hussein saw that things could only end badly for him and Monk, so decided to go out fighting. He was a big man, but surprisingly agile, and not in the least encumbered by his kneeling position. He seemed to pop up, landing flat on his feet and immediately springboarding to grapple my gun away. Monk was a second slower to move, but even he scurried forward, again going for the MAC-10s.

I shot Hussein, catching him in the gut. But a single 9 mm bullet will rarely stop a big man who's already committed to an attack at close quarters. I saw the impact reflected in the hot sheen of his eyes as he crashed into me. Then he had one huge hand around my windpipe and another on my wrist. He thrust me backwards and I smashed into the counter. He loomed over me, face inches from mine, and his wide mouth opened in a wolfish howl as he attempted to crush my throat to mulch. His saliva sprayed my features. My eyelids screwed momentarily in response, but I forced them open again. All the better to see him with. He had control of my wrist, but not my gun: I twisted it towards him. It's the beauty of a Glock. You squeeze the trigger and bullets come out. I slotted him three new holes in his left side, most or all of which found his lung. He was already slumping aside when Rink hammered him from behind, his KA-BAR plunging into the soft flesh behind Hussein's right collarbone.

Monk had his hands on a machine pistol.

Before he could use it to kill us he had to aim it, and he wasn't too successful with his damaged hand and gimpy legs.

Even as Hussein crashed down, I side-kicked Monk's knee, and as the MAC-10 flashed it did so into the ceiling. Even suppressed by the SIONICS silencer, the noise was like the angry flapping of giant bat wings. I returned fire: a close grouping of three bullets to Monk's chest. He sat down hard on his backside, and the MAC-10 slid from a hand now lifeless. He slumped at the waist, head deep between his splayed knees, almost as if he was attempting to kiss his butt goodbye.

Rink and I again looked at each other.

'Well that turned into a damn clusterfuck,' Rink said.

He'd get no argument from me. Besides, there was no time. Monk and Hussein had been sent back to their temporary armoury to bolster their team's firepower during an impending assault. Harvey and Trey were in danger, and we couldn't help them while we were on the opposite side of Biscayne Bay.

A safe house is only such until its location is discovered. By the very nature of its clientele, using the motel as a hiding place was always risky. There was no telling who had dropped the tip to Cahill and his goons – it could have been a member of staff, another customer, or one of the prostitutes plying their trade in the area. It was always a problem for Trey that many of her husband's sex workers knew her by sight, and that even those who'd managed to get away from him to work on patches governed by other pimps still knew who she was. Harvey suspected that Viskhan or Cahill had enrolled streetwalkers and local hoods into their army of seekers. Whoever had given them up didn't matter, only that their safe house was anything but, and it was time to leave.

Trey had no belongings to gather, and Harvey wasn't far behind her. Everything he'd brought to Miami with him he stuffed into a large carryall – electronics equipment and all – and he slung it on his back as if he was heading out on a mountain trek. They had no vehicle – Rink's rental car was their only mode of transportation – so they had to move on foot, and fast. The telephone call from Rink had been short, left no room for clarifying the threat, but its urgency told Harvey everything he needed to know. Their safe house was compromised and they had to flee. Thankfully they made it out of the room before their hunters arrived.

Harvey led them not back towards the main road, from where their hunters would surely arrive, but through the motel's parking lot to a low chain-link fence that separated it from the adjoining property.

'I thought I was done with climbing fences and walls,' said Trey, referencing something that she'd been forced into the previous night. She offered a meek smile to show she was only trying to lighten the situation.

Harvey stepped one leg over the fence. His long frame made easy work of it. Then he forced down the uppermost wire with both hands, lowering its height and making an easier climb for Trey. She balanced herself on his shoulders and almost leapfrogged over. Harvey followed, cursing under his breath when he snagged the material of his trousers on the tip of a twisted wire. He pursed his lips in mild anger when he felt the frayed edges of a hole in his trousers. 'Every time I get involved with Hunter I end up needing a new outfit,' he told Trey.

She took a quick glance down at her own makeshift costume. 'Tell me about it. Just don't tell me I'm going to wind up at the bottom of another creek.'

'I can't promise that,' Harvey said as he urged her away from the fence, 'but if we're chased I'll do everything I can to keep you safe.'

His announcement proved both prophetic and problematic.

Two vehicles pulled into the motel's parking lot, one of them staying near the entrance gate to cut off any escape in that direction. The other sped directly for the room at the end of the block. Men disgorged from both vehicles: two from each. In response, Harvey and Trey crouched low. It was dark now, but there was ambient light from the trailer and RV park behind them. If any of the men looked their way they'd be spotted, but for now all attention was on the motel room.

'That's Sean Cahill,' Trey whispered, indicating a sturdy-built man with reddish hair and moustache who was directing his men. Even as Harvey checked him out, he saw Cahill slip a sidearm from under his jacket and hold it tight against his middle. Cahill turned briefly to signal one of the two men approaching along the path outside the row of rooms. 'That's Dan StJohn,' Trey added. 'I don't know the names of the others.'

The team moved with familiarity, experienced in the tactics of room clearance. Cahill covered the door while his companion moved to the right, covering the side of the building so nobody could escape through the bathroom window. StJohn and his pal approached, and they too now had their sidearms prepped, but held close to their bodies. The blinds were still shut in the room, though Harvey had left the lights burning inside. Before leaving, he'd also switched on the TV, loud enough so it would be heard through the closed door. StJohn and his pal skirted the path, keeping away from the window until they were in place. Then StJohn set his back against the wall adjacent to the door. He looked at Cahill, received a nod. He tried the handle. The door had locked shut behind Harvey and Trey as they vacated the room. Instantly the third man in the team kicked directly beneath the handle and the flimsy door was smashed into the room. Cahill followed it, going in fast and low. StJohn was a beat behind him. The third man covered the door while the fourth man never took his aim off the bathroom window. Within seconds all four were back on the sidewalk, peering around, conversing urgently. Harvey cautioned Trey not to move: even a flinch could be enough movement to draw their gazes.

A slim figure appeared from towards the opposite end of the motel, having been concealed in an alcove housing an ice dispenser. It was a girl barely out of her teens, dressed in a skimpy top and skimpier shorts: obviously the person responsible for giving up their safe house, and she hadn't stopped spying on them while waiting for Cahill's team to arrive. She gesticulated wildly, wafting her stick thin arms in Harvey and Trey's direction. All four men turned and stared directly at them.

'Run!' Harvey said, and grabbed Trey's elbow to usher her ahead of him.

They were at the perimeter of the RV and trailer site, an unusual inner-city feature to Harvey. The land was generally flat, as was most of the terrain around those parts, but had been landscaped to add character and a sense of privacy to the site. There were trees and shrubs and low hedges. There were also dozens of RVs, the occasional trailer and even some tents erected throughout the site. Plenty of places of concealment, but also many innocent lives could be put at risk if they hid among them. Even as they ran they passed a family group sitting out for their evening meal under an awning. The kids gaped as they charged by, then jumped up for a better look, even following for a few steps before being hailed back by their concerned parents. Harvey hoped that Cahill's team wasn't trigger-happy.

A quick glance showed him that two of the men were in pursuit, already clambering over the wire boundary fence. Distantly the thrum of engines indicated that the cars were being used to cut them off. Harvey stabbed a finger at the gap between two parked trailers. 'That way!'

Trey took the instruction without comment, merely swerving down the aisle between the trailers. She hurdled a low hedge used to conceal a standing pipe. Harvey swerved around it, encumbered by the heavy bag on his shoulders. His leather-soled shoes weren't designed for running, and slipped with each step on a lawn recently watered by sprinklers. Mud and blades of grass adhered to his trousers as high as his knees. He was a well-groomed man but not vain. He could give a damn about his appearance when the alternative was much worse. He'd rather be a living mess than a tidy corpse. Behind him he could make out the slap of feet in pursuit. They dodged to the right around the trailer, across a gravel path and between an RV and trailer on the opposite side. With no idea of the layout of the park, there was no telling if they were heading for an exit or not. As long as it was away from their pursuers it didn't matter, but they didn't want to run into one of the cars speeding to cut them off.

They ran all the same. Dodging again around more parked vehicles, and pushing through a stand of shrubs tall enough to conceal them from view. Harvey caught Trey, told her to wait. They crouched, using the foliage for cover, and peered back the way they'd just run from. Their pursuers had split up, one of them following the same route that they had between the trailers and RVs, the second man moving parallel but about fifty yards further to the right, trying to reach a position where they could converge from different angles on their prey. Luckily the second man had miscalculated their direction and had gone the wrong way. He jogged directly across the latest path and between a large Winnebago and a stand of pine and palmetto trees.

Harvey checked behind them. He spotted a path that led towards some buildings forming the central hub of the site. Leading the hunters in that direction held mixed results. There would be more potential witnesses, who might deter their pursuers, but also more in the way of collateral damage should the gunmen employ their weapons. They had to be pragmatic: Harvey indicated the path, told Trey to run again. She set off and he fell in behind her, and was rewarded by a brief shout when the nearest gunman spotted them. The retort of the silenced handgun was lost on them as their feet scattered gravel, but Harvey heard the bullet smack a nearby tree trunk, saw a chunk of bark pinwheel away from the impact point. By its trajectory the bullet must have missed him by mere inches. Unfortunately the second shot didn't miss. The bullet drilled his carryall, but thankfully it didn't make its way through his stuffed-in belongings. Harvey barely stumbled, then picked up pace. The gunman could give a damn about witnesses to a shooting, then! He exhorted Trey to speed up, though he could tell her wind was already sapping.

They cut left, heading again for another bunch of trees, these sturdy enough to offer concealment and also protection from their pursuers' bullets. The man who'd shot at them had lowered his gun to concentrate on chasing them down.

'Keep going,' Harvey urged Trey, and pointed out a blaze of lights beyond the trees. From the same direction could be heard a buzz of muted conversation and the occasional splash. He ducked low, and ran at an angle away from Trey, making as much noise as possible as he thrust aside branches. Immediately he halted, then reversed direction, this time gently easing aside the bushes as he moved through the copse.

Mere yards beyond him he heard the drum off feet, then their nearest pursuer came to an abrupt halt. Harvey could hear rasping breaths as the gunman took stock of the situation, trying to determine which way they had gone. If the gunman went to his left around the trees, then Harvey's only chance at taking him by surprise would be wasted. But he doubted the man would take that option when his pal was already heading that way. Harvey cast around, spotted a stone on the ground and reached for it. He threw the stone the same direction as he'd run a moment ago, heard its clattering trajectory even as the gunman sucked in a breath and plunged into the foliage in pursuit. Harvey waited a few seconds to allow the man to be fully submerged in the bushes, while he slipped his bag off his shoulders and then charged. There was no finesse to his attack, only daring. He hurtled through the bushes with his carryall held before him, and this time he felt the solid impacts of the bullets striking the pack. One bullet snapped by his left hip, taking a tuft of material and a sliver of skin with it. Then Harvey crashed into the gunman, the carryall jammed between them, trapping the gun against its wielder's body. His dive took the guy down and, before there was chance for him to fight back, Harvey pounded the man's head with both fists. Uncommonly for Harvey, he swore savagely as he continued to beat the man relentlessly.

The gunman was no slouch in a fight. He weathered the initial blows to his skull, but then he swarmed back, hoping to free himself from the encumbrance of the stuffed carryall, trying to bring his gun to bear even as more punches rained down. He yanked his left hand from under the pack and jabbed fingers at Harvey's eyes, forcing him back. Swore a racist slur for Harvey's sake. Then his right knee battered up, striking Harvey between the legs. Luckily, most of the impact was on his butt, but still. Harvey woofed in pain, but didn't relent. He threw his weight on the man, again crushing the bag tightly between them, and he too drove fingers at the man's eyes.

The fight was taking too long! Harvey knew he'd seconds before the second gunman arrived and, on the ground, scuffling with the first man, he'd be an open target. So he went for broke. He got his thumbs in the sides of the man's mouth, bore down with all his body weight and slammed his forehead down. A flash of pain went through his own skull, but it would be nothing compared to what his target experienced. Harvey reared back, then arched forward again, and this time their foreheads didn't clash; his found the bridge of the man's nose and crushed it. Still the gunman clung to consciousness and his weapon, but Harvey wasn't done either. A third time he butted the man's face, and he heard a deep-throated groan escape him, felt the spray of bloody saliva on his face. Harvey pushed up onto his knees, wrenched aside the bag and caught hold of the gun. He yanked the pistol out of the spasming hand, and stood. Aimed it at his foe's beaten head, and was seriously tempted to pull the trigger. At the last second he pivoted slightly and, instead of ending the man's life, took away his ability to chase them any further. He shot him once in each foot.

He checked that the second gunman wasn't near, but couldn't tell by sound alone because the man he'd shot was making too much racket as he thrashed in semi-delirium among the shrubs. If he were in a gun's sights he'd probably be dead by now, he decided. Harvey snatched up his holed carryall, slung it over his shoulder and rushed after Trey. Before he broke from the cover of the trees, he heard a commotion ahead.

Without any concern for his own wellbeing he crashed from among the brush, trying to make sense of the clamour of movement and noise he'd burst into the midst of. Despite the late hour, the swimming pool was still in use. Other people had gathered at the poolside to share beers and stories. Those people were scattering, seeking cover, hollering in fright and confusion. Deckchairs had been upended, and an impromptu barbecue had been knocked down, spilling glowing coals on a paved patio next to the pool. People in shorts and T-shirts ran along the far side of the pool to get away from the gunman standing directly opposite. Amid the chaos it took Harvey a moment to differentiate Trey from the others running for their lives. But she became evident when she halted, turned towards the gunman and held out both palms in attempt to dissuade him from firing. The gunman snapped a response that was harsh and loud, but it was swallowed by the cacophony going on around them. Harvey saw him settle his aim, prepared to shoot and take Trey down in one bullet to her central mass.

'No!' Harvey charged forward, shooting as he ran.

The gunman flinched in response, just as his suppressed pistol discharged. But Harvey caught sight of Trey folding and tumbling into the pool even as he continued forward, emptying his pistol's magazine. Shooting while running was no easy task, and most of his bullets were wasted on the branches of trees beyond the shooter, but two hit. One low in the man's side, the other in the muscles of his upper right arm. The gunman twisted from his original target, gun swinging on Harvey, and he fired at almost pointblank range. Harvey experienced the impact as a dull thud to his upper chest, but his momentum wasn't slowed. For the second time within minutes, Harvey relied on his football skills to tackle his enemy and they too pitched over the edge and into the pool.

There were lights beneath the waterline, and the glow from them turned scarlet as their blood spread and mingled.

'So who do you think the friggin' buck nigger was?' Dan StJohn asked in his usual intolerant manner as he drove Sean Cahill across MacArthur Causeway towards Miami Beach.

Cahill didn't flinch at his friend's inherent racism, because he was used to hearing much worse. Anyone who wasn't a heterosexual WASP was to be derided, in StJohn's opinion. He didn't bother replying at all, because he hadn't a clue. It didn't take much figuring out, though. Joe Hunter had more friends in town than they had first assumed, and all were proving dangerous foes. Trey had obviously been left in the black man's care while Hunter and Rington left on another errand, and since he hadn't heard from either Monk or Hussein in the past hour he'd grown to fear the worst for them. And now Craig Parkinson and Jed Frost were down and out of the coming battle. Parkinson would recover from his smashed-up face long before he could hobble further than a few yards on his severely injured feet. Frost had almost drowned, and had taken two rounds. The bullet in his side was minor – a flesh wound that would soon heal – but the one to his upper arm was troubling for a man who made his living handling a gun. He'd been fortunate that he still retained the strength in one arm to drag himself from the pool and backtrack to where Parkinson lay like a crippled dog in some bushes.

Finding his team in disarray, and in need of immediate extraction before the police arrived, Cahill had been forced to give up on the pursuit of Trey and her new minder. From what he had patched together from Frost, he'd shot both of them but they'd got out of the pool before he'd dragged his sorry ass to dry land. They had fled, along with the civilians in the area, so Frost had no idea where they'd gone. Cahill had hauled his injured men into his SUV, and made it out of the trailer park with the sound of approaching sirens howling nearby. StJohn had prowled around the edge of the campsite, but with no luck in finding their prey, before making off and barely escaping the secure cordon the police were throwing up around Flagami. Conversing over their phones they'd arranged a rendezvous in downtown Miami, where Cahill had already called in a 'no questions asked' medic to perform emergency field medicine on his crippled men. Parkinson and Frost were stitched up, but only the latter was still standing: in his current state Parkinson was good for nothing. Frost was in a mixed state of mind, both ashamed that he'd been gotten the better of, lost their target, and carried injuries certain to slow him down, but also determined to finish what he'd started with the black guy.

But Cahill was tempted to call off the hunt.

During a brief status update on the phone he'd suggested as much to Mikhail Viskhan, and been rebuked.

He'd also tried to convince Mikhail that the impending operation in South Beach should be aborted. His argument was simple: his team had been severely compromised, and with Trey still at liberty it was only a matter of time before she told the cops what she knew of their plans. Mikhail's counter was also simple: 'So find and shut the bitch up!'

Cahill acquiesced.

He'd alerted his street-level watchers to be on the lookout for Mikhail's estranged wife, and now added the description of the black man to the list of targets along with Hunter and Rington. He wasn't hopeful that his prey would make the same mistake a second time: luck had placed the young hooker in the correct place at the right time when Trey had first been brought to the motel in Flagami. The odds were that a similar serendipitous whore wouldn't be around where they'd fled to this time.

It was unlikely that they'd go to their operating base in the SoBe restaurant, but Cahill wanted to check the place out. He didn't believe for one second that Monk and Hussein had decided they'd be better off a continent away and skipped out after he asked them to fetch some heavier armament from their stash. They had run into trouble of the worst kind, proof of which was their continued silence. He regretted sending them for the machine pistols now, when it had become patently obvious that the heavier firepower wasn't necessary at the motel, whereas a couple of extra bodies involved in the chase would have helped catch Trey and her bodyguard. As StJohn parked the SUV in the loading area behind the restaurant Cahill had a fatalist's sense of what they'd find inside, but he wanted to take a look. Whatever, there was clean-up to be done.

After alighting the vehicle, they withdrew their sidearms. They kept to the side of the building, out from under the scrutiny of any potential witnesses on the main street, and approached the same entrance Monk and Hussein would have entered via earlier. They communicated with nods and gestures, and then StJohn led the sweep. He entered, darting inside with Cahill following suit, and they cleared the corridor then the room beyond within seconds. Hunter and Rington might still be there, Cahill thought, though it was doubtful. They entered the dining room with the same professional calm, immediately saw their comrades lying dead, but continued their sweep and clearance of the building before going to them. StJohn checked the crawl space in the basement; Cahill went upstairs and moved from room to deserted room before he was satisfied there were no nasty surprises waiting for them.

StJohn moved on to check the area behind the kitchens, paying close attention to the open doors of the walk-in chiller compartment and its bare cells and torture chamber. Those doors had been shut tight last he knew. He rendezvoused with Cahill back in the dining room.

Cahill hunkered over the body of Ernest Monk, checking his vital signs. It was a wasted gesture because Monk was dead – cut and shot through in various places – but Cahill felt he owed the man that small consideration. He glimpsed up at StJohn. 'Earlier I was for giving up, but even if we weren't being paid for our trouble I'd happily hunt those bastards to the end of the earth now.'

'Omar has bought it too, huh?' StJohn asked pointlessly.

'And then some,' said Cahill.

Hussein was face down, arms and legs akimbo, and on first perusal his only visible injury was a single puncture wound to his upper shoulder. Cahill recognised its mortality, though: a blade had been forced down behind Hussein's clavicle and pierced the upper chambers of his heart. If that had been Hussein's only wound he still would have perished, but then they began discovering other bloody holes in his side, and a pool of dark blood had leaked from a gut wound. Both their comrades had been put through the meat grinder before they died, and judging by their differing wound patterns it hadn't been instantaneous. The piercing of Monk's hand almost smacked of torture. What had Hunter and Rington learned of their plans from their dead brethren? One thing Cahill was certain of: neither of his friends would have easily given them up, but enough had been forced from them to wreck their surprise element when it came to storming the motel.

'The guns are gone,' StJohn announced.

'Yes.'

'The fuckers know about the holding cells in the back.'

'Hard to miss.'

'So what now, Sean?'

'I think it's time we got out of here, Dan.'

StJohn peered down at their fallen comrades. 'What about these guys?'

'They deserve better, but there's not a lot we can do for them now. May as well leave them here.'

'You want to burn the place with them inside?'

'Don't see as we have any other choice. Those bastards know about this place now, and it's inevitable the cops will learn of it: we need to cover our tracks, Dan. Go get the gasoline while I finish up here.'

'You going to say a few words over them?'

'Wouldn't know where to start,' Cahill admitted. 'I don't even know if either of them were religious men.'

'All soldiers get religion when the bullets start flying,' StJohn quipped – at least he didn't use the old cliché about there being no atheists in foxholes. 'Me, I prefer to give Old Nick the wink. Don't know about you, Sean, but I know where I'll go when my chips get cashed in, and I bet it'll be hotter even than this place will be in a few minutes.'

Cahill would have preferred to remove the corpses of his men. When he said they deserved better he meant it. But what was the alternative? They would be buried in an anonymous grave out in the boonies, so perhaps a funeral pyre right there was the best send-off for them. While StJohn fetched the can of gasoline from the SUV, he stripped Hussein and Monk of any immediate identifiers, digging through pockets, removing their wallets, their cell phones, and then got down to the nastier stuff. He stomped Monk's mouth until it was a wet hole full of ragged stumps. He had to roll Hussein onto his back to repeat the process. The fire would burn their fingerprints, and their features, and the only speedy way to identify their corpses would be through matching their dental records – he'd taken that option away now. Their DNA would finally identify the men, but that would take time, and by then Cahill and the others would be long gone. He made another quick check of the surroundings, and found nothing that would point directly at his team.

StJohn returned, lugging the gasoline.

'Make sure the guys are well doused,' Cahill instructed.

StJohn breathed heavily through his nostrils, a harsh rasp, but it was his only sign of sympathy towards his fallen colleagues. He was as pissed as Cahill, but he was also a pragmatist. He poured fuel directly over the men's upper torsos and faces before widening his circle, splashing gasoline on the floor and furniture. Then, without instruction, he trailed a line through the kitchen to the open doors of the chiller and splashed gasoline in there too. He returned to Cahill.

'Want to do the honours?' Cahill offered.

'Seeing as you got the messy part, I don't mind.' StJohn set down the gas can and pulled out a disposable cigarette lighter. He snatched up an old menu card, lit it and held it up so that a flame brightened and danced along one edge. 'Best step back, Sean.'

Cahill backed for the entrance corridor.

StJohn dropped the burning paper on the sodden carpet alongside Monk's corpse. There was a hush, a sense of time standing still, and then the fumes of the spilled gasoline ignited and flames suddenly wreathed both dead men before it popped and became a conflagration. Another ribbon of flame swept beyond the service counter, into the kitchen, and seconds later there was another significant ignition within the cells. StJohn didn't stand around. He grabbed the gas can and retreated, joining Cahill outside in the loading yard. They shared a nod: it was a job well done for a change. Pity that the rest of their encounters with Hunter and his gang hadn't gone so well until now.

They left the area. It would be minutes before the fire raged enough that it would alert passersby and it would be minutes after that before fire crews would reach the scene, a good while later before the seared corpses were discovered in the wreckage. They had plenty of time to get away, but Cahill didn't trust their luck: it had been against him ever since he'd sent those punks after Joe Hunter and Trey at the hotel. To prove his point he spotted a MPD patrol vehicle streaking towards the restaurant before they were even two blocks north. The car went without sirens, but urgently enough to have its light rack blazing. It peeled into the kerb to the rear of the restaurant and one cop got out, talking animatedly into his radio. The cops had been dispatched to investigate the scene long before any calls went in concerning a fire.

'You think those bastards tipped the cops off about what they found inside?' StJohn wondered, echoing Cahill's thoughts.

'It sure looks that way.' The only alternative was that somebody had spotted StJohn and him entering the building and construed their actions as suspicious, but it was unlikely as they'd been in and out of the restaurant on dozens of previous occasions. 'Things are rapidly going to shit, Dan.'

StJohn's eyebrows rose towards his hairline. Again he repeated that harsh exhalation through his nostrils. This time it wasn't an expression of sympathy. 'I already gave you my thoughts on the matter.'

'You did. And I gave you mine. Going to shit or not, we're still committed to our side of the bargain.'

'We're down to three now, Sean, and I doubt Frost will be able to hold an assault rifle let alone fire one. I hope Mikhail will do the right thing and recompense the team for our losses.'

'You mean recompense you, Dan, for going above and beyond the original agreement?'

'I think he needs to up the payment, yeah. Our fucking workload has trebled in the past forty-eight hours.'

'Put it this way,' Cahill reminded him. 'The fee I set was for the team, the team has shrunk dramatically, and there was no agreement from me to send their pay to their next of kin…ergo your share of the pot has grown exponentially because of it.'

StJohn rocked his head. 'Well, when you put it that way…'

Cahill grunted in mirth. 'I knew I could win you around, buddy.'

'Like you said, even if we weren't being paid millions there's a matter of getting even with those bastards that killed our pals.' StJohn shrugged without taking his hands from the steering wheel. 'But being paid even more is like putting a cherry on the icing on the cake.'

'You and your crazy metaphors,' said Cahill. 'But yeah, I tend to agree.'

Another police cruiser swept past them, lights flashing. 'Looks as if they might've discovered the bonfire we set,' said StJohn.

'When you said things were going to get hotter than hell, you weren't kidding. Don't know what you think, Dan, but cruising around waiting for somebody to spot Trey isn't the best thing we can do. Let's go join the boss man and make sure he's aware of the clusterfuck his bruised ego has caused.'

First Jim McTeer, and now Harvey Lucas had been shot because I'd offered protection to Tracey Shaw, while Raul Velasquez was possibly being put through the mill wherever he was being held: his interrogation wouldn't involve bright lights and rubber hoses, but it'd still be unpleasant. As a group we'd already paid sorely for getting involved on Trey's behalf, but I didn't hear any complaints. Harvey had done enough muttering and under-his-breath cursing since we'd picked them up but his admonishment was as much about his ruined clothing as for the pain in his body. He'd been shot twice. One wound to his side was little more than a graze, while the second was more troubling. Thankfully the wound to his chest was a through-and-through of his left pectoral muscle, the bullet glancing off his ribs and exiting below his armpit. If it had penetrated the ribs, no doubt about it Harvey's lung would have been torn apart and he'd be as dead as our friend McTeer.

In pain, saturated, and running for their lives, it was Trey who had grabbed a cell phone from another fleeing woman and pressed it into Harvey's hands so he could call Rink for an immediate extraction. We'd already been making speed back towards Flagami from the Chinese restaurant when he'd given us directions to a church wedged between an elementary school and Cooper Park, eight or so blocks south of the motel they'd escaped from. Police had swarmed all over the area, responding to the reports of gunfire, but we made it through the cordon and collected them without raising any alarm. With no other destination in mind, we headed south of Miami; at least it was away from the hot zone. Both Harvey and Trey were soaked through, and Trey had made fun of the irony that twice since she'd met me she'd almost drowned, but at least this time she stank of chlorine instead of brine. In the back seat of Rink's rental car, she helped staunch the blood from Harvey's wounds, using a spare shirt pulled from his equally sopping carryall bag, while between them they related the details of their recent near miss with Cahill's team. We heard how in Trey's case she'd tumbled headlong into the water after a bullet came so close to killing her that it lifted a lock of hair off the side of her head. Unhurt, and determined to help her saviour, she'd dragged Harvey from the pool, and got him moving again, and mingling with the fleeing campers, from one of whom she'd stolen the phone.

In turn we told them what we'd discovered at the restaurant, the awful containment and torture cells. Shamed by her association with her husband, Trey had wept. When I tried consoling her, she reminded me that she'd endured similar physical and mental torture after being forcefully coerced into the sex trade in Eastern Europe. In the years that she'd been held prisoner, first as a plaything for brutal men in Bulgaria, then as the unwilling wife of a more brutal man, she'd been aware that hundreds of other women and girls suffered a similar fate. It pained her that she had not turned on Viskhan before now and saved all those others their terrible maltreatment at his hands, though she swore she'd no knowledge of what was happening in the restaurant – she'd eaten there, for God's sake! The thought made her feel sick, and we had to pull over while she purged her guts onto the kerb. When we continued, Trey was as bleary eyed as Harvey, and it didn't help her state of mind when we related our violent encounter with Monk and Hussein. We didn't go into the goriest of details, but she got the message, especially when she figured out our warning to get out of the motel came only after we'd forced the info from our prisoners. If she wondered what kind of monsters she'd traded Viskhan for, she didn't mention it, but I caught the occasional glimpse of her where she frowned and bared her teeth.

In first order we needed to find refuge, next Harvey's wounds required attention, and he and Trey must get dry and dressed in new clothing. Everything else could follow. Rink directed us to a mall where he visited a couple of different stores, using cash to buy dressings, antiseptic creams and painkillers, and also gathering what clothes he could: he was better at shopping than me, and even thought to grab underwear and socks. I snagged a pair of boxers from the pack he bought for Harvey; I was still wearing the same ones I'd taken a dunk in when the van crashed into Indian Creek last night and by now they felt like cardboard. For Trey he went for practicality over style; the costume he bought her wasn't too dissimilar to the one I'd chosen early that morning. Then we went to another hotel in Coral Gables – this one more upmarket than the last motel, and less likely to be the hangout of observant prostitutes.

Safely in our room, we cleaned and dressed Harvey's wounds, while Trey showered and then got into her new outfit of jeans and shirt. I then took to the shower and when I emerged, feeling fresher and more comfortable, I found my friends holding an impromptu war council. Someone turned on the TV, selecting a local news channel: I thought it was to check out what was going on in Flagami, but the reports were more concerned with the heightened state of alert happening in South Beach. The cameras showed police cars, uniformed officers, and even police helicopters buzzing overhead. It seemed that our warning had been taken seriously after we delivered Jeff Borden and his videoed confession to the Chief of Police's office.

That Mikhail Viskhan was the subject of an intense manhunt was both good and bad for our purposes. How could he now go ahead with his planned attack while every stone was being turned to find which one he'd crawl out from under? But if he was keeping out of sight that'd make it more difficult for us to find and stop him once and for all, which happened to be the consensus we'd all come to. We held an ace card in that respect, though, because Trey was more familiar with Viskhan's boltholes than the police would be. Though it was soaked through, Harvey had brought with him the list they had collated concerning Viskhan's potential hiding places while they were at the motel. While I'd showered, the three of them had been going through and striking off the most obvious places.

They'd shortened the list dramatically, and those that I could see remaining I thought would be difficult for us to check on with the police activity so high.

'Isn't it safe for us to go to the police now,' asked Trey hopefully, 'now that they know who the real bad guys are?'

'Sadly they won't differentiate – we'll all be the bad guys until we can clear things up good and proper,' I said. 'They've taken our tip-off seriously, but they still won't understand the full implication of the attack from what we've been able to tell them. Your testimony will mean a lot more than any half-truths they've gotten from Borden since we dropped him off, but there's nothing more you can add to what you already recorded in your statement, right?'

'There are these locations we're going through. Where they might find Mikhail before it's too late.'

Rink interjected. 'I'd rather we take a look at his hiding places before the cops start sniffing around.'

'Isn't it more important we stop the attack than you get revenge on Mikhail?'

'Of course it is,' said Rink, 'but even better is if we can do both.'

I nodded in agreement. Turned my attention back on Trey. 'Stopping the terror attack is on the authorities now, they've the resources and the manpower.' I gestured at the TV screen, and again saw helicopters swooping over South Beach, aiming searchlights down on the streets. There was no hope of catching Mikhail Viskhan in their lurid glare; the lights and show of force were more about a visual deterrent designed to dissuade anyone foolish enough to tempt the wrath of Miami PD. 'Stopping Viskhan is on us. We can't afford for him to escape, not when we've thwarted his plans. For as long as he lives, he'll hunt you...and us. You said the cops know who the bad guys are now, but sadly that isn't true. We're criminals to them and will be treated as such, unless there's something we can give them as a bargaining chip.'

Rink scowled: he'd heard Walter Hayes Conrad in my voice. 'He's not getting handed over alive.'

My words were only partly for Rink, more so for Trey. I gauged the reaction to the death sentence I was placing on Viskhan's head, and saw only relief as she returned my perusal. It was unnecessary adding, 'It has to be done if you're ever going to enjoy a normal life again.'

She inhaled deeply, sat on the hotel bed alongside where Harvey had gotten himself propped against the headboard. She looked Rink and me each in the face before nodding to herself. 'Then let's go get the son of a bitch,' she proclaimed.

I held up a steadying palm.

'*We* go get him.' My finger waggled between Rink and I. 'You and Harvey are staying put.'

Harvey's face clouded at my announcement, but he didn't argue. He knew his limitations. Bearing a chest wound, he would only slow us down, whereas he could still offer protection to Trey right there in the hotel room if the worst happened. He was armed this time, and though injured could still shoot one of the MAC-10 machine pistols we'd taken from Monk and Hussein. Trey momentarily looked as if she would argue, but she wasn't stupid. The coming battle with her husband and his henchmen was no place for her. She wanted to be more proactive, though, and I understood. So I gave her an out. 'We need you to look after Harvey for us. He's injured and needs to rest. Somebody will have to stay alert so a repeat of what happened at the last motel doesn't happen again. After you pulled him out of that swimming pool I'm sure he trusts you to save his ass a second time.'

Harvey took my jest in good humour, and even Trey found no offense at what could have been misconstrued as patronising. 'Maybe it's best I don't join you. Being almost drowned twice already, the third time might be the charm. I think I will stay here where it's nice and dry.' She indicated the current view of South Beach displayed on the TV screen. The cameras had centred on a female news presenter who stood before a backdrop of yachts and cabin cruisers as she reported on the latest news. 'I've just thought of another place where Mikhail might be hiding.'

The view across Biscayne Bay shimmered gently, a tidal surge pushing rolling waves northward. The lights of the cities on both sides of the bay were reflected in the deep turquoise water, dancing and jiggling as the sea contorted with metronomic regularity. On the nearby bridges that spanned the bay traffic came and went, some of them emergency vehicles denoted by their flashing red and blue lights. Helicopters were a regular feature in the skies overhead, but there were more than normal – police and news choppers – dancing and swooping, rotors chattering incessantly, some of them beaming down searchlights: it almost looked like aliens had arrived to subjugate the earthlings to their command. Out on the water the coast guard and police patrolled the bay, and probably the easternmost shores of the barrier islands too.

Mikhail Viskhan fumed.

He was under no illusion what the heightened cause of activity was about, or whom the authorities were seeking. He firmly suspected that by now the FBI and other federal agencies were involved in the hunt and had mobilised teams in the area. His operation was severely compromised – though he was not yet ready to call it off – and all because of his whore of a wife. He had trusted to Cahill the task of silencing Trey, and had entertained full trust that his right-hand man would get the job done. Instead, Cahill had proved an abject disappointment: in his magnificent failure he'd even managed to lose most of the professional soldiers required to ensure that his operation went without a glitch.

And the son of a bitch had the cheek to point the finger of blame at *him*! Cahill took some smug pleasure in reminding Viskhan that he had argued against punishing Joe Hunter, as it was a complication they could all do without and a problem firmly of Viskhan's making.

Viskhan kept his back to Cahill and StJohn. He refused to look at them. Instead he stared out over the bay, the dancing lights swimming in and out of focus. His eyes watered, but it was through fury. He could feel a deep tremor at his core, as agitated as boiling water about to spill from him in an eruption of scalding violence. He gripped the railing, both hands digging into the wood until his manicured fingernails dug tiny crescents in the veneer. Containing his rage was one of the hardest fights he'd ever taken on. Overhead a helicopter clattered inland, the sound echoing between tall tower blocks. Viskhan averted his face, should anyone onboard have access to a camera with a telescopic lens. He took the motion as a cue to turn and regard his men.

Cahill and StJohn stared at him without comment. They'd said their bit; now that they'd aired their complaints they awaited a response.

He exhaled heavily.

'When was the last time either of you slept?' he asked.

As amiable as it was, his question came out of left field. The two PMCs shared a glance.

'I have pushed you too hard,' Viskhan went on, 'expected too much of you. My selfishness has caused you undue work and stress.' He held up a palm to Cahill. 'You warned me about following a personal vendetta, Sean, and your argument was valid. In chasing Hunter you have lost men, *good men* we could have used tomorrow. Now I have put at risk the successful completion of our operation...'

Again the mercenaries looked at each other. This was unlike the Mikhail Viskhan they both knew. Being humble and reasonable were not aspects of his nature. It was only a prelude to his next words.

'Have I slept? Have I pushed you any harder than I have pushed myself? I *pay* you to *work* for me. Is it unreasonable or selfish of me to demand a good return on my investment?' Viskhan's eyes had stopped watering; hot and dry, they now looked as hard as marbles. 'You, Sean, you argued that punishing Hunter was merely about soothing my bruised ego! How do you feel about that when you've lost your men to him?

How does your fucking ego feel? Do you want your hands around his fucking throat as badly as I do? No! Don't answer yet. *I am not finished*.'

He stalked towards them. Dan StJohn shifted marginally, but Cahill held his ground. He merely stood, hands hanging loosely at his sides, taking the berating. Viskhan halted directly in front of him and stared him in the face. 'My personal vendetta,' he stated, 'was about avoiding *this*!' He swept up a hand to indicate the nearest helicopter, in truth meaning the entire raised alert state that Miami was under. 'Trey ran to Hunter, seeking his protection. What do you think she might have said to him to gain his sympathy: that she was an abused wife? She would have made me out to be a monster, and what better way than to paint me as a demented terrorist?'

StJohn's eyebrows rose and fell at the irony, but Viskhan didn't look at him; all his attention was on his closest ally.

'You say I've risked our main operation,' Viskhan snarled, 'when it is your ineptitude in killing one man and a wayward whore that has risked *everything*!'

'Hey,' StJohn said. 'Steady on there, Mikhail.'

Viskhan spun on him, a finger jabbing perilously close to StJohn's face. 'You do not speak unless spoken to.'

The mercenary rolled his neck, staring not at the warning finger but at its wielder's face. His right hand was mere inches from the butt of his pistol: he could draw it and follow through with his suggestion of shooting Viskhan dead in less than a second. Out of the corner of his eye, StJohn caught the warning shake of Cahill's head. He sniffed, as if he couldn't give a shit. But he held his peace, and allowed his hand to relax. Instead it was Cahill that spoke.

'I was tasked with killing Hunter and Trey, and I accept that I've failed, but not through lack of trying. When you first set me the task, neither of us knew what kind of man we were up against, or that he had a team of his own to back him up. If we had I'm sure we both would have followed a different path.

We clearly underestimated our enemy, proof of which is in the loss of some good men, and yes, this.' Now it was Cahill's turn to gesture at the circling choppers. But then he shrugged. 'This police activity is inconvenient. But I'm confident they won't find you here. And when I've thought about it, it doesn't preclude your operation from going ahead: it isn't too late to re-jig the parameters of the attack. We could feint at South Beach, and while the country is watching, hit them harder at our original target.'

StJohn frowned hard at Cahill's announcement. Viskhan wondered if the PMCs had discussed a different course prior to arriving. But Viskhan didn't care for the Brit's dissatisfaction. And, he had to admit, Cahill made a good point.

The authorities were wrongly concentrating their attention on South Beach, and would respond with all their might against an imagined attack on their turf. While they were thus engaged they would be unprepared for the actual attack fifty-five or so nautical miles to the north.

'Trey might have grown aware of our plan to launch an attack, but she could never have grasped the specifics,' Cahill went on. 'Actually, when I think about it, her blabbing to the cops might have actually worked to our favour. Even the fact that Jeff Borden was taken in by the cops helps, as he is a coward and will by now have admitted to his part in smuggling weapons into Miami. Add to that the fact we've conducted a number of running gun battles here already, and the local cops will be anticipating much worse at any minute. What might've appeared as a complete fuck-up on my part might just prove to be beneficial.'

A begrudging nod was forced from Viskhan. He stepped back from Cahill, and a smile dawned on his features. 'You know, you always did have the ability to put a spin on things. It reminds me of why I value your support, Sean.'

'It's why you always pay me so well for my support.' Cahill glanced at StJohn, offering a surreptitious wink. 'Speaking of which, I still expect full payment for my team, considering they lost their lives in your service.'

Viskhan waved aside his concern. 'What, you are going to send money to their widows and children? You are growing soft in your old age, Sean.'

'Not soft,' StJohn put in, 'just fucking sensible. We want everything that was promised to us. In fact, how's about sending across an advance to my account right now?'

'Did I not ask that you kept silent until spoken to? Ha! Forget it, I can be a reasonable man, no?' Viskhan shrugged expansively. He dug in his back pocket for his wallet and held it up before him. He snapped it open and counted off a short stack of hundred dollar bills. All the while StJohn eyed him sourly. Viskhan held out the bundle of notes.

'One thousand dollars,' he announced.

'A grand? What the hell am I supposed to do with that? Don't insult me, Mikhail.'

'Oh,' said Viskhan, and alongside him Cahill gave a little wince. 'You misunderstand. This is not an advance on your fee.'

Without warning Viskhan turned side-on, his right leg chambering at the knee, and he whipped a foot into the side of StJohn's head. The mercenary staggered at the blow, and had to throw out a hand to steady himself. His mouth hung open in disbelief as he blinked at his boss. 'Wh...what the fuck was that for?'

'A return on my thousand bucks,' said Viskhan. 'For the private sparring session.' In disdain he threw the cluster of notes on the floor at StJohn's feet. 'Would you like to earn some more pocket cash?'

Viskhan looked unaffected; StJohn's gaze was murderous. His hand began a slow creep towards his holstered pistol. Before things got further out of hand, Cahill interjected between them. He grasped StJohn's wrist, stopping him from drawing his pistol, while concealing the action with his body. 'Let it go,' he said *sotto voce*.

'I have to stand here and let the prick kick me like I'm a fuckin' mongrel?' StJohn snarled.

Cahill didn't release any pressure from his friend's wrist. 'Let it go,' he said again, and this time it sounded more like a warning than good advice.

Behind Cahill, Viskhan chuckled. 'Stop whimpering like a girl, Dan: you just made more money than most pro boxers do going the full twelve rounds.'

StJohn shook loose from Cahill, but his pistol remained in its holster. He touched the side of his head. His skin was hot, tender beneath his fingertips. What with his recent bruising encounter with Jared Rington, and now this, his head felt twice its normal size. He glared at Viskhan, who again showed no concern for his discomfort. Glancing down, he saw the scattered bank notes. He kicked at them in revulsion and strode away. Viskhan watched him go. He turned and appraised Cahill, wearing a smug grin. 'Dan is very touchy these days,' he said in a singsong tone. 'Have I done something to upset him?'

'Man, Mikhail, you didn't have to kick him in the head. For Christ's sake, I'm having enough trouble holding everything together without you pissing off my best man.'

'I couldn't help myself. But what do you expect? I've struggled to stop from killing him since you told me he suggested that you murder me and take over.'

Cahill darted a glance after the retreating mercenary. StJohn was well out of earshot. 'He has no idea I told you, Mikhail. I'd rather he stays ignorant to the fact and continues thinking he has my confidence. That way he will keep on fighting for me. Don't worry, I would never let him harm you.'

Without warning, Viskhan leaned in and placed a kiss on Cahill's cheek. Mildly startled by the gesture, Cahill took a step back, his fingers going to the spot caressed by Viskhan's lips. Viskhan laughed at his friend. 'Worry not, Sean. That was not a kiss from Judas. I trust I will never receive a Judas kiss from you?'

Lowering his fingers, Cahill didn't know what to do with his hands. He made do with digging them in his trouser pockets. 'I swore to you, Mikhail, that I'd never betray you.'

'Hmm, you did. And I trust your word, and apologise for doubting you earlier. It's such a shame my wife doesn't share your loyalty.' Viskhan again peered heavenward. The nearest police helicopter was about a mile away; more concerning was the relative closeness of a coast guard patrol. It sped by a hundred yards away, churning the water to froth in its wake. Viskhan stepped further away from the rail, but didn't duck for cover. The super-yacht he was aboard was familiar to those waters, the property of Fedor Stepanov, a Russian magnate who invested much of his wealth in the Miami-Dade shipping industry, and who was known to throw lavish parties on his boat when entertaining guests. Nobody would expect a Chechen rebel to find refuge with his supposed greatest enemies.

I managed to grab a few hours of much needed sleep. The previous night we'd made our plan, prepped what weapons we had and also eaten a room service meal, Harvey and me hiding in the bathroom while Rink and Trey played at being a couple for the waiter's sake; if the four of us had been present when the food was delivered it might have raised an eyebrow and some awkward questions from the hotel management. Sated on food and coffee, I took the bed fully clothed while my friends continued plotting and was unconscious in seconds. As dawn broke on the 4th of July Rink woke me – time had passed almost instantaneously to me – and I sat up, gave myself a mental shake and stood. My sleep had seemed brief, but I felt a hundred times better than I had before sprawling on the bed. Without any preamble, Rink handed me the carryall we'd appropriated from Monk and Hussein. I tucked the Glock taken from Dan StJohn in the small of my back: at the restaurant I'd used eight rounds, which left nine in the clip. Rink had a similar pistol elongated by the addition of a suppressor tucked into his jeans – courtesy of Harvey, who hadn't relinquished his grip on it even after he'd taken the plunge into the swimming pool. We both had knives. But for the coming assault we'd be relying more on the machine pistols in the bag.

Harvey had one of the MAC-10s primed and ready to go, too, should the unlikely happen and Viskhan's people discover Trey's hideout a second time. None of us shared any heartfelt goodbyes. Emotion couldn't play a part in what we planned. Unless you counted righteous fury: we all had enough of that to go around.

Rink drove the Chrysler, I sat in the front passenger seat – the carryall was in the trunk. There were a lot of cops around, and I was a fugitive. But the cops were looking for me accompanied by Trey, not a brooding Asian American dude. We managed to make it all the way out of Coral Gables, into downtown Miami and onto the McArthur Causeway without being pulled over. Next stop, Watson Island. Adjacent to us a string of cruise liners were moored at Dodge Island: they looked as if a row of tower blocks had toppled and lay partly submerged in the azure sea.

We made a brief stop at Watson Island, checking the moored boats at both a marina and a private yacht club. To be fair, neither of us seriously expected to find the boat we were looking for as neither port was large enough to accommodate it, but we weren't to know that without looking. Back in the car we continued on the causeway, passing Terminal Island, and could see the Miami Beach Marina before we were even off the bridge. From the marina was direct access to the Atlantic through Government Cut, a channel between the southern tip of Miami Beach and the exclusive Fisher Island, the domain of billionaires. There were half a dozen super-yachts moored at berths outside the marina itself, the large boats needing the extra space to manoeuvre when putting back to sea. As we swept over the last section of the causeway, I stared at each yacht in turn, wondering if Viskhan was hiding aboard one of them, as Trey had surmised. Occasionally, she'd said, she'd accompanied him to parties aboard the yachts of various playboys and celebrities. Viskhan had thrown some of those parties; he wasn't averse to chartering multi-million-dollar boats to impress certain business clients.

'D'you see it?' Rink asked.

We were seeking a particular yacht, the one Viskhan was fondest of. Trey said we couldn't miss it. The other boats were huge, sumptuous affairs, but the one that Viskhan favoured outshone them all. It was eighty-two yards long, could accommodate twelve guests in six lavish staterooms, as many as twenty-six crew members, and was equipped with a cinema, dining room, a passenger elevator through three decks and a gymnasium. It also had a tender garage and launching dock and, its most striking features, a heli-pad and chopper. Only one of the moored luxury yachts had a heli-pad that I could tell, but it wasn't the boat were looking for – this one was an older converted naval minesweeper more akin to an expedition boat than the toy of the mega-rich. We were on the lookout for a sleek, futuristic craft, not something left over from the Cold War.

'It's not there,' I said, 'but we have to check out the others. If we have no luck, we're going to have to put Harvey on the case. Think he can discover the *Nephilim*'s whereabouts from the port authority or elsewhere?'

'If they've logged a course, I guess. But what are the odds they'd come clean about their destination when it's being piloted by a wanted terrorist?'

'What kind of guy loans a boat worth tens of millions of dollars to Viskhan anyway?' Trey had told us that Fedor Stepanov had recently flown to conduct business in the Far East, and offered the use of the yacht to her husband while he was away

'Someone with more to lose than money. You heard what Trey said: Viskhan regularly supplied Stepanov with girls, and the younger the better.'

'Yeah,' I said. 'Shame that paedophilic bastard won't be aboard his yacht when we find it. I wouldn't mind sparing a bullet meant for Viskhan on him.'

'He'll get his comeuppance.' First, though, he meant, we should concentrate on Viskhan and his buddies.

Rink drove us along the approach route to the marina. Luxury condo- and apartment-blocks towered over the masts of more conventional sailing boats. Entrance to the marina was restricted to members only, and the rule enforced by a guard post: it smacked of elitism, the barrier-controlled gate there to keep out the unwashed hoi polloi. We weren't deterred by gates or rent-a-guards.

'What say we go for a poke around?' Rink suggested. 'Maybe somebody on the marina knows where to find the *Nephilim*.'

'Hold on. Do you see that?'

Rink followed my gesture. A banner was strung between poles, fluttering in the warm morning breeze. It advertised a regatta event scheduled for later that day; apparently a flotilla of pleasure craft and boats were putting to sea off South Beach to mark the national holiday. It coincided timing-wise with the planned celebratory parade down Ocean Drive and accompanying fair on Lummus Park. Where better to hide a yacht than alongside hundreds of other boats?

We shared a wondering glance: was the *Nephilim* already there, sitting off shore where Viskhan had a commanding view of the coming attack? Without consultation, Rink spun the car about and headed for the historic Art Deco District. Finding a parking spot proved tricky, but Rink muscled the Chrysler into a spot that didn't look big enough to contain the dimensions of the car. We got out, making sure our shirts covered the guns in our belts, and took a wander through the adjoining streets onto Ocean Drive. The preparations for the day's celebration were underway, with tents being erected as temporary market stalls and fun attractions, and mobile food and drink concession stands situated at regular intervals at kerbside, but as yet the crowds hadn't begun gathering. The cops were out in numbers. I was surprised that the parade hadn't been called off, but maybe it was too late in the day to change the arrangements, or the Chief of Police had only taken our warning with a pinch of salt. Those officers I could see were alert, but they were watching for possible terrorists, not two guys out apparently enjoying their vacation. In their minds they'd be watching for people with browner skin than mine – clichéd, yes, but the truth. Despite that, I diverted to a store selling beachwear and bought a baseball cap and sunglasses to blend in with similarly attired vacationers in town: Rink had fetched his own shades from the rental.

Unlike many of those cops, we allowed our attention to range further than checking out the usual suspects. Unfortunately terrorists came in all shapes, sizes and skin colours, and it was less their outward appearance that I was looking for than any suspicious body language or activity that was out of context with the surroundings. The main problem was, by the time any of us – the cops included – spotted anything untoward it would probably be too late. In recent years the tactic of choice of many terrorists was to drive a vehicle into a packed crowd, mow down as many innocent bystanders as they could before their rolling battering ram was brought to a halt, sometimes beneath a hail of police bullets. There was little to nothing Rink or I could do to halt such an attack. Ocean Drive was a long thoroughfare, and adjacent to it Lummus Park stretched a good distance too. The odds of being in the right place at the right time to halt a suicide run by a mobile terrorist would be akin to winning the lottery.

Our only hope of averting the inevitable was to stop it at its source. We had to find Viskhan, take out the leader. Our walk had taken us to a point mid-way along Lummus Park, where the Miami Beach Ocean Rescue Headquarters was situated on the park. Being as it was a department of public safety I was tempted to go inside and alert them to our fears. The parade should be cancelled and civilians evacuated from the area. But to do that would expose us, and most likely it'd be us under the guns of the police even if we were allowed to walk out of the building unchallenged. We cut past the building, through Lummus Park and stood between some sculpted dunes to see over the beach. I checked the locale for any sign of the super-yacht *Nephilim*. There were larger boats on the horizon, but at that distance the haze rising off the ocean made it impossible to distinguish yachts from tankers or cruise liners. Already there were beachgoers by the hundreds on the white sand and out in the surf. Boats sculled back and forth, and further out speedboats towed water-skiers behind them.

I exchanged a sour grimace with Rink.

'Do you get the feeling that we might be barking up the wrong palm tree here?' I asked, and received a smirk for my lame cliché.

We continued our walk, retracing in part steps I'd taken two nights ago while fleeing with Trey from Sean Cahill. Once we reached the end of Lummus Park we turned and strolled south again. As we kept watch for anything suspicious, our conversation turned to Raul Velasquez, who hadn't yet been released from custody. It wasn't a good sign; the cops obviously intended charging him. Stamping somebody to death probably wasn't acceptable as a self-defense plea. Our buddy probably wasn't helping his case by sticking to the assertion that he was also responsible for the death of the man I'd speared on Trey's shoe heel. Once we were done with Viskhan we both agreed that we should concentrate on getting Velasquez out of jail.

Somewhere nearby a marching band struck up for a matter of seconds before the music degenerated into a cacophony of random beats and notes: an impromptu rehearsal. I smelled frying onions and cotton candy. In the short period we'd walked along the beach, the carnival atmosphere had grown adjacent to us. I could tell Rink was as frustrated as me, but without going direct to the police and telling them what we suspected, there was little we could do there. We'd both hoped to spot the *Nephilim* sitting offshore, but with no hint of the yacht out there, I was flummoxed.

'This is a waste of time,' I announced.

Rink adjusted his shades without comment. He dug out his cell and phoned Harvey. By the lack of any urgency in Harvey's reply, I deduced all was fine back at the Coral Gables hotel. Rink asked our pal to do his magic on his laptop and find the current location for the *Nephilim*. A visible scowl formed on Rink's face. He bears a scar on his chin courtesy of a fight with a demented knifeman, and when he gets angry it blanches of all colour, as it did then. He made his goodbyes, hung up and turned to me. 'Well that idea's fubar.'

'What's up?'

'When Harvey fought those gunmen back in Flagami his laptop took a couple rounds intended for him: it's trashed.

Harve is gonna see if the hotel has an IT centre where he can do some searches but he isn't hopeful of gettin' what he wants in time to help us.' Rink held out his phone. 'As much as I hate to admit it, brother, we're fucked. It's the only reason I'm gonna ask you to call Walt. I don't mind sellin' out to the devil if it means he can help find Viskhan and stop him. If it means we have to take a back seat to Homeland, then so be it: the safety of innocent civilians trumps us gettin' revenge for Mack.'

'I'll call him,' I said, 'but when I ask for his help it'll be with a caveat.'

A hundred yards or more to the south another marching band launched into an impromptu rehearsal, this time the snare drums accompanied by an out of tune alto saxophonist. The music was more chaotic than before. Bystanders collectively lifted their voices in disapproval.

That was as long as the illusion held.

The snare drum rattle was that of automatic gunfire, the saxophone the squeals of terrified victims, the roaring of disapproval was actually dismay and panic.

People fled from Ocean Drive through Lummus Park. On the beach, holidaymakers all turned towards the sounds of gunfire. Then they too were fleeing, a stampede of humanity, away from its source.

North of us another gun began a staccato beat.

The crowds wheeled in confusion like a flock of birds disturbed by an electromagnetic pulse. Some people plunged into the surf. Others dove flat on the sand, seeking any hole to hide in. Some scrambled over friends and strangers alike to get away.

A third gun joined the assault, this one further away to the south, then a fourth, much closer to where Rink and me had gone to cover behind the boles of some palm trees. Across the park people fled in terror, parents carrying or hauling children to safety. A temporary food stand had been erected about fifty feet away, seats and tables set on the grass for the convenience of customers: people ploughed over and through the flimsy aluminium furniture, some becoming entangled in the legs of chairs and falling before scrambling up again and racing for their lives. Although I couldn't see where, other similar pockets of chaos reigned: I could hear the bleating panic, the rumble of fleeing people. The guns continued their rattling assaults.

Viskhan's spectacular was underway and there wasn't a damned thing we could do about it.

I'd hoped that with the heightened alert status and the number of armed police in the area, the terrorists would have aborted their operation, but no. They'd gone for broke, in a concerted and coordinated attack on at least four fronts. At that moment I dreaded to think how many casualties there had already been, how many were to come, and I was ashamed that I hadn't done more to halt the attack in the first place. But that was as long as my regret lasted: I fell into the trained response of the soldier who'd spent fourteen years combatting terrorism throughout the world, as did Rink alongside me. While the civilians around us ran from the sounds of gunfire, we headed directly towards it.

Various things became obvious within a few seconds, and the first we should have figured out, considering we'd been given hints through the truck used to collect the smuggled weapons from the port, the use of a Chinese restaurant as an operating base for Cahill's team and the fact that Viskhan trafficked some of his human slaves through other service and catering outfits. Their weapons had been smuggled to various locations alongside Ocean Drive hidden within various mobile concession stands, the terrorists posing as servers at the food counters until it was time for the coordinated attack. The second thing that struck me was how the attack felt premature; it had been launched before the parade had gotten underway, when the greatest impact would have been felt. There were a large number of people in attendance, but come midday when the festivities and accompanying regatta were due, the crowds would have swollen tenfold and therefore the casualties would have been exponentially greater. I wondered briefly if one of the terrorists had been uncovered by the police and had responded with a hail of gunfire, setting off the others in a deadly chain reaction, or if one of them had simply lost their nerve and gone for broke, causing the same domino effect. Or had Viskhan been behind the early triggering of the attack for reasons yet unknown? Not to underplay or trivialize the horrific event, but it was less a *spectacular* than a half-arsed attempt to go out in a lacklustre fizzle.

I considered these points even as I ran through Lummus Park for the main street, concluding the wrongness of the situation even before I spotted the first shooter. Rink was moving adjacent to me, about thirty feet to my right so that we didn't offer a single target. We were yet to pull our guns out: It'd be a poor end to our day if we were mistaken for the bad guys and brought down by an armed police officer. Civilians streaked past us, hurtling towards the beach, faces stricken, pale, mouths wide open in that age old question: why? An elderly man fell, losing his walking stick. I sacrificed a few seconds to drag him behind the bole of a tree, and commanded him to stay down before I charged on. My actions were so automatic I couldn't recall a single detail about the man's features a second after I'd left him. Rink had gained on me, but had come to a halt where the park met the street. I went to a knee alongside a tree, using it as a shield. We exchanged looks, and Rink nodded. I followed his gesture and spotted a skinny young man standing in the centre of Ocean Drive, indiscriminately pulling the trigger of an assault rifle. He was screaming wordlessly, and as much in horror as those scattering for cover. Having launched his attack from a hot-dog stand, he wore a paper cap on his head and an apron tied at his middle. He had the fair hair and deep-set pale eyes of an Eastern European, not your typical jihadist portrayed by the media and pop culture.

He didn't know how to shoot well. With each burst of his rifle, the barrel pulled up and to the right, and most of the bullets were spent in the walls of the buildings on the far side of the street. Only misfortune had placed some running civilians in his way, and I spotted at least three casualties crumpled on the far sidewalk. The youth turned around, trying his luck firing down the middle of the street. Brass shells ejected from his rifle tinkled on the asphalt. From our positions either of us could have dropped the youth with a shot to his body, but Rink didn't shoot and neither did I. It was unnecessary. An armed MPD officer shot him dead and saved us the trouble. The cop advanced on the youth, hollering at him despite him being dead, then kicked aside his gun even as other officers moved in to secure his body and weapon. Further along the road, other cops were in the process of directing people away from the shooting, towards the beach or into buildings where they could take cover. A female officer accompanied by a medic rushed towards the first fallen casualty on the sidewalk.

Guns competed to either side of our respective positions. Police sirens squawked. Pointed commands were hollered, directed at the shooters to lay down their weapons. Screams and shouts echoed off the stores and hotel fronts. More gunfire. The response was concerted. The gunfire fell silent, but none of the rest of the sounds adding to the cacophony.

I didn't hear the cop moving in behind me until he challenged me. Caught with one knee on the ground, I had to turn awkwardly to look up at him. Through my sunglasses I stared up at the muzzle of his service pistol. I held up my empty hands. The cop was a Marine Patrol Officer – denoted as such by the insignia on his uniform – and must have been patrolling the beachfront when things kicked off. He'd come upon me while trying to evacuate other civilians away from the fighting. In my baseball cap and shades, crouching fearfully behind a tree, I looked like many others caught up in the atrocity. He quickly scanned the fallen terrorist on the road, the huddle of cops around him, and decided he'd serve better to get more civilians to safety.

'Sir, get behind me and make directly for the beach.'

I gave him no cause to believe anything less than I was grateful of his assistance. I rose up, keeping the tree between the road and me, and nodded emphatic thanks at my saviour. He covered me while I moved back, and then inserted himself in the space I'd just vacated, his pistol still held at the ready. He spotted Rink, who'd crouched similarly to me, but behind some shrubs. Rink was watching, and accepted the cop's instructions when he too was waved back towards the beach. We retreated at a running crouch, exactly as any other innocent civilian might have under the circumstances. Only when I was out of the cop's line of sight did I swerve towards Rink.

'That was a close one,' I said.

'Yep, you might just have dodged a bullet, brother.'

If the cop had recognised me as the fugitive responsible for shooting dead three gunmen a few blocks away, and engaging

240

in a high-speed escape from other gunmen in a stolen van, things could have ended badly for me, if not for him. Rink wouldn't have let him take me in, and it could have become an armed confrontation on all sides. Neither of us would willingly shoot a police officer, but the same might not have been the case for him or the dozens of other cops now swarming the area.

There was still an overall state of alarm, but there was no hint of gunfire any more. I'd counted four shooters during the initial launch of the attack, and hadn't heard any more join the fight. Law enforcement officers had taken out, or captured, the other three terrorists: somehow I didn't believe any of the three was Viskhan, Cahill or StJohn. The police wouldn't now be complacent: if anything they would be at an even higher alert as they braced for more attacks. Soon they would begin a controlled sweep of the area, seeking other threats.

'We'd best git,' Rink suggested, 'before they shut SoBe down tighter than a clam.'

He wasn't wrong. The last we wanted was to be caught within a tightening cordon while armed and with a bunch of illegal firearms in the trunk of our car. Besides, there was nothing more for us to do there, and the last I wanted was to cause any undue work for the honest cops already overwhelmed with mopping up on Ocean Drive. We jogged along the perimeter of Lummus Park, out of sight of the various pockets of activity, blending in with other fleeing civilians, then when it was safe to do so we cut across the main street, found access to an alley and through to where we'd left the rental.

As Rink drove us off the island, I scanned Biscayne Bay for any sign of the *Nephilim*. When it again eluded me, I took Rink's cell phone out and called Walter Hayes Conrad. Before I'd ended the call, Rink hit the gas and we tore up the I-95 expressway, hurtling in pursuit of the super-yacht that was already sailing off the coast somewhere between Boca Raton and West Palm Beach. Viskhan hadn't hung around to observe the aftermath of the terror assault he'd arranged, but had made himself scarce, possibly intending to sail to some pre-arranged flight out of the US...but was that it? His spectacular had been anything but; what if it was only the precursor to something much worse?

36

The *Nephilim* had a healthy lead on us, but Rink jammed the throttle to the floor and every second we gained on it as we rocketed up the expressway. My buddy drove as if he was auditioning for the next movie in the Fast and Furious franchise, pushing the rental car to extremes. He overtook slower-moving vehicles, whipping around them on whatever lane was clear, and left them almost standing in his wake. How a keen-eyed highway patrolman didn't spot us and give chase I'll never know, but am thankful for. As we hurtled northward, I periodically scanned the sea for signs of the super-yacht, without ever losing course of the conversation I was engaged in.

Walter Hayes Conrad was sequestered in some government office on Capitol Hill, but to hear his breathless voice it was as if he were along for the chase with us. After agreeing to use his resources to find the *Nephilim*'s current whereabouts and setting us in pursuit, he'd been busy. Due to the reports coming out of South Beach he had fully bought into our assertion that another attack was not only possible but also imminent. Against our wishes, he was rallying a team of Navy SEALS to board the *Nephilim* and contain the situation. The SEALs were already en route. But we were still ahead of them.

'I want your eyes on them only,' he ordered. 'You report back to me, do you hear me, Joe? Do not engage.'

'I hear you, Walt.' I exchanged a wry smile with Rink. We heard; it didn't mean we'd obey.

'I mean it, goddamnit! Stay out of the damn way and leave Viskhan to—'

I cut him off. 'Who, the professionals? Do you forget who we are, Walt, what we did for you in the past?'

'I'm not questioning your abilities,' Walt snapped. 'I'm trying to protect you boys.'

'We're big enough and ugly enough to take the knocks,' I told him. I caught a glimpse from Rink, and under his breath he whispered something about me being ugly enough at any rate, before he went back to undertaking a freightliner by accelerating along the shoulder of the expressway: the truck driver pressed angrily on his horn as we shot past and swerved back onto the road. 'Walt, Viskhan ordered my murder, and that of his wife. He killed one of our closest friends, Harvey got shot too, and Raul is currently in jail because of him. He's just triggered a shoot-out in South Beach and innocent people died. Believe me, if he's in my sights, I'm not going to stand there with my dick in my hand.'

'He will be dealt with.'

'So you say. But that's not good enough. You owe us, Walter, don't ever forget that. You *owe* us big time.'

He was silent for a moment. Possibly he was weighing up the amount of debt he was in to us, mentally ticking off the times he'd used us for his personal political agenda, and not least saving the lives of his granddaughter and great grandson. Finally he showed signs that he was weakening in his resolve. 'I can't buy you any time; I can't take a chance on Viskhan getting away. But if you're there before the SEALs...'

'We'll do everything in our power to hold Viskhan until they arrive,' I said. 'Just ensure they know there are a couple of friendlies in the firing line.'

'I'll do what I can do, but there are no promises.'

Before he could backtrack, I changed the subject. 'So any hint yet on what has motivated Viskhan?'

'From what I've been able to learn he has no religious or political allegiance, unless you count the Chechen Republic of Ichkeria he once fought for. Even then, intelligence suggests he has no current affiliation with the CRI or any other Chechen rebel group, and until you mentioned his name he wasn't on any Homeland watch list. Well, that isn't exactly true: MPD vice and Customs and Border Control have been on his ass for years, but...well, you know how successful they've been.'

'He is being protected,' I said, as contritely as I could. 'He is paying off certain key authorities, or blackmailing them, but there's more to it. Is he a CIA asset, Walt? A fucking foreign national with ties to a terrorist group doesn't get to run a criminal empire in the US without somebody looking the other way.'

'I couldn't possibly say.' He meant he wouldn't. 'So don't press me. We have been able to confirm that Sean Cahill, Daniel StJohn and the others you've contacted are listed as private military contractors, but with the exclusion of Cahill none have raised an alarm that they've ever worked for our enemies.'

'Cahill?'

'His daddy was Real IRA. Cahill enlisted with the British Army, allegedly in rebellion with the sins of his father. He was suspected of getting involved in the drugs trade while serving in Afghanistan, but was never caught. After leaving the army he resurfaced as a mercenary, worked for us in Iraq, and later in Libya and Syria. Which brings us back to what we think this is all about. It's unconfirmed, but through Viskhan, Cahill's team have been hired to launch a counter-strike against the US for the recent bombings of IS bases, in particular the one where we took out thirty-six of their people when we dropped the MOAB.' The GBU-43/B Massive Ordnance Air Blast, more commonly known as the Mother Of All Bombs, was allegedly the most powerful non-nuclear explosive ordnance employed by the US, and it had targeted a cave system in Afghanistan that Islamic State employed as a base: use of the bomb had caused political furore and international condemnation, and even prompted fears of a Third World War when North Korea grew defiant at President Trump's overt show of military power. 'There's also thinking that the Assad regime could be responsible for Viskhan's actions, after we bombarded that air base in response to him gassing his own people.'

'Yeah, well, whoever's behind him is your job to find out. I'm not interested in the politics, only stopping the bastard.'

'You aren't listening, Joe, but why doesn't that surprise me?'

Rink had been party to the conversation throughout, and despite driving at speed, had absorbed exactly what Walter referred to. And made the connection where the *Nephilim* was heading.

'Mar-a-Lago,' he intoned.

I shot him a look of incomprehension.

He glimpsed away from the road long enough to explain.

'The Southern White House.'

Walter heard, said, 'The *Nephilim* is headed towards Palm Beach and the presidential retreat. This could be an attack directed at the POTUS in response to him ordering those recent attacks.'

'You've got to be kidding me? Is the president even at his retreat?'

'No. He's safely out here in D.C., but it's not about killing him, but hitting him where it hurts most personally. He bombed their house, so they're going to return the favour.'

'If that were true, why haven't you had the *Nephilim* sunk already?'

'We can't. Not until we know for sure Viskhan's intentions and that he poses a credible threat. We don't know if he's even onboard, and until we do, and confirm an imminent attack, we can't shoot him out of the water. The SEAL mission is as much about confirming the specific threat, and if they are unable to take the boat, they're going to laser paint it for a missile strike.'

'That's what you meant when you couldn't make any promises about protecting us from friendly fire?'

'It's why I warned you to only take an eyes-on approach,' he confirmed. 'If you're onboard and the threat to Mar-a-Lago is deemed *credible* and *imminent*, a fighter jet will be scrambled and I won't be able to stop that missile: you'll be burned along with everyone else.'

Mar-a-Lago is an historic estate in Palm Beach, built by a socialite called Marjorie Merriweather Post in the 1920s. Post envisioned the southern mansion as a winter retreat for American presidents and foreign dignitaries – possibly with the idea of currying favour from such highly placed politicians rather than through altruism – but it went unused by any president until purchased by Donald Trump. It was almost as if he'd foreseen the future when Trump, a successful businessman at the time, snapped up the beachside estate as part of his expanding property portfolio back in the 1980s. Since his inauguration as the 45th President of the United States of America, he had used it as his Camp David-style retreat.

I knew little more about the estate as we headed for it except for a few snippets I'd watched on the news when last Trump was in residence. I'd learned enough to know Mar-a-Lago currently housed a private members-only club, guest rooms, spa and hotel-style amenities, and that the president maintained private quarters in a separate area of the house and grounds. I'd also heard rumours that the estate came equipped with bomb shelters and a sensitive facility for direct communications with the White House Situation Room and Pentagon. I did not doubt that at that moment, messages were flying to and fro from that facility, and that a lockdown of the estate was under way. When the POTUS was in residence, air and shipping operations were restricted in its vicinity, and the Coast Guard and Secret Service secured the two waterway approaches to the estate by sea and lagoon. The Secret Service also restricted access to surrounding streets. When the president was home, Mar-a-Lago was almost impregnable to outside threat. Unfortunately, Trump wasn't in the house. Therefore neither were the resources to counter the abrupt threat, though I suspected they were being marshalled as Rink drove us at speed along Gateway Boulevard in Boynton Beach for the shore of Lake Worth Lagoon. At random Rink took a left into an area of lakefront property called Hypoluxo. As expected almost every man, woman and dog that lived on the lagoon owned a boat.

Grabbing the carryall from the trunk of the car, I charged after Rink and we hijacked the first seaworthy vessel we could get going. A couple of teenage boys had to be chased off it first, and they hollered curses at us as Rink pointed the prow towards a narrow inlet from the lagoon, the only access to the open sea nearby. I trusted to Rink's inbuilt navigation system, because I'd no idea where in relation we were to the presidential retreat when we roared out into the Atlantic Ocean. He got a fix immediately, sending the speedboat in a tight curve to take us north, then pulled down on the throttle. Time was ticking away, and every second wasted was a second closer Viskhan got to his target.

There were other craft on the sea, but I gave them little notice. I watched out for the Coast Guard, and for an incoming missile. Primarily I searched the heat-hazed horizon for the super-yacht, even as I pulled from their bag two of the MAC-10 machine pistols and readied them for action.

Mar-a-Lago, it turned out, was still a few miles north of us, situated at Palm Beach on the narrow strip of land between Lake Worth Lagoon and the Atlantic Ocean, another of those barrier islands that had featured heavily since my arrival in Miami. Beachfront condos, golf courses and tennis clubs dominated the land we scudded past. Rink didn't spare the horsepower.

'Do you see her yet, Hunter?' Rink had to shout over the roar of the outboard motor and the slapping of the hull as it bounced over the waves.

'Couple of ships out to the east, but I can't tell if any of them is the *Nephilim*.' I had braced myself against the hull of the speedboat to avoid being thrown overboard as we crested the higher swells. The ships I could see were little more than hazy blotches on the horizon. 'I don't see anything up ahead that is big enough.'

'What if we got ahead of her?' Rink suggested.

We had no idea of the yacht's cruising speed, or even if Viskhan had flogged the engines. At some point as we hurtled up the coast we could very well have gotten ahead of it, despite its early lead. Another consideration: what if we were wrong about its destination and the yacht had swept on past Mar-a-Lago?

'Wait!' I said, and craned as tall as I could without losing balance. 'There! Do you see it?'

Rink was at the stern, which was at a lower point in the water. He couldn't see what I'd spotted.

I'd only been able to picture the *Nephilim* in my mind, and had overexaggerated its actual appearance. It was as long as I'd thought, but had sleeker and lower lines. From a distance its white hull blended perfectly with the spume cloud stirred in its wake as it forged north. Rink swung the speedboat side-on for a better look. 'Sure looks like a super-yacht to me,' he confirmed. 'D'you see that? Not only has it a heli-pad, there's a chopper onboard.'

The appearance of the helicopter didn't come as any surprise. A narcissist like Viskhan didn't strike me as the type to launch a personal suicide attack; he'd have a rapid escape strategy in place. I gave his getaway chopper scant notice, instead turning and scanning the heavens for any hint of incoming aircraft. As yet the Navy SEALs were still en route.

'So are we doing this?' I asked.

'Never a backward step, brother.'

'Then let's go get the bastards.'

Rink throttled up and sent the prow directly towards the distant *Nephilim* like a dart.

There was none of Fedor Stepanov's regular crew aboard the *Nephilim*. Mikhail Viskhan had replaced them with a crew of his own choosing, each and every last man and woman as expendable as the yacht, in his opinion. They were a mixture of radicalized jihadists, criminals and other cannon fodder bullied into obeying him. Of the latter Viskhan knew that a slave would be defiant if they were the only one punished for their rebellion, so instead he threatened those dearest to their hearts: their wives, their children, their parents. Occasionally he caught dark looks from some of those coerced into his plan, and he knew that they would prefer to turn the guns he'd given to them on him, except for the genuine fear that his omnipotent reach would still extend to the throats of their loved ones. But should anyone decide the temptation was too strong to resist, he had given them unloaded guns. His quartermaster would pass around magazines to them only when they were approaching their target. In the meantime, the reluctant suicide assault team was under armed guard by those radicalized and chomping at the bit to give up their own lives – and to take as many innocents with them as possible.

Sean Cahill had always been uneasy about using innocent people in the attack, though not through any sense of compassion: he simply didn't think that they would be reliable when their hearts weren't in the job. He fully suspected they'd throw down their weapons the instant opposition was shown. Viskhan thought otherwise. People terrified for the welfare of their loved ones were more determined fighters than any religious fanatic he'd ever met.

They were quickly approaching Mar-a-Lago. The next fifteen minutes would tell who was correct.

Because they were nearing their target, the activity onboard had grown hectic. To avoid detection as they sailed from Miami, all signs of the yacht's actual battle capability had been concealed under tarpaulins. The yacht had been retrofitted as a floating war machine. Those forced into – or willingly in the jihadists' sakes – storming the beach were literally there to draw fire while Cahill's people did the real damage from the decks. Dan StJohn had overseen the situating of a pair of L1A1 heavy machine guns, fixing them to the decks with weapon mount installation kits, and also a number of L16A2 81 mm mortar and 40 mm grenade launch points. With a range of half a mile, mortar rounds could easily be dropped within the grounds of Mar-a-Lago where most destruction was Viskhan's desired result. This had never been about an assassination attempt on the president, but showing him that his house too could be bombed. Nor could Viskhan give a damn about the political ambitions of his Islamic State employers, because this was about payback on two fronts personal to him: the Yanks had almost killed him that time they pounded the Taliban stronghold in Afghanistan, where only Cahill's selflessness had saved his life, but also bombs had murdered his father, mother and siblings during the Battle of Grozny. On that occasion it was the Russians who'd made him an orphan, but arguing was semantics when Trump and Putin were being too pally for his liking.

He knew his decision to send Sean Cahill's team after Trey and Joe Hunter had jeopardised his operation, in that he'd lost the professionalism of men trained in the weaponry onboard, but he was a man driven by the need for revenge. His wife forsaking him, and being knocked on his backside by a lesser man – both were good reason to chase them to the ends of the earth, in his opinion. He didn't personally regret the loss of Sean's men apart from the fact he was yet to be avenged, but he did regret losing their expertise. Sean, though, assured him that the crew had been sufficiently trained in the use of the weapons, and all the land assault team need do was point and squeeze. In one matter the decimation of Sean's team was fortuitous: there had always been an issue problematic to Sean, in that escape from the yacht of his entire team would become difficult once the attack was launched. Originally the plan was to attack the presidential retreat under darkness, and then abandon the yacht while the team escaped in RIBs to points on the mainland where they had vehicles waiting. Now Viskhan's escape strategy had been altered for the better, where he and Sean would take to the heavens in the *Nephelim*'s helicopter, the rigid inflatable boats would not be required. If any of the surviving crew decided to take the spare skiff they'd brought, then that was on them – in daylight they'd be shot out of the water before they made landfall.

Dan StJohn could have proved a sticking point in their arrangement. The Englishman had always shown loyalty to Sean, but he had placed a question in Sean's mind when suggesting they slay Viskhan and take over his criminal activities. It would only be a matter of time before StJohn decided that Sean too was extraneous to his ambitions and would invite a bullet to his brain. Any attack made on Viskhan was to be treated severely, be that a sneaky punch in the manner of Joe Hunter or the suggestion of assassination by StJohn. There was no seat on the getaway copter for the treacherous son of a bitch, and Viskhan would take great pleasure in killing the bastard before he flew off. Last night he'd almost forewarned StJohn of his intent when kicking him in the head – a foolhardy thing to do, but he wasn't lying when he told Sean he was finding it difficult containing the urge to murder the Brit. Though he had to admit, kicking him had offered a small degree of satisfaction and somewhat energized him after previous disappointments.

Sean knew of his plan to murder StJohn. If he didn't approve, he didn't protest, and Viskhan was confident he never would. Sean's loyalty to him was unquestioned; the man was smitten with him. Not in an unhealthy sexual manner that Viskhan could not tolerate, but Sean loved him with the depth of a brother. Viskhan's feelings for Sean didn't run as deep, but he let him believe so; it made Sean malleable to his will. Ironically, had he employed a similar pretext with Trey, perhaps his wife would not have betrayed him. He scorned the notion of irony. He would not lie to her; Trey was a whore to be used, and he had been determined she'd learn her place.

It angered him that she hadn't learned the supreme lesson yet: he was not to be crossed. Once he was done here and had returned to Chechnya, he would raise a bounty on her head. He'd toyed with the idea of having her brought to him alive so that her torment could be endless, but he'd be happy enough that she was dead because of the trouble she'd caused. But then, as had the slaying of most of Sean's team, her betrayal had also brought opportunity. Through reports to Sean from Parkinson and Frost, the injured PMCs left behind in Miami, he'd heard the attack in SoBe was dominating the news and the nation's collective attention was pinned to the aftermath of the short but shocking gun battle. His four-man suicide squad had managed to kill six people, including one police officer, injure dozens of others and send a shockwave of dismay through the populace. As far as terror attacks went the results were negligible, but as a distraction had worked as well as Sean promised it would: any pugilist knew that a swift jab was the best prelude to the knockout punch. The hammer blow he was about to launch from the *Nephilim* was the spectacular that would really have the world talking.

He took a last lingering look at his surroundings. Stepanov was about to lose his boat, but Viskhan couldn't give a shit. He'd played the Russian into loaning him the yacht on the promise of a fresh batch of nubile virgins on his return from the Far East. Instead, Stepanov would be forced into hiding or face scandal next time he set foot in the U.S.; that or implication in an IS terror plot. Losing his yacht would prove the lesser of Stepanov's concerns in the coming months, especially when Viskhan delivered proof of his sexual deviance to the FBI. Discounting personal enemies but above all others he hated Russians, and Fedor Stepanov wasn't an exception.

Rapid footsteps approached.

Viskhan turned and greeted Sean Cahill with a rictus grin. The Irishman's mouth was set in an equally tight grimace.

'Is everything in order?' Viskhan asked needlessly.

'We're minutes out, Mikhail. Soon we'll be in mortar range of the estate, and Dan's prepping the RIB to send the landing party ashore...but we might have a problem.'

'Tell me.'

'We've a boat incoming on our rear.'

'Gunship?'

'No, but there appear to be two armed men aboard.'

Viskhan laughed in scorn. 'That isn't a problem to us. In fact, let's get things underway. It's time to try those machine guns out; have your gunners shoot that boat out of the water for me.'

Nodding sharply, Cahill turned away, hollering commands to the nearest men. The tarpaulins were deftly removed, uncovering the tripod-mounted heavy machine guns. The guns were belt-fed, fifty 12.7 mm rounds a time, and had an upper cyclical rate of six hundred and thirty-five rounds per minute: at full continuous fire fifty rounds could be expelled in seconds, reducing its target to scraps. The aft gunner swung the HMG on its gimbal, lining up the approaching boat, and let loose hell.

The noise was tremendous, the yacht shuddering under the recoil of the gun. A few hundred yards distant, bullets strafed the waves and the gunner adjusted his aim to accommodate their trajectory. The next volley punched the boat repeatedly, blasting holes through it with impunity, scattering debris high in the air. The men aboard the boat were ripped apart, their rag and bone corpses as full of holes as the sieve they died in. The gunner didn't let up, firing until the belt was empty, and after he was done, all that remained whole of the boat were random chunks floating on the water and a ragged hull wallowing amid the destruction.

Viskhan felt a tremor of pleasure go through him. Sean approached, his features set in stone. 'I can confirm the heavy machine guns work,' he announced, and squeezed out a smile.

'Yes. Quite a show you put on, Sean. I didn't expect my request to be taken so literally.'

'That was just the appetizer to the main course,' Sean said.

'Excellent. I'm growing impatient with waiting. Send the RIB, Sean, and start softening up the landing zone for them.'

Again Cahill strode away, issuing curt commands. To aft the RIB was already situated in the tender dock and, without seeing them, Viskhan could hear his landing team boarding it. Suicidal jihadists were the most vocal; those less willing to die kept their prayers to themselves. Viskhan remained out of sight as his quartermaster – StJohn – had by now passed around fully loaded magazines. Only once he heard the roar of the outboard motor and the RIB began a charge at the nearby beach did he approach the port rail and observe the boat's progress. To either side of him mortar rounds began popping, and he saw their detonations as puffing clouds of raining dirt before he heard the explosions. It was only moments later that he picked out the first wail of terror, taken up a second after by fleeing beachgoers. The HMGs opened up again, this time aimed at the beach and the nearest buildings discernible through the subtropical foliage. Tracer rounds zipped in arcs over the turquoise water and flashed brightly where they struck. Grenades were launched and joined the assault on the beach, their detonations sending sand and bodies skyward. He rocked back on his heels in satisfaction: this was the spectacular 4th of July fireworks display he'd envisioned. And he'd only just got started.

The brief roar of heavy machine-gun fire made us fruitlessly duck in the speedboat. If we were the targets the bullets would have shredded us along with the boat, but our response was only natural. The machine gun fired a second time, more sustained. Because we were still alive it was safe to assume that we were not in the gunner's sights. I bobbed up to scan the scene ahead, even as Rink returned to the boat's controls and took us in a wide curve away. I saw enough before ducking again that hell had been visited upon a larger craft than ours, and though it was torn to pieces, much of it scattered now across the sea, it bore the decal of the Coast Guard. The boat hadn't been a gunship but only an exploratory craft sent out to investigate the *Nephilim*. The servicemen onboard hadn't stood a chance, their deaths coming so suddenly they wouldn't have had an opportunity to cry for their mothers, let alone summon help.

We'd been working on a strong hunch that Viskhan was captaining the *Nephilim*, and that he had planned a second atrocity at Palm Beach: well, here was undeniable proof. It also stood to reason that Walter – and who knew how many other government officials and military officers – observing the progress of the yacht hadn't missed the destruction of the Coast Guard boat. Those Navy SEALs, most assuredly waiting at a nearby staging post, would get the green light to take the yacht. They'd be inbound very rapidly, so our window of opportunity was slim. We could, as Walter had suggested, stand down and allow the pros to do their jobs, but I don't mind admitting to selfishness. I wanted to kill Viskhan and his friend Cahill myself. One glance at Rink told me he hadn't had second thoughts either.

'Murderous bastards!' he growled under his breath as he took us in a sweeping curve to the yacht's starboard.

Smoke trails arced from the decks of the *Nephilim*. I knew what they signified before the mortar rounds detonated, sending up fountains of sand and parts of innocent people into the air. A string of curses ran from me faster than the machine guns that opened up and sent a hail of bullets among fleeing beachgoers. The beach was packed with holidaymakers – men, women and children – and the casualties were many. Every innocent life taken was one too many.

An RIB, bristling with armed men, roared from a tender docking bay at the rear of the yacht and swept in a direct line for the shore. The bastards were on a mission to kill more innocent people.

We could have chased them, opened up on the crew with our MAC-10s, but Rink powered back on the motor, sent the speedboat towards the yacht. If we were sighted we could end up destroyed by the heavy machine guns as easily as the Coast Guard boat, but all weapons were currently aimed landward. If our boat had already been spotted then we'd been disregarded as just another couple of vacationers out on a pleasure cruise – there were other boats previously scudding about nearby, most of them now making beelines in the opposite direction. We got to within twenty feet of the yacht before a figure appeared at a deck rail above us. It took the bearded man a few seconds to process what he was seeing, make up his mind we were dangerous and raise his gun. By then I'd already let rip with my machine pistol. He was dead without ever firing a round.

Our boat and the *Nephilim* bumped hulls. As I covered him, Rink grabbed for a hanging buoy rope and went up it with simian ease. He swarmed over the rail and I heard his MAC-10 blaring. Who he shot at I didn't see, but it was apparent he'd won the brief gunfight when he leaned over the rail and gave me the all clear. I slung my MAC-10 on its shoulder strap, then grabbed for the rope, my soles bracing the hull as I dragged myself upward hand over hand while Rink covered my ascent.

Safely on deck, and MAC-10 back in hand, I covered fore and Rink took aft.

'We're up against it, brother,' Rink said, stating the obvious, 'but we have to stop 'em hurting any more civilians. If we spot Viskhan, he goes down, but right now those gunners are the real threat. We have to take 'em out and give those poor folks on shore a chance to escape.'

'So let's do it,' I said, and we advanced together along starboard for the front of the yacht, Rink keeping an eye on our six while I concentrated ahead. Our recent gunfire had been buried under the cacophony coming from portside. But we had to make sure that no sentries had been set to watch for incoming threats on our side, or on the upper decks. Even as we advanced I caught the drum of footsteps overhead, and also movement inside the yacht. A door opened, and a man rushed out. His back was to us: I'd no compunction about shooting him in the spine, and he sprawled dead on the deck. He had been armed with a machine pistol similar to ours. I grabbed it, slung its strap on my left shoulder and advanced again holding both guns like a Western gunslinger.

Rink gave the corpse a nudge with his foot, rolling the man to study his features. His wasn't a face familiar to us: some unknown punk bought by Viskhan to do his dirty work. We continued on, the blaring of the heavy machine gun on the prow drawing us towards it. As we neared the front, we had to take more care. The upper levels swept back sharply from the prow, offering clean and aerodynamic lines as well as a clear view over the lower deck from the bridge. Anyone standing above us would have us in their sights before we knew they were there. I spun, stepped backwards, staying tight to the wall as I took a quick look. I caught the shadow of movement, but then whoever had cast it had moved. Mortars popped. The HMG at aft continued its hellish roar, but the one forward momentarily stopped shooting, probably so another ammunition belt could be fed into it. I snuck out for a look.

The HMG's tripod mount had been bolted to the foredeck. One gunner sat with his feet straddling the tripod while a second man knelt alongside him, feeding the greedy gun's appetite for destruction. They were in the process of reloading, and confident that they faced no opposition. As the gunner searched for new targets on the beach, swung the barrel round on his choice of victims, I emptied the clip of one MAC-10 in him and his pal. My rounds didn't have the same devastating effect as the larger projectiles they were sending towards the beach, but they did the job of chewing up their soft flesh.

Until that point we'd avoided detection – anyone who'd spotted us was dead – but slaying the machine gun crew tipped the scales. Instantly the battle switched from land to sea. A figure in paramilitary-style fatigues and bulletproof utility vest leaned out from concealment, and his eyes widened a fraction in recognition a split second before he fired at me. I jerked back, and his bullets tore up the deck and rail I'd momentarily been standing in front of. I hadn't come face to face with him before, but had heard how Rink had rearranged his features when they tussled at the port. The guy's misshapen nose and bruised eyes gave up his identity.

'StJohn,' I told Rink.

He had been covering our backs and watching for anyone leaning out from the upper deck. He half-turned to nod acknowledgement, but without compromising his attention. 'Maybe I should've taken the time to finish that fucker off last time we met, saved us the effort now.'

'I'm sure you'll happily put in the effort given the chance.'

'You ain't wrong, brother,' he said.

Another figure emerged from the same doorway as the guy I'd felled with a shot to his spine, and stared in confusion. Again this guy was struggling to process what was happening, and that we were enemies. Before he ever came to a conclusion, Rink fired. The guy jerked and shuddered at the impact of bullets and then fell gracelessly against the starboard rail. He wasn't dead, but neither was he fit to continue the fight. Nevertheless, Rink put him down permanently. Another guy witnessed his death, and didn't waste any time figuring us out. He leaned out from the open doorway and fired at us, spray-and-pray-style. The bullets came wickedly close to hitting Rink, and I also felt the snapping impact off a ricochet tug at my baseball cap. I'd forgotten I was wearing the damn thing. I swiped it off, didn't need to bother with the shades; I'd already lost them somewhere between SoBe and here. Bullets chewed the rail to my rear: Dan StJohn or somebody else was moving past the fore cabin, trying to pin us down with crossfire.

Rink pinned down the shooter in the doorway while I crouched and prepared to confront StJohn. If we stayed put we'd be caught in an exposed position. I glanced up. The deck overhead was clear and there was a handy set of steps offering access only a few feet from Rink. I gestured to him, and he got the message. Staying close to the wall, he laid down a barrage of bullets that impacted the doorframe where the other shooter hid. He deliberately stopped shooting. I swivelled on my heels and put my back to the rail just as the gunman bobbed out to shoot at Rink. The angle I'd made between us offered him up as a bigger target. I fired, both MAC-10s this time. It was a blistering hail that forced the shooter back inside, hopefully wounded. Immediately Rink went up the steps, and I was on his heels as soon as he gave me the all clear. I lobbed the first MAC-10 away, flinging it so it went over the lower deck rail and into the sea: I'd emptied the clip. I had extra magazines stuffed in my pockets, but the empty gun was a hindrance I didn't have time, or a spare set of hands, to reload.

I swapped the gun I'd kept from left to right hand, estimating the number of rounds in its clip. Not many. But enough to save our arses while Rink reloaded: he did so perfunctorily. Once he was done, I dropped the clip on my gun, slapped in a fresh one and chambered the first round. Seconds had passed. Already the dynamics of our enemy had shifted. Below us and to the front I could see the two machine gunners I'd slain, and also a hint of movement directly below: StJohn again? I fired down, forcing whoever was below us to dive through the doors of the fore cabin. A second later he was firing up at us through the cabin's ceiling. Few of the rounds made it through, and those that did had lost their killing force, but the impact of the others made the deck shudder beneath my feet and I danced backwards, pressing up against Rink. He braced his feet, steadying me. I took stock of our surroundings.

I'd have bet bikini-clad girls were the usual occupants of the deck on which we stood. I couldn't see evidence of the last party held there, but imagined nubile young things reclining on the comfortable loungers while Fedor Stepanov or Mikhail Viskhan ogled and pawed them. I imagined champagne and canapés, and shrieks of laughter – maybe shrieks of pain if it was one of *those* parties. That was as wide-ranging as my perusal went before I rushed across to the portside and leaned out for a quick check on numbers down there. Viskhan had arranged his people along the length of the deck so that they could maintain a constant barrage of the beach and the presidential compound beyond. There weren't as many left aboard as I'd feared. There were three mortar crews, two individuals with grenade launchers and two men at the aft HMG: the odds weren't insurmountable. Then again, I'd no way of telling how many were inside, or had moved across to starboard to confront us. Viskhan, Cahill and StJohn were nowhere to be seen. A brief pang shot through me; what if Viskhan and Cahill had abandoned ship before they'd reached the war zone? I doubted it, because the RIB had headed directly for shore and Viskhan didn't strike me as the suicidal type. Besides, the chopper wasn't there for decoration alone. It would be the choice of getaway vehicle should the Coast Guard surround the *Nephilim*.

There was a distinct lack of response from the sea: I had to assume the Coast Guard and Secret Service had been ordered to stand down and leave the yacht to the incoming SEAL team. On shore I could imagine heroic actions underway, with

261

innocent victims being evacuated to safer zones while defenders struck back against the armed landing party. The deserted RIB wallowed in the low surf, and I couldn't determine a terrorist from a defender on the beach for all the drifting smoke. Distant rifle fire competed, barely audible because of the racket still emanating from the yacht. Mortar rounds and grenades arced beyond the beachside shrubbery, now exclusively targeting the Mar-a-Lago estate. Those rumoured bomb shelters would be very handy additions to have access to for those within the members' club and presidential retreat.

I sent a blizzard of bullets along the port rail, and lessened the intensity of the bombardment by half. Those nearest the front of the yacht would have been aware already that they were under attack, but those at aft had been blissfully ignorant. Now the fuckers knew! They began seeking cover and, I bet, swapping out their unwieldy weapons for sidearms and rifles. I'd just invited all their fury to come down on our heads. But that was fine; Rink and me were in the business of fighting. Innocent holidaymakers in shorts and sun lotion weren't.

Directly behind us was an open doorway. It led into a once sumptuous living area, one now littered by the refuse of men who couldn't care less about its appearance. Towards the rear of the room a swing door allowed access to mid-ship. Through it came the voice of a man organising a response to us. I recalled Sean Cahill's sibilant voice from when Trey and me played dead at Indian Creek, and was positive it was he. I was tempted to go through the room and find him, but that would be walking into a trap.

'Up and over,' I suggested to Rink.

'You go,' he said. 'I'll stay on this level and draw their fire. Take out that other machine gun post, brother. If it's still in action when the SEALs arrive they might not chance boarding, they'll just strafe the fuckin' yacht with their own cannons.'

His fear was the same as mine, and he was correct. The HMG had to be shut down. He winked at me, and I nodded: platitudes were unnecessary. I swarmed up a ladder, and was peering inside the bridge within a few seconds. It was currently deserted. I couldn't resist the opportunity, so pushed inside and emptied the remainder of a clip into the array of high-tech controls. I slapped in a fresh mag, gave it another short burst and watched sparks fizz and pop, and smoke rise from the console. Unsure if it was enough to disable the yacht, I kicked and hammered at other levers and knobs. Below me there was gunfire, and I caught the shrill yelp of somebody injured. The intervening walls dampened the blare of the aft HMG, but it didn't trivialize the weapon's destructive efficacy. It got me moving again. Going along the top deck was leaving me open to shots from below so I went through a door from the bridge into a narrow corridor. Even there in that utilitarian space the décor was plush, and the carpet underfoot so thick it absorbed my jogging footsteps.

It also absorbed those of the man coming inside from a side door.

I ran directly into Mikhail Viskhan and we rebounded, each of us juggling our weapons. He fired first.

It was only minutes between the first mortars streaking towards the beach and Viskhan shooting at me. But in the intervening space hundreds, more like thousands, of rounds had been fired. The majority of those bullets would have been spent in surf, sand and foliage, only a small number of them hitting fleshier targets. I was lucky that the first to strike me glanced off the mound of my left forearm and didn't embed in my face, Viskhan's target.

I'd clashed with him as he emerged from the door, and my MAC-10 had been knocked aside, but I wasn't without my full senses despite the jarring impact. Even as he rocked back, hauling up his pistol, I lunged and swept up my left arm just as he squeezed the trigger. The bullet intended for my skull went overhead, burying itself and a sliver of my forearm in the ceiling. I backhanded the MAC-10 into his chest but it slapped harmlessly off a bulletproof vest he'd donned. Still, it forced him sideways, and his next bullet to fly wider again. I brought my gun fully around and pulled the trigger. Vest or not, the impacts kept him from aiming, and blood spattered the wall beside him.

Sadly most of my rounds had gone centre mass, ripping the outer material of the vest to shreds, and only one of them had found his flesh. I'd no idea where, and didn't waste time checking. I went for a headshot, but he ducked and lurched aside. In desperation he unloaded his weapon blindly, three shots on semi-automatic that deterred me from following too closely.

In the next instant he was through the door again, and to follow him would be stepping into his sights.

I leapt past the open portal, slapped my shoulders against the wall and crabbed away down the corridor.

'You!' Viskhan screamed after me. He was as much struck by disbelief at my sudden appearance as stung by my bullets. 'Come out! I will kill you!'

'Why don't you come back inside?' I taunted, but continued to move away, my MAC-10 up and ready for the instant he showed his face.

In response he snuck his gun around the doorjamb and fired. His bullets didn't trouble me, too far to my left and too high. I peppered the doorframe with a short burst of bullets and he retracted his gun. 'Bastard!' he yelled. 'I swear I'm going to kill you!'

'I'm only sorry I didn't stamp on your fuckin' throat the first time I knocked you on your arse,' I hollered back. 'Trust me, I won't show pity next time.'

'Next time will be very soon, my friend.'

'Bet on it.'

Before he could throw another angry retort, I backed through a door into what amounted to a floating man cave. The requisite pool table took centre stage among all the other boys' toys. Glass doors opened on to the heli-deck. They swished open and admitted two armed figures. Initially they didn't spot me in the subdued gloom at the far end of the room, and aimed their weapons outward. But the instant I fired it got their attention: or at least the attention of one of them, because the other was too busy crashing to the floor. I knew not who I'd killed, and didn't care. And I was set on killing the second man. Sadly my MAC-10 ran dry, and I'd no time to reload.

I hurtled forwards, throwing down the machine pistol and snapping my hand round to my lower back, groping for the Glock. Bullets traced a halo inches around me.

Shit!

When I ran full pelt into Viskhan, the Glock must have fallen out of my waistband!

I still had a knife, but you know the old adage about knives and gunfights. Instead I snatched up a pool ball and hurled it at the gunman. It didn't strike him, but it made him cower to avoid the rebound. There was some kind of stool, a silver metal pedestal topped by a white leather cushion. I grabbed and hurled it at the same time, throwing it more as a distraction than anything, hoping to entangle his legs and spoil the gunman's aim as he righted himself. The stool was lighter than expected, or my strength more desperate. The cushioned end flipped and sent the metal base into his torso. I was only a second behind it so it hadn't even begun to fall away when I crashed into it, the cushion against my abdomen. It worked as a brace between us, me forcing him against the wall, him trying to shoot me. But I'd also got a hand on its barrel and forced his gun aside. The barrel was hot, growing searing as he unleashed a storm of bullets among the rich man's playthings. Ignoring the blistering of my fingers, I pounded my other fist into his face twice. We continued jostling and the stool fell between us. I threw my shoulder into his chest and, as he bounced off the wall, I wrenched on the gun and pulled him off balance and rammed a headbutt into his face. He tripped over the stool and went down heavily on his front, with me now on top. Now the gun had been dealt with it was the right time for the knife. I yanked it out of its pouch and plunged the combat blade repeatedly into the back of his neck. The man shuddered beneath me; his blood was hot on my hand. He was no longer a threat, but I stabbed him again for good measure, wishing it were Mikhail Viskhan I was kneeling astride.

Viskhan's life could be measured in minutes, I swore, but before I could take the fight back to him I still had to stop that HMG before the SEALs blasted us all out of the water. I grabbed the dead man's gun and emerged back into sunlight on the heli-deck.

Most of the bombardment of the beach had come to a halt as those on the yacht realised the *Nephilim* had been stormed. Mortars stood abandoned on the deck below while Viskhan's people searched for us, wielding weapons befitting close-quarters combat. I'd no idea of where Rink had got to, but he was still alive if the sound of battle towards the front was anything to go by. I heard the chatter of his MAC-10 and corresponding retorts from handguns and rifles. To aft the shooting had fallen silent, but for one. The heavy machine gun was still active, crystallizing my intentions. Using the helicopter as cover, I moved on its position.

A quick scan of the coastline showed pockets of destruction. Smoke hung in clouds over the churned sand and splintered or toppled palm trees. Fires raged beyond, where I guessed the estate's buildings had taken hits. The gunner on the aft deck below continued to rain projectiles towards land, but it was largely a gesture, because I couldn't spot a living soul. None of Viskhan's landing party were in sight, having moved inland to storm the presidential retreat: I wondered how that was going, because there was no gunfire apparent from their end now. The heavy machine-gunner was shooting for shooting's sake, enjoying his job too much for my liking and encouraging a fatal response. From the south, hugging the coastline, a helicopter was incoming and it would only be minutes until it arrived. If the trigger-happy gunner decided to switch his attention on that chopper the consequences for us all would be dire.

I briefly checked over the assault rifle I'd appropriated. It was a semi-automatic civilian AR-15 – infamously tagged the 'mass shooter's weapon of choice' because, cloaked by the Second Amendment, it was easily available in the US. Supposedly a restricted modern sporting rifle, it was still a killing machine. And I was happy to put it to good use.

While Hunter brought chaos to the uppermost deck, Rink hadn't been topping up his tan on the sun deck. He had paid back some of the hell the *Nephilim*'s crew had rained down on Mar-a-Lago. In doing so he'd drawn much of the fire away from Hunter, his plan all along so his friend could stop the HMG, but had placed himself in an untenable position. He was surrounded, with no clear escape route and his options for survival dwindling.

He was fighting a battle on three fronts and all dimensions. Those on the fore and lower starboard decks could only pin him down, but sporadically he had to contend with a shooter from above, near the bridge. Minutes ago he'd listened to Hunter wrecking the controls, then engaging in skirmishes as he progressed through the yacht, but it was apparent he hadn't killed everyone up there. Some dude with a handgun occasionally crept out of cover to try and shoot him from above, and he was the most troubling enemy to contend with. Rink couldn't retreat through the cabin; there were shooters within the yacht, and they were being organised into a three-pronged assault. They were seconds from swarming along both decks and through the cabin, and he had no chance of ascending to the lower deck without being cut to pieces by those below. His only way out was up the same ladder Hunter used to gain the upper deck, but not while the gunman waited for him to show his face. But it was better that he faced one gun rather than many...or it wasn't.

Behind him the orders had curtailed, and that meant only one thing: the assault on his position was underway. *Time*, he thought, *to move!*

Going up the steps was tantamount to suicide. So was going down, and if he chose to skirt round one of the decks he'd meet the forces coming those ways and then get pinned by a pincer move. There was no safe passage through the cabin. He wasn't afraid of death, but wasn't keen on meeting it just yet. So he took the only thing left to him: he charged for starboard, rattling off bullets to deter anyone coming around the corner at him, and then cast the MAC-10 aside to free his hands.

He vaulted over the rail, arcing out in a swan dive for the sea. Around him he could feel the sonic cracks as bullets whizzed by, experienced blazing heat across his shoulders and right calf muscle. Then he plunged head first into the water. His dive took him deep, and bullets trailing streaks of bubbles zipped and darted around him. He was hit a third time, not with killing force but enough to send a flash of agony the length of his spine. Air leaked between his clamped jaws, but he held on to most of it in his lungs while kicking like a frog and pulling at the water to get deeper. More bullets ploughed after him, but most of their velocity was slowed by the water pressure. Those that hit him had less force than a thrown pebble. He tucked in the water, righted himself by observing the rising bubbles around him and peered up through an indigo twilight. Way above he spotted concentric circles of froth marking where more bullets were sent into the deep after him. Up there gunmen shot furiously but blindly, in the hope of finishing him off. They were wasting ammunition.

Blood clouded the water around him, and no doubt some of it had already formed a discolouration of the sea. Let them think he was mortally wounded. He knew he wasn't, because he was still functioning. The brine stung his wounds but he could ignore the discomfort in the knowledge that he'd taken glancing nicks rather than being holed through. Worse than the itchiness across his shoulder and lower leg, the pressure in his chest was building as his need for oxygen kicked in. But he didn't claw for the surface. First he felt where he'd taken the third hit. His lower back was sore, but he'd been saved a severed spine by the suppressed pistol he'd earlier tucked in his belt. He found where the bullet had struck the grip, indenting it instead of his vertebra. He left the gun in situ, checked for his KA-BAR. Good, he still had the tools of his trade, because his job was not yet done.

His wild dive into the ocean wasn't about escaping but expanding his options for helping Hunter to kill Viskhan. Anyone of right mind would swim a safe distance from the yacht before surfacing, so Rink ignored good sense. Through the murk he spotted the hull of the *Nephilim* and he curved towards it. His fingers found its slickness, and he used it to direct him aft as he fought to rise to the surface and gasp for air. It was too soon to come up; somebody would still be watching for him, and he had to make them believe he'd been killed and had sunk to the ocean floor. Overhead he spotted another shape. It was the speedboat they'd arrived in earlier. It bobbed adrift, but very close to the *Nephilim*'s hull. He pulled for the speedboat, got it between him and any observers on deck and then gratefully sucked in lungfuls of air. Taking a peek around or above the boat was out of the question, so he listened. Those who'd laid down a blizzard of lead where he'd dived into the sea were still on the decks, all talking and shouting excitedly, so he waited long enough for them to begin filtering away, chasing other imagined enemies, but also going to join the fight against Hunter.

He ducked beneath the speedboat and surfaced again just high enough to clear his nostrils and peered up at the sweeping hull of the *Nephilim*. He was yards away from the buoy line he'd climbed the first time, but he wouldn't take a chance on it now. Keeping close to the yacht, hidden from above by the curve of its hull, he swam for the rear and the tender dock. Again he submerged to come up within the shelter of the open-ended dock where a skiff was moored on a bracket extending over the water from the dock. He stayed between the bodies of both boats so there was less chance of being spotted, timing his exit from the water with the braying of the HMG on the next deck up.

He strong-armed himself up, braced on both palms and hoisting his hips and bent knees upward like a gymnast taking to a pommel horse. As his soles found the deck he pushed up and came to his feet, then immediately swept beneath the overhanging upper deck, out of view of the gunner up there. Steps allowed access up, or he could enter a corridor to the aft staterooms. He decided neither were suitable and instead went to port and took a quick glance along the deck. Most of the terrorists had abandoned their posts when they'd been summoned to kill him. Mortars were lined up along the deck, but sans operators. He spotted an assault rifle on which was mounted an M203 grenade launcher propped against a box of 40 mm grenades. A grim smile played across his lips.

Time to level the playing field.

Drawing the silenced pistol, he snuck along the deck. Was within spitting distance of the grenade launcher when a familiar figure rounded the corner ahead. Rink snapped up the pistol, fired thrice in rapid succession. His aim was good, but the suppressor and the intervening fifty or so yards played havoc with the gun's accuracy and Dan StJohn was lucky to survive. He hollered the alert, summoning assistance even as he brought up his own weapon and returned fire. Rink ducked and dived, plastered his body into a recessed doorway and came out of the brief encounter unscathed. As others joined him, StJohn thrust them ahead of him and two reckless fools began a suicide run at Rink, shooting as they advanced.

Disregarding the pistol and the bullets chewing the deck, walls and rail all around him, Rink lunged for the grenade launcher. He toppled the ammunition box towards him and grenades spilled around his feet as he again pushed into the recess. It took him less than three seconds to chamber a grenade and bring the gun up. His two would-be killers were already retreating, not bothering to shoot as they fled for their lives. The grenade Rink fired struck the lattermost and obliterated him. The other man was thrown ten feet in the air as he somersaulted out to sea.

Forward of where they died, StJohn ordered another two terrorists to get Rink, and when they cowered back around the corner it saved their lives as a second grenade scuffed the deck, bounced a few feet and then struck the prow. The detonation still threw them down, as it did StJohn, but they were spared the instantaneous obliteration suffered by the first man to be struck. Shedding seawater, Rink charged down the deck even as he racked in a third grenade, the last he'd managed to snap up. It was time to finish what he'd begun that time at the Miami-Dade County Seaport with StJohn.

For the briefest of seconds I feared that the incoming SEAL team had launched a salvo of rockets at the *Nephilim*, but part of my mind told me I was wrong. The two detonations, terrifically deafening so close by, weren't the result of rockets, but by less destructive armament. Grenades was my best guess, fired from one of the terrorist's own guns but striking on the lower deck instead of the beach. If pushed to bet on who was behind the explosions my money was on one man. I grinned in feral joy: trust Rink to turn things noisier.

The fact that an enemy had gotten his hands on a grenade launcher wasn't lost on the duo working the HMG. It fell silent as they checked they weren't next to be blown to smithereens. Their attention was directed front of ship, from where smoke plumed for the heavens. The gunner's mate jogged away, moving for an angle where he could see over the rail, to check out the lower deck. Above him, and over his left shoulder, I went undetected. I centred the AR-15's sights between his shoulders and let rip a three-rounds volley. Somebody once described that being shot by a handgun was akin to being stabbed with a thimble, while being shot by an AR-15 was more like being perforated by soda cans. The bullets – at such close range – put holes in his torso that I could've shoved a fist through.

I immediately turned on the machine gunner.

But he had heard the retorts of my rifle, saw his pal cut to ribbons and began to target the HMG on me. The gun swung fluidly on its gimbal, but he wasn't as nimble as he shuffled around after it. Before he'd any hope of getting a bead on me, I moved quickly to the right, rushing past the cockpit of the chopper, making it even more difficult to follow me, and then came to a straddling halt. I prompted him to fire and his bullets ripped through Viskhan's getaway helicopter, feet away from me. My AR-15 blatted out three rounds with each caress of the trigger. The first three missed the gunner but forced him to release the gun and scramble for his life. Taking better aim, I sent another grouping of three shots into him and a chunk of bloody meat was ejected across the brass-littered deck. He wasn't dead, but he was dying. He still had the determination to pull out a sidearm and swing it up at me, but he'd barely any strength, and less clarity of vision. His bullets troubled the seagulls flapping noisily in the sky but came nowhere near me. It was almost too easy when I rested into the stock, sighted on him and put three rounds in his sternum. As he sprawled dead on the deck a third grenade exploded at the prow, and the shockwave that travelled the length of the boat could be felt through my soles. That Rink.

The heaviest weapons had been taken out of commission, the attack on the land redirected, and now the *Nephilim* was taking hits: hopefully it was enough to deter an immediate and devastating response from the SEALs, or an incoming rocket from a fighter plane. After a studious check of my surroundings – no enemy in sight – I looked again for the incoming chopper. It hove into view a few hundred yards off port, standing between the yacht and the mainland. It was a huge twin-prop Chinook CH-47D troop transporter, but beyond it, skimming over the bombarded presidential retreat, were two sleeker craft, Boeing AH-64 Apache attack helos. The Apaches had initially secured the battleground but were now coming to offer supporting fire to the Chinook. The monstrous twin-prop descended, and I could figure out why. SEAL frogmen didn't rappel from the chopper; they weren't required when the tailgate could be lowered to spit out an RIB full of steely-eyed Special Forces guys who meant to board the *Nephilim* and quell all opposition. Briefly I wondered if Walter's warning had fallen on deaf ears, but then the fact there were friendlies on the yacht was hard to miss, no less the evidence of my taking out the HMG which had given them the opening to storm the boat.

In another minute some of the most capable warriors on Earth would swarm aboard, and I didn't want to be confused as a terrorist. But neither did I lay down my weapons and lace my hands on my head. Rink was still fighting for his life, and there were still some specific people I wished to meet in person. I sprinted around the destroyed chopper for the starboard side, and took up the hunt for Mikhail Viskhan.

The third explosion onboard the *Nephilim* told Mikhail Viskhan that the battle had turned for the worse. That was what happened having lost the use of actual trained professionals who knew how to fight – he now regretted wasting Sean Cahill's team on a personal vendetta – and relying on big-mouthed criminals who talked the talk but couldn't walk the walk. Joe Hunter and a companion, most likely Jared Rington, had gone through his hired *killers* like a barbed-wire enema, reaming a butthole in the yacht. How many had died aboard was to be seen, but it wasn't so much the deaths as the chaos they'd wrought among his people that was important. Whilst fighting the invaders, they weren't bombarding Mar-a-Lago or the civilians on the beach. Hunter and his pal had shut down both his heavy machine guns and his mortar crews had abandoned their stations while they took up guns to help defend him – more likely defend themselves. And now, minutes after he'd supposedly died in the sea, Rington had turned one of their grenade launchers against them.

Without any supporting fire, his landing party was exposed to counter-attack, and the general lack of gunshots from the estate told him that they had all been killed, or surrendered. Smoke wreathed the heavens over the presidential retreat but he'd no way of telling how much damage had been done. But did it actually matter? The attack was more about symbolism than causing destruction, and in that case his operation had been an unquestioned success. Pretty soon the world's press would be on the scene and images of the attack's aftermath beamed to every household on the planet. His Islamic State sponsors would be more than thrilled with the impact – he'd promised them something spectacular and he'd delivered. They must now give him the promised riches, the position and land he'd demanded, and the protection he was due. He could finally go home.

But for one important fact: his getaway helicopter was trashed, shot to pieces by his own gunner during a firefight with Hunter. Even if it hadn't been turned to scrap, his helicopter no longer offered a way off the yacht as the Apaches would have blown it out of the sky. He had expected that once the attack was underway a swift response would be launched, but Viskhan had counted on it being by a Coast Guard boat or two, which he was confident could be handled by his gunners, not from the military. By the time any Special Forces could be mobilised against him, he had planned on being far away from the *Nephilim*. Judging by the rapid response of the three Navy helicopters, he had to now accept that they'd been forewarned about his intentions and had only been waiting for the green light to launch a counter-assault. His money was on Trey being the leak. But his wife had never been party to the plans he'd made to target Mar-a-Lago, only the initial, and subsequently diversionary, suicide attack on the South Beach parade. Still, only Trey could have known about his association with Fedor Stepanov, and the depraved Russian's pleasure boat. She must have sent Hunter and Rington in pursuit of him, ruining everything, and together they must have concluded where he was going, and to what reason. Her betrayal of him had cost him a magnificent victory, and had definitely thrown the proverbial wrench in his getaway plan.

He thought furiously of a way off the yacht. Only the yacht's skiff remained to be taken. If he could get to it he might still be able to slip away while all the attention was on taking the *Nephilim* from his men that remained board. He'd planned with Sean that they'd escape together, but as it was, Sean would have to look after himself this time. Being abandoned, Sean would be devastated, but Viskhan couldn't concern himself with his old friend's feelings: his weren't as mutually strong after all, and besides, if Sean cared for him so deeply then he'd be happy that Viskhan had escaped.

He was currently in the living quarters at aft of the second deck, and through the glass doors could see that the balcony area was clear of opposition. After his brief skirmish with Hunter upstairs he'd used the elevator as a secure escape route, but had gotten off at the next floor down so he could easily ascend to the heli-deck. He'd witnessed the aftermath of the battle between Hunter and his gunners, seen the steaming wreckage left of his chopper's cockpit and had even spotted his nemesis slinking away even as the Navy helicopters thundered into view. Instead of going up he'd stayed put, craning to watch the Chinook launch an RIB bristling with armed Special Forces soldiers in full combat gear. The inflatable boat was currently scudding across the sea towards the *Nephilim*. He checked his weapon, a pistol holding half a mag of ammunition, and his tattered anti-ballistic vest. He wasn't equipped to take on a team of highly trained and superbly armed soldiers, and that was before he discounted his wound. Hunter had shot him, drilling his left tricep and his arm was almost useless.

Quickly he shucked out of his vest, kicking it behind a plush leather easy chair, where he also dumped his pistol. He checked out his reflection in a mirror. His hair was disheveled, his faced pained and lacking colour, and better yet his shirt and arm were sodden with blood: he didn't strike a threat. If he could get to the skiff unchallenged, he might yet make it to the mainland where he could blend with the dozens of innocent victims of the battle. He could then slip away and make it to the private jet waiting for him at Lantana Airport.

Deciding on the ploy as his best chance of escape, he set off, going down an internal stairwell, and making it outside. From his position he couldn't see the RIB, but the Chinook had flown to a higher elevation so that its guns could be brought to bear on the *Nephilim*. Only one of the Apaches was visible, streaking low towards the prow of the yacht. There was a second attack copter somewhere nearby: if he were spotted launching the skiff, they'd destroy him in the water. Suddenly he wasn't as confident in plan B, so he decided on C. Launch the skiff, set it adrift, and then enter the water and use it as a shield until it had drifted clear of the battle zone. From there he could swim ashore, and then plan B would kick back into action.

Taking care to make as small a target as possible, he slunk down into the tender docking bay and unslung the rope tethering the skiff in place on its bracket. He rolled the lightweight aluminium boat over in the water so that it capsized and offered him a breathing space where he could hide beneath the upturned hull as it drifted away. He grinned, feeling confident of escape again. Set his left foot to the rung of a ladder and began to lower himself into the water.

'Going someplace?'

The voice startled him into immobility.

He stared up at the figure on the balcony above him, and at the AR-15 Joe Hunter aimed at his heart.

The third grenade Rink launched had left a smoking crater in the foredeck of the yacht. Scattered around it were lumps of twisted metal, splintered decking, warped duct housing and misshaped machine parts. Also there were the eviscerated corpses of three men and one woman. He gave them no pity. Minutes ago they'd been dropping mortar rounds and grenades on innocent vacationers on Palm Beach, so their violent ending was somewhat karmic. He was only sorry that Daniel StJohn wasn't among their number. The guy who'd ordered his death only moments earlier, sent men running to their deaths while he stayed behind cover, had made himself scarce the second Rink turned the tables with the M203.

He was unsure if StJohn had sprinted around the corner onto the starboard deck before he'd fully leaned out and point blank blasted the foredeck and the four fighters taking shelter behind the various machine and equipment housings, or if he'd skipped back inside through doors now smashed to a million glittering shards. Wherever he'd gotten to, Rink intended hunting him down. But not unarmed. He'd dumped the suppressed pistol when going for the grenade launcher, and now without any shells it was useless to him. He checked the weapons of those he'd slain, but their rifles had been damaged in the blast. Even the HMG was bent out of shape and lying on its side alongside the port rail, and besides, Rink was inordinately strong but it couldn't be easily wielded by a man unless he were a Hollywood action hero.

Downwash from rotors buffeted him.

The SEAL team was incoming, and two of their choppers were taking strategic positions overhead, clearing any opposition. One of the Apaches opened up with its Chain Gun, strafing the upper deck, and the thunder of 30 mm projectiles shredding the yacht almost buried the screams of the dying terrorists it targeted. Holding the M203 grenade launcher, Rink invited friendly fire. He quickly cast it aside and held his open hands overhead, but only as he retreated towards the smashed doors into the living quarters. As soon as he was out of line of sight, Rink drew his KA-BAR: to be fair, he'd gone to war with less in the past. He took stock of his surroundings. He was in a dining room. A better description was a space once reserved for fine dining, except now the shrapnel from his final grenade had tarnished the image. So too did the bloody figure sprawled over a toppled dining table at one side of the room. So StJohn hadn't fled like a rat; he'd been knocked through the glass doors by the detonating grenade.

Striding rapidly towards him, Rink spotted the PMC's assault rifle lying under the wreckage beside him, but out of reach of his twitching fingers. Rink stepped on the rifle, then slid it a few feet away to pick it up. But before he could, StJohn moaned in a mixture of anger and frustration and pushed up to his feet. He was bloody in numerous places, the front of his utility vest shredded, but none of his wounds was immediately life threatening. He was unaware of Rink's presence and his first instinct was to rub at his face and scalp to force some lucidity into his spinning brain. StJohn staggered as he pulled free of the overturned table, and then he turned to scan the destruction caused by the grenade he'd luckily survived. His view was blocked. Rink took a moment to enjoy the look on the Englishman's battered features before he slammed a kick into StJohn's chest.

StJohn somersaulted over the table and crashed to the floor. Rink swerved around it after him and met the merc as he was rising. He slashed his KA-BAR and opened up another hole in the fabric of StJohn's vest. The body armour had saved him from grenade shrapnel, and also Rink's knife, but it wouldn't deter everything Rink had in mind for him. Rink kicked him again, purposefully in the chest to keep StJohn moving and unable to mount an effective defence. The merc was still reeling from being blown into the room, but Rink recalled their fight at the dock and how their battle could easily have gone a different way. He stabbed for the man's face, and StJohn whipped his head aside even as he tugged something from his utility vest. Rink thought knife until the small cylindrical object clattered beside his feet. StJohn sneered, then dove away, and Rink leapt the other way. The grenade detonated like a thunderclap, sound and fury. Both men had escaped its immediate killing range but were peppered by the debris cast by the explosion. Thankfully Rink had made it behind another overturned piece of furniture that took the eviscerating force out of the flying shrapnel, but not the concussive effect that left his ears ringing and his vision blurred. He moved on impulse, wary of another grenade being thrown at him, but dropping the grenade had been a desperate move that StJohn wouldn't risk a second time. As Rink got his bearings, working his jaw to relieve the whistling in his ears, he spotted his enemy through a drifting curtain of acrid smoke, scrabbling through broken furniture for his dropped assault rifle.

Rink rushed him.

StJohn grabbed the shattered remains of a chair and hurled it at him. Rink smashed it aside with his forearm, took a deep lunge to spear StJohn. The KA-BAR gashed the merc's shoulder as he dodged aside, then sent a sidekick into Rink's knee. Thankfully Rink was flexing for another attack and his knee didn't shatter. Nevertheless he wobbled, and StJohn struck at his face. Knuckles raked Rink's cheek but he took the blow to land one of his own. This time he employed the butt of the KA-BAR to hammer the side of StJohn's head. The man staggered under the blow, but didn't go down. He snatched for another chunk of broken furniture and swung it into Rink's chest. Weathering the pain that pierced his sternum, Rink powered in with a headbutt that almost put out StJohn's lights, and yet the merc retained a fighting man's instinct to keep on throwing bombs even when he was almost out on his feet. His punches slammed Rink, but he had fought in knockdown Kyokushinkai karate matches much of his adult life, where combatants gladly accepted punishment to deliver theirs in return. He swept a shin kick into StJohn's left thigh, a kick he could snap a baseball bat clean in two with, and the merc almost passed out at the debilitating nerve pain that flashed through his entire body: a Charley horse from hell. His abused leg collapsed and he went to one knee, just in time for Rink's second shin kick to slash into his ribs. The body armour took away some of the kick's force, but not all. StJohn fell to all fours, wheezing for breath. Rink could have killed him then, but there was something that required doing first. He waited while StJohn struggled to stand and then sway in place. From overhead the guns of the Apaches rained down suppressing cover for the SEALs storming aboard. Rink had limited time to end things with StJohn.

'I'm betting you feel like crap right now,' he said. 'Would be unfair of me to kill an unarmed and injured man, right?'

StJohn deflated visibly, his shoulders rounding. 'Mate, this was never my idea of a fair fight.'

'You're a merc, and you took Viskhan's money.'

'I was never along for that insane fucker's sake. I was pulled into this bullshite through my employer. I didn't like it, man. I'm a professional soldier not a fucking cowardly terrorist!'

'So it's only about the money for you, huh?'

'Yeah, and isn't that the joke? I've never seen any fucking payment.'

Rink shrugged. 'Don't think you're ever going to.'

'So if I'm never going to get paid, what's the sense of keeping this up? This bullshite has nothing to do with me now. We aren't enemies any more. There's no need for us to fight again, is there, mate?'

'Isn't there?' Rink's left hand snapped forward, clasping StJohn's right wrist. He squeezed, forcing the PMC's hand down so that it was trapped against his thigh. He did so even as his right hand plunged in and thumped into StJohn's abdomen. 'In that case you won't be needing this.'

Rink stripped away the knife StJohn had been in the sneaky act of drawing. The merc looked down at the hand still planted tight to his unguarded lower abdomen, watched in dawning horror as Rink withdrew it and the KA-BAR he'd buried to the hilt. Blood seeped through StJohn's clothing, a rapidly expanding patch. StJohn staggered back on his heels until an upturned table checked him. His blood began dripping between his feet, the stain growing on the once plush carpet. The amount of blood was proof that Rink's knife had severed a major artery.

'Y-you took away my knife. Wh-why did you have to gut me?' he croaked.

'Unfinished business,' Rink replied. 'I shoulda killed you first time we met, saved me the trouble now. You're not important to me, bub, I want your bosses dead.'

StJohn's hands went ineffectively to his wound. He tried to staunch the flow but his life could now be measured in minutes.

'You...you didn't have to kill me.'

'No, I didn't. But go tell that to Jim McTeer and ask him if I did something wrong.'

The name meant nothing to StJohn. If he'd heard the name of the man first murdered on Viskhan's orders, then it hadn't been important enough to retain. He only gawped up at Rink as his knees buckled and he sat down hard. Rink dropped StJohn's knife and stepped in, cupping a palm against the side of the merc's head. It was no touch of empathy; it was to brace him while he drove the length of the KA-BAR through his neck, but in the end it was a stroke of kindness. Severing his throat meant StJohn died instantly instead of lingering in agony while he bled out from his gut.

Taking a step back, Rink swiped the KA-BAR to one side, flicking off clinging droplets of gore. They spattered the floor, as did StJohn's spurting blood. Rink moved to avoid the shower as StJohn flopped sideways. The arterial spurts ebbed to a slow trickle; StJohn was dead. Rink eyed the corpse of his enemy, grim-faced. StJohn's death had been easier than that of others who'd died through Viskhan's madness. He gave himself a mental shake. He could hear shouted commands, brief controlled bursts of gunfire. The Navy SEALs had stormed the yacht, and standing there over a murdered corpse probable wasn't the way he should be found by the good guys.

Despite that, he dragged up StJohn's assault rifle and strode deeper into the yacht, looking for Hunter. Where his friend had gotten to, so too had Viskhan he'd bet.

'I surrender,' said Mikhail Viskhan and raised his hands. He struggled to lift the left one, and it pained him to do so. His shirt was soaked with blood all down that side, especially at his upper arm: evidence of where I'd hit him during our skirmish in the corridor.

'What? You think I signed up to the Geneva Convention?' I glared over the sights of my gun, seriously tempted to empty the clip into his body. 'You don't get to surrender, *you piece of shit*! The only way you're getting off this boat is in a fucking body bag.'

I'd made him get off the tender dock and stand on the lower deck where there was less chance of him plunging into the sea. But in doing so, I'd had to adjust my position on the deck above. I was exposed on my right flank to the SEALs storming the yacht, and from my left to the same doorway I'd recently emerged from, and from above by the circling Apache attack choppers. I should shoot the bastard and get it over with. But I wanted him to understand why he was about to die, and surrender was not an option.

'You murdered my friend,' I said. 'You probably don't care, but he was a good man, and you had him shot to death.'

'It should have been you,' he replied, and his tone made no apology for the mix up.

'It should have,' I answered, as equally as contrite. 'But know this, Viskhan, if it had you'd still be right here, right now, about to die, because my friends would have avenged my death exactly as I'll avenge McTeer's.'

He began to lower his arms.

'Get your hands up where I can see them,' I snapped.

Groaning, he strained to lift his left arm. Playing the pity card. It didn't wash with me. I pulled the trigger and the bullets struck the deck beside him. His left arm snapped up, his mouth in a tight grimace.

'Don't fucking try me again,' I said.

But I'd made an error. By not shooting him instantly it gave him hope. He concluded something about me.

'You're not a murderer.'

'Tell that to your people I've killed.'

'I didn't say you weren't a killer, just not a murderer. I can see it in your face. In battle you'd gladly shoot me, but not like this. Not in cold blood.'

'For you I'll gladly make an exception.'

'I don't think so.' He shook his head, believing he had the measure of me. His sneer made my stomach clench. An Apache attack chopper hove overhead, and he eyed it as if it were his guardian angel, sent to snatch him from certain death. 'I surrender,' he hollered, 'I am your prisoner.'

I switched the selector switch over on the AR-15. Single shot. I put one through his right thigh, and firing at that range the damage was extreme: the bloody hole was the size of a soda can, as the analogy had promised. Viskhan collapsed, keening in agony but also in realisation that he'd assumed wrong about me and his would-be saviours in the helicopter which swept from view. While he squirmed to sit and grab at the horrendous wound in his leg, I descended the steps and stood feet away from him.

'Trey told me you fancy yourself as a kickboxer.' I sneered down, unimpressed. 'Try kicking someone now, you bastard.'

'Coward!' he roared. The sclera of his eyes was scarlet, and spittle frothed from his lips as he aimed a bloody finger at me. 'You shot me because you're afraid to face me man to man. Even with only one good arm I'd have ripped your fucking head off!'

'I'm the coward, huh? Who was the one I found sneaking away from the fight? Trust me, I'd have loved nothing more than proving you wrong. Actually, that's untrue. Seeing you dead is all I want.'

'Then get it over with. Shoot me like the coward you are!'

'Oh, don't worry, I'm going to shoot you again,' I promised.

'I won't beg for my life.'

'Good. You'll be saving us both the time.'

I shouldered the weapon, and was happy when he averted his face, screwing up his features in anticipation.

I shot him in his other thigh.

Viskhan went crazy, flopping and screaming in agony, but mostly in outrage. He'd prepared for death, and I'd prolonged it. Ordinarily I took no satisfaction in torture, but Viskhan was the exception to my moral rule. In fact, I wasn't done yet. Trey had told me how the sadist had regularly beaten her, how he'd kicked, punched and raped her...and many others. It was obvious who'd gotten most pleasure out of the torture chamber we'd discovered at the Chinese restaurant. So he was fond of beating up and raping the defenceless? When the bastard arrived in hell, I was determined he wouldn't have a limb left with which to defend against the devil's toasting fork. I aimed for his right shoulder, squeezed off a round. It only nicked him, but that was good enough, because the shock of a full-on impact might have sent him to oblivion. I wanted him conscious when I finally blew off his balls. I kicked his ankles apart, lined up.

A body crashed into mine. My shot went wild, skipping off the deck to who knew where.

My feet got caught under one of Viskhan's knees and I went sideways, borne by my attacker along the platform from which the overturned skiff had recently been launched. For the briefest of times I thought I'd been tackled by a SEAL – otherwise why hadn't Viskhan's defender shot me dead rather than wrestle me away? – but then a disciplined Special Forces soldier wouldn't have gone for the dramatic; they'd have got the job done. This attack felt more personal. Proof of that were the snarling curses spoken into my ear as the man struck me repeatedly with one hand while trying to wrench the AR-15 out of my grasp. I let it go, primarily so I could defend myself but also for the fact I knew the clip was empty: I'd been counting and saved that last round for Viskhan's testicles. The raised end of the tender dock checked my fall, and at the same time I heard the clatter of my assault rifle as it hit the deck, then slid away, perhaps into the sea. I made a wild swipe with my elbow and struck my attacker. I followed it up with a headbutt and then forced my shoulder into him, shoving a few feet back, and only then got a look at his face.

Sean Cahill's rage was almost palpable as he spat out a curse, and then he was coming at me once more, his fists flashing for my face. He drove each punch with fury, but they were poorly guided and struck my forearms and shoulders instead of the intended target. All the while he swore repeatedly, promising to beat me to death. His attack wasn't backed by a rational mind, and I guessed why. There was a firearm holstered at his hip, but he hadn't shot me. He'd come upon me torturing his friend and, incensed at Viskhan's treatment, had given in to his base instincts. His mistake.

I struck back, driven by equal rage, but mine was cold and contained. My right fist rammed into his solar plexus, knocking the wind out of him, and before he could pull in another breath the web between my left thumb and index finger was in his windpipe, forcing back his head. He slashed at me with the side of his hand. It glanced off the top of my skull but was a strong enough blow that I saw sparks. I planted a kick in his abdomen and he staggered back, and this time he got caught up on his fallen pal, and fell over on his backside. The cabin wall behind supported his shoulders. He looked first at me – who was charging in – then at Viskhan, and finally down at the pistol on his hip. Sudden clarity struck him and he grabbed at the gun, got it halfway out of its holster. I jumped over the Chechen, both heels coming down on Cahill with all my weight behind them. Bones could have been broken, I'm unsure, but there was definitely soft tissue damage. The shocking impact had taken his mind away from shooting me, but only for a second or two. By then I had grabbed at his gun, clenching my hand around his. We struggled for control and I softened him up a bit more, ramming my right knee into his face more times than I could keep count.

Cahill, for all he'd allowed his anger to control him, was tough and a dangerous fighter. Most men would have wilted under the pounding my knee gave his head, but he fought on, even forcing upright once more and trying to bite out my throat. He got his teeth on my skin, his jaw working to drive them deeper, and my only recourse was to grasp and squeeze his balls. He was so infuriated it took longer to release his bite than I'd expected and by then there was blood pouring down my shirtfront. Even as his mouth writhed open in a deep-throated groan, I gave his testicles an extra ounce of crushing force and a wicked twist before releasing him.

He was suffering, but not yet ready to fold. He kicked at my thigh and the pain in my leg was sharp and deep, my mobility compromised. He wasn't so steady on his feet either. I kind of hobbled with him sideways, still grasping his gun hand, and we came up against the jamb of the cabin door. He struck with a left punch to my ear, then clawed at my eyes. I battered my forehead into his face. And then he had his left arm around my neck, and had partially clambered onto my back and jostled to sink in a chokehold. Slamming him backwards against the doorjamb didn't shake him off, but partly through the fact I wouldn't relinquish my grip on his gun. But I did throw it high, so that his right arm was extended over my shoulder. I wrenched down, locking his elbow so he'd no escape, then without warning allowed my numb leg to collapse down to a knee. The judo move somersaulted him over me, but with his left arm wrapped around my neck it was never going to be a clean throw. He dragged me down to the deck with him, and we were almost cheek to cheek, lying like an inverted V to each other. I'd lost my grip on his pistol and was in a poor position to protect myself. We both scrambled, rolling to our knees and lunging. Both Cahill's hands were empty.

Our heads clashed and I saw more stars, and then I was slightly atop him and bore my weight down to flatten him on the deck. He fought free, scooting sideways, but forcing him down was only ever a feint. I buried the tip of my right elbow between his shoulder blades and, still on his knees, he cramped over, his shoulders rounding as the shock rode the length of his spinal column. I wrapped my right arm round his neck and squeezed. On our knees, I'd no leverage to sink in a finishing choke and he strained to loosen my hold.

'You're fucking good...I knew we were alike, that you were...almost my equal,' he wheezed out, 'but I'm still going to kill you for what you did to Mikhail.'

He was showing gruff respect for his opponent, and I had no clue where the need to do so came from. For my part I'd no respect for the piece of shit. He was barely a wafer-thin step up the evolutionary ladder from the pond scum Mikhail Viskhan was. 'You should be more concerned with what I'm going to do to you,' I hissed into his ear, 'instead of your girlfriend.'

My words galvanised him to reach for my face, where he tried to dig his nails into my eyeballs. As he pushed forward, I snapped my hips up, cleared my lower legs so I could throw them out from under my backside, and I rolled with him. I never let go of the hold around his neck, and he lunged into me, thinking I was off balance. That was his undoing, because I planted my heels in the angle made by his thighs and upper body and forced away. Cahill's body was stretched out. Before he could scramble for position I locked my legs around his waist and threw my head and shoulders back. The edge of my radius bone dug into his throat, cutting off his air. He struggled, his fingers still clawing for my face. He fought back to his knees, kneed my butt ineffectively, swung punches into my ribs, but I was going nowhere. I arched my spine, exerting crushing pressure on his windpipe, and was rewarded by a shrill squawk as the last of his air escaped his throat. As he weakened, I grabbed my right fist with my left, and rocked my shoulders side to side, sawing my forearm deeper.

Cahill passed out.

I kicked free. Stood up, gasping and bleeding.

Sprawled face down, Cahill spasmed. His hands grasped at the slick deck. He forced his head up to glare in hatred at me. Blood stood in shivering beads on his moustache, some of it mine.

Earlier I'd told Viskhan I wished I'd stamped on his throat that time I knocked him down in the posh hotel's washroom.

'I won't make the same mistake twice,' I told Cahill.

I brought down my heel on the nape of his skull.

'That's for Mack,' I told his corpse.

Then I turned back to Viskhan. I'd still to finish punishing him on behalf of Trey and who knew how many other women he'd abused, and for the innocents murdered and hurt today at Miami Beach and at Mar-a-Lago.

Viskhan had somehow gotten seated, wedged in the corner formed by the cabin wall and tender station deck. He was a bloody wreck, with barely enough strength to support his injured right arm. And yet he'd found Cahill's dropped pistol, and there was still enough mad determination in him to aim it at my heart.

'You have ruined everything,' he said. 'You and my whore of a wife.'

'Yes I have,' I answered, 'and I can't tell you how pleased I am. You're fucked, Viskhan.'

'Go to hell,' he snarled, and began to squeeze the trigger.

The bullet never left the gun.

Beside me Rink let loose with an AR-15 on full auto, and didn't release the trigger until the magazine ran dry. It would be hard work identifying Viskhan's remains once Rink was done.

My buddy looked at me. Then down at Cahill. 'I guess that's them all,' he announced.

'StJohn?'

'Speared like a frog on a gig.' He made a jab of his thumb back the way he'd come from, and I understood that it was StJohn's corpse he'd taken the assault rifle from.

'That's them all then,' I agreed.

As it was, the Navy SEALs still had some mopping up to do. There was the occasional gunshot, and plenty of shouting and commands to be heard. During the violent minute or two I'd been engaged with Viskhan and Cahill I'd almost forgotten the *Nephilim* was currently under siege. As clarity settled in my mind once more, I was suddenly aware of the roaring of the overhead choppers, and of the riot of activity onboard. I eyed the skiff, but discarded the idea of setting sail in it, and our speedboat would have been commandeered by now or drifted away. There was no way we could leave safely at any rate. So I did the only sensible thing. I went down on my knees, held my open hands above my head. After a second, Rink hurled the smoking AR-15 in the sea, and knelt beside me.

And it wasn't a moment too soon.

Navy SEALs challenged us from both sides, guns unwavering as they hollered throaty commands.

'Relax, fellas,' I called over my shoulder. 'We're with the good guys.'

We were still treated like potential threats. Roughly forced down and patted head to toe for weapons, the only cache confiscated from us was my dagger and Rink's KA-BAR. Plastic ties were fastened to our wrists behind our backs and none too gently. I didn't begrudge the rough treatment; under the circumstances the SEALs were doing what we'd done to others in the past. But then we were hauled back onto our knees and one SEAL in full combat fatigues grabbed my chin and pulled my head back. For one heart-stopping second I thought the SEAL wanted payback for the deaths of the innocents on the beach, and for the Coast Guards murdered in the first salvo of the battle. I braced for a blade swiping across my throat. And was thankful instead when he held a laminated card directly alongside my face. A second SEAL loomed over me, comparing my face to the one on the card. 'It's him,' he confirmed.

The process was repeated with Rink, and this time it was a foregone conclusion that he too would be positively identified.

'On your feet, Hunter,' the first SEAL snapped gruffly. He helped me up, dragging me by an elbow. 'You're coming with us.'

Beside me Rink was also assisted to stand. We exchanged the briefest of glances, and I caught the arching of Rink's eyebrow. Then we were escorted off the *Nephilim* and onto the RIB for a short ride to where the Chinook hovered over the sea. We were pushed up into the arms of the helicopter crew, but this time with less roughness.

There could only be two reasons why the SEALs carried identifying photographs of us, and I didn't think it was the first. We hadn't been identified for arrest; Walter Hayes Conrad could be a conniving weasel, but this time he had come through for us.

'To Mack,' said Rink, and raised a glass. Me, Raul Velasquez and Harvey Lucas also picked up our shots of bourbon.

'Mack.' Our chorus came as a salute as we clinked glasses and then knocked back our drinks. Rink sloshed more bourbon into each glass. We were arranged around a table on the raised deck at the back of Rink's condo. The bourbon wasn't the only bottle getting our attention, but for the sake of the toast we'd chosen our dead friend's tipple of choice. Our gathering was in his memory, a celebration of his life; the sad goodbyes were due to come in the following days.

When the police released his body, McTeer's wife claimed it and had him repatriated to New York, where he'd be interred in the family plot. We were scheduled to fly up to attend his funeral in a few days, but after we had gone through a series of interrogations and debriefing sessions, we had been allowed to return to Tampa. Happily, Velasquez was also released and had travelled with us home. Harvey had also stuck around: it was pointless going back to Little Rock only to have to follow us to New York a few days later. We'd all convened at Rink's place at Temple Terrace, holding the impromptu memorial for our fallen brother, and the beer and liquor had flowed. I didn't normally overindulge, but I made the exception as we engaged in several rounds of toasting McTeer's memory. But my somber mood meant that the alcohol had little effect on me. I'd feel the effects the following morning, but as we replayed the events down in Miami and afterwards, I was sober in body and mind.

That we were at liberty to imbibe was not so much a miracle as it was the result of political and governmental machinations. When we had been snatched from the *Nephilim* by the SEAL team we'd been taken to a temporary staging post at Palm Beach County Airport, also known as Lantana, where we'd been deposited in a secure office within a hangar. The airport was growing used to military and federal operations

ساسس

conducted there since the inauguration of Donald Trump as POTUS – for three consecutive weekends the previous February the airport had been shut down while Trump held a summit with visiting Chinese politicians. The Secret Service had shut the airport down again, this time mid-week, while we were their guests of honour. Yes, we were treated with respect and with gratitude. If not for our timely intervention the attack on Mar-a-Lago would have been much worse, and the fact that we'd taken out the heavy machinegunners and sent the mortar teams into disarray gave the Navy SEALs the opportunity to board and take control of the super-yacht without resorting to extreme measures. For all intents and purposes, to the watching world, Mar-a-Lago had been saved by the arrival of the Special Forces, and nobody need know otherwise. In return for our sworn silence about our part in the battle to take the yacht we were exonerated of all our crimes – including those in the days leading up to the attack on the presidential retreat – in a secret deal rubber-stamped by Mr Trump himself. We agreed to keep silent, but only after making some demands of our own. Velasquez must be released without charge; Harvey Lucas must be exonerated for his involvement in the fight at the RV site; and Trey Shaw must be given a new identity and protected from anyone who might attempt to avenge her dead husband. Donald Trump didn't attend the parlay in person –he was represented by the Director of National Intelligence – but agreed to our terms and afterwards and off the record he did extend his gratitude for our patriotic service to the country – no less saving his Southern White House from being reduced to rubble – through Walter Conrad. If not for the deaths of so many innocent people, McTeer prime among them, it would have been a satisfactory end to a potentially more serious incident.

The Miami Police Department had proved reluctant to meeting our demands at first. Discounting the terrorist attack on Ocean Drive, they still had a number of other unsolved murders on their books – the running fight with Cahill's team had left a number of bodies in its wake at various locations, and then there was Albert Greville-Jones, and the men killed at our hotel alongside McTeer – and their only suspects were being taken away from them. But they bent to pressure from on high, and in the end the series of violent encounters and killings was put down to inter-gang rivalries within Mikhail Viskhan's organisation. Sean Cahill and Daniel StJohn were painted as the true villains of the piece: the fact they'd been spotted fleeing the scene after torching the Chinese restaurant added to the suggestion they were behind the murders of Hussein and Monk, and probably of the others too. They became our fall guys and as far as I was concerned it was the only good either of them had ever done. Another thing that appeased the MPD was that most of those killed happened to be scumbag criminals, and was in some way restitution for the innocent lives taken on the 4th of July.

In all, Viskhan's spectacular had burned brightly, but only briefly. It had become apparent that the attack in SoBe was a distraction tactic, and the quartet of radicalized punks who'd pulled out assault rifles smuggled to the site in the chiller compartments of food carts had never been expected to do more than cause minimal damage and fatalities. They had all been killed by the responding law enforcement agencies. But the strike at Mar-a-Lago was supposed to go better, if not for our intervention where we'd taken out the *Nephilim*'s heavy guns and mortar teams. Even ashore the attack had been repelled: lacking the expert supervision of Cahill's team – who we'd thinned considerably – the landing party had proved an undisciplined rabble, and those among them who'd been forced to take up arms were the first to drop their guns and surrender the instant they met opposition from the Secret Service, while the more fervent jihadists were all shot with extreme prejudice. The Coast Guard had lost two good men. There was loss of innocent life, and other people seriously injured on the beach, but far fewer than if we hadn't pursued him and then disrupted Viskhan's attack.

Foiling the attack had become a massive propaganda coup snatched from Islamic State, too. They initially claimed responsibility, crowing about how they could strike at the very heart of the nation, but everyone soon realised it was an unmitigated failure. They soon retracted their statement and disassociated themselves from Viskhan. According to Trey, Viskhan had planned a triumphant return home to claim land, titles and glory: if he had escaped us it was probable that an IS hit squad would have been waiting for his flight at the other end. His spectacular had been a complete bust.

We drank to that.

But then I stood from the table and went to the edge of the deck. When drinking to the memory of a good friend, ours didn't feel like a victory. Besides, our actions hadn't initially been driven by the idea of diverting a terrorist attack; it was all about avenging McTeer, and when all came to all, he wouldn't be dead if I hadn't punched out Viskhan in that washroom and attracted his twisted attention.

I thought about Trey when first I'd laid eyes on her at the gala evening, how she had looked in her designer dress and heels, her styled hair and make-up, how beautiful she was, but also so sad. When last I saw her after our release from custody she was wearing the off-the-rack goods chosen for her by Rink, hair pulled back and held in place with an elastic band, her only make-up the shadows of fatigue around her eyes and in the hollows of her cheeks. How happy and grateful she was by comparison.

She had held my hands while she thanked me, then when that wasn't enough to express the depths of her gratitude she wrapped her arms around me and held me tight. I returned the hug, then gently eased out of her embrace. 'You'll be safe now, Trey,' I promised her. 'You're no longer a prisoner. You can take back your life and do whatever you want, with whomever *you* want. But do me a favour, huh? If you ever remarry, do it on your terms, right, and don't go picking a bad boy again.'

'No more bad boys?'

She eyed me, and for effect I fiddled with my shirt collar. 'Well, I suppose one more wouldn't do any lasting harm.'

We both laughed.

'Seriously though, I've no plans right now, certainly where marriage is concerned,' she admitted. For years she had been controlled, her every move, every thought, the way she dressed and acted, all had been ordered by her domineering husband. Now she was free to make her own choices it had to be a frightening prospect. 'Apart from one thing. I want my marriage to Mikhail annulled.'

'Rink already took care of that when he blew the bastard to hell.'

She nodded at the finality of my statement, but I also watched a shadow pass behind her features before she lowered her gaze. Despite hating him with a passion, she didn't need to hear the gory details of Viskhan's death. Something I shouldn't forget either; there were many people trapped in abusive relationships who still loved their partners, despite everything. It wasn't the person but their behaviour they grew to despise.

'Sorry,' I said, 'I didn't mean to be insensitive.'

'He deserved what he got,' Trey assured me. 'No. Getting the annulment is about taking back the power he held over me. I don't want to carry his name any longer, and I want it struck from all official records. Viskhan was never my name by choice.'

'Understandable.' What I didn't understand was Viskhan's deal with Sean Cahill. 'Can I ask...was there, I dunno, something going on between Viskhan and his pal, Sean?'

'You mean romantically?' At first Trey scoffed at the idea. But I knew I'd hit on something she'd obviously wondered about too. 'Mikhail was driven by sexual aggression, but as far as I can say, it was always aimed at me or at another girl. He abhorred gay people. But then, I can't remember a time I ever saw Sean with a woman, not intimately. He did have an unhealthy fascination with my hus—' she checked herself '—with Mikhail, and wasn't averse to showing his envy of me. Maybe there was something in their relationship, that Sean loved him more than as a friend, but I'm positive it was unrequited. What I am certain of, Mikhail loved nobody but himself.'

I didn't push the subject. I'd nothing against his sexual preference, I was simply trying to figure out why Cahill had fought so savagely to defend Viskhan at the end when it was obvious he had intended bailing out on him. Rink had related his final encounter with Dan StJohn, and how that guy was driven only by the promise of reward, but Cahill had been different and had paid the ultimate price for his infatuation. There's a recognised term for Cahill's fixation on Viskhan, to whom Trey told me Cahill owed his life. It's a form of hero worship, a White Knight Syndrome, where when a person's life is saved they then go on to pledge it to their saviour. Similarly where someone is nursed or tended to following life-changing injury or illness they can form a relationship with their caregiver known as the Florence Nightingale Effect. While I couldn't see Viskhan in either virtuous role, I suppose Cahill viewed him from a different perspective. Also, I understood the ties of brotherhood often formed between soldiers, and how I too would risk anything to defend my closest friends. Perhaps Cahill had a bond similar to the one I had with Rink, and had died for it.

Too many people had died because of my war with Viskhan and, to be fair, I had to share some of the blame.

We said our goodbyes, and Trey again held me, this time for longer. We parted with a kiss on our cheeks. She was still in protective custody while the last of Viskhan's people were being mopped up, and afterwards would be relocated to a place of her choosing. The two wounded PMCs Harvey fought – Frost and Parkinson – had already been apprehended when they tried to skip out of Miami, but there were still some of Viskhan's retinue of criminal associates at large. Some of them might try to hurt Trey in retaliation, though I thought it unlikely. For now the fighting was done, and it was time for us to return home...wherever that might be. If I returned back to Mexico Beach, would I be greeted by pitchforks and flaming torches?

Rink joined me at the edge of his deck, resting his meaty forearms on the railing, gently sloshing bourbon in the glass he held. For a while we just stood there in silence.

'Mack expressly asked me to keep my hands to myself,' I finally said.

'Brother, if that was me in that washroom I'd have kicked Viskhan's ass too.'

'Undoubtedly,' I said. 'But I can't help feeling this is my fault. I attract trouble. I told you I feel as if I'm about to be run out of Mexico Beach, and I'm betting I'm not too welcome in Miami after this either. I'm beginning to wonder, Rink, if maybe it's time for a fresh start.'

For a while I'd been feeling uneasy, restless, and it wasn't until then that I realised it was homesickness. It had been years since I'd been back home to England. Placing an ocean between us might save my other friends from the next round of trouble I attracted.

'The booze is making you maudlin, brother,' Rink said. 'And the best cure for that is to drink some more.'

I'd purposefully left my replenished glass sitting on the table. Rink offered me his. I declined. Rink rested his right hand on my left shoulder, gave it a squeeze. 'It's not that you attract trouble, Hunter,' he said, 'it's just that you can't walk away from it. That's the definition of a good man in my book. Don't dwell on the ones you hurt, or those you failed to protect, think about the lives you saved. Think about the difference you made to Trey.' He glanced back to offer a nod of acknowledgement to Harvey. 'Trey told Harve that she'd been praying for an opportunity to escape from Viskhan ever since he'd lost his hold over her after her parents died, and you were it. Viskhan was about to drag her to Chechnya to who knew what kind of hellish life. You came along at just the right time and place, like her guardian angel, and you gave her the strength and courage to get away. You don't attract trouble, brother, you're attracted to it, and who knows, maybe there's some purpose behind it.'

I snorted at the suggestion. 'The booze is having a weird effect on you too, Rink. The only higher power that ever guided me was Arrowsake, and I'm glad that's behind us now.'

He grinned. But then grew sombre. 'Walt ain't finished with us, especially not after pulling the strings for us this time.'

'It's partly why I'm thinking of going away for a while. You know Walter; he'll call in my debt before long. I'd prefer if you and the guys aren't sucked into whatever shit he has in mind for me. I don't want another of your deaths on my conscience.'

'I appreciate your concern, but it's like you told Walt: we're big enough and ugly enough to take the knocks...all of us. It's not on you when any of us gets hurt, brother. If Mack were here now he'd tell you the same damn thing. Besides, we're all in his debt – when Walter calls it will be for all of us. Doesn't matter where you are, brother, he'll reel you back, and if not him, I will.'

'And I'll come.' I faced him. 'But right now I need to get away. There's people I need to see, people I need to make my peace with.' I was talking about my ex-wife, Diane, and my mother. McTeer's death had reminded me how instantly we could blink out of existence, and though the possibility of being killed in action had been an aspect of my adult life, it had never struck me so hard before. 'I'm thinking of going back to England,' I announced.

He shrugged. 'As long as you come back.'

I nodded.

'And you don't go before Mack's funeral.'

'I'll be there, no question. But afterwards, I'm going to take a flight home out of Newark.'

'If you gotta do it, brother, then you do it with my blessing. But you'd better hurry on back, y'hear?'

I squeezed his shoulder. He laughed, but it was forced. He was feeling the maudlin effects of the alcohol too. He gave himself a mental shake. 'Now come on, Hunter. This is supposed to be a celebration of Mack's life, goddamnit, and there's still bourbon to be drunk.'

Harvey and Velasquez had both been aware that we had shared a moment, and had held a respectful silence. But as we returned to them at the table, they bucked the mood in the right direction, raising their glasses in salute of us this time. And it was then that another epiphany struck me. I wasn't suffering from homesickness; how could I be when the people most important in my life were right there with me? I was with family. But was I home?

Matt Hilton
Thanks

My thanks go to the following people whose assistance was invaluable to me during the writing of this book: Denise Hilton, Luigi Bonomi, Jordan Arran Hilton, Michael Bhaskar, Becca Allen and Tracey Shaw (the latter of whom kindly allowed me to use her name as inspiration for a major character). My thanks are also extended to my friends and readers who urged me to get the latest Joe Hunter thriller written.

Lightning Source UK Ltd.
Milton Keynes UK
UKHW040948130219
337247UK00001B/38/P